OF ASH AND EMBERS

JENNA WOLFHART

Cover Design by The Book Brander

Character Art by Ruby Dian Arts

Map by Allison Alexander

Chapter Art by Etheric Designs

Editing by Practical Proofing

For those who believe dreams are worth fighting for.

Author's Note

This series is intended for adult readers and will contain dark elements. To see a full list of potential triggers, visit www.jennawolfhart.com/books/content or scan the QR code below.

THE FAE OF AESIR

ELITE FAE

All the common fae
powers, as well as
additional magical
abilities related to
their bloodline.

COMMON FAE

Immortal life-span.
Enhanced senses,
strength, and speed.

LIGHT FAE

Power over fire.
Power over light.
Ability to create shields.

SHADOW FAE

Power over mist.
Animal communication.
Telekenesis.

STORM FAE

Power over wind.
Power over rain.
Power over lightning.

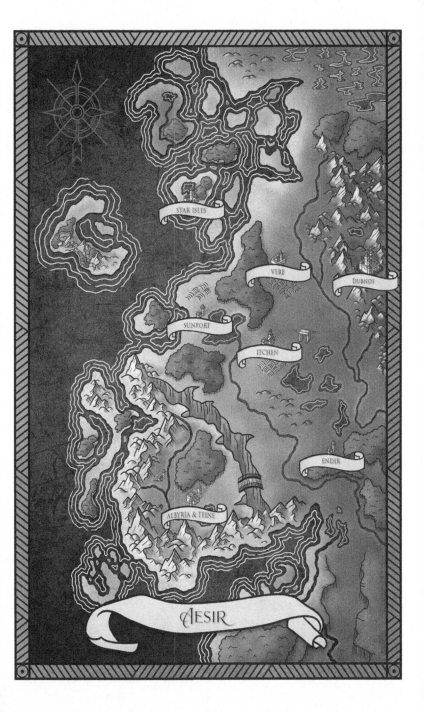

THE STORY SO FAR

In case you need a refresher...

In book one, Tessa Baran defied cruel King Oberon by stealing his powerful gemstones from the chasm. He caught her and punished her by choosing her to become his next mortal bride. Once he took her from her loved ones, he terrorized her and tricked her into believing he'd killed her sister.

Eventually, she escaped with the help of Morgan, one of Oberon's guards, who secretly works with the Mist King—Kalen Denare.

Kalen found her in the mists and took her back to his kingdom in the mountains. There, he offered her a deal. If she would sneak back across the barrier and kill King Oberon with the Mortal Blade, he would find a safe haven for her people, and he would help her find her family, currently lost somewhere in the mists.

She agreed.

They traveled together, dodging attacks from dangerous monsters and enemies from the Kingdom of

Storms. When they got trapped in a castle in Itchen, they grew closer. But half of the God of Death's power was also trapped in that castle. She offered Tessa the life of her sister in exchange for her release.

Tessa denied her and tried to destroy her as a way to stop the god from muting Kalen's powers any longer. It was the only way she could help him fight the storm fae, who had been attacking them for days.

It worked. Kalen got his powers back, and they survived.

Soon after, a letter arrived from Kalen's kingdom. Tessa's mother and dearest friend had made it there safely, against all odds. Eagerly, she returned to Kalen's homeland to reunite with them, only to discover the note was faked.

Kalen had betrayed her. According to Morgan, her family was trapped in Oberon's dungeons, and Kalen had known about it the entire time they'd been traveling together.

With vengeance in her heart, she stabbed him with the Mortal Blade, and then returned to Albyria where she stabbed Oberon as well.

Unfortunately, she soon discovered the blade was a fake. Oberon didn't die, and neither did the Mist King.

King Oberon then threw her into the dungeons, where she discovered her sister was still alive. That night, when she slept, Kalen visited her dreams.

"Hello, love," he said. "Surprised to see me?"

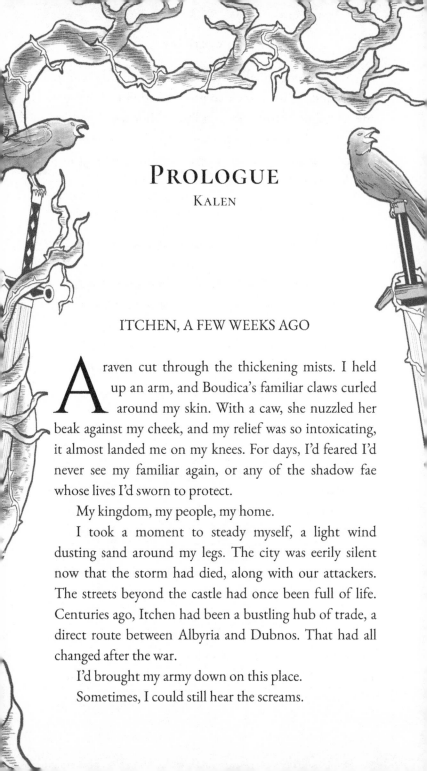

PROLOGUE
KALEN

ITCHEN, A FEW WEEKS AGO

A raven cut through the thickening mists. I held up an arm, and Boudica's familiar claws curled around my skin. With a caw, she nuzzled her beak against my cheek, and my relief was so intoxicating, it almost landed me on my knees. For days, I'd feared I'd never see my familiar again, or any of the shadow fae whose lives I'd sworn to protect.

My kingdom, my people, my home.

I took a moment to steady myself, a light wind dusting sand around my legs. The city was eerily silent now that the storm had died, along with our attackers. The streets beyond the castle had once been full of life. Centuries ago, Itchen had been a bustling hub of trade, a direct route between Albyria and Dubnos. That had all changed after the war.

I'd brought my army down on this place.

Sometimes, I could still hear the screams.

With a long exhale, I turned away from the empty homes and unfurled the two notes Boudica had brought me. Good news from home, I hoped. But when my eyes landed on the words, written in Niamh's familiar scrawl, my hope plummeted like a broken body tumbling into the depths of the Great Rift.

Kal,

    Everything is fine here, but I have bad news. I've spoken to one of our spies in Albyria, and things are worse than we feared. Oberon caught Tessa's family before they could escape. They've been in his dungeons this entire time.

    But there's more.

    Tessa's surname is Baran. You know what that means and who her father was.

    I don't know what she's trying to accomplish, but I worry it's nothing good. It seems she's fooled us all.

    Stay safe,

    Niamh

I crumpled the note in my fist as a wave of cold rushed through me. Niamh had to be wrong. Or there was some other explanation. With a thundering heart, I stumbled to the side and leaned against the onyx building, the world blurring before me.

Tessa *Baran*.

She'd never told me her surname. I hadn't even thought to ask. We'd been so focused on our mission—find her family and kill Oberon—that we'd hardly discussed much else. There was obviously much I didn't know about her.

Including, it turned out, who she was.

"Fuck," I muttered, suppressing my desperate need to shout the word into the wind.

Tessa had mentioned her father's death, but she'd told me that Oberon had killed him. If she genuinely was a Baran, then that wasn't the truth at all. *I'd* been the one to end his life. It had been the only way to stop him from dooming the world. And now Tessa would doom it too.

Fuck!

Pacing just outside the castle's front door, I glanced at the second note. Niamh had written this one as a fake to show to Tessa. It said Val and her mother were in Dubnos. It would be a way to lure her back to my city without arousing suspicion.

I tried to roll the tension from my shoulders. The last thing I wanted was to deceive her. We'd been traveling together, trying to save her family. And somehow, over the course of a few weeks, she'd knocked a hole in my defenses. It was hard to imagine the girl with fire in her eyes as my enemy. How much did she know? Did she truly believe that Oberon had killed her father? I could tell when she was lying, but...what if she had found a way around that?

I glanced up at the sky. No sign of any comet so far, thank the moon. But...

She'd been so insistent on visiting the god trapped inside this castle. Just like her father. She'd broken the gemstone to help me fight the storm fae, but what if that had been nothing more than an excuse to gain access to the god? When I'd first found her crossing the bridge from the Kingdom of Light, she'd been so against me helping her that she'd stabbed me.

Perhaps this was why.

The thought stung far more than I wanted it to. I'd seen her bravery. I'd seen her love for those she'd sworn to protect. My hands fisted as I thought through the implications. There *was* a chance that she hadn't betrayed us and that Niamh was wrong. But there was also a chance that she'd been playing me. I needed to get her back to Dubnos, talk things through with the others, and then see if I could discern the truth.

It meant lying to her about something that was unforgivable: the fate of her family. But if I didn't—if she was exactly who Niamh thought she was—the world would never survive. Not as long as she lived.

Before I could talk myself out of it, I squared my shoulders and headed inside to lie to the only woman who had made me feel something in a very long time.

"You did the right thing, Kal." Niamh dropped her hand onto my shoulder and squeezed tight as I gripped the side of the war table. My breath puffed out of my flared nostrils. During the ride back to Dubnos, silence had hung heavy around Tessa and me. More than once, I'd opened my mouth to demand the truth. But a conversation with my mother kept ringing through my memory, stopping me every time.

"The gods still search for a way to return to this world.

You must never let them, no matter who stands in your way."

"Why me? Why not you?"

"Just promise me you'll do whatever it takes to stop them. Vow to me, Kalen."

"I vow it."

Centuries had passed, and yet I still heard those words in my mind as clearly as if she had spoken them yesterday. She'd woke me from my bed, the clouds in her eyes as heavy as the ones in the sky and she'd made me vow, right then and there, that I'd save the damn world when the time came. Not if, but *when*. She'd been certain of it. All this time, I'd thought Oberon was the one she'd been warning me about, but now...

No matter who stands in your way.

"Kal," Niamh said, gently nudging her shoulder into mine. "Come on, say something."

"I don't want this to be happening," I managed to say.

"Yeah." Alastair sighed. "Neither do I, Kal."

I lifted my eyes from the war table to meet his gaze. The flickering torchlight was reflected in his brown eyes, and his broad, muscular body bowed forward. "It just doesn't make any sense. She would have had to lie to us at some point, but we can scent it when she does."

"Well, we don't know exactly what she can and can't do." Niamh moved around the war table and dropped a new token on the map. The miniature onyx dragon gleamed, the shadows of its sinewy wings stretching toward the city of Itchen. "Perhaps she's been given the power to dampen our senses when it suits her."

"Or maybe our spy in Albyria was wrong."

"Could be." She nodded and exchanged a quick glance with Alastair. "But I think we need to assume he wasn't wrong and act accordingly. Tessa seems intent on leaving Dubnos in the morning to go in search of her family again—if that's actually why she wants to leave. We can't let her. If she tries to bring back the gods...Besides, we can't risk the storm fae getting their hands on her."

A pained noise rumbled in the back of my throat as my grip around the edge of the war table tightened. "I hate this. I fucking hate it."

It served me right for opening up to someone, especially a mortal girl I'd known for only a few weeks. But, of course, it felt far longer than that. I'd been visiting her in her dreams for months before we ever met in person, and even though I'd been guarded then—and lying to her about who *I* was—I'd looked into her eyes and seen her heart. Or at least I'd thought I had.

Shaking my head, I closed my eyes. No wonder she'd called out for help, reaching toward me in her dreams. All this time, I thought she'd done it accidentally because she was lost and scared, but it must have been a ruse. A way to draw me in. But for what? What was her plan here?

Alastair rubbed the back of his neck. "Want me to go collect her from her room and take her to the dungeons?"

Tessa, back in another cell. For moon's sake, I hated the thought of it, regardless of who she was.

"No," I said with a heavy sigh. "I'll do it. First thing in the morning. She's exhausted. Let's give her one night in a normal bed. She won't try to leave tonight."

But what I didn't know then was that Tessa Baran

currently stalked through the silent hallways of my castle, readying herself to stab me with the fake Mortal Blade. And then she would leave me for dead, confirming my worst fears about her.

She was the enemy my mother had always warned me about.

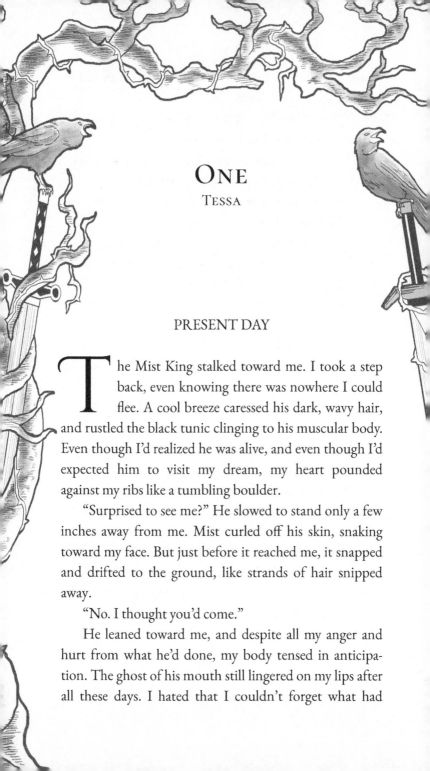

ONE
TESSA

PRESENT DAY

The Mist King stalked toward me. I took a step back, even knowing there was nowhere I could flee. A cool breeze caressed his dark, wavy hair, and rustled the black tunic clinging to his muscular body. Even though I'd realized he was alive, and even though I'd expected him to visit my dream, my heart pounded against my ribs like a tumbling boulder.

"Surprised to see me?" He slowed to stand only a few inches away from me. Mist curled off his skin, snaking toward my face. But just before it reached me, it snapped and drifted to the ground, like strands of hair snipped away.

"No. I thought you'd come."

He leaned toward me, and despite all my anger and hurt from what he'd done, my body tensed in anticipation. The ghost of his mouth still lingered on my lips after all these days. I hated that I couldn't forget what had passed between us. I hated that I still yearned to feel his touch. Most of all, I hated *him*.

"Tell me," he said with a tone as cold as steel, "was it a trick the whole time? Were you using me?"

That was the last thing I'd expected him to say. I frowned. "I could ask you the same question."

A bitter smile curved his lips. "There's no need to pretend anymore. I know who you are."

My eyes widened as a dagger appeared in his hand, its hilt elaborately decorated with glittering sapphire gems. I glanced at his blade and then at his face. My boot crushed the swaying grass as I took a step back.

"Why are you carrying a dagger?" I whispered, even though I already knew the answer. I'd tried to kill him, and now he would get his revenge on me. He wanted me dead. The fae who stood before me had never been my friend. He was my enemy, and now he would shove a blade into my heart and watch me bleed out beneath a blanket of stars.

Just like I'd tried to do to him.

"Because I have no other choice." The Mist King's voice went sharp, and the look in his eye reminded me of who exactly I was talking to right now. He was a ruthless king who had killed thousands in the war. He might not have burned down the human kingdoms, like Oberon had told us, but he wasn't innocent. He'd even admitted that himself. When he saw someone as his enemy, he crushed them.

And I was his enemy now. Maybe I always had been.

I fisted my hands, ignoring the flash of hurt in my

heart. "If this is how it's going to be, at least let me go down fighting."

"Very well," he murmured. "Arm yourself."

When I called forth a weapon to aid me, my fucking wooden dagger appeared in my hand. Of all things. I wanted a real blade, one like the weapon Kalen held, but no matter how hard I tried to conjure something more deadly, the wooden dagger remained as stubborn and as unchanging as a statue of a king.

"That won't do you much good."

I could have sworn he smirked.

For once, he looked just like I'd always imagined. He was a tall, imposing figure in the mists with venom in his eyes. He was the ruthless fae who had destroyed the Kingdom of Light and had trapped the mortals of Teine beneath Oberon's heinous rule. Gone was Kalen, the fae who had tended to my wounds, fought for my life, and braided my hair. But that Kalen had never truly existed. He'd been a lie.

"You know what, Mist King?" I whispered, too scared to speak any louder for fear he would hear the tears in my voice. "It doesn't matter. You're not wearing armor. If I stab you in the right spot, a wooden blade can do as much damage as one forged in steel."

His eyes almost softened. "You always were so brave, love."

"Don't call me that," I snapped.

"Don't call me the Mist King."

"All right. What would you have me call you then?"

"Oh, there are *many* things I would have you call me. Unfortunately, fate has decided otherwise." He flipped

the dagger, and then speared me with his sapphire gaze.
"Are you ready?"

No.

"Yes." I clutched the wooden dagger and bent my
knees, bracing myself for his impending attack. We'd
trained for days together. He'd shown me all his tricks. I
knew how he moved and what he thought and how he
approached a fight against his enemies. First, he'd feint to
the right, and then he'd swoop low before he tried to gut
me. If that didn't work, he'd feint again, only this time to
the left. His opponent would expect the feint after the
first and shift their focus. And that would be when he'd
shove his blade into the left side of their head.

I watched him, and he watched me. Only our ragged
breaths filled the silence.

Mist pulsed off Kalen's body. It seeped from his skin,
got sucked right back in, and then pulsed out again and
again, as if in rhythm with his heart. His face was
inscrutable, but his body betrayed his emotions. The curl
of his hands. The tension in his shoulders. The power
that washed over me like a wave of unyielding darkness.

My hands twitched by my sides, yearning to reach out
and touch him, to feel that power beneath my fingers.

And then he moved.

Kalen rushed to the right, and I smiled as I danced
further right to dodge his blow. But he didn't swoop low,
like I'd expected. He stayed on the right and slammed his
body into mine, knocking me off my feet. My back hit the
ground. All my breath rushed out of me. I got my
wooden dagger up between us just as he pinned me to the
grass, his blade against my neck.

A rushing sound filled my ears as death stared me in the face.

His muscular body shifted against me. "I'm sorry. I knew you'd expect the feint."

"Why are you apologizing?" I hissed up at him, my heart rattling in my chest. "Just cut my throat and be done with it."

He leaned forward, mist roiling from his skin. It curled around my cheek, a soft caress that shot shivers down my spine. I waited for him to sink the blade into my neck and for the brutal pain that would follow. But all he did was shift against me. His thighs pressed tightly against my waist, and his free hand cupped my shoulder.

I should've been afraid, but a thrill went through me instead. His lips were agonizingly close, and his breath was hot against my cheek. Warning bells clanged in my mind, but I didn't whimper in fear. I returned his hard gaze with one of my own, meeting his anger with mine.

He wrapped his hand around my dagger, tugged it from my grip, and then tossed it into the grass. The steel left my neck a second later. He hurled his dagger away to join mine.

"What are you doing?" I whispered.

His eyes went dark. "I don't want to kill you."

My breath rattled in my lungs. "Then you've just made a very big mistake. Because I definitely want to kill you."

He lowered his face to mine so that our noses brushed. A tremor went through my core. "Is that truly what you want, love?"

"I said don't call me that," I breathed, my heart pounding so hard that it drowned out the distant birds.

Slowly, he rose to his feet. I tumbled to the side, grabbed his dagger, and pointed it right at his heart. I stood on shaky legs, watching him watch me with an infuriatingly flat gaze. It was impossible to know what he was thinking.

"That won't work," he said. "We can't harm each other in our dreams."

My stomach turned. "Then, why did you just try to...?"

"I was forced to try."

Silence stretched between us. Even in a dream, the tension was palpable, thick and heavy like sap from the trees. It coated my tongue, and my words stuck to my mouth until I was choking on them.

"Why?" I finally asked him, stepping so close that the point of the dagger pierced his tunic. "You're the one who lied to me. For whatever reason, you led me around your mist and shadow filled lands, pretending to help me find my family. *You* were the one who betrayed me, not the other way around."

His eyes narrowed. "How are you able to lie so easily? I should be able to tell, but I can't."

"What in the name of light are you talking about? Nothing you've said makes any sense."

"I know who you are." He took the dagger from my hand and tossed it even further away, power humming from his body. "Because I'm the one who killed your father."

Shock punched me in the stomach. All the blood

drained from my face. The ground seemed to tip beneath me, throwing my head into a wild vertigo. I reached out to grab something, but all I found was air and mist and Kalen's terrible power.

"That's impossible," I choked out. "Oberon killed my father."

"No. He took credit for it, likely to make a point," he said quietly. "I found your father in the mists, and I had no choice but to take his life, just like I had no choice but to put that dagger against your neck. If I could harm someone in dreams, I would have been forced to kill you, too."

My lips parted. "You actually mean this. It's not some cruel joke?"

"I'm afraid I mean every word."

Fists clenching, I glared at him, horror snaking through me. The Mist King had killed my father.

Kalen had killed my father.

Burning tears filled my eyes.

"I was right about you," I hissed. "I actually regretted stabbing you with that fucking blade, but now I wish I really had killed you. Everything Oberon has ever said about you is true. You're a monster. You kill mortals for no reason."

He stiffened. "I didn't kill him for no reason. He was trying to release the god's power, and I had no choice but to stop him. If I hadn't done something, he would have destroyed the—"

My entire body went tight.

"No." I shoved at his chest, but he was an immovable stone. "Stop lying. Stop talking about him!"

Kalen grabbed my wrists and tried to hold me still, his eyes sweeping across my face. "He told me his daughter would follow in his footsteps. That you would finish his quest to release the god, no matter what I did to him. Is that true, Tessa? Be honest with me for once."

I stopped struggling against him and just stared into his face, dumbfounded. None of this made any sense. It was lies. *More lies.* All he'd done since I'd first met him in that stupid dream was lie to me. About who he was, what he was, and what he wanted. And now he seemed determined to turn me against my family. But *why*?

"Tell me," he repeated insistently, "when we were in Itchen, were you trying to release the god? All those visits you made to her...what were you really trying to do?"

"What do you think? Her twisted offer was a cruel joke. Nellie isn't even dead, did you know that? She's locked in Oberon's dungeons, along with me." A tear slipped down my cheek, but my hands were still trapped in his, so I couldn't brush it away. "Let go of me."

He released his grip on my hands. I twisted away and stared up at the stars with tears streaming down my face. I didn't want to hear anymore. None of it made sense. Father would never do anything like that. He was a good man. And the Mist King had killed him.

I can't trust anyone.

"You don't know about any of this," he murmured, "do you?"

"Just leave me alone."

"Did he ever mention anything about the gods to you?" he asked. "About his plans and what he would do to bring them back?"

"Please, no more of this. You've already done too much," I breathed. "Stop talking about my father. I won't listen to it, especially after you lied to me about where my family was. Everything you've ever told me has been a lie."

A strand of mist curled around my body, and it caressed my cheek. I ached to lean into it, but I wouldn't. Not now.

"Not everything, Tessa. I truly didn't know where your mother was until we were in Itchen, when Boudica arrived with letters. Niamh found out through one of our spies. She reached out to him when we started suspecting that Oberon was using Morgan more than we thought. He fully controls her, giving her commands she's forced to follow. That's also how Niamh found out who you are. I didn't know what to do after that. I thought you were working against me, using me to get to the god, especially after you smashed that stone. And so I took you back to Dubnos because I didn't know what else to do. I was going to try talking to you about it after you got some rest, but you made your move first."

When I tried to kill him.

I closed my eyes. "How am I supposed to believe a word of this? You even lied to me about the damn Mortal Blade. The one you carried with you was its twin."

"Because I had a feeling you'd try to use it against me at some point."

I frowned.

"Turn around and look at me."

My body shaking, I turned to face him. He reached out and brushed a strand of hair away from my face.

Everything within me tensed. "Stop. You can't do that. It's not fair. Not after everything you've just dumped on me. After everything you've done. Kalen, I—"

Something tickled the back of my neck, and a strange sensation swept down my spine, like the fingers of Kalen's mists. But his mists were nowhere near me. Frowning, I glanced over my shoulder, half-expecting to find someone standing behind me. But no one was there. Just a sparkling horizon full of stars.

"I know," Kalen said. "I shouldn't have. I'm sorry. But I won't lie and say I'm not worried about you being trapped in Oberon's dungeons. That's the last thing I wanted, even when I thought you were following in your father's footsteps."

I turned back toward him, saw the sorrowful look on his face, and felt my shoulders droop as resignation replaced my boiling anger. "Please tell me you didn't mean any of this. My father would never do something like that. He wouldn't bring back one of the gods."

"I wish I could." He glanced toward a gathering of shadows. "Niamh is calling for me. It might be about the army outside our walls. I must go."

"Wait." I lifted my hand toward him but then yanked it back when I realized what I was doing. Still, the words poured out of me before I could stop them. I hated him and I didn't trust him and yet..."I'm set to wed Oberon in a few days, and then I'll be stuck in the Kingdom of Light for eternity. I'll never see the stars again."

He palmed my cheek with his strong, steadying hand. "As long as dreams remain, so do the stars."

A breath later, the dream began to fuzz around the

edges. The night-encased forest whispered away, the trees transforming from living, breathing things into nothing but dense fog full of shadows. I blinked and sat up, gazing around at the barred cell and my sister sleeping soundly beside me.

The Mist King and my dream were gone.

I squeezed my eyes shut and fell back onto the pillows, my head pounding with the weight of what I'd just seen and heard. Kalen had killed my father because he'd been seeking a way to release the god's power. It made little sense. All my memories of Father...he never would have done something like that.

Kalen had to be wrong. The Mist King had killed an innocent man, and then he'd wanted to end me too. That made sense. That fit into everything I knew about the world.

But I'd been wrong before. My reckless anger and distrust had landed me here, along with everyone I loved.

Kalen had no reason to lie to me about any of this. I was trapped in this cell and couldn't go anywhere or do anything. I wasn't a player on the board anymore. Which meant...I'd stabbed Kalen for nothing. He had never betrayed me, not truly. Morgan had.

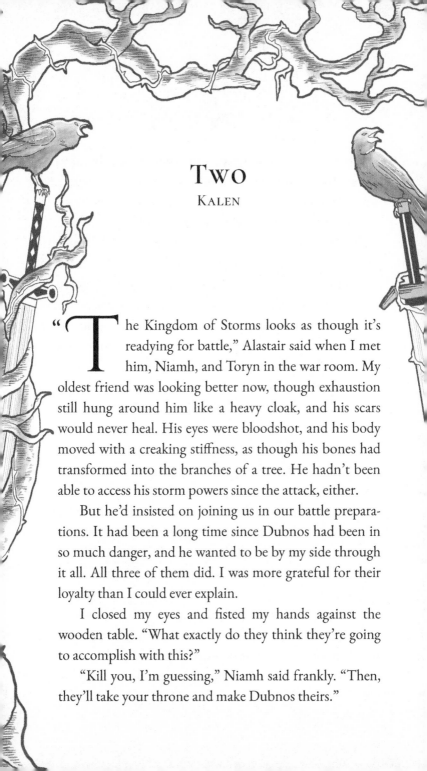

Two
Kalen

"The Kingdom of Storms looks as though it's readying for battle," Alastair said when I met him, Niamh, and Toryn in the war room. My oldest friend was looking better now, though exhaustion still hung around him like a heavy cloak, and his scars would never heal. His eyes were bloodshot, and his body moved with a creaking stiffness, as though his bones had transformed into the branches of a tree. He hadn't been able to access his storm powers since the attack, either.

But he'd insisted on joining us in our battle preparations. It had been a long time since Dubnos had been in so much danger, and he wanted to be by my side through it all. All three of them did. I was more grateful for their loyalty than I could ever explain.

I closed my eyes and fisted my hands against the wooden table. "What exactly do they think they're going to accomplish with this?"

"Kill you, I'm guessing," Niamh said frankly. "Then, they'll take your throne and make Dubnos theirs."

"Oberon has clearly gotten to them," Toryn said, running a hand along the top of his buzz cut hair. "He's offered them an alliance. Together, they'll find a way to bring back the gods."

It was what Oberon had wanted almost four hundred years before, though I'd never fully understood it. The gods would be no kinder to him and his people than they'd been to those they'd destroyed centuries ago, when they'd first claimed these lands. They would not care to make a fae king one of them. In fact, they would likely smite him for having the audacity to believe they'd lower themselves to his level.

"Let's say that's true," I said, staring down at the cluster of swords outside my border. "Why would the storm fae want that? They were against him centuries ago. Why aren't they against him now?"

"Oberon must have promised them something," Alastair said with a grunt. "And it was enough to tempt the bastards."

"Perhaps we could use a valerian fog against them. Knock them out before they can attack the city," Niamh offered.

I shook my head. "And then what? Drag them somewhere? Toss them into our dungeons? We don't have enough space for their entire army, and besides, I don't know if we have enough valerian for that. Oberon is the only one with a cache that large."

My eyes drifted back to the city of Albyria, trapped behind its chasm walls and the mountain range that swept around the western edges. I curled my lip at that miniature crown and its glittering colors. I wanted to wrap my hands around that king's neck and snap the life out of him. Now more than ever.

Niamh gave me a knowing look. "Manage to get anything out of Tessa?"

"More than I expected. I saw the look on her face when I told her about her father. She had no idea that he was trying to release the god's power. I don't think she was trying to do it, either. We were wrong to suspect the worst."

"I told you," Toryn said, folding his arms. "You should have given her a chance to explain herself."

"Well, shit." Alastair fiddled with the rings in his ears, the bright silver a contrast to his deep bronze skin. "What are you going to do, Kal?"

"I don't know. Oberon has her." Something in my gut twisted. If I'd been upfront with her to begin with, she never would have run off to take care of him by herself. She wouldn't be in this mess, trapped and forced to wed her cruel king.

Albyria was a short journey from Dubnos, but the distance felt insurmountable right now. With the attacking army at my doors and Oberon's barrier keeping me out, it was impossible for me to reach her. The thought filled my veins with acid. Despite what she'd done to me, I could not bear the thought of her trapped in Oberon's dungeons, waiting in the darkness for her wedding day.

She'd never be free from him once she made the marriage vow. Not until his death.

I would not wish such a fate on my worst enemy. Not

even on the mortal girl who had stabbed me with a blade she thought would turn me into a pile of ash.

"I know you must think I'm mad," I said to the three of them. Well, maybe not to Toryn. "She did stab me."

Alastair just chuckled. "You wouldn't be you if you didn't still want to help the girl."

"I don't think you're mad," Toryn said quietly. "She's been given a bad lot in life, and Morgan presented her with a truth she couldn't ignore. No matter that it was exaggerated. We can likely thank Oberon for that, the bastard. He controls Morgan far more than we've wanted to admit."

I nodded, but there was a heaviness in my heart that was impossible to ignore. Of course Tessa had believed Morgan. Swallowing the lump of pain, I turned away from Albyria's pocket of land and stared down the border between the Kingdom of Shadow and the Kingdom of Storms. Tessa had no reason to trust me over anyone else. We barely knew each other, even if it felt like she'd been in my life far longer than a few months.

She had been pitted against me since birth. She'd been taught to fear and hate me. And somehow, she'd seen past all that for a brief moment in time. She'd thrown away her prejudice against me, even when I'd told her I wouldn't change a damn thing I'd done in the war. I thought she'd understood me.

And now she knew I'd killed her father. Any hope of reconciliation was gone.

"What do you want to do, Kal?" Toryn asked as he hobbled a few steps closer, his eyebrows pinched with pain and worry. "Tell us the plan."

With a deep breath, I nodded. "I'll speak with a few of our spies inside Albyria. See what they can tell us about Oberon's plans for Tessa and her family. I might be able to persuade one of them to smuggle her out, though it'll be hard to do that a second time. Oberon will expect it."

Toryn gave me a tight smile. "I meant with this battle. What are we going to do about the Kingdom of Storms?"

"Ah." I pressed my lips into a thin line. "That one is much easier to answer. If they attack our city, we'll have to kill them all."

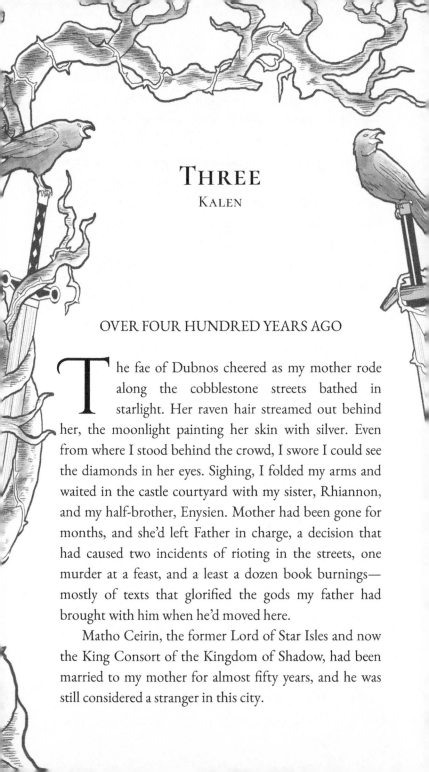

THREE
KALEN

OVER FOUR HUNDRED YEARS AGO

The fae of Dubnos cheered as my mother rode along the cobblestone streets bathed in starlight. Her raven hair streamed out behind her, the moonlight painting her skin with silver. Even from where I stood behind the crowd, I swore I could see the diamonds in her eyes. Sighing, I folded my arms and waited in the castle courtyard with my sister, Rhiannon, and my half-brother, Enysien. Mother had been gone for months, and she'd left Father in charge, a decision that had caused two incidents of rioting in the streets, one murder at a feast, and a least a dozen book burnings—mostly of texts that glorified the gods my father had brought with him when he'd moved here.

Matho Ceirin, the former Lord of Star Isles and now the King Consort of the Kingdom of Shadow, had been married to my mother for almost fifty years, and he was still considered a stranger in this city.

"Queen Bellicent Denare! I'm so glad you're home."
The Queen's Shadow, a warrior named Niamh, walked
toward my mother with a smile, her braided violet hair
trailing down her back. She wore black leather armor that
blended with her dark skin, and she moved with a confidence no one could ignore. My mother swung off her
horse and embraced the warrior before striding over to us.
My father had been in charge in Mother's absence, but
Niamh had done her damndest as my mother's right
hand to keep the crown in check. She'd been the only
reason the brief riots hadn't escalated into something far
worse.

"My babies. My beautiful, beautiful babies." With a
magnificent smile, Mother opened her arms wide, just as
she'd done when we were still toddlers racing barefoot
down the castle hallways with the cold stone biting our
skin.

My sister hugged her fiercely. "Thank the moon
you're back. But when are you going to stop acting as
though we were frozen in time at age eight?"

"Never," my mother whispered into my sister's short
dark hair. She pulled back and turned to my half-brother.
"Not you, either, Enysien, though it's getting harder by
the day to ignore."

Enysien had grown hard these past few years and
spent most of his time training in the courtyard with the
Queen's Shadow. Like his father, he was a common fae
and couldn't wield any shadow magic. Normally, a queen
—or king—would seek out an elite fae to shore up
strength. But Matho had been the Lord of Star Isles,
home to thousands of ships, including ones crafted for

war. When my father had first come to Dubnos, he'd passed down his title to his eldest son from a previous marriage, who had stayed behind in Star Isles. Linking our families had been a strategic move on my mother's part.

Unfortunately, he'd brought his love of the gods here with him.

Mother embraced Enysien quickly, and then placed her gloved hand on my arm. "Kalen, I need to speak with you privately about something quite important. Come with me. Now."

I frowned and glanced at my sister, who merely shrugged. Mother had been acting strangely the past few years, and she'd left in a hurry a few months ago with a cryptic explanation. *The knowledge is out there, you see,* she'd said. *And I need to find it before it's too late.*

She'd never explained anything more than that. One day, she'd hopped on her horse, surrounded by two dozen warriors, and rode off to chase down answers. There had been moments I'd wondered if she would ever come back.

Mother led me to her private quarters where a fire blazed in the hearth. I eased into an armchair and watched her pace from one end of the drafty room to the next, still clad in her boiled leather armor. It was then I noticed that the faint lines around her eyes were deeper than they'd been before, and a single strand of gray shot through her glossy midnight hair. When fae reached adulthood, they stopped aging. Most of the time.

"Something has happened." The chair creaked as I shifted. "You ran off on some wild adventure with barely a word, and when you return, you do this? What's the matter? The way you're acting...you're making me think someone's died."

She paused and gazed into the flames. "If you don't do exactly what I ask of you, a lot of people *are* going to die."

I frowned and sat up a little straighter. "What are you talking about?"

With a sigh, she spun around the opposite chair and sank down, dropping her head into her hands. Strands of her dark hair leaked out between her fingers. "I found something in your father's books that alarmed me. We know so little about the history of Aesir. All that knowledge has been lost over the centuries, but mostly, we know hardly anything about the gods."

"Matho certainly does," I countered.

She frowned at me. "Are you still not calling him your father?"

"Do you blame me?"

"He's not a bad man. He's just confused."

I let out a bitter laugh. "Matho worships the five winged riders who brought destruction to this world. The fae of this city are revolting against him, against *us*. He tried to erect a statue of the gods while you were gone. Did you know that? Riots broke out in the streets."

"Niamh told me everything," my mother said tightly. "And he will be dealt with. He just...he doesn't know what he's doing. Star Isles has always worshipped the gods. It will take time for him to come around to our beliefs. He just needs to see that what he's been taught is wrong."

"And so that's why you sailed away? To find something that could convince him?"

"No." She folded her hands in her lap. "I was seeking the truth about when they first came to these lands and how we once banished them. Something in your fathers' books made me worry they might soon return."

I furrowed my brow. "Return? Here, to Aesir?"

She nodded.

"But..." I trailed off. "It's been centuries. Mortals and fae bound together to rid this world of them. Surely it's impossible for them to come back."

"There's a prophecy," she whispered. "It speaks of a time when the gods will return, and I fear that time is imminent. I need you to make a vow to me, Kalen. A binding vow, laced with magic. You know what this means."

I swallowed hard. Fae rarely made binding vows these days, at least in Dubnos. "I'll be physically forced to follow through on whatever I vow."

"That's right," she said. "I need you to do this for me. You know I would not ask if it wasn't important."

"Tell me what it is first. I can't agree to something that I don't understand."

She nodded. "All right. There are two parts to this vow. First, if you learn that someone is trying to bring back the gods, you need to act with haste. You will do whatever it takes to stop them, even if that means killing them. Even if that means using your destructive power against them."

I frowned. My powers had proved almost impossible to control. Mother had assured me by the time I reached twenty-five, I'd know how to handle the mists and the telekinetic power that could blast from my hands. But I was a man of twenty-eight now, and it still eluded me.

"Second, if you see a comet in the sky, burning a bright white, it means a god is returning. You need to kill whoever caused that to happen. If you don't, you will never be able to save this world. That person must die, Kalen. Do you understand me?"

For a moment, I couldn't breathe. Until now, Mother had rarely spoken to me about the gods, especially in such a fervent manner. Any time Matho brought them up, she dismissed his ramblings and moved on to something else. But her eyes were alight now, her entire body curving toward me with anxious energy.

"What is this?" I asked. "What's brought this on?"

"The gods still search for a way to return to this world. You can never let them, no matter who stands in your way."

Shaking my head, I sat back in my chair, heart pounding. "We don't believe in the gods in Dubnos. We worship the land, nature, the moon in the sky. Not some horrible beings that tried to make this realm theirs by killing us all."

"Exactly," she hissed, grabbing my hand. "Which is why we can never let them come here again. Vow to me, Kalen."

"Why me? Why not you? Why not Rhiannon? She's the eldest. She's your heir."

"Your power is formidable."

"It's erratic," I countered. "The last time I tried to use

it, I blew an entire house apart. If anyone had been inside at the time..."

Her bony fingers squeezed tight. "Just promise me you'll do whatever it takes to stop them. Vow to me, Kalen."

I stared into her diamond-studded eyes. No one was able to say no to my mother, not even Matho Ceirin, who chafed against the rules of her reign. It was why he'd waited until she was gone to try to turn the city away from Druidism and to his gods instead.

The five winged riders were full of fire and vengeance. Matho believed they were fated to rule this land, punishing the wicked, and granting immortality amongst the stars to anyone who followed them. He would be rewarded for bringing them back. He'd always been...obsessed.

"You're worried about Matho, aren't you?" I pushed up from the chair and waved at the closed door. He'd be outside, pacing and wondering why we'd holed up in here together. Thankfully, the stone walls where thick enough to trap our words within. "You think he's the one who's going to do it."

Mother actually laughed. "He's far too useless for that."

"But then what has you so spooked?"

"I'm telling you, son. They *will* return soon. And you're the most powerful fae I've ever met. Will you please make this vow to me? One that must carry on beyond my death."

I closed my eyes. A binding vow. One to fight against powerful beings I knew next to nothing about. "Will you tell me what you've found out about them? If you expect me to stop this, I need to know what I'll face."

"What little knowledge I have will be yours," she said.

"All right then." Something in my chest tightened, though I didn't quite understand why. "I vow it, Mother. I'll do what you've asked."

The magic burned through me, forever fusing my life to my words. The only way to escape what I'd promised would be my death.

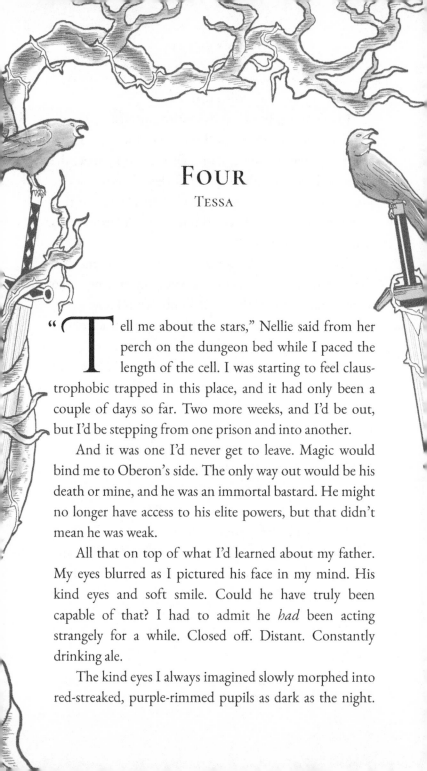

FOUR
TESSA

"Tell me about the stars," Nellie said from her perch on the dungeon bed while I paced the length of the cell. I was starting to feel claustrophobic trapped in this place, and it had only been a couple of days so far. Two more weeks, and I'd be out, but I'd be stepping from one prison and into another.

And it was one I'd never get to leave. Magic would bind me to Oberon's side. The only way out would be his death or mine, and he was an immortal bastard. He might no longer have access to his elite powers, but that didn't mean he was weak.

All that on top of what I'd learned about my father. My eyes blurred as I pictured his face in my mind. His kind eyes and soft smile. Could he have truly been capable of that? I had to admit he *had* been acting strangely for a while. Closed off. Distant. Constantly drinking ale.

The kind eyes I always imagined slowly morphed into red-streaked, purple-rimmed pupils as dark as the night.

He'd lost his way at some point. I'd seen it with my own eyes. But had he really fallen that far?

I blew out a breath and focused on Nellie's words, thinking back to the forest dreams and those nights I'd spent roaming the mists. Through the murky haze, the stars had been difficult to spot, but there'd been that one night in Itchen when the mists had cleared. The stars that swept through the sky had shone like millions of souls lighting up the dark.

Sighing, I stopped my pacing to join her on the bed, the rusted springs creaking beneath my weight. "You want to know about the stars? I don't even know where to begin. We think of the night like the pitch black of our bedrooms in Teine where we cannot even see our hands in front of our faces. But night is nothing like that, not out there. The stars and the moon drench the world in silver. You look up and you realize this world is a beautiful, enormous place, and we're only a small part of it. It sounds scary, but it's not. If anything, it just makes me believe that things don't have to be the way they are. If the universe is that big, there's hope for things to be different. We can have a better life, Nellie."

If only we could get out of this place.

As if reading my mind, my sister reached out and clasped my hand. A watery film covered her eyes, and she shook her head. "Maybe others can, but I think this is it for us."

"No," I said fiercely, squeezing her hand. "Don't you say that."

"What are we going to do? Escape?" She let out a bitter laugh I'd never heard from her before. It made my heart ache. I wasn't the only one who had been beaten down by this place—by these fae. By *Oberon*.

Furious fire whipping through me, I leaned forward and hissed, "I am going to get us out of here, and then I'm going to kill him. This time, I won't fail."

"You sound so certain."

"Because I am."

"But how?" She flicked her gaze down the hallway, where the guards stood watch beside the door leading out of the dungeons. There were six of them, and they seemed to rotate at regular intervals. They were too far away to hear our words if we spoke quietly enough, but I was still wary of saying too much. One could never be too careful around the fae.

"Don't you worry about that," I said.

I didn't want to tell her what I was planning, partially because I was likely to fail. It would be my last resort, and it was one I hoped to avoid. On my wedding day, I would grab whatever sword I could off any soldier nearby and chop Oberon's head off. Or at least die trying.

Unless I was lucky, I'd never even get close to succeeding.

I had to find a way to get Nellie out of here first, though. Otherwise, her life would be in danger the second I fought back.

My sister gave me a frank look, one I'd seen from her before. She always knew when I was hiding something. It was how she'd found out about my gemstone stealing and midnight visits to the captain—to the Mist King. She knew me too well. "You're planning something. I already don't like it, judging by that look in your eye."

I opened my mouth to tell her not to worry, but the sound of door hinges creaking snatched at my attention. Turning toward the guards, I spotted Morgan striding down the passageway with her silver hair pulled into a tight bun and her steel armor glistening as if it had just been polished.

The rest of the guards stayed back and allowed her to approach on her own. A breath whistled out from between my clenched teeth, but I tried to keep my face blank. I couldn't let her know that I'd spoken to Kalen, that I had doubts about her and what she'd told me. If Oberon was using her, I couldn't risk him finding out any of this.

"Good morning," Morgan said, easing to a stop outside our cell. "Sleep all right?"

My heart pounded against my ribs. Did she know about Kalen's dream ability? "Not particularly. Being trapped in a cell while your loved ones are being threatened doesn't lend itself to relaxation."

Far too late, I realized the snap in my tone. One of my worst faults. I couldn't seem to keep my emotions at bay, especially when they were raging inside me like a bonfire.

She frowned in at me. "Has something happened? You seem angrier than you were last night."

"I'm a very angry person, Morgan. This is just my natural state."

Her frown deepened. "Is this because I'm not able to do anything to help you right now?"

"Well, you probably could do *something*. You could cause some sort of commotion and leave the key where I can get to it. Five minutes is all I need to get us out of here."

I knew what her answer would be before she spoke it.

"I told you. I can't go against Oberon's orders, even when I want to."

"But why not?" I asked, leaning forward. "You've done it before—at the wedding when you got me out of Albyria. Is there another reason you're not able to go against his stated orders?"

Morgan's face remained blank and unreadable. She flicked her gaze behind me to where Nellie still sat curled up on the bed. "That's an interesting question, and I'm afraid I can't explain it to you."

"You can't? Or you won't?"

She pressed her lips together. "*I can't.*"

Darkness flashed behind her eyes, and a strange, twisting sensation went through my gut. Nodding, I dropped my voice to a whisper. "That's what I thought. You really are trapped. Whatever he tells you to do, you have to do it."

She didn't answer. Instead, she took a single step closer to the cell's bars and narrowed her eyes at me. A million emotions seemed to war inside the silver, a million thoughts I didn't know how to read. And it was that— this single look from her that told me everything I needed to know. Kalen was right. Oberon was controlling Morgan, and there was nothing she could do to help me now.

Chills swept down my spine.

"I think you should go," I said.

She pressed her lips together. "What about your mother? And Val?"

"I can't trust you to take care of that, and you know it. I'm going to have to find a solution myself."

"You can't help them. He'll never let you out of here," she warned. "He didn't give me any orders about your family. Nothing regarding your mother and—"

"How can I be sure that anything you say is true?" I whispered around the lump of pain in my throat. As much as I wanted to hate her for what she'd done, I couldn't. She was just as much a pawn in Oberon's game as I was. Maybe even more so.

He was the one behind it all. But as much as I understood her predicament, I wouldn't trust a single word that came out of her mouth.

Hurt flashed in her eyes, but she nodded and took a step back. "You're making the right decision. I wish it weren't true, but it is. I hope I see you on the other side of the bars one day, Tessa. And I do mean that. I hope one day I can make it up to all of you."

She whirled and took off down the corridor, leaving me to grip the bars and stare after her. Nellie stepped up beside me and frowned as we both watched Morgan leave the dungeons. "What was that all about? Why don't you trust her?"

I still hadn't told Nellie about my dream with the Mist King, and I didn't know how to tell her now, especially when it came to everything I'd heard about my father.

"I'll explain later," I told her, frowning when another guard started down the corridor toward our cell. "All you need to know is that you can't trust anything she says to you. If she ever comes here when I'm not around, don't believe a word, all right? Even if she tells you I sent her and that she's trying to get you out of this cell. Even if she's as convincing as the sun. Don't believe her."

"Didn't she help you escape before?"

I held a finger up to my lips as the guard approached. He was tall and broad-shouldered, but there was little else I could tell about him. His face and body were hidden behind steel—everything except his scowling lips. "Let me guess. You two are plotting a way to break out of here. Good luck with that, *mortals*."

His disdain was meant to consume me like a crashing wave, one that could tug me into the bottomless depths of despair, but I let it roll off my back. I could weather their insults all day long. They'd done far worse to me than this, and I'd risen up from their attempts to break me each and every time.

I smiled. "I'll be sure to tell Oberon you wished us luck in our endeavors to escape him."

His scowl dropped. One thing I'd learned during my last captivity, many of the fae were as just as scared of Oberon as the mortals of Teine were. He was the definition of a tyrant, and he controlled every aspect of their lives. The trouble was, a lot of the fae didn't seem to realize how much they were like us. They thought they were above it all when they were just as entrenched in his cruelty.

All because they believed he had the power of the sun.

If only they knew the truth. Perhaps it was time they found out.

"Don't worry," I told the guard, "you'd probably win if he fought you. He's weaker now that he doesn't have his elite powers."

The guard frowned in at me. "What in the name of light did the Mist King do to you?"

"Pardon me?"

"Your words don't smell like lies, but you aren't telling the truth." He cocked his head. "Or maybe it's because you're...yeah, that has to be it."

My eyes narrowed. "Maybe it's because I'm what?"

His smile froze my bones. "Maybe if you're a good girl, you'll get to find out."

With that, he shoved a key into the lock and hauled open the cell door. I bit the insides of my cheeks as a sudden rage burned through me, filling my veins with liquid fire. For a moment, the world around me went black, and all I could see was his smug smile and the sword belted around his waist. He probably didn't expect me to fight back. I could catch him off guard. I could drag his own blade across his neck and get out of this city for good.

Something inside me rose up, hungry to give in to my vengeful thoughts and follow through with it, just like I always had. When something punched me, I always punched back. Or *stabbed* back, really.

But look where it had gotten me. More importantly, look where it had gotten Nellie, Mother, Val.

My actions had put them in these dungeons. All three of them. And if I did something rash now, deep down I knew it would only make it worse for them, as impossible as that seemed. At least they were alive. At least they had hope that one day they might find themselves back in Teine beneath the baking sun, laughing as they lounged on the river banks with their bare toes in the water.

I closed my eyes and shoved down my rage. It would have to come out to play another time. Next time I made a move, I had to be certain it was the right one.

"Are you coming or what?" he asked.

"Coming where?" I snapped back.

I wouldn't stab him, but I had no intention of being nice, either.

He chuckled. "The king has plans for you. And he's ordered me to kill one of your loved ones if you make a fuss. We'll start with Nellie here, if you'd like."

"Don't you dare speak her name." Heart pounding, I took a step toward the door. Nellie gripped my hand, but she didn't try to pull me back. She knew it was useless to do anything but go along with whatever Oberon had planned for us.

"Tessa," she whispered.

"I'll be back soon," I promised her. "He won't kill me. It'll ruin his wedding."

Oberon had gone to a lot of trouble to get me back. And I would find a way to make him pay for it.

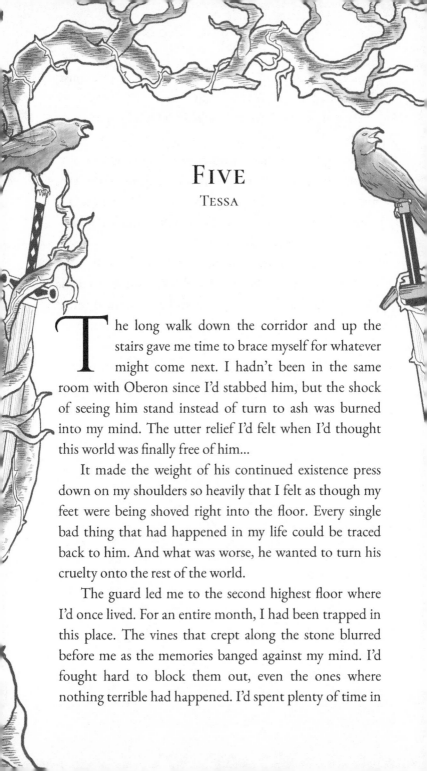

FIVE
TESSA

T he long walk down the corridor and up the stairs gave me time to brace myself for whatever might come next. I hadn't been in the same room with Oberon since I'd stabbed him, but the shock of seeing him stand instead of turn to ash was burned into my mind. The utter relief I'd felt when I'd thought this world was finally free of him...

It made the weight of his continued existence press down on my shoulders so heavily that I felt as though my feet were being shoved right into the floor. Every single bad thing that had happened in my life could be traced back to him. And what was worse, he wanted to turn his cruelty onto the rest of the world.

The guard led me to the second highest floor where I'd once lived. For an entire month, I had been trapped in this place. The vines that crept along the stone blurred before me as the memories banged against my mind. I'd fought hard to block them out, even the ones where nothing terrible had happened. I'd spent plenty of time in silence, or just staring out the window at the mist-enshrouded mountains in the distance.

But those memories were laced with a grief so great I'd thought I might die. I'd lost the will to fight. Even breathing had felt hard. I never wanted to feel that way again, but I knew Oberon would do his damndest to take me back to that place again. He wanted to shatter me. He wanted to watch me curl up into a ball and mewl in pain, a mere creature beneath his boot.

He wanted me to be the one that burned to ash.

"Here we are," the guard said when we reached the old bathing chamber I'd once used. Dread crept through me at the sight of the gold-plated tub. Steam curled off the water, transforming the room into a world of fog—or mist. But unlike before, Queen Hannah was nowhere to be seen. In her place stood two maidservants I'd never seen before. Both human, both young. Their heads bowed; they did not speak a word.

"What's this?" I asked, turning to the guard.

"You're the king's betrothed, and the rules remain the same as they were before." He smiled. "No speaking, except in your private quarters. This time, that's your dungeon cell. So, shut up and get in the bath, mortal."

I tensed. "No. I can't follow that rule again."

"You can." He shoved me toward the bath, and my ankles twisted beneath me. "And you will. Because if you don't, you know what will happen. We have three of your loved ones. How many times are you willing to defy us? Once? Fine. You'll lose one family member. Twice? Three times? Going to sacrifice them all just because you refuse to play by our rules?"

I ground my teeth together. Without another word, I pulled off my dirtied fighting leathers and stepped into the tub, refusing to be embarrassed as the guard's gaze tracked my every move. When his eyes lingered on the curve of my thighs, I didn't react. I eased into the soothing heat and tried not to sigh.

Truth be told, the hot water soothed my sore muscles, my tired feet, my aching skin. I'd run myself into the ground trying to get back here, and a full night's sleep had done little to help me recover. Back inside Oberon's protective barrier, I was healing fast, but my ankle still throbbed with phantom pain.

The cocoon of the bath tugged at me, dragging my tired body away from the horror of my life, if only for a moment.

And then Oberon appeared at the door.

I felt him before I saw him. The tension was electric, and pinpricks of heat flared to life across my skin. But nothing about this heat felt warm. There was something dark and twisted about it, like it had been doused with poison before being lit. Like it would eat me apart if I sat too long beneath it. I stiffened in the tub and tried not to turn my head to look, but I couldn't stop myself. With a shuddering breath, I gazed behind me.

King Oberon, the crimson one-eyed dragon, lounged just inside the open door with crossed arms, leaning against the frame. His twisting horns curled out of his head and his ember eyes glowed like a bonfire in the deepest part of the night. An onyx neck-lace glittered at his throat—the one that felt like the shadow of the god. He'd taken it back from me after knocking me out in the moment I'd feared would be my last.

He smiled at the look on my face. I could only imagine what he must see. Despite all my hatred toward him—despite how deeply I wanted to look strong—I was still afraid. He had my family. He had me.

I would fight my damndest against him, but deep down I knew it would be next to impossible for me to beat him.

I had no weapons.

I had no help from Kalen this time.

I had nothing and no one but me.

I tensed when he pushed off the doorframe and strode into the room.

"Well, you're not looking much better, but it's a start." His voice scraped across me as his eyes dipped down. I did nothing to cover myself. I wouldn't give him the satisfaction, but his gaze felt like thousands of spiders crawling over me. "You have two weeks to sort yourself out. And then you're mine."

I would never be his.

He smiled when I didn't answer. I knew what he was doing—trying to goad me into breaking his precious rules. "You can pretend all you'd like that you're going to be a good little betrothed and do as I say, but I can see the hatred in your eyes. You did stab me, after all. Don't think I've forgotten about my promise to you. You will pay the price for what you've done. Your mother and your friend will die."

I flinched. Water sloshed over the sides of the bath and poured onto the timber floor, the soap like white paint across a dark canvas. My anger was a bitter lump in my throat, so thick I almost choked on it. Words begged to spill from my lips. I needed to speak. I needed to scream and shout and rage—anything to fight him—but I couldn't.

I sucked them in and held them close. I'd made some terrible mistakes. I'd acted rashly. Awful things had happened because I could not control my anger, because I let everything that had ever happened to me drive me forward with no thought to the consequences.

The three most important people in my life were in that dungeon. I would *not* give him any reason to harm them.

He arched his brow. "You have nothing to say to me?"

I glanced at the guard.

"Your Highness." The guard dipped his head. "I ordered her not to speak."

"I know you did," Oberon shot back. "What surprises me is her willingness to listen." He turned his gaze back to me and narrowed his eyes. "You're up to something."

Oh, if only that were true.

With a terrifying speed, Oberon closed the distance between us and leaned down so that his glowing eyes were only an inch from my face. The scent of him flooded my senses, that sickly lavender smell that clung to him like the leeches from the sea beyond the mountains.

"What if I hit you? Would you speak then?" When I didn't answer, he smiled. "What if I dropped your sister's bloody head at your feet?"

My entire body flinched and I glanced away, my eyes burning. That memory flashed through my mind like a wild storm. Even though Nellie was safe and sound, the trauma from that day still hung around my neck like a noose, cutting off my air and branding itself in my skin. I hadn't lost my sister, but for weeks, it had felt like I had, and that feeling wasn't going to just vanish now that I knew she was alive.

And Oberon knew that.

He let out a low chuckle and flicked his finger against my cheek. It didn't hurt, but I winced nonetheless. Anger punched my ribs, and a desperate need blinded me. I wanted to hurt him. Badly. So badly that I yearned to taste his blood and smile as the light in his eyes died.

So badly that I'd risked everything just to get my revenge, ruining my life in the process. My blind rage had landed me here. Now I couldn't help my family. I was just as trapped as they were.

With a victorious glint in his eye, Oberon stood. "Good. It seems you've learned your lesson. Surprising, given our history. But make no mistake, if you put a single toe out of line, I have your sister, your mother, and your dearest friend. I spared your sister's life once, but I will not do it again."

A chill swept down my back, despite the heat of the bath. Oberon's smile widened at the look on my face, and then he spun on his feet and vanished out the door. I gripped the side of the tub and stared down at the wooden floorboards coated with the water that had splashed over the side. I swallowed the scream of rage clawing up my throat. He was right. I couldn't do a damn thing. I was well and truly fucked.

"Betrothed," one of the maidservants whispered, her

shaky voice cutting through my thoughts. "We need to finish your bath now. Can you...please let go of the tub so that we can wash you?"

I glanced down at my hands, at the knuckles growing white. Hissing through my clenched teeth, I relaxed my grip, but the rest of me wasn't so lucky. Every muscle in my body was wound as tight as a harp string. I would snap if anyone plucked me too hard.

The maidservants finished washing me with gentle hands and then helped me towel off before leading me over to a chair situated just beside a window overlooking the small pocket of land that Oberon ruled. Bathed in light, the village of Teine looked cheery, hopeful, and glossy, despite the ramshackle homes. Happiness lived there.

I dropped into the chair and gazed down at the village while the maidservants got to work brushing out my tangled mess of hair. Every time they hit a snag, it reminded me of how Kalen's hands had felt combing through my strands. When he'd braided my hair. When we'd been trapped in that onyx castle with no one but each other, and my heart had begun to soften toward him.

How little I'd known then. He'd killed my father.

Blinking away the tears, I dragged my gaze away from Teine and looked toward the mists. *His* mists. The dense, dark fog pushed at the far edge of the Bridge to Death, swallowing up Oberon's endless sun, but...

I sat up straighter, causing the maidservant to jerk on my hair, but the sharp stab of pain was nothing compared to the sudden pounding of my heart. I'd stared at the edge of the mist on the other side of the chasm at least a thousand times in my life. Maybe even more. I'd memorized the look of it, and I knew precisely where our world ended and *his* began.

Never, not once, had it changed.

Until today.

The mists. I almost said it out loud as I lifted a shaky finger, but I swallowed the words down. Instead, I pointed insistently, leaning forward in my chair. The mists had moved. They were further across the bridge than they had ever been before, like they were...starting to come into the Kingdom of Light.

But how could that be? Nothing had changed. Oberon still ruled this land and kept the mists out. It had been that way for centuries.

One of the maidservants gasped and dropped my hair. She scurried over to the window and peered outside. "Something's happening. The mists are coming in."

"That's impossible." The other maidservant continued to work on my hair. "Just some trick of the eye, that's all."

The maidservant beside the window turned, and our gazes locked. She pressed her lips together. There was no denying what we both saw. Somehow, Oberon's barrier was failing. That only meant one thing.

The mists were coming.

Did that mean he was, too?

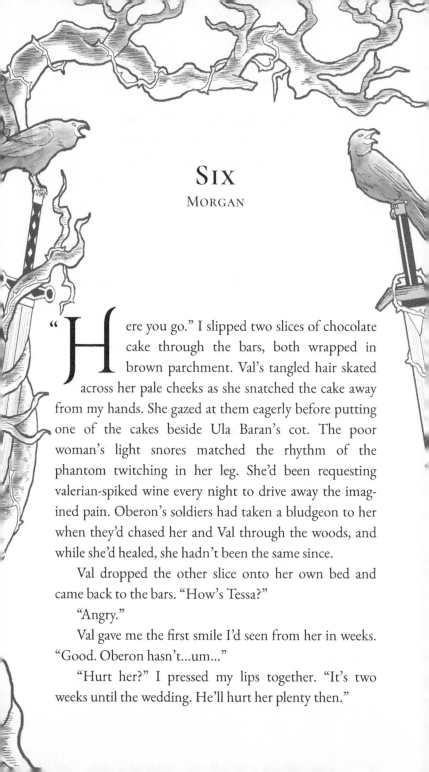

Six
Morgan

"Here you go." I slipped two slices of chocolate cake through the bars, both wrapped in brown parchment. Val's tangled hair skated across her pale cheeks as she snatched the cake away from my hands. She gazed at them eagerly before putting one of the cakes beside Ula Baran's cot. The poor woman's light snores matched the rhythm of the phantom twitching in her leg. She'd been requesting valerian-spiked wine every night to drive away the imagined pain. Oberon's soldiers had taken a bludgeon to her when they'd chased her and Val through the woods, and while she'd healed, she hadn't been the same since.

Val dropped the other slice onto her own bed and came back to the bars. "How's Tessa?"

"Angry."

Val gave me the first smile I'd seen from her in weeks. "Good. Oberon hasn't...um..."

"Hurt her?" I pressed my lips together. "It's two weeks until the wedding. He'll hurt her plenty then."

The smile dropped. "You have to get her out of there."

"I can't." My hand tightened around the sharp edge of my dagger. It pierced my palm for the hundredth time, and droplets of blood painted the floor. In a moment, the wound would be gone, but the blood would remain—along with the other dried splotches I'd left here—until a nameless maidservant scrubbed the stone. It was my only rebellion that ever made even the slightest mark, but it wouldn't last, either.

Val's eyes tracked the blood. "You need to talk to someone about this."

"About Tessa's fate?"

"No, what you're doing. The pain you're inflicting on yourself."

"And who am I supposed to talk to? You?" I asked. "What good will that do?"

"You're suffering," she said softly.

I tightened my grip on the blade, and pain lanced my palm, skittering up the side of my arm. "This small wound is the worst I can do to myself. He made sure of that, just like he made sure of a million other things. Why would you care anyway? I'm the reason your friend is in that dungeon. He made me convince Ula that the Mist King knew where you two were this whole time. And then he made me send a letter to Tessa to make sure she found out."

"Which means you *aren't* the reason, Morgan. He is. You need to stop blaming yourself for what Oberon commands you to do."

I shook my head and stepped away from the bars. "I

was the one who made this vow in the first place, even if it's trapped me here. I could have said no."

"And what would have happened to you if you had?"

Oberon had not always been a cruel king, and I'd once served him gladly. But four hundred years ago, things began to change. Whispers of dark deeds filled the halls of this castle, murmurs that the king had turned his back on the Druids and started to look to the gods. Not long after, the Druids left the Kingdom of Light, and all the ravens flew far from here, as if they sensed an impending storm. I still wasn't sure what had compelled me to warn the Kingdom of Shadow and their new ruler at the time, Kalen Denare. I had just sensed something changing, like the ravens had.

"I did something traitorous, and he caught me," I finally said to Val. "If I hadn't vowed to follow his every command, he would have taken my head. But that's no excuse. I should have chosen death over binding myself to him."

A door slammed in the distance. I stepped back and glanced down the dark corridor, shoving my blade into my belt. "I must go. Someone is coming."

"Wait," Val said, pulling her body up against the bars. "Can you please find a way to get Tessa out of here? You can't let her marry that monster. She'll be forced to make a vow just like yours."

A tremor went down my spine. The truth was, Tessa faced something darker than Val could even imagine. The Mortal Queens suffered a fate far worse than death. But I'd been forbidden to speak about that too. Oberon controlled my tongue.

"Do you have any other favorite foods? I can bring whatever you like next time I visit, just so long as the kitchen here has it."

Val lowered her forehead to the bars and sighed. "Some ale would be nice."

"I'll see what I can do." With a furtive glance over my shoulder, I jogged down the passageway and spun around the corner just as the door near Val's cell creaked open. Heavy footsteps thudded against the stone, drowning out my thundering heart.

I listened from my hidden spot around the corner, and the footsteps stopped just outside of Val's cell.

"Did I hear you speaking to someone?" the guard barked at her. I didn't recognize his voice, but he was likely one of Oberon's half-mortal sons. He liked to hand them swords and put them to work.

"What makes you think I'm not just talking to myself?" Val replied, cleverly avoiding an answer. "I'm bored out of my mind."

The guard grunted. "Better bored than dead."

I eased down the final stretch of the passageway and then climbed the nearest stairwell. Oberon was waiting for me when I stepped out into the castle halls. His horns glinted beneath the sunlight streaming in through the atrium windows, matching the harsh glow of his ember eyes. He curved his lips into a wicked smile when I stopped short.

"Ah, Morgan. You're so predictable. Visiting the prisoners again, are we?" he said in that eerie voice that sounded so unlike the fae I'd once known. Even after all these years, I could still picture the lopsided smile he'd once worn as easily as a cloak.

"I was just taking some food to them. They need to eat."

He walked toward me and flicked my armor. "The last time I checked, you're a soldier of mine. Not a maid-servant. Shall I swap your armor for sackcloth?"

All my arguments stuck in my throat. The last thing I wanted was an order to stay out of the dungeons. Despite Tessa's insistence that I leave everything up to her, I did want to help Val and Ula escape. So far, Oberon had barely given those two a second thought. That would all change if he knew I'd struck up a friendship with them.

"You can take them food all you like." His smile widened. "They'll be dead soon enough. In the meantime, I order you to do *nothing* that would lead to their escape."

My hands twitched to reach for my blade. Not to hurt him. I knew that was impossible. But I needed to feel the bite of steel against my palm. I wanted my blood to run down my fingers and paint the floor. I hadn't moved fast enough, and now the door had slammed on any hope I'd had of getting anyone out of this castle alive.

Oberon shook his head and laughed. "You truly thought you'd be able to help them? When are you going to give up, Morgan?"

"Never," I whispered.

"I wouldn't expect anything else." The bastard tapped my nose, causing me to flinch. "Which leads me to why I've sought you out. I have another order regarding my betrothed."

I lifted my chin and stared right into the depths of his eyes. "Whatever you've come up with, it won't be enough. She's going to be the end of you. Mark my words."

The king let no one else speak so boldly. For whatever reason, he'd never given me an order to stop. Sometimes, I thought he must find great joy in it, hearing my hatred toward him and knowing I could do nothing but strain against the bonds he'd forced around me. It would not entertain him if I just bowed my head and whimpered beneath his gaze. He wanted me to fight.

So, he merely rolled his eyes. "The mists across the bridge are acting strangely today."

"Strangely?" I went still. "How?"

"It's likely nothing," he said, waving his hand dismissively, but I didn't miss the tensing of his shoulders. "They've come a little further onto the bridge, that's all."

My heartbeat quickened. "The barrier is failing?"

"No," he snapped. "Of course not. My magic is keeping the mists out, the same as it has for almost four centuries now. But I need to know what's caused it to shift. Is it the Mist King? Is he trying to attack me somehow? You need to find out."

"He won't tell me a damn thing, not after the little trick you had me pull on Tessa."

"Then find out what my betrothed knows," he countered. "The timing is suspicious, is it not? She spends time in his dreadful mists, and when she returns here, they start coming across the bridge."

"I thought you said it was nothing."

He narrowed his gaze. "It is nothing, but they're both

clearly *trying* to work against me, and I need to know their plan. This is an order, Morgan. Start by questioning her sister. And see if the guards have noticed anything odd. Now go."

Without another word, Oberon left me in the glittering corridor to stew in my thoughts. He wanted me to believe it was nothing, but that clearly wasn't the case. His powerful barrier had kept the mists out for centuries. They wouldn't move unless his magic was failing.

We might have hope yet. If only I didn't have to ruin it.

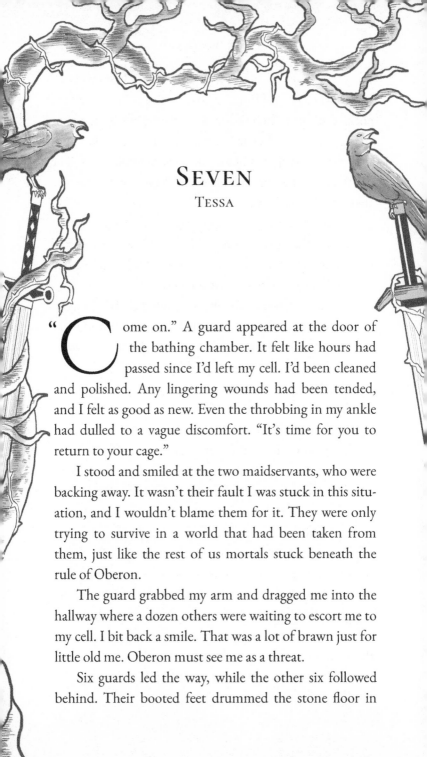

SEVEN
TESSA

"Come on." A guard appeared at the door of the bathing chamber. It felt like hours had passed since I'd left my cell. I'd been cleaned and polished. Any lingering wounds had been tended, and I felt as good as new. Even the throbbing in my ankle had dulled to a vague discomfort. "It's time for you to return to your cage."

I stood and smiled at the two maidservants, who were backing away. It wasn't their fault I was stuck in this situation, and I wouldn't blame them for it. They were only trying to survive in a world that had been taken from them, just like the rest of us mortals stuck beneath the rule of Oberon.

The guard grabbed my arm and dragged me into the hallway where a dozen others were waiting to escort me to my cell. I bit back a smile. That was a lot of brawn just for little old me. Oberon must see me as a threat.

Six guards led the way, while the other six followed behind. Their booted feet drummed the stone floor in unison, a song of brutal force and cruelty. It was one I'd heard far too many times in my life. Every time the king enacted his punishments on a mortal traitor in Teine, he brought a score of guards with him. They marched into the village and spilled blood onto the trampled dirt. The courtyard reeked of lavender and death for hours, and that steady *tha-rump, tha-rump, tha-rump* of soldier boots echoed in the silence of the terrified village.

It was the same sound I'd heard when Oberon had strung up my father, and the memory of it brought a sick taste to the back of my throat even now.

But it had not been Oberon, not like I'd thought. He'd shown my father's broken body to the mortals of Teine as a warning, but he'd taken credit for the worst of it.

The Mist King had done it.

Kalen had done it.

My heart burned in my chest.

We wound down the steps, taking us past the Great Hall. Voices drifted out through the open door, and I recognized the loudest of them instantly. Oberon was inside.

"These are traitorous accusations." The thunderous boom of his voice echoed like a shout in the chasm. I sucked in a breath and cut my eyes to the side as we passed the open door. The king was inside the hall, perched on his crimson throne, but the tension in his body betrayed him. He sneered down at a cluster of courtiers I recognized from my month spent trapped in this castle. His closest confidantes. His allies.

A horned fae with jet black hair scowled and folded

his arms. "How is it traitorous to point out the obvious? The mists have moved. We demand to know what's going on, Your Grace."

Oh, this was interesting. I tried to slow my steps so that I might linger outside the Great Hall, but the steady thump of the soldiers' march urged me onwards.

"The mists don't move. My barrier prevents that. Whatever you thought you saw is wrong," Oberon answered.

One of the courtiers barked out a laugh. "Oh come now, Oberon. You can't expect us to ignore what's right in front of our eyes. The mists haven't moved in centuries and yet they're further across the bridge now. It's obvious to every single fae I've talked to today."

"*Your Grace*," Oberon seethed. "You will address me with my proper title or I'll banish you from this discussion at once."

But that was the last I heard. The conversation was soon drowned out by the heavy footsteps. I mulled over the words as we made our way down to the dungeons. The other fae nobles had noticed the mists, and they weren't happy about it, especially because Oberon seemed determined to ignore it was happening.

Excitement rushed through my veins, as heady as a bucketful of ale. If the barrier was failing, had the Mist King found a way to get inside the Kingdom of Light? But just as quickly as I smiled, my stomach dropped. That wasn't a good thing. If the Mist King came, so would the monsters that lurked inside his mists, and the mortals of Teine wouldn't stand a chance.

And he'd killed my father. Who was to say any of us would be safe if he took over this land?

When we reached my cell, I breathed a sigh of relief seeing Nellie perched on the bed flipping through a book. She was safe and sound. Well, as safe and sound as she could be in this place. The guards opened the door, shoved me inside, and then twisted the key in the lock.

Nellie snapped the book shut and leapt from the bed. "You're all right."

"I'm fine, Nellie."

She nibbled on her bottom lip. "I was worried."

"I know." Sighing, I wound my arms around her and breathed her in. "But he needs me. Don't forget that."

She pulled back and frowned. "To become his bride. But why you? Why is he so determined to marry *you*?"

"I don't know." I crossed the room and sat on the edge of the bed. "But listen, something's happening." Quickly, I filled her in on what I'd seen and heard. Nellie's eyes grew wider with every word I spoke.

"What do you think that means?" she asked when I'd finished explaining.

"It means the barrier is failing." I leaned forward. "Whether it's because Oberon's powers are dying or because the Mist King has found a way inside the Kingdom of Light, it doesn't matter. The result is the same."

"The mists are coming," she whispered.

I nodded. "And whenever that happens, we need to be gone from this place. You, me, Mother, and Val. All the mortals in Teine. Oberon lied to us about a lot of things...I think. But there's one thing I can swear to you is true. The mists are full of dangerous things, and they will kill us all if they come here."

Nellie shivered and hugged her arms to her chest. "You're scaring me."

"I'm sorry. I just want you to be prepared for what's to come." I took her hand and squeezed. "This could be a good thing, when all is said and done. Oberon's courtiers aren't happy. If the mists keep pushing across the barrier, he'll lose control of his court. The wedding won't happen. I won't have to make that marriage vow. And then we can get out of here."

"Speaking of the wedding...Morgan came by earlier, asking lots of questions." Nellie glanced at the guards standing watch at the end of the passageway. "She questioned them too. Loudly."

I leaned forward. "What was she asking about?"

"You, mainly. She wanted to know if you'd made some kind of plan with the Mist King."

"Some kind of plan," I murmured, putting two and two together. "Oberon's convinced that I have something to do with the mists coming across the bridge, so he ordered Morgan to investigate. What did you tell her?"

"Well, I told her the truth. You and the Mist King aren't exactly on good terms right now. He lied to you about Val and Mother. And then you tried to kill him. How would you two be working together?"

I stood from the cot and started pacing the cell. "That's good. She needs to think we're at odds."

"*Aren't* you at odds?" Nellie shook her head and laughed. "I mean, you tried to kill him, Tessa."

"Yes, we're at odds, but...it's more complicated than

that." Even I didn't know how to explain it. What Nellie had said was true. And a single dream—one where we both leveled blades at each other—hadn't changed that. Especially when the truth was far worse than I would have guessed. The Mist King had killed my father.

But something in me yearned to speak with him again.

I needed to know if what he'd told me was true.

Nellie cocked her head and dropped her voice to a whisper. "For the love of light, Tessa. Are you actually working with him?"

"No," I said quickly. "I'm not, but...he might be behind this."

"Well, don't say anything about it to anyone, because Morgan is snooping around," she whispered back. "She even asked the guards if you've been talking in your sleep about it."

I stiffened. Did Morgan know about Kalen's power over dreams? "What did they say?"

"They told her you had a nightmare last night, but that all you did was mumble." She took my hand, pulling me toward her. "It's happening again, isn't it? Your dreams. That's why you're being strange."

Nellie knew about the dreams. I'd told her back when the captain—who we now knew was the Mist King—used them to speak to me about the gemstones.

I nodded.

She hissed. "You can't trust him, Tessa. He lied to you about Mother and Val."

"That was mostly Morgan," I admitted.

Her eyes widened. "So that's why you warned me about her."

A few moments passed in silence before my sister spoke again. "She asked the guards to tell her the next time you have a nightmare."

"That could be at any time," I said. "I don't control the dreams. He does."

It could be tonight. An unwanted storm of ravens rushed through my stomach at the thought.

"Right. I won't sleep, just in case," she said with a nod. "And if you start mumbling about anything, I'll wake you up. That way, they won't hear anything important."

I sat hard on the bed beside her and tipped my head toward hers. "That's not fair to you."

"We're in this together, you and I." She cast a quick glance over my shoulder as the guards started toward us, likely seeing our actions as suspect. "Tell him about the mists. Find out if he has a plan. I don't want to trust him, but..."

"He might be our only way out of here."

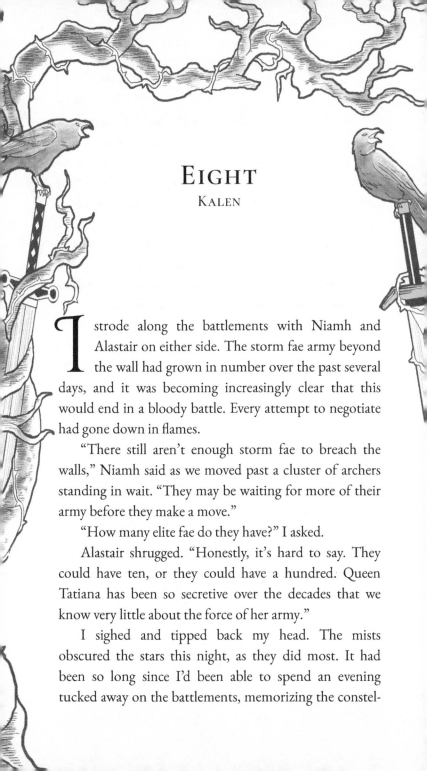

EIGHT
KALEN

I strode along the battlements with Niamh and Alastair on either side. The storm fae army beyond the wall had grown in number over the past several days, and it was becoming increasingly clear that this would end in a bloody battle. Every attempt to negotiate had gone down in flames.

"There still aren't enough storm fae to breach the walls," Niamh said as we moved past a cluster of archers standing in wait. "They may be waiting for more of their army before they make a move."

"How many elite fae do they have?" I asked.

Alastair shrugged. "Honestly, it's hard to say. They could have ten, or they could have a hundred. Queen Tatiana has been so secretive over the decades that we know very little about the force of her army."

I sighed and tipped back my head. The mists obscured the stars this night, as they did most. It had been so long since I'd been able to spend an evening tucked away on the battlements, memorizing the constellations. Everyone blamed me for bringing ruin upon us all —which was true—but what few understood was that I'd destroyed my own happiness too. I missed the starlight. If only I could control the mists, I'd send them away.

"Then we should move forward expecting an attack from a hundred elite storm fae, just in case. They could bring down this wall if they blasted their enormous strength at it."

"I think that probably means they don't have a hundred." Niamh paced, rubbing the bottom edge of the scar on her face. She always did that when she was itching for a fight. "Or they would have done it already."

"Now is not the time for this." I gripped the stone edge and leaned out into the mists. "This battle is a fucking distraction and nothing more. I need to get to Albyria."

Niamh and Alastair exchanged a glance.

"Don't," I warned them both. "I know what you're thinking, and you need to keep those bloody thoughts to yourself."

"It's just..." Alastair couldn't help himself. He grinned. "You seem awfully worried about the girl who tried to kill you."

"Oberon is winning. He's marrying her soon, and then he'll bind his forces with the storm fae. The whole damned world should be worried."

"Right, Kal." Niamh patted me on the shoulder. "That's the only reason you're worried."

"Of course it is. If it was anything more than that, I'd be an idiot."

"Well," Alastair chuckled, "at least you said it and not me."

A low growl rumbled in the back of my throat. "I don't have time for this. I—"

And that was when I felt it. A familiar voice calling in the back of my mind, tugging me toward her dreams. Stiffening, I stared out at the growing storm fae army. In the past, I'd always answered her call, but I couldn't any longer. Things had changed irrevocably between us, and the truth was like the gaping Great Rift that stood between me and the Kingdom of Light. We could never breach it. She was Tessa Baran. And I was the bloody Mist King. We could never be allies, and we could never be friends.

Let alone anything more.

"I know that look," Alastair said quietly. "Go on then. See what she wants."

Furrowing my brow, I glanced at him. "You would have me go to her, even after everything she's done?"

"It's like you said. Oberon's got her. We don't want that. So maybe by talking to her, you can find a way to get her away from him again."

"She doesn't want me to help her. I killed her father."

"She's calling for you, Kal," Niamh said with a sad smile. "Go see what she wants."

Tessa often dreamt of the forest, and while I could take her anywhere I'd been in the world, I let her lead me to that place filled with bird-song, sap, and shadows. Normally, I found an empty tree bent with age, its bark forming a seat beneath the drooping evergreen leaves. But she took up that space now. She sat with her arms wrapped around her legs, her chin on her knees. As I approached, my boots crunching fallen twigs, she closed her eyes, like she couldn't stand the thought of seeing me.

A dagger of pain sliced my heart. Why did this have to be so fucking complicated?

"I wasn't sure you'd come," she said by way of greeting. "Since you seem to hate me and my family."

She had a right to be angry. I still held a grudge against Oberon after all these years for what he'd done to my mother. And calling it a "grudge" was putting it lightly.

"I don't hate you."

"You have an interesting way of showing that," she said with a bitter laugh.

"You're one to talk." She looked so innocent sitting there, with her legs tucked up to her chest, but I knew what she was capable of. "Why did you call me to your dreams? To argue? To see who could wield their words with a sharper blade? Because if so, I have better things to do."

I turned to go but she cleared her throat before I got more than half a step away. "These better things you need to take care of. What are they, anyway?"

I leaned against the tree and folded my arms. "Why would I tell you that? I'm not sure I can trust you."

"I don't trust you, either," she said with a frown. "I don't trust anyone."

"Good. I'm glad we got that cleared up. Anything else?"

"Are you outside of Albyria? Out in the mists on the other side of the Bridge to Death?" she asked, lifting her chin from her knees to gaze up at me. Her bottomless brown eyes seemed to pierce right through me. Dammit.

"The Bridge to Death? Is that what you call it?" Oberon really had woven quite the tale for the mortals. Perhaps for his own fae as well. To cross that bridge was to walk straight into your final day in this world. For many, I had to admit, that was true. But not because I wanted to roast people alive and consume their flesh. I'd done a lot of terrible things in my life, but that kind of monstrous indulgence—a practice begun by the gods— was one thing I would never do.

"Seems like a pretty accurate title, if you ask me." She dropped her legs on either side of the branch and gave me a frank perusal. "You have no idea what I'm talking about, though, do you?"

My eyebrows pinched together. "What?"

"I can tell by the look on your face. You don't know why I'm asking you if you're outside of Albyria, which means..." Her voice dropped to a whisper. "It isn't you."

Annoyance burned through me. "Stop speaking in riddles. *What* isn't me?"

Victory lit her eyes as her lips curled into a smile. She swung her leg over the branch and hopped down, fallen leaves crunching beneath her boots. As she stalked toward me, I held my body still, forcing my heartbeat to remain steady. But my gaze wandered from her face, drifting to the cascade of silken hair around her shoulders, to the curve of her breasts beneath the snug tunic, to the hand tucked behind her back where I knew she hid a dagger.

I took every single inch of her in, and I reveled in her.

"I'd hoped you had a plan, but this is almost as good. Because I know more than the Mist King does for once," she said with a luxurious laugh. Delight danced in her eyes. "Now, get out of my dream."

Mist seeped from my skin as I curved over her. She tipped back her head, and her throat bobbed as she swallowed hard. "You forget. I'm the one in control here. Not you."

"I don't want my father's murderer in my dreams."

"You called me. You always do." A smile tipped up the corners of my lips. "You always have."

Her eyes narrowed. "I said get out."

Suddenly, she whipped the wooden dagger out from behind her back and shoved the pointy end right into my throat, though she stopped before the sharp end could draw blood, not that it could in a dream. Her eyes flashed. "You killed my father. I should kill you for good this time."

"Unfortunately for you, we're in a dream. And you know the truth about your father. I had no other choice but to kill him."

Her gaze swept across my face, her brow pulled down. "How can I be sure you aren't lying to me about that? He never said anything to me about the gods. I'll admit he was acting strangely the last few months I saw him, and he did leave Teine to search the mists for something, but..."

"Perhaps he didn't tell you because he didn't want you to know."

Her face tightened. "That doesn't make sense. And besides, even if everything you say is true, that doesn't change the fact you stole his life from him. There must have been another way to stop—"

"I made a vow," I said before I could stop myself, my heartbeat thundering against my ribs. "To my mother—centuries ago. It's one I've never been able to turn away from, no matter how hard I try. She made it so that even if she died, I could never escape it."

"A vow?" Her arm dropped heavily to her side.

"A binding one, the same kind we shared when I asked you to kill Oberon for me. It's one of the reasons I released you from it. I didn't want it to have the same hold over you as mine has over me. It's made me do things that will haunt me for the rest of my life, and it will continue to make me do things I don't want to do. That's why I killed your father, Tessa. I had no other choice."

"I..." She took a step back, and the wooden blade in her hand tumbled onto the leaves. "Why are you telling me all this?"

"Because I want you to understand," I said. "I know how it feels for someone to steal a loved one from you. That anger. That hatred. And I know what you must think of me. I don't expect that to change, but I do want you to understand."

"Why?" she asked, tipping back her head to gaze up

into my eyes. "I tried to kill you. We're not even friends. We're enemies."

"Are we enemies?" I murmured. "Or have we merely misunderstood each other in a very horrible, twisted way?"

"It's quite the misunderstanding," she whispered back. "You, showing up in my dream and putting a dagger against my throat. Me, shoving a real blade into your chest, thinking it would turn you into a pile of ash."

"Except it didn't."

"It could have."

"But it *didn't*."

For a moment, neither of us even breathed. Her neck bobbed as she swallowed, and my eyes followed the path of the tear that traced a line down her flushed cheek. Heart aching, I stayed my ground, knowing that if I made a move toward her, she'd only push me away.

But then she wrapped a hand around my tunic and tugged me close. "Tell me about this vow."

I loosed a breath, all too aware of how close her body was to mine. "That's a long story, one I still don't fully understand, even now. When I was younger, my mother sailed to the human lands to seek answers about the history of Aesir. She came upon a prophecy that convinced her the gods would soon return to this world. And then she made me vow to stop it from happening, and to kill anyone who brought them back. I'm to look out for a white comet in the sky."

"A white comet," she said with a frown. "What's that supposed to mean?"

"She believed it would herald their return, and

whoever caused it must die, or else that would be the end of this world. For a long time, I thought the person to do this would be Oberon, but the years have passed, and no comet has come."

She released her grip on my tunic. "You could be lying to me about this."

I tucked a finger beneath her chin and leaned toward her. "I swear it on my mother's memory."

Suddenly, the dream blinked away, and my quarters back in Dubnos solidified before my eyes. Tessa and the forest were gone. Frowning, I stood from my chair and cracked open the door to see if someone had been calling for me, but there was nothing in the passageway other than the dancing shadows from the torches mounted along the walls.

I shut the door just as I heard her call for me again.

A breath later, I'd returned to her dream. But this time, we stood in the mists just outside of Itchen, the imposing onyx castle a blur of shadows that stretched up toward the hidden stars. Tessa's hair whipped around her, and she stood shivering in the icy darkness. She frowned as soon as she saw me.

"Where did you go?" she asked. "Why are we here now?"

"I don't know. The dream stopped for me too." A shiver crept along the back of my neck. Something was wrong. "And I didn't choose to come here. You must have."

She shook her head, jaw tensing. "This is the last place I'd want to be."

"Take my hand," I shouted into the wind. We needed

to go somewhere else. It would be too difficult to continue our conversation here. "Let's go back to—"

My voice cut off as soon as I saw him. Brown hair whipped around a lined face pockmarked with bloodshot eyes and a cluster of burns along his right cheek. He raced through the mists toward the onyx castle, his tattered boots slipping on the sand. Cold plunged through my body, as if I'd suddenly been dunked into a frozen lake while the ice closed in over my head. I couldn't breathe. I couldn't move. Until I remembered that Tessa *was standing right there*.

I moved in front of her, but it was far too late. She'd spotted him.

She took two slow steps before breaking out into a run. "Father!"

"No." I snatched her arms and hauled her back. "You don't want to see this."

"Let go of me." She struggled against me. I closed my eyes and turned her away from the sight. I needed to stop this. I had to gain control of this dream, but the core of my power seemed to slip through my fingers, like the sand that billowed around us. "Kalen, stop!"

"This is a memory you don't want to see," I said into her ear. "Just trust me on this. You don't want to look, and I can't control this, or I'd take us far away from here."

She stilled, gripping my hand as a familiar voice called out in the distance. My voice. "You cannot go inside there."

Tessa breathed out. "Let me see."

"Please, you don't—"

"I need to see it, Kalen."

This was the last thing I wanted. I hadn't brought her here on purpose, had I? Deep down, I knew she needed to understand the truth about her father, but not like this. She should not have to see the moment the life left his eyes. Eyes that she had loved, that she had trusted. No matter what he'd done, I didn't want her to experience a loss this harsh.

But it was her decision, not mine. And so I released her.

She stumbled away from me, toward the castle. I followed just behind her, my heart twisting into tangled ribbons of guilt. She stopped just as her father and another man reached the guard at the entrance to the castle. I—the me of the past—strode purposely behind them with a sword in his hand. In *my* hand. My face was hard and tense and cruel. I could see the truth in it now. I looked like the Mist King.

The guard shifted, frowning at Tessa's father. "You cannot go inside."

Nash Baran walked right up to the guard, unarmed, while the other man held back. The guard narrowed his eyes, but he was fae and did not see this human as a threat. The old me shouted into the wind, but it did not matter. Nash placed his hands on the fae's neck and then jerked his head with a strength he should not possess. The guard was dead within seconds. His body hit the ground.

Tessa cried out, her hands flying to her throat. She stumbled into me, and her back hit me hard. I held her arms to keep her steady, but I didn't force her to turn away. If she needed to see this, then so be it.

"What did he just do?" she breathed. "How did he—?"

The past me closed the distance and came up behind Tessa's trembling father. "I can't let you go in there. I know what power it is you're playing with, and I won't let you release it."

Nash turned toward me with a vicious glint in his eye. Tessa flinched. "You can't stop me. I'll just kill you too."

In the memory, I took a wide step back. "You won't get close enough to me for that to work. What is your name?"

Her father wet his lips. "Nash Baran of Teine. The savior of our village, as soon as I release the god's power and use it against Oberon. And against you, if you don't leave me to it."

"Step away from the door, Nash. Go with your friend back there and never return to this place," I said gently. "I don't want to kill you, but I will if you refuse to leave. Go back to your home in Teine. Go back to your family."

"Yes, Nash. Come on. It's time for us to leave," the other man said, his voice soft and full of fear.

Nash hissed. "You can't stop this. Even if you kill me, my daughter will follow in my footsteps. She and I, we're the same."

"Step away from the door. Now."

But her father just laughed, twisted toward the door, and reached for the handle. Tessa's body began to shake. I closed my eyes, wincing at the sound of my sword slicing through flesh. Tessa's shaking turned violent, full of anguish and pain. And then the world beneath my feet dropped away.

We landed in the castle courtyard in Dubnos, my hands still wrapped around Tessa's arms. She yanked away from me, opened her mouth to likely rail at me for what I'd done, but I didn't hear a word she said. I was too busy staring at twenty-eight-year-old me, with my half-brother in front of me and my sister behind.

The image of my younger self was a stark contrast to the towering, brutal fae king we'd just seen. In this memory, I shuffled uneasily—face pale, eyes full of fear. Rhiannon wore a pale blue gown and cried into her shaking hands. Enysien's smirk tore right through me.

"No." I fell onto my knees. "I can't watch this."

"What's going on?" Tessa started toward me, but I couldn't bear to answer. I turned away, jaw clenching, tension wracking my body. The worst moment of my life sprang into action just beyond my line of sight, but I didn't need to look. Every second of it was forever burned into my mind.

"Get away from her," the younger me shouted at Enysien. "I won't let you kill her."

"Kalen, what's going on?" Tessa repeated.

But my lips were nailed shut. I bent over the ground, dug my fingers into the dirt, and clung, knowing the words that came next.

"The crown will be mine," Enysien said. "Our father

said Rhiannon's line will be the end of us all. I won't let that happen."

Steel sang as Enysien rushed forward. My younger self bellowed, loosing my erratic power. It exploded with an avalanche of mist and brutal pain. Enysien hit the ground, and Tessa gasped. A second thump soon followed, and my younger self's screams echoed through Dubnos when he—*I*—turned to see my sister's broken body on the ground.

"No!" The younger me moaned as he fell to his knees. He pulled my sister's lifeless body onto his lap and howled at the stars, tears streaming down his face. "I didn't mean to, I didn't mean to. I was trying to save you!"

Tessa shouted into the wind as we hurtled toward the ground, crashing heavily onto the battlements that wound around the edge of Dubnos. Matho held another version of my younger self over the edge, his face red, his neck bulging. Younger Kalen just hung there limply as my father shouted into his face.

"You killed him, you bastard," he hissed at younger me, his spittle spraying. "I won't let you get your hands on that fucking throne!"

I knelt on the stone and stared, numbness creeping over me. I couldn't take any more of this. But any time I tried to reach out to my magic, it whispered away from me like leaves on the wind.

Tessa's hand gripped my shoulder. "Kalen, what's happening? Why are we spinning through your memories like this?"

I just shook my head. My voice had left me.

"Let him go," my mother's calm, clear voice rang out in the silence.

Father scowled, but he pulled younger me back over the ledge and dropped him onto the stone. "He fucking killed him. I will have his head."

Mother walked right up to her husband and slit his throat.

Another flash. Another memory. I couldn't even bear to open my eyes, knowing exactly what this one would show. It was the last remaining piece of my twisted past. The truth I'd fought so hard to ignore all these years.

We were in the Great Hall, my mother and me, sitting at our table alone. There were three empty seats that surrounded us. As if I was reliving it all over again, an unsettling loneliness, combined with a deep-seated grief, pushed down on my shoulders.

"I've received some unsettling news about the other kingdoms," Mother said, her fork scraping her plate. "They've heard of our...troubles. I believe Oberon intends to cease trade with us."

I lifted my head to watch my younger self frown. "We can't lose their trade. Why don't you go meet with King Oberon? You were friends with Bronwen, his mother. I'm sure if you speak to him face to face, he won't be able to renege on our trade deals. No one can ever say no to you."

Mother nodded and smiled. "What an excellent idea. I'll make plans to leave by the end of the week."

Mercifully, the memories stopped. One more stab at my fragile casing, and my soul would shatter. The star-filled sky spread before me, and at long last, I collapsed to the ground, crushed by the weight of my past. I glanced up at the ink above, but it did little to comfort me now.

Tessa settled onto the ground beside me. What must she think?

"I'm sorry you had to see all that." I couldn't bear to look at her. Any hope we'd had at reconciliation was gone, all because I'd lost control of the dream. She'd seen *everything*. "You must hate me even more than you already did."

Tessa edged a little closer and dropped her head onto my shoulder, her hair whispering against my cheek. I stiffened beneath her touch, but I didn't dare move away. "No, Kalen. I can't hate you for that."

"But you saw me kill your father. You saw me kill my sister, my half-brother. That's who that was, Tessa. My family." My voice broke, but I continued on, the words spilling out of me now, like a poisonous gemstone had cracked open inside of me, washing acid through my veins. "I was the reason my father died, even if he was a bastard who loved the gods. And I told my mother to meet with Oberon. He eventually killed her, which means I'm responsible for the death of my entire family. Everyone except for one. My other half-brother, who lives in Star Isles. He refuses to speak to me, even after all these years, and I do not blame him."

The weight of Tessa's head was a soothing comfort, and when it vanished, a part of me felt adrift. She shifted sideways, took my face in her in palms, and captured my gaze with earnest eyes. "It's not your fault."

I opened my mouth to argue, but she shook her head.

"Listen to me," she said gently, still cupping my face. "I understand how you're feeling. I've felt the same way too. Look at what I've done. Not just to you, but to everyone else. I know what it is to want to rewind the past and choose a different path. One that can save everyone, even if it means losing myself along the way."

I captured her hand and pulled her closer, wanting to feel the warmth of her body against mine. "You understand."

"More than you'll ever know," she whispered. "More than most ever could. I'm so sorry for what I did to you, Kalen. If I could take it back, I would."

And I knew at once that she meant every word. Her own pain and guilt reflected right back onto me, and I wanted to erase it all. I wished she did not have to hurt the way I did. Fuck the fact she'd stabbed me. It didn't matter, not when Oberon had been pulling her strings and poisoning her mind. Not when I understood exactly why she did it. I would have done it too.

"I'm the one who is sorry. You shouldn't have had to witness what happened to your father, and I never would have shown it to you like that." I furrowed my brow. "I don't understand it. It was like I lost complete control over my powers. That's never happened before. Except..."

Tessa pulled back, her face grim. "Except when we were in Itchen and the god muted your powers."

My entire body went taut. "No. Surely not. It can't be the god's power."

"It's the only explanation," Tessa whispered, glancing up at the stars. "I thought I hadn't released her."

"There's been no white comet," I pointed out. "If you'd released her, we would have seen it by now."

"That was only half of her power. Oberon has the other half in his necklace." Tessa gripped my hand. "I tried to take it from him, but he got it back after he hit me in the head and I lost consciousness."

"He did *what*?" I asked in a growl, climbing to my feet, the venomous snake inside of me lifting its head.

"None of that matters now." She rose from the swaying grass and then tilted her head. "No, I'm not done yet. Wait a—"

And then she blinked out of the dream. I reached for her, and my fingers brushed the wind. Even the stars fell from the sky, drenching me in darkness. If it weren't for her faint scent on the air, it would have been like she'd never been there.

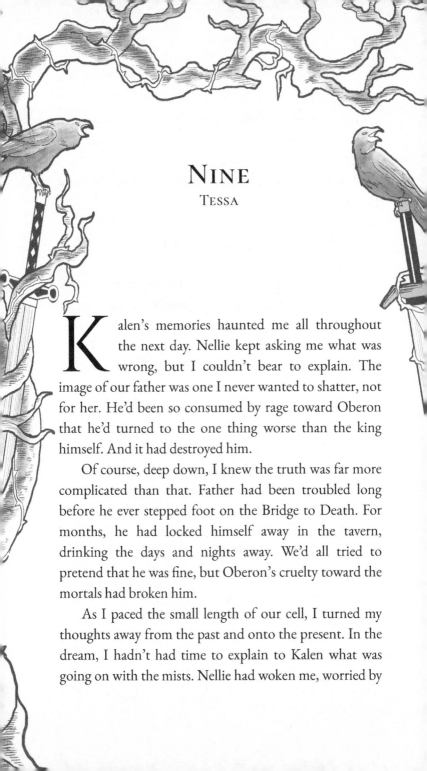

NINE
TESSA

K alen's memories haunted me all throughout the next day. Nellie kept asking me what was wrong, but I couldn't bear to explain. The image of our father was one I never wanted to shatter, not for her. He'd been so consumed by rage toward Oberon that he'd turned to the one thing worse than the king himself. And it had destroyed him.

Of course, deep down, I knew the truth was far more complicated than that. Father had been troubled long before he ever stepped foot on the Bridge to Death. For months, he had locked himself away in the tavern, drinking the days and nights away. We'd all tried to pretend that he was fine, but Oberon's cruelty toward the mortals had broken him.

As I paced the small length of our cell, I turned my thoughts away from the past and onto the present. In the dream, I hadn't had time to explain to Kalen what was going on with the mists. Nellie had woken me, worried by the tears streaming down my face, concerned that the guards would notice my nightmare. Dreams were only dreams, but the emotions I felt in them were sometimes more true than reality itself. And after that, sleep had eluded me.

I couldn't stop thinking about Kalen's loss of control. Had I released half of the god's power? And was she now visiting my dreams?

"Someone's coming," Nellie whispered from her bed. She leapt to her feet as the door at the end of the passageway swung wide and a handful of guards stormed inside. My shoulders tightened, and I moved between Nellie and the bars. I tracked the guards as they rushed toward us. Keys jangled in the nearest one's hands. I braced myself for whatever Oberon might throw at me next.

I would not let them take Nellie from me.

The guards stopped just outside our cell, and the one holding the key unlocked the door. He pointed a gloved finger at me, ignoring Nellie. "You. Come with us."

Nellie grabbed my arm, and she tugged me back. "Where are you taking her?"

"Don't worry about it," I whispered to her. "It's fine."

She raised her voice. "Where are you taking her?"

The guard scowled. "Quiet, both of you. The king is waiting, and you do not want to make him angry."

Nellie's grip on me tightened, but then she let out a hiss and released my arm.

I stepped through the open door and joined the

guards in the passageway. After locking the cell door again, they led me through the dimly lit dungeons, up the stairs, and through the crimson halls to where Oberon waited for me inside the Great Hall.

The vast room was silent and empty for once. Oberon lounged on his crimson throne, one leg crossed over the other, arms relaxed. His curving horns rested on the back of the chair as his eyes narrowed on me. I stood at the end of a narrow carpet that led toward him. Where tables once sat—holding lamb stew, bone broth, buttered potatoes, spinach soaked in bacon fat, plum pudding, and sweet sponge cakes—now sat a guillotine. A fire raged in the open hearth, and it splashed orange and yellow light across the one-eyed dragon banners that hung along the walls.

Oberon's gaze hardened as he dismissed his guards, leaving me alone with my worst enemy. The door slammed behind me. "My betrothed. The bearer of my future children. And the thorn in my side."

My lips twitched with the threat of a smile, but I held it back. I wouldn't let him goad me into action. All I had to do was keep my head on my shoulders long enough to come up with a plan that could actually work.

"Do you know why I brought you here?" he asked, leaning forward and resting an elbow on his knee.

For once, I had no idea. Did it have something to do with the Mist King? After a long moment passed, I shook my head.

That was the wrong answer.

With fire in his eyes, Oberon stood and stormed

toward me. His crimson hair trailed behind him like a wave of rippling blood. I backed up, but I had nowhere to go. He reached me, seized my shoulders, and shook me so hard that my teeth collided in a sharp crack.

"Why are the mists coming into the Kingdom of Light?"

I shook my head.

"You've done something," Oberon growled into my face. Droplets of his spit landed on my chin, and I twisted away from him. "Stop it right now. Undo it. Take it back. Or I will kill every single person you love in this godforsaken world. I will rip their flesh from their bones and make you watch them scream."

My heart pattering my ribs, I tried to pull myself away from him, but he gripped me by the arm and yanked me back. "I am your king. Answer me!" His voice boomed in the silent hall, filling my head with his rage-filled words.

"I don't know," I said. "I saw the mists coming across the bridge, but I don't know how or why or who is doing it."

"You know who is doing it. It's that fucking Mist King, the one who stole you from me."

Except it wasn't. I'd seen the confusion on Kalen's face when I'd brought it up. It wasn't him. But I couldn't explain that to Oberon without letting him in on my secret. I didn't want him to know that I could communicate with Kalen. He'd find a way to use it against me. Or worse, stop me from ever dreaming of him again.

"If he's the one doing it, I don't know how, all right?" I said, hating the pleading sound of my voice. "Whatever he's trying to do, I have nothing to do with it. I tried to kill him, remember?"

Oberon scowled, though he stopped shouting in my face. One good thing about the fae's ability to smell mortal lies was that Oberon now knew I was telling the truth. He might not like it, but he couldn't ignore what his senses told him.

With a hiss, he released his hold on my arm. "I find it difficult to believe that you have nothing to do with this. My barrier has never faltered. Not for a moment, for all these centuries. And yet it shows a weakness right when *you* return from your little adventure?"

I met his gaze. "I've done nothing to your barrier, King Oberon. I'm a mere mortal."

He stiffened, and his eyes narrowed to slits. "I don't know what you're up to, but it stops here. Take off your shirt."

I blinked. "What?"

"Take off your fucking shirt." Oberon stalked toward me, grabbed the material, and ripped the tunic in half. He yanked off the rest of it and tossed it into the flames of the roaring hearth.

Swallowing, I covered myself. "What are you doing?"

"Punishing you. Turn around." When I did nothing but shake my head, he grabbed my shoulders and shoved me around so that my back faced him. I realized what he planned to do a second too late. He roughly clutched me around the waist and shoved his thumbs against my old scars, the ones he'd given me six years before.

The ones that ached even now.

Pain ripped through me. I sucked in a gasp and bit

down on my tongue so hard I tasted blood. Oberon laughed and released his grip. I sagged forward, my breath coming out in frantic gasps. Whatever he'd done to me all those years ago still followed me even now and—

"Lie down on the floor," he ordered.

I stayed frozen with my feet rooted in place. Stars danced in my eyes.

"Do what I say, or one of them dies."

Tears streamed down my cheeks. Memories of Nellie's face flashed in my mind. Not as she was now, but as she'd been then, only seventeen and scared out of her mind. She'd waved that broom around, brown bristles against a clear blue sky. Oberon would have killed her that day if I hadn't taken his punishment. And he'd kill her now too.

I shook as I lowered myself to my knees and flattened my body against the cool floor. The rough stone scraped against my cheek. I curved my fingers against it, clinging on as best as I could, but I'd find no soothing comfort here. Nothing but hard, rough stone.

The rustle of cloth soon filled my ears. Oberon was opening his little pouch again, the same one he'd had with him that day he'd made the cuts on my back. I didn't know what he stored inside that thing, but whatever it was, it came from fire. Just like him.

"You think you can defy me," he said, as he lowered himself to the floor and pinned me in place with his muscular legs. "But you still haven't learned. You cannot kill me, Tessa Baran. You cannot stop me. And you certainly cannot overpower my magic. Whatever you think you're doing, it ends now."

He poured the salt on my scars, a drizzle of sand against my skin. Sudden agony seared through me and transformed my body into one gigantic bleeding wound. The pain was an endless, all-consuming torment that burned up my mind until all I could see was blinding crimson. The red bled into black as I lost consciousness.

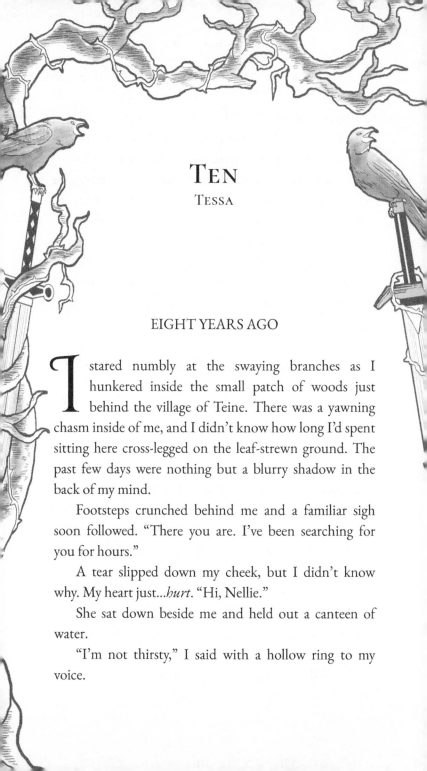

TEN
TESSA

EIGHT YEARS AGO

I stared numbly at the swaying branches as I hunkered inside the small patch of woods just behind the village of Teine. There was a yawning chasm inside of me, and I didn't know how long I'd spent sitting here cross-legged on the leaf-strewn ground. The past few days were nothing but a blurry shadow in the back of my mind.

Footsteps crunched behind me and a familiar sigh soon followed. "There you are. I've been searching for you for hours."

A tear slipped down my cheek, but I didn't know why. My heart just...*hurt*. "Hi, Nellie."

She sat down beside me and held out a canteen of water.

"I'm not thirsty," I said with a hollow ring to my voice.

"It's a hot one today," she said gently. "You need to drink."

"I don't want to."

"Too bad. Remember our deal?" She placed the canteen in my lap and leaned against the tree behind us.

I released a heavy sigh before turning my watery gaze on her. She was a blur of colors through the tears, all russet and burnt orange against the brightness of the sky. "I'm to listen to you when I feel this way."

She leaned in and brushed the tears from my cheeks. Her kind smile was like an anchor back to life, back to the sun and away from the shadows of my mind. "That's right. Just do what I ask you to do, and you'll feel better soon."

That anvil weight dragged down my heart again. "But what if I don't want to feel better?"

"Well, then my question would be, why don't you?" She pointed at the canteen. "Drink up first. Then answer."

I did what she told me to do because I didn't have the energy to fight against her. Besides, she was right. We'd agreed, years ago, to do this. It was a familiar dance. Something inside me would break, and Nellie would pick up the pieces. It was as constant as the eversun.

After I tipped the water into my parched mouth, I tried to conjure an answer that made sense, but I came up empty. "I don't know, Nellie. I just...don't. There's something wrong with me."

"And do you know why you feel wrong in the first place?"

"No." I shook my head and furrowed my brow. "I don't even know how I got here."

She pressed her lips together and turned away.

Frowning, I sat up a little straighter. We knew each other so well that even the slightest change in her posture could tip me off to what she was thinking. "Wait a minute. *You* know why, don't you?"

"So do you." She palmed my face and dropped her forehead against mine. The scent of fresh apples filled my head. "When you're ready, you'll understand. But I can't tell you, Tessa. I've tried before, and you block me out. So, I won't push you like that ever again. You'll know when you're ready to face the truth."

I blew out a breath and pulled back. "That's not fair. I need to know what is making me feel this way."

"I agree. And I hope you're ready to face it sooner rather than later. But I'm here for you in the meantime. For as long as it takes."

All I could do was shake my head. None of this made any sense.

Leaves crunched in the distance, and Nellie's back went straight.

"Tessa!" Father's voice drifted toward us. "Nellie! Are you girls out here?"

I opened my mouth to call out to him, but Nellie clamped her hand over my lips and shook her head. Frowning against her palm, I stayed still until the sound of his footsteps faded. Then Nellie leapt to her feet and took off through the woods, motioning for me to follow.

My breath was ragged by the time we reached the edge of the chasm. Wind whistled up from the deep, twirling the strands of my long golden hair around my shoulders. Nellie smiled as she tipped her head back to face the sky. She seemed to glow from within, as if she held more of the sun than the sun itself.

"What was all that about?" I asked after I'd caught my breath. "Why did we run from Father?"

"I just want it to be you and me today," she said. "Look at the chasm and all those gemstones."

I stared down into the Great Rift, my heart pounding. A thousand jewels glimmered beneath the sunlight, as if they contained a touch of Oberon's fire. According to legend, they did. "Gemstones, yes. But shadowfiends too. We're dangerously close to the edge."

"The beasts won't come up this far," she said. "We're inside the barrier where it's safe. Not out there."

I lifted my eyes from the shadows of the chasm to gaze out into the mists. They crept along the opposite cliff, pushing and prodding at the invisible barrier that Oberon had erected centuries ago. It kept us safe from the horrors of the Mist King, though I'd often questioned just how safe we truly were.

A pair of dark wings cut through the mists. A flash of feathers flared wide, spinning closer and closer until the bird cut to the left, and then slowly transformed into a vague shadow battling the harsh winds of that world.

"A raven," I said. "They won't cross the barrier, either."

"No," Nellie replied sadly. "Oberon scared them off. I doubt they'll ever return."

"Not until he's dead."

Her lips formed a thin line. "And that won't happen in our lifetime."

"Someone needs to do something," I said boldly, feeling a little more reckless and defiant now that the strange fog in my mind had finally lifted. "He says he did all this to protect us, but he kills us if we do anything he doesn't like. He's not our savior, Nellie. He's the enemy."

Nellie wrapped her arm around my back, pulled me close, and sighed. "I wish we could fly away from here, like the ravens."

"Maybe one day we will."

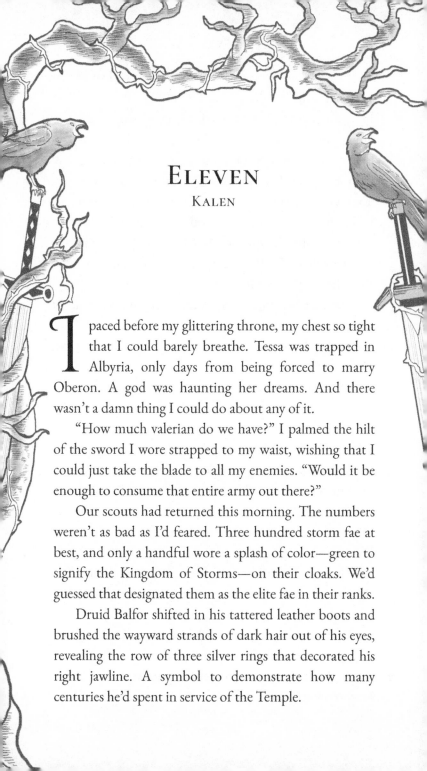

ELEVEN
KALEN

I paced before my glittering throne, my chest so tight that I could barely breathe. Tessa was trapped in Albyria, only days from being forced to marry Oberon. A god was haunting her dreams. And there wasn't a damn thing I could do about any of it.

"How much valerian do we have?" I palmed the hilt of the sword I wore strapped to my waist, wishing that I could just take the blade to all my enemies. "Would it be enough to consume that entire army out there?"

Our scouts had returned this morning. The numbers weren't as bad as I'd feared. Three hundred storm fae at best, and only a handful wore a splash of color—green to signify the Kingdom of Storms—on their cloaks. We'd guessed that designated them as the elite fae in their ranks.

Druid Balfor shifted in his tattered leather boots and brushed the wayward strands of dark hair out of his eyes, revealing the row of three silver rings that decorated his right jawline. A symbol to demonstrate how many centuries he'd spent in service of the Temple.

"We have the usual stocks," he said in a soft voice that betrayed how little he spoke. The Druids did not believe in excess chatter. They argued it led to gossip and calculating politics. They were right in that, at least. "But we do not have enough for some kind of war strategy, and even if we did, I would ask that you not use it for that, Your Grace. These are meant to be used as medicinal herbs and nothing more. To heal. Not to harm."

"It would prevent bloodshed." I stopped my pacing and frowned. "If the storm fae are not awake to fight, then there is no need for war."

"Be that as it may, we don't have enough valerian for this plot of yours to work. I'm sorry, Your Grace."

I sighed and nodded. "Thank you for your time, Druid Balfor. You may go."

He bowed his head and left the throne room, a cloud of spiced herbs scenting the air in his wake. I watched him go, almost envious of his simple life in his drab brown robes. The Druids did not like to involve themselves in war and politics. They lived in peace and cared for nature over material things. I would have liked a life like that. But someone had needed to step up when my mother had vanished, and that person turned out to be me. There had been no one else.

"It was a nice idea, Kal." Toryn eased up the stairs to the dais, wincing with every step. "But I think we both know there is only one way for this to end."

The throne's seat was hard and cold as I settled onto it. "I hate what they did to you."

"I don't want you to seek vengeance against them, just on my account."

"They almost killed you. And they took something away from you that you will likely never get back. Your storm fae powers."

Toryn flexed his hands. "I'm fairly certain that was their intention."

"Why aren't you more angry?" I shoved up from the throne, too wound to sit calmly. "They came across the border and lured us into that village. It was a pointed attack. At first I thought they did it as a way to hurt me, but it's clear there was something more behind it. Your mother did this. She wanted to make you hurt."

"It's the price we both knew I'd eventually pay, Kal. I left my kingdom to follow you. My mother was never going to let me go that easily. She tried to fight you for me once before, and she's doing it again, only now she has Oberon on her side."

"What would you have me do?"

"We can't afford to meet the storm fae on the battlefield. They only have a few elite fae, but it's enough to do serious damage to our forces. If they take out a quarter of our warriors, we will be left far too vulnerable if Oberon ever decides to attack, and he might very well do that if things go his way." Toryn gave me a steadying look. "We can wait this out and let them attack our walls when they're ready—they will never be able to take down this city that way. Or you can use your powers against them and finish this in one fell swoop."

My hands fisted. "You know I don't want to use my powers like that."

"Then we wait," he replied.

"But Tessa..."

"Needs our help."

I rubbed my jaw. If I used my power to attack the storm fae, hundreds would die in an instant. They were warriors, sent to fight a war against my kingdom, but still. I'd hated doing it almost four hundred years ago, and I would hate doing it again now.

"I'll speak with Tessa again tonight," I said. "She was trying to tell me something about the mists outside of Albyria, and she seemed to think I might be nearby."

Toryn frowned. "What do you think that could be about?"

"I have no idea. She didn't seem alarmed."

My old friend searched my gaze. "And what about you? Those memories couldn't have been easy to face again, after all these years."

I let out a bitter laugh. "I face them every fucking day, Toryn. The only difference last night was, Tessa faced them right along with me. And she did not turn away."

A silent moment passed. And then he said, "We need to find a way to get her out of there."

"I know." My hand tightened around the hilt of my sword. "But let's say we defeat the army and leave straight away. What the fuck am I supposed to do? I can't cross Oberon's barrier. There's no way for me to get to her."

But I had to find a way. Because I would not let King Oberon bind her to him. If I had to rip that entire chasm apart to get to her, I would.

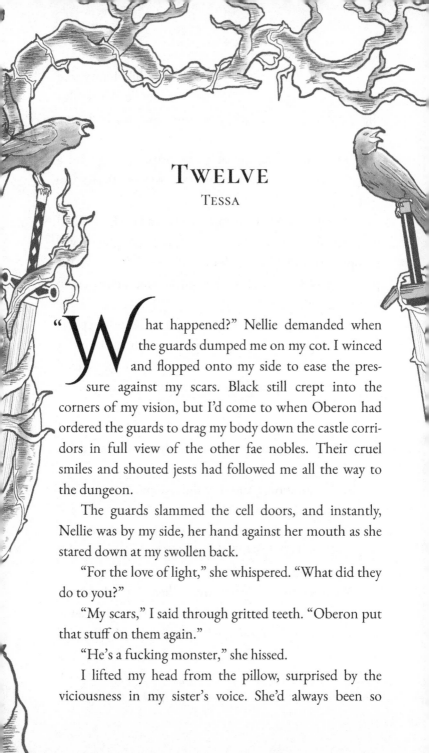

TWELVE
TESSA

"What happened?" Nellie demanded when the guards dumped me on my cot. I winced and flopped onto my side to ease the pressure against my scars. Black still crept into the corners of my vision, but I'd come to when Oberon had ordered the guards to drag my body down the castle corridors in full view of the other fae nobles. Their cruel smiles and shouted jests had followed me all the way to the dungeon.

The guards slammed the cell doors, and instantly, Nellie was by my side, her hand against her mouth as she stared down at my swollen back.

"For the love of light," she whispered. "What did they do to you?"

"My scars," I said through gritted teeth. "Oberon put that stuff on them again."

"He's a fucking monster," she hissed.

I lifted my head from the pillow, surprised by the viciousness in my sister's voice. She'd always been so demure in the face of the fae's cruelty. While I answered with reckless rage, she responded with meek silence. But the sister who stood before me now was no shrinking violet.

"Those words are music to my ears," I said with a slight smile. "Just don't let him hear you say things like that."

She perched beside me on the bed and took my hand in hers. "Why did he do this to you? I thought he was prepping you for your wedding. All the bathing and the primping. Why has he gone from looking after you to torturing you again?"

"He thinks I'm making the mists come over the bridge." I pushed up onto my elbow and winced at another flash of pain. "It only started to do that after I came back to Albyria. This was his way of getting me to stop it, I guess."

Her face paled. "But you're not the one in control of them. What's Oberon going to do when the mists don't stop?"

Good question. And I didn't want to know the answer. Because when the mists remained, the rage he felt toward me would only escalate. He'd believe that torturing me hadn't worked. So then he would turn his knives onto someone else.

"We need to get you out of here," I whispered, flicking my eyes toward the end of the passageway where the guards stood watch. "You and Mother and Val."

"If I'm leaving, you're coming, too." She frowned. "But that's impossible. We're locked up in here and those guards never leave their posts. They'd kill us before they'd let us take a single step out of this cell."

"I need to find a way to beat him at his own game. I just don't know how to do that yet. There's still over a week until the wedding, though. I have time."

"Less than that if he's going to treat you like this in the meantime." Nellie's eyes dropped to my back. "Now let me take a look at your scars. We need to figure out how long it's going to take you to recover."

I read between the lines. A fight was coming for us, one way or another. And I needed to be at full strength—what little that was compared to the fae—as soon as possible. If Oberon came for me again, my swollen scars would be the least of my worries.

Wincing, I leaned to the side to expose my back to her. My sister gently lifted my tunic away from my skin and stared down at the wounds for a good long while before she let out a hiss between her teeth. It reminded me of all those times she'd tended to me when we were children. My younger sister, the mother hen.

"Whatever he did, it's somehow broken the skin again." Her voice was hard. "The wounds look as fresh as the day they were made. They've looked like this before. They should close up in a few hours, but you'll likely feel their pain for several days."

"What in the name of light is that stuff he put on them?" I mumbled into my pillow. "We're behind the protective barrier. I shouldn't even have a scar anymore. Six years have passed, and it's still so fresh that—"

"Six years?" Nellie asked sharply.

"Yes." I lifted my head as she released the tunic, and

the material brushed against my aching skin. "Oberon came into the village six years ago, after Father tried to return from his quest or whatever it was...it feels like so much longer, but I remember like it happened yesterday. Don't you? You were there, waving that broom at him. It's always stuck with me, you know, how brave you were that day. It made me love that bloody broom."

Nellie pushed up from the bed and wandered over to the bars, her back to me.

I frowned. "Nellie, what's wrong?"

She turned back toward me and shook her head. "You're the one who needs to *remember*."

My heart pounded as I slowly eased off the cot to stand on unsteady feet. Nellie wouldn't look at me, and a strange sensation prickled the back of my neck, like there was something unseen and unknowable standing right behind me. A ghost from my past that turned to shadows when I tried to look at it. Even now, it felt as though I was looking through an opaque window. The haze consumed my mind, drowning me in mist.

"Remember what?" I whispered. "I don't understand what you're trying to say."

"Twenty years ago." Nellie frowned. "You were five. I was three. That was when he first tried to cut it out of you. It was going to be me, because I was younger, but you insisted he choose you instead. You've always protected me. Always. And I'll always protect you, too."

"What?" My heart dropped as the entire world seemed to tilt beneath me. "Are you saying Oberon came for me twenty years ago, and that I...that I don't remember it? That's impossible. It doesn't make any sense. I—"

I didn't have the scars before that day. Six years ago, that was when Oberon had cut my back.

Something screamed inside of me. An animalistic mewl that echoed through the caverns of my mind. I tried to push it away, to cling on to what Nellie was trying to tell me, but it felt as if claws were scraping through my mind. I clamped my hands over my ears, bending over on myself, sitting hard on the cot behind me.

Nellie appeared beside me in an instant. She pulled my hand away from my ear and gave me a sad smile. "I'm sorry. Forget what I said. I think I'm just confused, that's all. You should get some rest. You'll heal a lot faster if you do."

"No. Wait a minute. A second ago, you were convinced—"

"Like I said, I was wrong," she whispered quickly. "I got confused. That was a nightmare I had last night. I'm getting everything all mixed up."

She wouldn't look at me.

I frowned. "Nellie."

"Get some rest." She wrapped her arms around my neck and buried her face in my hair. "I love you, Tessa. We're going to get you out of here."

I shook my head as my sister padded across the cell and climbed into her bed. What was going on? What had she been talking about? However she'd tried to turn it around, I knew she wasn't talking about a recent nightmare. She truly believed Oberon had attacked us that long ago, and that I'd somehow forgotten it had ever happened. But how could that be?

Easing back onto the bed, I tried to think back to those early days, but my memories of childhood had always been blurry. I'd thought that was normal. As the years passed, new memories pushed aside the old. But try as I might to stay awake and figure this thing out, sleep soon claimed me, as if a part of me didn't want to wander into the past.

I sensed him. It was something electric in the air, as if the world shifted just slightly to accommodate the ultimate power of him. Mist and snow swirled toward me on the chilly wind, and as I turned, my belly did a little flip at the sight of him.

His razor-edged ears cut through the dark hair blowing around his angular face. Just like the last time I saw him, he wore snug trousers and an unbuttoned tunic that highlighted the ridges of his abs. His powerful hands tensed beside him as his sapphire gaze speared my soul.

For a moment, I could barely breathe.

"I'm glad you're all right," he finally said. "When you vanished last night, I didn't know what to think."

"Nellie woke me," I said. "I was mumbling in my sleep, and she was worried the guards would hear me. We didn't want Oberon to find out I can talk to you."

A strange tension thumped between us. After the previous night's dream, it was as if we'd come to an awkward truce. The things I'd seen...they made me understand him more than I had before. Our journey together through the mists had really only scratched the surface of knowing him. Guilt and duty weighed heavily on his shoulders. He wanted to do what was right, but his past was tainted with pain and violence and betrayal. And he was stuck in a vow he could never escape.

I wanted to be angry at him for what he'd done to my father, but I couldn't be. As hard as it was to reconcile my memories of my father with what I'd seen in Kalen's memories, I knew he'd needed to be stopped. And Kalen had been forced to be the bearer of that duty.

"I need to ask you about the mists," Kalen said, his steady voice cutting through the thickening tension. "What did you mean before when you asked me if I was outside of Albyria?"

"The mists are coming across the bridge. Not by a lot, but they've definitely shifted closer. Oberon has no idea why. He's frantic about it, and the courtiers are demanding answers. They think the barrier might be failing."

Kalen stilled. "The mists have moved."

"Do you know what it means?" I asked. "If you aren't the one doing it then—"

A shiver stole down my back. It was that same feeling as before, when it had felt as though someone's eyes were burning holes into my back. I shifted to face the wind that tugged at the wild strands of my hair, and a clap of thunder tore through the star-studded sky.

"Tessa," Kalen warned just as he grabbed my hand.

"What's going on?" My pulse ticked faster.

"Pookas are coming. Three of them. We need to run."

Pookas—the shadow fae's name for the monstrous shadowfiends that hunted in the mists. How were they here?

I narrowed my gaze at the shadowy landscape, and yes, just there...in the distance, three large forms were hurtling toward us. I took a step back, bumping up against Kalen, and his hand tightened around mine. But even the warmth of him could not chase away the sudden chill in my bones.

"I don't understand. They can't hurt us, right?"

"I don't know," Kalen growled. "I didn't bring them here. I'm not in control. *Again.* And I will not risk your life to find out just how much damage they can cause. We need to go. Now."

The pookas grew larger, and they were close enough now that I could see their elongated fangs flashing in the moonlight. Memories from the mists stormed through me, bringing a sick feeling into the back of my throat. It was as if a giant's fist had curled around my heart and was choking the blood out of it. I knew I needed to run. But I couldn't force my feet to move.

"Tessa." Kalen pulled me toward him. "We have to go."

My feet were as heavy as stone, but something in Kalen's words got them moving. He pulled me after him, and I stumbled in his wake, my vision drowned in a haze of mist. This couldn't be happening. We were safe here. The shadowfiends—the pookas—shouldn't be able to invade our dreams.

We raced from the field and into the dense woods, plunging deep into the brush. Leaves crackled beneath our hurried steps, and twigs snapped like the breaking of bones. As we ran, I focused on Kalen's steady strength, the determined set of his shoulders, the way his hair curled across his neck. The pookas screamed in the distance, a sound that scraped through my soul. They were gaining on us fast.

When we pushed out of the woods, we reached the chasm edge that separated this part of the fae world from the rest. Kalen's brows furrowed as he gazed down into the murky depths. "This shouldn't be here. Not in this dream. I didn't conjure this."

"What do we do?" I asked. "Where do we go?"

Kalen glanced over his shoulder as the shadowfiends crashed through the forest. Any moment now, they'd be on us, their fangs and claws ripping through our flesh. Would we ever wake again?

He turned back toward the chasm and looked down, and then he turned to me, his hand still holding mine. "Do you trust me, Tessa?"

My heart kicked my ribs. "Why? What are you going to do?"

"Do you trust me?" he repeated.

I stared up into his eyes and swallowed hard. "Yes."

As a pooka lunged from the depths of the woods, Kalen pulled me to his chest, wrapped his arms around me, and...leapt. Wind shook around us as we plunged into the chasm. A scream built in my throat, but my terror held it there like a lump of molten rock. Heart throbbing, I buried my face in his chest, breathing in the scent of ice and snow, willing this to stop.

But on and on we fell.

Kalen suddenly twisted to the side, angling his body toward the chasm floor. I opened my mouth to scream at him to stop, but the ground slammed into us. The whole world shattered, and chunks of rock stormed around us in a whirlwind of deadly debris.

And then everything stopped.

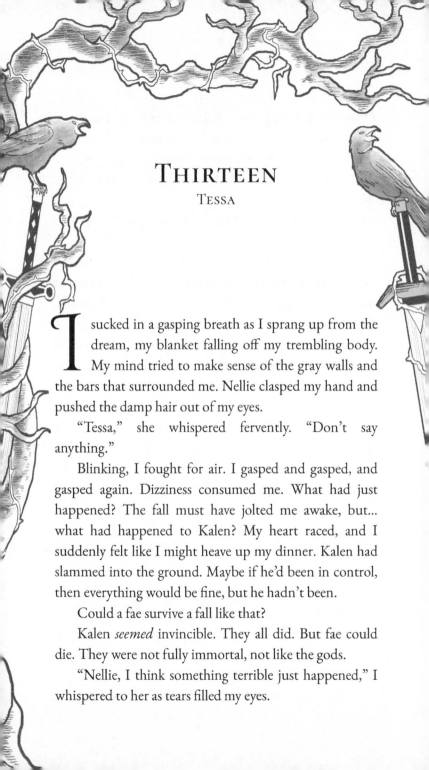

THIRTEEN
TESSA

I sucked in a gasping breath as I sprang up from the dream, my blanket falling off my trembling body. My mind tried to make sense of the gray walls and the bars that surrounded me. Nellie clasped my hand and pushed the damp hair out of my eyes.

"Tessa," she whispered fervently. "Don't say anything."

Blinking, I fought for air. I gasped and gasped, and gasped again. Dizziness consumed me. What had just happened? The fall must have jolted me awake, but... what had happened to Kalen? My heart raced, and I suddenly felt like I might heave up my dinner. Kalen had slammed into the ground. Maybe if he'd been in control, then everything would be fine, but he hadn't been.

Could a fae survive a fall like that?

Kalen *seemed* invincible. They all did. But fae could die. They were not fully immortal, not like the gods.

"Nellie, I think something terrible just happened," I whispered to her as tears filled my eyes.

She shoved her finger against my lips.

"And what would that be, my dear betrothed?" Oberon's slithering voice snaked toward me. I stiffened and turned to find him in the passageway, along with Morgan. They were both watching me intently. I pressed my lips together. How much had they seen? "Have a bad dream?"

My heart pounded. I turned to Morgan. She winced and glanced away.

"Guards!" Oberon called out, holding up a goblet overflowing with a deep crimson wine. "Feed this to my betrothed. If she resists, hold open her jaw and pour it down her throat. She will never dream again."

"No," I whispered, despite my every intention of remaining calm and silent in Oberon's presence. The scars around my heart were rubbed raw, and the thunderous sounds of my dream still echoed in my mind. He couldn't do this. The dreams were my only escape from this brutal reality, my only hope when faced with a lifetime—an *endless* lifetime—stuck by his side. Stuck in this castle. Once we were married, I would never see the sky again unless he let me.

I'd never see the stars again.

Tears dripped down my cheeks. I couldn't stop them.

Oberon just smiled.

"You have been communicating with the enemy," he said. "You should be glad I'm not punishing you far worse than this. I just have one question before I put you under."

The guard opened the door, and Oberon walked

inside. He came over to my cot and flicked my cheek. I bit my tongue to stop myself from flinching.

His lavender-scented breath rushed toward me. "What is the Mist King planning?"

"He isn't planning anything," I said in a rough voice. "Your barrier is failing all on its own."

His gaze narrowed.

From the passageway, Morgan cleared her throat. "I know it's surprising, but she doesn't know anything. I can scent she's not lying."

I kept my gaze on Oberon's face, despite my curiosity. The last thing I'd expected was for her to speak in my defense.

"Maybe he made it so that she can lie without detection." Oberon leaned closer and sniffed. "All I smell is mist."

It took everything within me not to smile.

"That's impossible," Morgan countered. "There's no magic out there that can suppress a mortal's lie scent. She's telling the truth. If he does have a plan, she clearly doesn't know about it."

"Fine." Oberon shoved away from my cot, and I allowed my body to relax—just slightly—now that his face was no longer an inch away from mine. "But that changes nothing. I cannot allow my betrothed to communicate with *him* any longer. These dreams end now."

"Wait," I blurted.

Oberon froze halfway to the open cell door.

"What are you afraid is going to happen?" I asked. "What is it you're so scared of?"

The king leveled his gaze at me with a predatory still-
ness. "I am not afraid of anything, least of all you. Enjoy
your sleep, my future queen."

He stepped back out into the corridor, and the guards
rushed inside. I wrapped Kalen's cloak around me, trying
to steel myself for what came next. If Oberon forced me
to have that valerian wine again, I wouldn't be able to
reach out to Kalen. I didn't even know if he was all right,
and I couldn't stand the thought of not seeing him when
I closed my eyes to dream.

"Oh, and give some to the sister, just in case." Oberon
smiled, nodded to himself, and vanished down the corridor, Morgan in tow.

I watched her and noted the stiffening of her back,
visible even beneath her armor. As if she could feel my
eyes on her, she cast a quick glance over her shoulder.
Sorrow filled her eyes.

"I'm sorry," she mouthed.

And then the guards closed in on me, blocking my
view. They shoved the goblet up to my mouth, and the
saccharine stench of the valerian-spiked wine clogged my
nose. The cold edge of the goblet bit my lips.

"Take it," the guard said roughly. "Don't make me
open your mouth and pour it down your throat."

I shook my head.

He shoved it closer, and it clicked against my teeth.
"Just drink the fucking thing, all right?"

I met his eyes. Unlike the others, he did not wear a
helmet. His crimson hair and curving horns gave him
away as one of Oberon's sons, while the deep brown of

his eyes exposed his human side. I couldn't help but wonder which Mortal Queen was his mother. And did Oberon ever let him visit the Tower of Crones, now that she'd been banished there?

"You're new," I said through clenched teeth, stalling for time.

His face went grim. "I'm replacing the previous head guard. He asked questions he shouldn't have. Now, drink."

My heart pounded. Asked questions he shouldn't have? Did that have anything to do with what I'd told him about Oberon's lack of powers? And then, if so...did that mean Oberon didn't want anyone to know about his missing powers, not even his guards? With the mists creeping closer to Albyria, he couldn't afford anyone questioning his strength.

With one hand still holding tight to Kalen's cloak, I took the goblet from the guard. Out of the corner of my eye, I could see that Nellie had already downed her glass. She'd settled back on her pillows, her eyelids weighed down by the intoxicating herbs coursing through her veins.

"Don't do anything rash now, Tessa," the guard warned.

I lifted my brow.

"You've earned quite the reputation around here. Your grit is impressive, but you need to learn when to kneel and when to fight. Now is not the time for the latter."

I downed the wine, chugging the sickly liquid until

the goblet was empty. When I handed it back to the guard, I said, "Which one is it for you?"

A ghost of a smile whispered across his face as dizziness washed over me. Before he could answer, shadows deeper than the mists filled my mind.

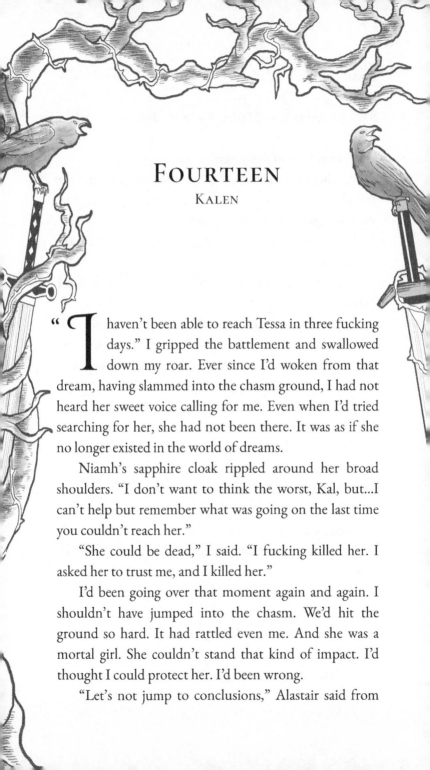

FOURTEEN
KALEN

"I haven't been able to reach Tessa in three fucking days." I gripped the battlement and swallowed down my roar. Ever since I'd woken from that dream, having slammed into the chasm ground, I had not heard her sweet voice calling for me. Even when I'd tried searching for her, she had not been there. It was as if she no longer existed in the world of dreams.

Niamh's sapphire cloak rippled around her broad shoulders. "I don't want to think the worst, Kal, but...I can't help but remember what was going on the last time you couldn't reach her."

"She could be dead," I said. "I fucking killed her. I asked her to trust me, and I killed her."

I'd been going over that moment again and again. I shouldn't have jumped into the chasm. We'd hit the ground so hard. It had rattled even me. And she was a mortal girl. She couldn't stand that kind of impact. I'd thought I could protect her. I'd been wrong.

"Let's not jump to conclusions," Alastair said from

my other side, his dark silken hair tied back from his face. "When you woke up, you didn't have a scratch on you. She's probably fine. Maybe not in the best situation, but fine."

"What kind of situation?" I demanded.

He held up his hands. "Don't you snap at me. I'm not the one who's got her. Oberon drugged her with valerian-spiked wine before. I bet he's done it again, leading up to the wedding. He can't afford for her to start acting like...well, like her."

I breathed out and tried to calm my pounding heart. "She does tend to act rashly."

"And Oberon knows that all too well." Alastair's lazy grin tried to pull me back down to solid ground, but I just kept thinking about her trapped in her wedding dress with his fucking hands all over her.

"I will rip out his heart if he touches her."

"He won't. Yet."

Still, I paced. The icy wind battled against me, but I'd faced far worse cold than this. "What if you're wrong? Have you heard from any of our spies?"

Niamh shook her head. "The king has put them to work guarding the chasm, and he hasn't let them near the dungeons for a few days. Tessa was right. The mists are moving across that bridge."

"I don't care about the mists right now. I need to know if Tessa is all right."

"You should care about the mists," Alastair countered. "I've been thinking."

"That's always a bad sign," Niamh mumbled beneath her breath.

I stopped and shot her a dark look. "Now is not the time for jokes."

Alastair's smile widened. "Well, then how about this? There can really only be one reason the mists are moving. The bastard's barrier is failing."

"That doesn't make any sense. Why would it be failing?"

"Didn't Tessa say Oberon has been acting unsettled?" Niamh asked.

"True." I frowned. "I just don't understand how that could actually happen."

"There's only one way to find out." Alastair thumped my shoulder. "We go to Albyria. And we try walking across that bridge. If the barrier still stands, nothing really changes. But if it's no longer there..."

My hands fisted. "We can save Tessa."

"Well, yes. But also, we can finally kill Oberon and end his fucking reign."

"Which stops him from bringing back the gods," Niamh added.

Heart pounding, I lifted my gaze to the storm fae army camped outside the city walls. Niamh and Alastair were right. If the mists were pushing into the Kingdom of Light, we might have a chance to get across that barrier for the first time in centuries. Oberon clearly didn't know what was happening, which meant he wasn't in control. I had to get there. I might not get another chance like this again.

Tessa's face flashed in my mind, and the way she'd looked at me after seeing my memories—the ones that had revealed the worst moments of my life. There had been no disgust there, but there'd also been no pity. Just understanding. And I could not let that monster control her for the rest of her life.

"I have to go to her." I leaned forward and breathed in the scent of impending war. Fires dotted the field, and smoke drifted with the wind, carrying the scent of cooking meat. There was a tension in the air that you could feel creeping along your skin—anticipation of the bloodshed to come. It took me back to that day, the last time the storm fae had taken up arms against us. It had been about Toryn then. It likely was now, too. Queen Tatiana had held a very long grudge, but I could hardly blame her for that. I'd never let go of my hatred for Oberon, either.

"Boudica," I said to my familiar, who perched quietly on a nearby stone ledge. "Go get Toryn."

The raven gave me a nod and soared toward the nearest tower before vanishing into an open window. Alastair folded his arms and leaned against the stone wall while Niamh joined me watching the army below. She draped her arms across the ledge and dropped her head against my shoulder.

"How are you doing, Kal? Be honest with me."

I wound my arm around her back. "I feel like my power is thumping against my skin. It wants out, in the worst way possible. The last time—"

"You've used it since then. In front of us. You killed our enemies, and we were fine."

"That was different," I said, my jaw clenching. "There were a dozen storm fae then. We're facing hundreds now."

"True." She lifted her head from my shoulder and stared up at me. "And what's the worst that can happen?"

"I could destroy this whole fucking city."

"You won't do that, and you know it."

I shook my head, the world before me transforming into a memory I hated to recall. Clouds of dust swirling through a black sky. The screams of dying men punctuating a mist-drenched night. Pookas charging toward us. So much blood. So much death. It took me a moment to catch my breath, to push aside the lingering pain I still felt all these centuries later. I'd done all that. It had been me. Perhaps if Tessa had seen that memory, she wouldn't have gazed at me with those knowing eyes. She wouldn't see my soul and keep looking. She would have turned away.

My voice was full of sorrow when I finally spoke. "What if I create another rift? What if I release more uncontrollable mist, and it consumes the Kingdom of Storms? I've already ruined two fae realms. I don't want to ruin a third. The only one left unmarked by my power's deadly touch."

"I have faith in you, Kal." She knocked her shoulder against mine. "We all do, including all your people in this city. They know your strength, and they trust you to protect them from those storm fae down there. That army is the enemy. Not you."

I let out a bitter laugh. "A quarter of my people left after my war against Oberon. They hated me and blamed me for the mists, and my mother's death."

"Your mother would be proud of you."

A burning dagger of pain cut through me. I closed my eyes and dropped my head, my hands gripping the stone. "I don't think she would be, Niamh. I really don't think she would be."

"Everything all right, Kal?" Toryn asked as Boudica settled on my shoulder. He came up on my other side and caught the look on my face. His eyes softened. "You're wondering if you should do it."

I clasped his shoulder and pulled him close. "These are your people. Your family. If I do this, I need you to swear to me that it's what you want."

"I told you before."

"I need you to swear it," I said, my voice cracking. "Your mother could be down there. If I do this, none of them will survive."

Toryn's expression darkened. "She's not down there. Trust me, I'd know."

"Well, then where is she?"

"She's in her castle in Gailfean, where it's safe. She won't fight her own battles."

I nodded, glancing at Niamh and then Alastair. "All three of you are in agreement with this?"

"If you want to get to the little dove before Oberon traps her forever," Alastair said, "this is your best move."

"Fuck." My power thrummed in my veins, as if it sensed my temptation to use it. It yearned to pour across the storm fae lands just beyond my city walls, destroying every living thing in its path. The need was almost intoxicating. For so long, I'd pushed this power down, forcing it to stay locked up inside me with iron chains. Knowing that Oberon was so close to securing Tessa for eternity ate away at those chains like venomous acid. It wanted out.

And with Toryn's encouragement, it was hard to find a reason not to give in to that desire.

"All right." I palmed the stone wall and narrowed my gaze on the storm fae army. "Get everyone inside the castle and the barracks. Now."

"Absolutely, Your Grace," Niamh said before grabbing Alastair's arm and leading him down the battlements. They'd gather my army, who was waiting for the impending attack, and they'd usher them back into the barracks where they'd be safe from my power. Even the archers. Toryn was the only one who stayed by my side.

"I'm a bad fucking king," I muttered to myself. "What's worse is, I don't know what I would have done if you'd said no. I think I would have used my power against them regardless. I can't reach Tessa. She could be dead. Or Oberon could be doing something terrible to her. I can't wait any longer, Toryn. I have to *do something*. She needs me."

"You care about her. More than you even want to admit, I think." His voice dropped an octave. "Truth be told, I'm a little jealous you found someone who can make you feel that way. I'll never get that now."

I glanced at my old friend, surprised he felt that way. "Don't say that. Any woman would be lucky to have you."

"No one wants a powerless fae covered in scars," he said so quietly that I almost didn't hear him.

"That's not true, Toryn."

Boudica stirred on my shoulder, twitching her wings. I turned toward the castle and saw Niamh waving at me from the courtyard. I nodded and whispered to my raven. She took off at once and fled for the skies.

"You should go inside," I told Toryn, my voice turning hard. "I don't want you to have to see this. And you're not safe standing this close to me."

"I'm staying right here, Kal. You're going to need me when that power leaves your body." Toryn stepped just behind me and leaned against the wall. "You don't have to be alone in this, even though you think you should be. You don't have to be alone in anything ever again."

"I am your king," I ground out. "I can command you to return to the safety of the castle."

"Let me be here for this. For you."

Closing my eyes, I nodded, relenting to his wishes. My power horrified me. It always had. It was too volatile, storming through my body as if it had a mind of its own, as if some other entity took over when that spark came alive beneath my skin. It was different than the mists. This power, the destructive part of me, it was something else. Sometimes, I felt like it wanted to consume the entire world.

"Just don't stand directly behind me," I said to Toryn without turning. "Go behind that pillar there. I won't have the same thing happen to you that happened to..." My voice broke. *Rhiannon.* It had been far too many years since I'd been able to speak her name out loud.

"All right. But I'm right there if you need me." His boots clicked on the stone battlement, carrying him away from me. He was still too close for comfort, but I knew this was as good as it was going to get. I wouldn't force him to go inside the castle. Not when I was aiming my powers on his people. He'd left them behind centuries ago, but I knew he held on to his love for them the same way I held on to love for my own. Fae emotions could burn hot for eternity.

I turned my attention back to the war camp. The storm fae were gathered around their fires, cooking their stew. A few bursts of laughter drifted toward me on the wind, and my stomach turned. They had no idea they were about to die.

"Are you ready?" I called to Toryn.

A pause. And then, "I'm ready."

Breathing in, I curled my fists and let my eager power build up inside of me, a windstorm of destruction racing through my veins. Tessa's face flashed in my mind, her brown eyes staring into my soul, unblinking. My breath rattled. For her, I could do this. For her, I would do anything.

Before I could back down, I loosed my power on the world below. The force of it knocked me back, and my knees slammed against the stone. A shuddering crack exploded outward, like an earthquake rushing across the war camp. Not a single scream raced up into the night. Instead, a horrible silence followed the thunder in my ears.

I knew without looking that every storm fae in the war camp was dead. At least they had not suffered. Even so, my entire body shook.

"Toryn," I said, palming the stone.

He was beside me in an instant, his hand on my shoulder. "Don't worry. I'm here."

I took a moment to steady myself, but I did not have all the time in the world.

"Get the horses ready." I brushed off the sadness that pressed on my shoulders, and I stood. "We leave for Albyria immediately."

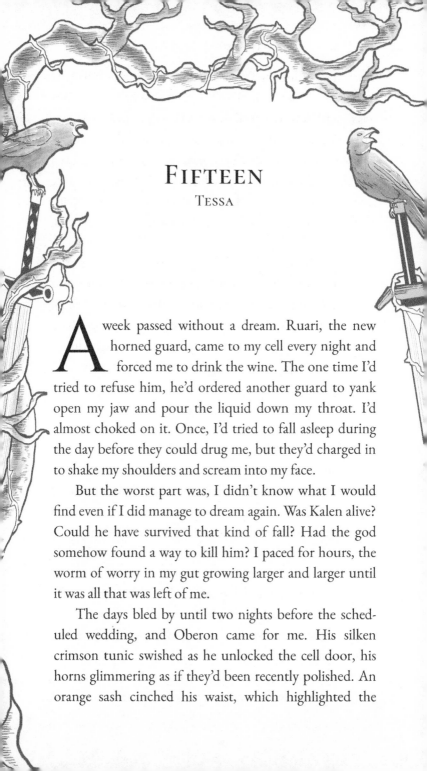

FIFTEEN

TESSA

A week passed without a dream. Ruari, the new horned guard, came to my cell every night and forced me to drink the wine. The one time I'd tried to refuse him, he'd ordered another guard to yank open my jaw and pour the liquid down my throat. I'd almost choked on it. Once, I'd tried to fall asleep during the day before they could drug me, but they'd charged in to shake my shoulders and scream into my face.

But the worst part was, I didn't know what I would find even if I did manage to dream again. Was Kalen alive? Could he have survived that kind of fall? Had the god somehow found a way to kill him? I paced for hours, the worm of worry in my gut growing larger and larger until it was all that was left of me.

The days bled by until two nights before the scheduled wedding, and Oberon came for me. His silken crimson tunic swished as he unlocked the cell door, his horns glimmering as if they'd been recently polished. An orange sash cinched his waist, which highlighted the broadness of his chest that whittled down into a sharp V. If he wasn't such a bastard, he might be handsome, but his cruelty was so etched into his face that it turned every attractive feature into an ugliness unlike any I'd ever seen.

Without a word, he beckoned me from my bed. Even though I desperately wanted to scowl, I kept my face expressionless and stood. As I walked toward him, Nellie gasped from where she sat cross-legged on her bed, reading.

He towered over me, reeking of lavender and blood.

"I'm throwing a ball tonight to celebrate our impending union," he said with a wicked smile. "You'll join me there for an hour at most. The courtiers have barely seen you since your return, and it's high time I show you off again. A maidservant will be by shortly to..." He waved a hand at my drab brown trousers and cotton tunic. "Make you more presentable for court."

I nodded, biting the insides of my cheeks. He'd barely let me leave my cell this past week. I was eager to get out and actually do something, even if that meant attending one of his horrible balls. I'd never forget the moment I'd doomed Raven, but I knew better than to make that kind of move now. No more stabbing kings, especially this one, not unless I could be certain the blade would slide into his heart.

Oberon left, and the guards followed him out of the dungeons. Ruari was the only one who remained. As soon as the sound of Oberon's footsteps faded, he was outside my cell, peering in at me and Nellie.

"Are you going to be on your best behavior tonight?" he asked me with arched eyebrows. "I think we all remember what happened during one of your other balls."

"You took away my wooden dagger," I said dryly. "What am I going to stab him with? My fingernail?"

He gave me a tight smile. "Knowing you, you might try. The king will expect it, too."

"I'm not going to try to stab him." I smiled right back. "You can smell the truth on me. So now you can run along and tell your father exactly what I've said."

Ruari just laughed. He always did when I spoke rudely to him, and he hadn't once told his father about my disrespect. It was the only reason I dared to do it. He didn't seem to care. It almost seemed, at times, that he reveled in it. Sometimes, I even swore I spotted a flicker of defiance on his face when Oberon ordered him around.

I didn't trust him, though.

"So, is that all?" I asked him.

"Hmm, no." He folded his arms and lounged against the bars of the cell. "Just thought I'd give you a little tip. You should be on guard tonight. Court is all aflame about this mist business. There might be some..." He flicked his gaze to Nellie. "...unpleasant moments."

My blood pooled in my gut, as heavy as a hammer of war. "What are you talking about?"

"Just be careful." He took several steps back from the cell and cast a glance over his shoulder at the closed door. "And if you've been conjuring up some kind of rash plan, now might be the time to execute it."

"I know what you're trying to do," I called after him. "It won't work."

"Trying to get you to trust me? No, I know that'd never happen. I'd be disappointed if you did."

"I've figured out who you are. You're his first-born son."

Ruari froze.

"You want his throne," I continued. "But you're part human. Even if you got rid of him, the fae of this kingdom would never accept you as his heir."

His gaze hardened into something I recognized in myself. "We'll see about that."

And then he turned, jogged the rest of the way to the door, and vanished up the stairs. With my heart thumping against my ribs, I trailed over to the bars and stared at the spot where he'd just stood. Cold crept along the back of my neck, freezing my spine.

I didn't trust him, but I knew that look. He would die trying to steal the throne, and he might just make that attempt tonight.

"What in the name of light was that all about?" Nellie whispered from behind me.

I jumped and almost released a pent-up scream. "For fuck's sake, Nellie. I didn't hear you come up behind me."

"That guard is like a snake."

"Don't be ridiculous. Snakes are much more pleasant than that guard, even when they bite you."

Nellie cracked a smile, but then her expression darkened. "Seriously, what was all that?"

My lips pressed together. I'd seen the look he'd cast toward Nellie, as quick as, well, a snake. I didn't want to tell her my worst fear—that Oberon had something planned for her—but hiding the truth wouldn't protect her. She needed to be as on guard tonight as I would be.

"I'm not sure," I told her. "First of all, we don't even know if we can believe a word he says. Oberon is his father. He's clearly one of them. Even if he wants to steal the throne. *Especially* if he wants to steal the throne."

She nodded, her brow pinched with worry. "I was about to say the same thing to you."

"I'm glad we're on the same page. I need you to be on guard tonight. Stay awake until I get back."

Her throat bobbed as she swallowed. "You really think Oberon might do something tonight? Or his son?"

"He might. They both might." I grasped her hand in mine and squeezed tight, staring into a pair of dark brown eyes that I knew matched mine, down to the orange rim along the edges. My heart pounded in my chest. "And if someone comes for you, I want you to fight your fucking heart out, do you hear me? Scream, thrash, punch, claw. Rip them to shreds. And then find Mother and Val, and get out of this place. Don't worry about me. I'll be fine."

Nellie's face paled. "I don't want to do that."

"I know." I pulled her close and wrapped my arms around her. "But when this is all over, we can fly away from here."

"Like the ravens," she whispered back.

Crimson painted nearly everything, including the goblets the fae clinked, the stretch of carpet cutting through the Great Hall that led to the king's matching throne, and the gowns, tunics, and cloaks that everyone in attendance wore.

Everyone except for me.

My flat pointy shoes pinched my feet, where I stood on the dais beside the king's throne. They were golden yellow to match the gown and its deep, plunging neckline. Long, gauzy sleeves covered my arms, despite the heat that baked the crowded room. Thankfully, the maidservant had agreed to braid my hair, which provided much-needed relief to the back of my neck. Bonus: the strands wouldn't get in my way if I had to fight.

My recollection of the balls I'd attended before was a meaningless blur. I'd been so wracked with grief that those moments were hazy memories, one bleeding into another, turning that entire month into one long, tormenting day. So, I didn't remember much other than that first ball where everything had gone horribly wrong. It had been a lively affair. Lots of drinking. Lots of sex. Lots of wicked smiles and glinting eyes.

This ball was much more subdued.

The courtiers wandered through the dense hall, whispering amongst themselves. Some of them cast nervous glances our way, while others stood by the nearest window, staring out at the border. The mist had advanced even further, until the bridge was nearly engulfed. Musicians played an upbeat tune, but no one danced. And no one was naked. Yet.

That, I was certain, was only a matter of time.

"Stop looking so sullen," King Oberon muttered from beside me. "You're here to look pretty. Smile."

The king knew exactly what to say to make me want to stab him. I stared blankly at the crowd and smiled.

"For light's sake." He sighed. "Nevermind, don't smile. You look deranged."

Satisfaction bloomed inside me. The corners of my lips dropped at once.

He sighed again and motioned toward the swelling crowd by the window. "This isn't working. They're supposed to see you and get distracted from that fucking mist. But you're old news now. We've already done this song and dance. I suppose it's time I do the one thing they can't ignore."

I didn't like the sound of that.

I shifted on my feet and frowned as he stood from his throne. A hush fell across the crowd almost instantly, as if they'd been waiting for him to speak. Every fae in the room gazed up at him solemnly. There were no smiles. No smirks. In fact, they hardly paid me any attention at all.

In any other situation, I'd be thrilled. But not tonight.

A movement flashed in the corner of my vision. I cut my eyes to the side to find Ruari skulking along the nearest wall, his hand pressed against the hilt of his sword. He gave me a slight nod.

My stomach turned.

"Welcome to tonight's ball," Oberon announced, his voice booming in the hushed space. "We're here to celebrate my resumed betrothal to your next Mortal Queen, once stolen from us by the bloody Mist King. But he cannot defeat us. I got her back from him, just as I will one day get back our stolen lands. This is a sign from the gods."

A rumble went through the crowd. I'd never heard Oberon invoke the gods like this. So blatantly. By the shocked looks on the faces before us, it seemed the courtiers hadn't, either.

"Quiet." He held up his hand, and the murmurs stopped. "With the blessing of the gods, we can finally defeat our greatest enemy, the Mist King, once and for all. But we need just one more thing." That was when he turned to me with a glimmer in his eye. "A blood sacrifice."

A ringing filled my ears as every face in the crowd turned to me. But I didn't even see them. I stared at Oberon, at his twisting horns, at the shadows in his eyes, and I felt my rage for him build up inside of me. So, this was his move. If the fae no longer cared about a wedding, he'd paint this floor with my blood.

For the gods.

His gaze left my face to land on someone just behind me. "Go get the mother and the friend."

A gasp ripped from my throat.

"I told you their lives were forfeit," he said to me. "This is your punishment for trying to kill me. And it is the Kingdom of Light's salvation."

I cast a desperate glance over my shoulder. Oberon's son had vanished. He must have been the one Oberon ordered to fetch my mother and Val. This was what he'd been alluding to earlier. He'd encouraged me to fight, no doubt because he hoped I'd take his father down.

But I couldn't depend on him to save my family. He had his own motivations, his own goals in mind. Mother and Val were nothing to him. If he had to bring them here for Oberon's sacrifice, he would.

So, I did the only thing I could do. I finally made my move. But this time, I would stab Oberon with my words rather than a useless wooden dagger. And they would make a mark.

Clenching my hands into fists, I turned to the gathered light fae. "Oberon no longer has his power. That's why the mist is coming across the bridge. His barrier is failing."

Horror—actual horror—flashed across Oberon's face. It was a fleeting expression, but I was close enough to see the widening of his eyes, the twitch of his shoulders, the flaring of his nostrils, before it was all gone—smoothed over. His eyes went hard.

The crowd erupted. All solemnity was cast aside as the fae pushed toward the dais, shouting questions and demands, all on top of each other so that their words were nothing more than a meaningless garble of fear and anger. Oberon didn't look at them. He just stared at me.

I gave him a smile and I whispered. "Did you really think I'd let you kill them?"

His nostrils flared again, and he turned to the crowd. When he yanked his sword from his scabbard, the room quieted to a dull roar. "Enough! This is a mortal! I am your king."

"Even so," a nearby courtier, a man with ginger hair

shot through with silver, called out, "the mists are closer, Your Grace. What's happening with the barrier?"

"Yes, why isn't the barrier working?" another called out.

A muscle in Oberon's jaw ticked. "Nothing is happening. The barrier holds strong."

"Why don't you prove it?" I raised my voice to be heard throughout the Great Hall. "If you're in control of the barrier and you haven't lost your power, then show us your fire. When was the last time you gave the court one of your infamous displays?"

He whirled on me then, his eyes flashing. "Shut up, mortal. Haven't you learned your fucking lesson yet? You've just killed your sister. You've just killed them all."

My heart pounded, but I kept my face blank. I'd been counting the moments since the guard had left to get my family. He should have reached the dungeons by now. A few moments more, and he'd return with them. I hoped it was long enough for the tide to turn.

"The mortal is right," that ginger-and-silver haired fae said with a frown. "I can't remember the last time we saw you use your power."

Oberon's skin turned ashen. "What kind of king would I be if I felt I had to prove my power to you? Don't listen to this mortal. She means nothing."

The fae's eyes widened. "She's right, isn't she? You don't have it."

Another rumble went through the crowd, and the scent of smoke filled the air. The expressions in the crowd had turned from open curiosity to something edged in steel. Some looked eager as Oberon's carefully constructed mask of power cracked beneath the weight of my words. I took the moment to back up to the wall.

"He doesn't have his power!" one of the fae called out. "He's no better than a common fae!"

"You don't know what you're doing," Oberon muttered, his steel singing as he raised it before him. "You do not want me to show you my power. It's the only thing holding back—"

The crowd parted, forming a circle around five elite fae with fire rippling wickedly in their open palms. Around them, five more fae had drawn their swords. They all stared at their king. The room crackled with tension.

I glanced at Oberon just as I hopped off the dais. "You're done."

"I'm afraid not," he said grimly. "You've left me no choice."

I didn't know what that meant, and I didn't want to stick around to find out. I edged closer to the door leading out of the hall. The elite fae lifted their hands. Oberon narrowed his eyes. He opened his arms wide just as they launched their power at the dais. A shock of light went through the room, blinding me. A boom shook the floor. The wall beside me cracked, dumping a cascade of crumbling rocks onto my back. I covered my head with my arms and stumbled to the side, trying to blink away the light. The scent of fire filled my nose, and slowly, the world came back into view around me.

Fae screamed. They ran past me, hurtling out the door as if a storm of beasts chased them down. But all I could do was stare. The entire dais was engulfed in flames, including the throne. A chasm gaped in the center of the room, a deep crack zigzagging from the dais to the far wall where Oberon's tapestry had been shredded. Smoke filled the air, burning my lungs. And everywhere I looked, there was fire.

I glanced around, coughing. Several fae were bleeding. Others were dead, a pile of burned bodies on the floor near the dais. Nowhere could I find Oberon's gleaming horns, or his crimson hair, or those ember eyes that had haunted my every step.

His words echoed in my ears.

I'm afraid not. You've left me no choice.

Had he done this? But how? And if he had, why was there no sign of him?

I didn't have time to find out. The walls began to crumble around me. Fire snaked through the Great Hall, consuming everything. If I didn't go now, I'd be trapped in the flames forever.

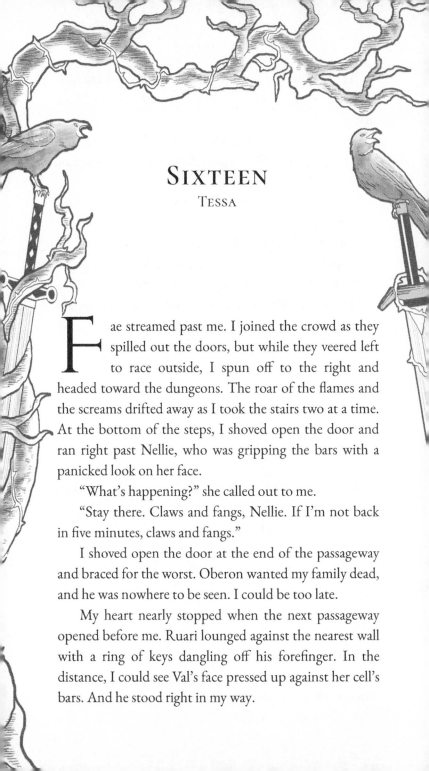

Sixteen
Tessa

Fae streamed past me. I joined the crowd as they spilled out the doors, but while they veered left to race outside, I spun off to the right and headed toward the dungeons. The roar of the flames and the screams drifted away as I took the stairs two at a time. At the bottom of the steps, I shoved open the door and ran right past Nellie, who was gripping the bars with a panicked look on her face.

"What's happening?" she called out to me.

"Stay there. Claws and fangs, Nellie. If I'm not back in five minutes, claws and fangs."

I shoved open the door at the end of the passageway and braced for the worst. Oberon wanted my family dead, and he was nowhere to be seen. I could be too late.

My heart nearly stopped when the next passageway opened before me. Ruari lounged against the nearest wall with a ring of keys dangling off his forefinger. In the distance, I could see Val's face pressed up against her cell's bars. And he stood right in my way.

He gave me a lazy smile when I stormed toward him. "What a relief. I was worried you might have lost your nerve."

I reached for the keys. He closed his fist around them and stepped back. "Not yet. Tell me what happened up there."

"You got your wish. Oberon's out. But the entire court is in chaos."

His smile widened. "He's dead?"

"I didn't see a body. Now can you give me the keys?"

"I shouldn't. You're dangerous, untethered."

I frowned. What in the name of light did that mean? "I will make your life fucking miserable if you do not give me those keys."

"I don't doubt it." He tossed them toward me, and I opened my palm to catch them. The cool steel cracked something open inside of me. Freedom was in my grasp. Freedom for Mother, for Val, for Nellie. For me. After everything that had happened, we could finally rid ourselves of this place.

"Take your family and get out of here," he said. "And don't come back. My father wanted to play with things he shouldn't have, but I won't do the same."

"What does that have to do with—"

A rumble shook the ground, coming from the direction of Nellie's cell. Ruari frowned and glanced up at the ceiling. "Go. We need to get out of here."

He didn't wait for an answer. Without another word, he took off down the passageway toward the stairwell. I tightened my grip around the keyring and shoved back through the door, going to Nellie first. I had the cell open within seconds. Chunks of rocks crashed only a few feet away from us.

Nellie grabbed Kalen's cloak and shoved it into my hands, following me back down the passageway. Despite the heat, I draped the cloak around my shoulders. The scent of mist surrounded me and soothed away the frayed edges of my nerves.

When we reached Mother and Val, they were both on their feet. My mother's face was lined with worry, and a watery film coated her familiar brown eyes. She wore a simple frock I knew well, though dirt stained the soft material. Dirt and blood. Her hand clutched her leg as she stumbled toward the bars.

My eyes went to Val as I unlocked the door with shaking hands. Her gaze betrayed none of her emotions, not like Mother's did, but I could tell, just by the bald spot above her ear, that she'd spent the past few weeks scared out of her mind.

The hinges creaked as I yanked open the door. For a moment, the four of us did nothing but stand there, as if our collective trauma had become like twisted vines trapping our feet to the floor. It was as if my mind couldn't comprehend it. I'd fought so hard to get back to them. With every step closer I'd made, they'd felt further and further away, even when they'd just been down the dungeon corridor.

I'd truly believed that I'd never see them again. Not alive, at least.

My mother was the first to crack.

"Oh, my loves." Her shaking voice was papery thin as she stumbled toward us. She reached Nellie first and clung to her neck, reaching out for me to join them. I folded my body into their embrace and grabbed Val's arm. She closed her eyes, leaned in. And we all stood there like that, holding on to each for dear life, sobbing.

Until the floor shook again.

I pulled back and wiped the tears from my face. "We need to go. The castle is burning. And maybe even falling down."

My mother cast a frantic look down the length of the passageway. "What about the guards? Won't they try to stop us?"

"They're busy. I doubt they'll pay much attention to us."

Together, we rushed down the corridor. Val ran in step beside me. She noticed the cloak I wore, but she didn't comment on it.

"Where are we going to go?" she asked, her breath huffing.

"For now, we'll go to Teine."

"Won't Oberon look for us there?"

"I don't think Oberon is going to be a problem right now."

His son might be, though. He'd told us to leave this place, and we would. But I didn't want to take my family across the bridge and out into the mists. It was too dangerous.

When we reached the castle's ground floor, smoke billowed toward us from the direction of the Great Hall. The corridors were empty, and the front doors had been thrown open in the fae's haste to escape. I covered my nose with the edge of the cloak and coughed, my eyes watering.

Outside, smoke coated everything, or at least we thought it was smoke. As we drew nearer, the thick fog that pushed through Albyria's streets became achingly familiar. I didn't know how I could tell the difference. Maybe it was the scent of it or the way the particles floated in the light breeze. Or maybe it was just how it felt like *him*.

"That's not smoke," I whispered. "That's mist."

As if to confirm my suspicion, a scream rent the air. My stomach turned. That scream could mean anything, of course. The fae might be turning on each other. They'd be breaking into factions now to fight for the throne. With all the mist and smoke and fire, some of the more undesirables of the city might start looting.

There were many reasons to scream.

But where there were mists, there were monsters. A fingernail of dread scraped down my spine.

Nellie stepped up beside me and gazed out the castle's open doors. "The sun is still in the sky. How's that possible? Shouldn't it be night now that the mists are here?"

"I don't know."

Mother clutched at the fabric near her heart. "He's dead. Oberon's dead. The barrier is gone."

"The Mist King will come for us all," Val breathed.

"Yes, about that. There's nothing to fear if he comes. He's my friend." *If he's still alive.*

"What?" Val asked sharply. "I thought you stabbed him."

"You heard about that?"

She grinned. "The guards are gossips. Was it not true?"

"It was a mistake," I said as a small shot of pain went through my heart. "He's..."

Kalen.

"Tessa," my mother hissed. "But Morgan said—"

"Morgan isn't trustworthy. She made a vow to Oberon to say and do whatever he commands."

Val frowned, but she didn't argue. Mother, on the other hand, looked bereft.

"Don't tell me you actually trust that monster." She gazed up at me, her eyes searching mine. "He's the reason we've been stuck here with these horrible fae all these years. He trapped us here. That mist, that dangerous mist, he controls it. He is our enemy, just as much as Oberon is. You cannot forget that, Tessa, no matter what he told you."

I looked at my mother and saw a reflection of my own self there in her eyes, angry and harsh. Her words haunted me, because they were the very same words I'd thrown into Kalen's face when he'd shown me nothing but kindness. Well, he'd shown me grumpiness, too, and he had lied about some things, but when it had mattered—*really mattered*—he'd taken care of me. He'd protected me.

He'd saved my fucking life.

And he'd let me shove a blade into his chest rather than raise a hand toward me in defense.

But Mother didn't know all that, of course. She'd never met him. She hadn't looked into his sapphire eyes and seen the way they gleamed. Not like a sword's murderous blade, but like the stars.

I grasped her hand. "He's not our enemy."

She scoffed and started to form another argument, but Nellie cut her off.

"We need to go." My sister's voice wobbled. "The fire is spreading."

We all turned. Plumes of smoke raced toward us. Fire licked the walls of the corridor now, having followed the path from the Great Hall to the rest of the castle. The orange light drenched the crimson carpet and the sun-gold walls, the perfect complement to Oberon's gaudy color scheme.

But it would all be ash soon enough. Us, too, if we did not leave this place.

Val grabbed my arm and tucked herself up against me. "I don't want to go into the mist."

"It's the fire or the mist," I said. "I'm afraid the mist is the better option right now."

"The shadowfiends. They'll be out there. And they'll rip us to shreds if they find us."

"Probably. But we'll be safe if we can find somewhere to hole up for a while. They don't like to go indoors." Most of the time.

"Then we need to warn everyone in Teine," Nellie said, her voice now steady, as if she'd gained control of her nerves. "The villagers might be running around outside, scared."

I nodded. "Mother?"

She grimaced and glanced over her shoulder at the approaching fire. "I don't like this, but I don't much like the idea of being burned alive, either."

"That settles it then. We're going to Teine." I led the

four of us out the doors and down the curving steps that took us into the mist-drenched courtyard. The sun cut through the dense haze, basking the city in an eerie orange glow that matched the fire raging behind us. Every now and then, another scream ripped through the city, a constant reminder that danger lurked in the shadows.

Our footsteps were light on the stone street that traced a path to the gates of the city. We raced toward it, hands clasping hands, our breaths ragged, our cheeks burning pink. None of us said a word. We didn't stop to calm our racing hearts or peek around corners. We did nothing other than run.

When we reached the dirt path that led down the hill to the tiny village of Teine, I risked a glance over my shoulder. The fire had spread. It consumed most of the castle and several of the nearby buildings. Only the Tower of Crones, quiet and dark, had been left untouched for now. It stood separate from the rest of Oberon's castle, but it was still close enough that it was only a matter of time. Would anyone think to get the former queens out alive?

A distant sound drifted toward us on the wind, snapping my attention away from the castle. It had been a scream or something like it, and it had come from Teine.

"Tessa," Nellie said, almost sobbing.

"It's all right," I said, even though it wasn't. "Even if a shadowfiend is already there, we can get everyone inside to safety."

My mounting fear for the mortals propelled my feet. Part of me wanted to run ahead and warn the village, but I couldn't leave my family behind. There was nowhere for them to hide. The river could not save them. The woods could not hide them. The chasm was especially dangerous now.

At least in Teine, we had walls and doors and buildings without windows.

We kept charging forward. Down and down and down we went until the vague forms in the shadows solidified into the familiar houses of my village. It was eerily silent compared to the chaos of the city. All I heard were our collective ragged breaths and my own thundering heart.

Palms slick, I snatched a stick from the ground and crept forward at the head of our little pack. Once again, I was armed with nothing but wood, but there was something oddly calming about it. This was a dance I understood.

The thunk of heavy steps sounded nearby. I stopped short and widened my arms to stop the others from moving forward.

Something raced around the corner. I braced myself and gritted my teeth and started to swing my—

A man thundered toward us with wild eyes. I lowered my stick and caught him by the arm before he could go charging off into the mists again. He trembled as he swept his gaze across us, though it was almost as if he didn't even see who we were.

"Shadowfiends," he whispered. "Two of them. At the back edge of the village, near the trees."

My eyes widened. That was near our house. We'd need somewhere else to hide until this was all over.

If it would ever be over.

"They've already killed at least six of us," he started to sob.

I pressed my finger against his lips and shook my head. With wide eyes, he suddenly stilled.

"Is there anyone else outside?" I breathed.

He nodded and held up his hand. Three.

"Only three? Everyone else is inside a building?"

Once again, he nodded.

"Where?" I dropped my finger from his lips.

"In the courtyard. I tried to get them to move, but they're too scared."

"All right. We'll go to the courtyard, grab them, and then hole up inside the pub."

"We need weapons," he hissed. "I'm going to the fae city to get some."

I glanced over my shoulder at the city burning orange, lighting up the mists. "Albyria is worse off than we are."

He scowled and wrenched free of my grip. "What do you think you're going to do? Bash a beast in the head with a stick? I'm going to the city. Swords are the only thing that can save us now."

Before any of us could argue, he took off. His footsteps were too loud. Grimacing, I grabbed my family and drew them close to the building. A moment later, the sound of thunderous steps drowned out his. I pulled the others after me and crouched low.

A moment later, a gurgled scream sounded his demise.

Mother clutched my arm. Nellie sniffled. Val hissed in my ear. Still, we pressed on, and when we reached the square, we found three humans huddling beneath

Oberon's statue. I recognized them. Teine was a tiny place, and every face had been burned into my memory. A girl my age, who had been one of Oberon's choices for a wife. She was with a younger boy and her mother. Their faces were pale, and their eyes were distant. Clearly shell-shocked.

I knelt before them. "You can't stay out here."

No response.

Together, the four of us hauled the humans from the ground and dragged them to the pub. We got them inside just as a roar bellowed from somewhere nearby. The shadowfiends were out there, hunting for more blood. I slammed the door, barred it, and then slumped to the floor, wondering how we would ever, ever get out of this alive.

SEVENTEEN
TESSA

SEVEN YEARS AGO

"I can't believe they're letting us have axes." Nellie stood beside me, watching a few of the village boys haul chopped logs over to the new building at the edge of our small, bustling town. After decades, our numbers were growing, and we needed more houses. Oberon, in an unexpected display of generosity, had sent down some axes to help. He'd sent some soldiers, too, but all they did was stand and watch with their swords at the ready, just in case a mortal decided to rebel.

Things were changing in Teine, but some things would always remain the same.

Val, on my other side, elbowed me when Aidan stopped to wipe the sweat off his brow and remove his tunic. Muscles gleamed beneath the oppressive light of the eversun. "How are things going between you two? Have you spoken to him since you kissed?"

"No." I turned away from the sight. "He's a nice enough boy, I guess. I just...well, it wasn't very exciting."

"Maybe it doesn't need to be exciting."

"It does for me." I hooked my arms into the crook of their elbows and steered them toward the village square. A few of the women had set out cakes and pastries to celebrate the momentous occasion. New homes meant growing families, which meant hope for the future of our village. We were more than surviving now. It was time for us to thrive.

When we reached the dirt-packed square, my eyes were drawn to my uncle. He vanished into the pub. Val's parents followed soon after, along with a few of the boys around my age. I frowned and slowed my steps. The day had only just begun and already they were seeking solace in their tankards? That wasn't like my uncle. *Or* Val's parents.

I nodded toward the sagging building that had seen so many better days. "Your parents are starting early. Are they not happy about the build?"

Val pressed her lips together. "They've been acting strangely for a few weeks now. Every time I turn around, they're always going to that damn pub, but the weird thing is...they never stink of ale."

"Maybe they're having council meetings." Nellie tugged my hand to pull us over to the tables of cakes near Oberon's statue in the center of the square.

I plucked a square sponge cake topped with strawberries. A rarity here. We'd had a good harvest this year, but most of the time, lack of rainfall killed any berries we tried to grow. Only the river winding down from the mountains beyond the border kept us going.

Val frowned down at the cakes. "My parents aren't on the council."

"Maybe our uncle brought them on board," I suggested, though that made little sense. Any new council members had to be voted in by the village, according to our laws. Of course, the council didn't hold any true power. Oberon allowed us to play at self-sufficiency, but he was the only authority in Teine. His soldiers were present at every meeting the council held, to ensure the mortals weren't planning a revolt against him.

"There are too many fae in the village today for them to be doing this. We need to tell them to stop."

"To be doing what, Val?" Suddenly, the aftertaste of the cake was far too sickly, far too sweet. "Is there something you're not telling us?"

"No, I don't know what they're doing. Maybe they're just...taking a break from the build."

Val did not sound convinced, and truth be told, I didn't have a good feeling about it, either. But I wasn't going to chase my uncle inside the pub and bring attention to it. Maybe they really were planning something, but what? There was little we mere mortals could do against the fae. They were as tough as nails, and it took more than just a stab in the gut to kill them. We needed to chop off their heads or burn their bodies. Anything else... and they'd just heal.

It wasn't as if we could escape this place even if we did kill them all. We were trapped on this side of the Great

Rift by the mists that plagued what had once been the rest of the Kingdom of Light, lands that now belonged to the monstrous Mist King. We had nowhere else to go.

"Sure," Val said tightly. "They're just having a rest. There's no cause for alarm..."

Two dozen fae soldiers marched into the square, their boots thunderous against the packed ground. My stomach roiled at the glint of their deadly swords beneath the eversun. They strode right past us with their eyes set on the corner pub. Val snatched my hand and squeezed so tight that my bones ached. Nellie dropped her cake, and it splattered on the dirt, a smashed pulp of sugar and flour and blood-red icing.

"What's happening?" my sister whispered, not daring to speak too loudly. We didn't want the soldiers to notice us hovering nearby like terrified ants beneath the boots of giants.

"I need to do something," Val said, her voice unsteady. "They're going into the pub. My parents are in there."

I clutched her hand and held her back. "You can't. They'll kill you if you try to stop them."

My father drifted into the square, saw us frozen by the cake stand, and rushed over. The haunted look in his eyes shook me to my bones. "You need to go on home, girls. Get out of here. Now."

Val pleaded with my father. "Mr. Baran, you have to stop them. My parents are in there."

"So is our uncle," Nellie whispered.

Father frowned down at my sister and reached for her

arm, but she flinched away. "I'll take care of it, but you can't be here. Go home. Now."

I met my father's gaze. "Take care of it? But—"

"Go to the house, lock the doors, and do not come out until I tell you it's safe." He grabbed Nellie's arm, and she hissed at him. "Don't make me drag you there myself."

He let go of her, and she stumbled away from him, her face pale. Val slowly shook her head as tears streamed down her cheeks. Meanwhile, all I could do was take slow steps down the path leading away from the village square. Something was happening. Something terrible.

Deep down, I knew we'd been right to worry about the mysterious meetings in the pub. My uncle and Val's parents were planning something. A rebellion against the fae. I wanted to be a part of it, but if I stayed, Nellie would stay. When blood sprayed, she needed to be safe.

"Come on." I grabbed her hand, and Val's, and tugged them toward the path. "Let's go."

Val took two strides back in the opposite direction. Her eyes were as wide as the eversun. "I'm staying here."

My leg muscles twitched with the urge to run. It was as if a rift had suddenly cracked open in my heart. On one side stood the rebellious girl with eyes full of fire, desperate to stay with Val and watch the fae burn. But on the other side, a girl trembled with fear, her hand entwined with her sister's.

I had never been a fighter. The fae were far too strong for us to hope we could win a battle against them. All my life, I had fallen in line. Sure, I whispered about them, cursing the king and his loyal fae subjects. But I'd never dreamed of turning my words into actions.

What kind of hope did a mortal have against a fae? That was the core of it. If I stayed, I wouldn't witness the triumphant victory of the Teine mortals against their fae overlords. Everyone who fought would die a gruesome death. That might include witnesses. Anyone Oberon deemed a traitor.

"Val, you can't stay," I pleaded with her before turning to my father. "Neither can you."

Nellie frowned at me. "Why are you—"

Screams rent the calm morning air. The fae charged the pub with swords raised, shouting at the mortals gathered inside. Val cried out and raced toward the building. Blood sprayed from the open door and soaked the front wooden steps.

"Val, no!" I ran after her with tears burning my eyes. If she went into that pub, they'd kill her, too. Dirt dusted around me. My bare feet pounded the ground. I kept my gaze on Val's stumbling form and blocked out the savage chaos.

A male grunt sounded in my ears as two strong hands grabbed my waist and tossed me into the air. I landed on my father's shoulder and kicked out my legs, trying to twist away from him so that I could get to Val.

He tightened his grip on me, carried me across the square, and dumped me far from the screams. Far from Val. My backside hit the ground hard, and my teeth slammed together. Pain lanced through me as I stared up at him in shock, blinking at the alien look on his face. His smile was gone, and so was the laughter in his eyes. In its place sat a mask of cruelty that could rival the fae's.

"How dare you?" I whispered as I climbed to my feet. "You can't stop me from trying to help Val."

"You're more important than she is," he said flatly. "And it's too late now for you to help her. She's already inside the pub."

"How can you be so heartless?"

"Go to our house, Tessa."

"No."

He grabbed my arm and shook me. My teeth knocked together. "You have to get out of here. Oberon will come. You can't be anywhere near him when he does. If he finds out—"

I blinked up at him. "If he finds out what?"

"You are *precious*."

Something within me broke at the look on his face. Father had been distant the past couple of years. He'd spent a lot of time in that damn pub, and he stumbled home reeking of ale most nights. He never talked about why. I'd overheard Mother ask him about it, but he brushed her aside, too. Every now and then, I saw the pain in her eyes when she looked at him. He was drifting away from us. We all knew it. And so the swell of emotion I saw in him now knocked past the flimsy wall I'd erected to protect myself from the pain of losing him slowly.

But still, it wasn't enough to shove it all aside so easily. "Val is precious too."

I turned away from him and walked toward the pub. He started to follow, but Nellie stepped into his path.

"Let her go," she said.

"I'm trying to protect her."

"Val needs her. It's over. Look, the fae have left the pub."

And so they had. Inside, I found carnage. Carnage and a broken Val, sobbing, her hands covered in her parents' blood. I knelt beside her. She leaned against me, and she swore to me that one day we would kill them all.

And I swore right back.

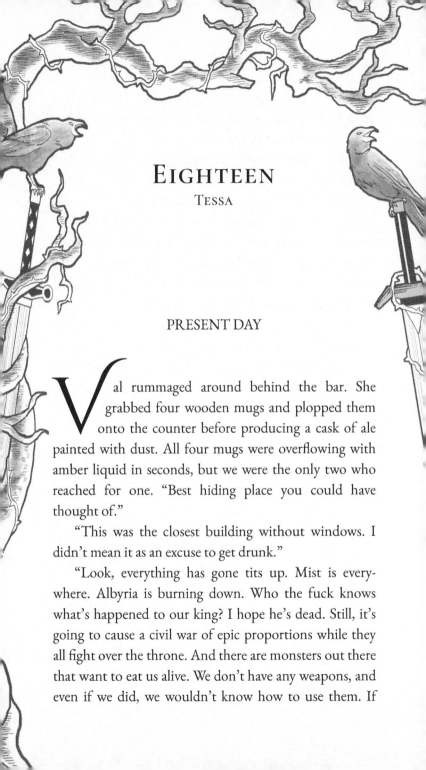

EIGHTEEN
TESSA

PRESENT DAY

Val rummaged around behind the bar. She grabbed four wooden mugs and plopped them onto the counter before producing a cask of ale painted with dust. All four mugs were overflowing with amber liquid in seconds, but we were the only two who reached for one. "Best hiding place you could have thought of."

"This was the closest building without windows. I didn't mean it as an excuse to get drunk."

"Look, everything has gone tits up. Mist is everywhere. Albyria is burning down. Who the fuck knows what's happened to our king? I hope he's dead. Still, it's going to cause a civil war of epic proportions while they all fight over the throne. And there are monsters out there that want to eat us alive. We don't have any weapons, and even if we did, we wouldn't know how to use them. If that's not an excuse to get drunk, then I don't know what is." As if to punctuate her little speech, she lifted her mug in a toast. Foam spilled over the sides, and then she downed the whole thing at once.

She poured herself another without letting a beat pass.

I hopped up on the nearest stool and stared into my drink. Nellie was in the back corner where Milly and her family hunkered down. Mother sat with them, but she wasn't engaging. She rubbed her leg and stared numbly at the wall, as if the reality of our situation had truly sunk in. The barrier had broken. If Oberon was gone, then everything we'd always depended on was gone too. No more enhanced healing. No protection from death.

And the Mist King, of course. I knew she feared him still, no matter what I said.

"We'll find a way out of this," I said.

Val gave me a frank look. "How?"

"I don't know. As long as everyone stays inside, the shadowfiends might get bored and go to the city. The fae can deal with them then."

"And then what? We just stay inside for the rest of our lives? The fae might be able to kill the few shadow-fiends that are out there now, but more will come. You know they will."

I took a sip of the bitter ale. "Once everything calms down, we can get everyone out of Teine. There are places in this world without mist. You can go there."

Val's brow arched, and she paused with her drink halfway to her lips. "Don't you mean *we*? We can go there."

"Right. We can go there."

She finished the second ale and then poured another. I took careful sips of mine, knowing that Val was one of the few people in the world who was capable of reading between my lines. Kalen was another, but I tried not to think about him too much. I hated not knowing how he was. If my nerves weren't completely fried, I'd try to dream of him, but I knew I'd never get to sleep right now.

"Is this about him?" Val asked. "You got a funny look on your face before. You've got it now, too."

"There's just something I need to do."

She folded her arms and leaned against the back of the bar, waiting for me to elaborate. I didn't want to explain. I didn't even really understand it myself. But Val was a more patient person than I was, and my defenses crumbled beneath the weight of her gaze after long moments stretched by in brutal silence.

I sighed. "I did something terrible to him. I made a mistake, and I need to apologize."

"Are you sure you made a mistake?"

"*Yes.*"

She nodded, more easily satisfied than I would have expected. "You still have that dream bond thing with him?"

"As long as I'm not being force-fed valerian." *And as long as he's alive.*

"So apologize to him that way."

My elbows dug into the hard wood of the bar as I dropped my head into my hands. "I already did. I have to do it in person, Val. The dreams aren't real, even if they feel that way sometimes. I need to speak the words out loud. He needs to hear them."

I expected another counter, another argument. Instead, she refilled my mug. I hadn't realized I'd drank the whole thing already. But the sharp daggers of my anxiety had softened from the swirl of alcohol through my veins, just enough to take the edge off. I sighed and took another sip. "Thanks, Val. Are you...have you been all right?"

"I'm fine." She dropped her voice to a whisper. "Your mother has been...well, this whole thing has been hard on her. She's been out of her mind with worry. For you. For Nellie. They wouldn't let us see her, you know."

I closed my eyes. "I'm sorry. That whole thing was my fault."

"No, you're not doing that." She snapped her fingers in front of my face, forcing me to reopen my eyes and look at her. "They took Nellie the same day they took you. Hours later, if that. Your mother was distraught and talked about breaking into the castle to go after you. I don't know how I managed to talk her out of it, but I convinced her to go with me to find the rebels in Endir, hoping they could help. Oberon's soldiers caught us before we even reached the bridge."

"So, that note Morgan gave me. The one you wrote to me. It was real."

"Very real. I thought I might go find your captain." Her lips quirked. "Turns out he was the fucking Mist King the whole time. I told you there was more to that mysterious cloaked fae than he let on."

I gave her a flat stare. "Go on then. Rub it in. You were right, and I was wrong."

Her lips split into a grin, and a sheen of tears covered her eyes. "For the love of light, Tessa. I've never been happier to see anyone in my entire life. I thought you might be dead."

"Likewise," I whispered, a deep, heart-splitting emotion swelling in my chest.

For a long time, neither of us said a word. We drank our ale and breathed in the musty air. A companionable silence settled around me like a gentle hug, only broken by the occasional trail of mist creeping through the cracks in the door. The others eventually fell asleep, even my mother. She looked frail, curled up against the table, shocks of white around her hairline. There were lines around her eyes that hadn't been there before, too. Already, she showed signs of Oberon's missing protection. Humans had still aged in Teine, but very few got grey hairs, and wrinkles only came near the end.

"Do you think Oberon is dead?" Val asked me, as if reading my mind.

I turned back. "He's gone, but he's not dead."

"How can you be sure?"

"Flames can't kill him, and I didn't see a body. The barrier is gone, and so is he, but he's still out there somewhere. And as long as he's alive, he'll try to bring back the gods."

Val looked alarmed. "The gods?"

I filled her in on everything I'd learned from Kalen. It was a lot to go through. I'd seen and heard so much during my short time spent out in the mists that it felt like hours passed before I finished my story. Val looked suitably gobsmacked by the information.

"Maybe it's time for another drink," she muttered. When she lifted the cask, I placed a hand on her arm to stop her.

"Let's not. Just in case."

She lowered the ale and reached for the golden chain around her neck. "You think the shadowfiends might try to come in here."

"If they get hungry enough, yes."

"Fuck."

I hopped off the stool and took in our surroundings, though I'd been in here often enough over the years to know what I'd find. Plenty of cobwebs in the corners. Old, worn circular tables and mismatched chairs. Plain floorboards. A handful of candles dripped wax onto their metal holders.

I crossed the room, removed a candle from a table, and added the metal holder to the stick I'd brought in from outside.

"That's not going to kill a shadowfiend," Val said dryly.

"Do you have any better ideas? All my wooden daggers are back in my house."

"*All* your wooden daggers? You had more than just that one?"

"Oh yes." I smiled. "I have a whole stash of them in the cupboard."

Val shook her head and laughed. "That's deranged."

"One of these days, those daggers are going to be useful." I frowned as an animalistic shriek echoed nearby.

"But I agree that's not today. We need something a little bigger."

"There's a hatch back here." Val kicked her boot against something behind the bar. "Maybe someone, such as my parents, hid some weapons inside. Like an axe."

Our gazes locked across the bar. "Val."

"It's all right. I'm all right." She brushed her ginger hair out of her face and tried on a smile. But she did not sound all right.

"I'll look." I rounded the bar and spotted the hatch she'd mentioned. A large rectangular door had been cut into the floor. Several casks of ale were stacked on top of it, almost as though someone had tried to hide it.

"Do you think an axe is inside?" she whispered.

I glanced at her. Val's eyes were pools of tears, but she wouldn't shed them. She never did. Not once since that day had I ever seen her cry. "I don't know if you want me to say yes, or if you want me to say no."

"I want the truth."

"I think it's possible," I said, thinking back to that day. I remembered the look on my father's face when the fae cornered the humans hiding out in the pub. His insistence I stay away. For a long time, I'd ignored that memory. Father had made me feel so uneasy, but I didn't want to remember him that way, so I'd pushed it out of my mind, replacing his scowls with the image of his smiling eyes.

But Nellie's words had scraped away the mask I'd placed on him in my head. They were like a chisel, carving away the lie. I remembered him more clearly now, even if it made my soul ache. There had been something going on that day. He hadn't been all right. For a very long time.

"I'm sorry," I said quickly. "I don't want to upset you."

Val curled her fingers into fists. "I hope we find an axe."

Together, we pulled the barrels of ale off the hidden door, careful not to wake the others or capture the attention of the shadowfiends lurking outside. When we finally pulled the door away from the floor, dust swirled up from a shadowy compartment only deep enough to hold a handful of items.

"Oh." Val's shoulders slumped. "That's not an axe."

I knelt. Kalen's cloak pooled around me as I gathered three leather-bound books and a pocket-sized journal into my arms. Val lowered the door as I stood. She didn't look at me, and I didn't press. If I were her, I'd have wanted to find an axe, too.

I spread the books out on the bar and began flipping through one that had no title or author labeled anywhere. The parchment was old and faded, but the ink smelled fresh, and the rough paper seemed to hum beneath my fingertips.

"My father put these books there," I said with a strange certainty. Something about this felt like him, and I remembered that day he'd brought me here, right before he'd run off into the mists, never to be seen or heard from again. His friend had been rummaging around behind the bar before he'd tossed my father's pack across the room. This book was his.

Val frowned. "Why would he hide some books under the pub's floorboards?"

"There's something in them. Something dangerous." My eyes slid to the journal, and my heart pounded. "Something he didn't want any of us to know."

"Then let's see it." Val snatched up the journal before I could stop her, so quickly I didn't even realize she'd done it until the pages fanned open before her eyes.

"Val," I said.

Her brows pinched together as she read. "This is weird."

"Val."

"What...?" Her eyes flicked up to me, and then back to the page. Something in me fractured. I didn't like this. I didn't like it at all.

"Books won't help us," I found myself saying. "We should put them away and then go back to searching for weapons."

"Tessa, you need to read this." Her voice held a strange softness that didn't sound like Val at all.

"I don't think I want to."

Her eyes speared me. "It's important." She flipped the notebook around and placed it on the table before me. I didn't glance down. I couldn't. "You should look at it, but...it's going to be hard."

My mouth felt dry. "That's really not convincing me to look."

"Don't you want to know what your father was doing?"

I sucked in a rattling breath. Muscles tensing, I glanced down at the page and instantly started. This wasn't what I'd expected at all. There, on the first page, was a name, nestled inside an ornamental square with a line branching off to another just like it.

Andromeda, it read, *the God of Death.*

And the box it connected to read, *King Ovalis Hinde of the mortal kingdom of Talaven.*

I jerked up my head, furrowing my brow. "What the fuck is this?"

"It's a family tree."

My blood curdled. I traced the line down the page to Andromeda's offspring. Another box with another name, connected to more boxes. I flipped the parchment over, following more lines, more boxes, more names I'd never heard of before. Years and years and years of it.

I kept going until I started to recognize the names.

Uther Baran of Teine.

Ruan Baran of Teine.

And then there it was.

Nash Baran of Teine, followed by the two final boxes in the notebook.

Tessa Baran of Teine. Nellie Baran of Teine.

Eyes burning, I hauled back the notebook and hurled it at the wall. The *thump* was loud. Too loud. It startled the others awake, and it filled my ears with the sound of it.

"No," I whispered hoarsely. "My father wasn't in his right mind for a long time. That's just some nonsensical scribblings. It isn't true."

The floor creaked as Nellie stood. "What's happening?"

"Nothing," I called out, meeting Val's steady gaze. "Nothing is happening."

But it wasn't nothing, and everyone in the pub could tell.

"Your father believed you to be a descendent of the God of Death."

"Yeah, I can see that, Val, but it's not true. I mean, can't you see how ridiculous that is?"

"You're really fucking strong."

"Because I spent months training."

"No." She shook her head, leaning forward. "I always thought it, Tessa, way before this. You shouldn't be able to do half the things you can do, despite all the training. You scaled the chasm, repeatedly, like it was nothing. Half the time, you didn't even hold on to the rope when you were prying out the gemstones. I tried to keep up with you, but..."

The blood in my veins stilled. "What are you saying? You actually believe this?"

"If he thought you all were descendants of a god, doesn't that explain why he went in search of her?"

"I..." It made more sense than I wanted to admit. Because it did explain a lot. Why Father had left. Why he'd been so determined to reach the god. Why it must have driven him mad. That didn't mean he was right about it, though. He'd been mistaken, or someone had lied to him, or he'd just lost his grip on reality. I couldn't accept the alternative. That maybe, just maybe, he'd been right. If I was a descendent of the God of Death, then that meant her dark magic ran through my veins.

I could kill people with my touch.

And I could not accept that.

I opened my mouth to say all this and more, but a deep bellow blasted through the courtyard. The hair on the back of my neck bristled. In unison, Val and I turned toward the door. Thunderous footsteps drew closer. The shadowfiends had found us.

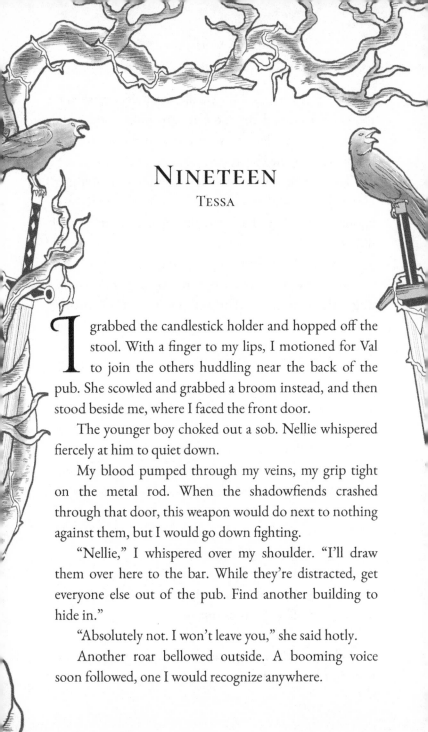

NINETEEN
TESSA

I grabbed the candlestick holder and hopped off the stool. With a finger to my lips, I motioned for Val to join the others huddling near the back of the pub. She scowled and grabbed a broom instead, and then stood beside me, where I faced the front door.

The younger boy choked out a sob. Nellie whispered fiercely at him to quiet down.

My blood pumped through my veins, my grip tight on the metal rod. When the shadowfiends crashed through that door, this weapon would do next to nothing against them, but I would go down fighting.

"Nellie," I whispered over my shoulder. "I'll draw them over here to the bar. While they're distracted, get everyone else out of the pub. Find another building to hide in."

"Absolutely not. I won't leave you," she said hotly.

Another roar bellowed outside. A booming voice soon followed, one I would recognize anywhere.

"Tessa!"

My lips parted, and the candlestick holder crashed to the floor. I crossed the room in two quick strides and ripped open the door to stare out into the mists, half-fearing I'd imagined his voice.

The orange-stained darkness consumed everything. Heart throbbing, I stepped out onto the front step and grasped the railing. I'd heard him. He was out here. I didn't know how, but he was.

"Kalen?" I breathed into the mists.

Steel sang from somewhere nearby, and an ear-splitting shriek rent the air. The wet sound of a blade cutting through flesh followed soon after, and then hurried footsteps, whispers, and another gruesome scream.

I scanned the foggy courtyard and tried to find the source of the sounds, but the air was too thick for me to see further than the steps. It had to be Kalen. It just had to be.

From behind me, my mother grabbed my arm. "Tessa, what in the name of light are you doing? Get back in here before you get killed."

"I'll be fine," I said as the wind carried silence toward us. "If those shadowfiends aren't dead yet, they will be soon. He'll kill them all to get to me."

"Tessa!" His voice ripped through the village, so loud and echoing that I could not tell where it came from, but he was near. There was so much anguish in it, so much rage.

I clutched the railing, desperate to run to him, but I wouldn't leave my family unprotected. If even one shadowfiend got into this pub, it would be devastating. Claws through flesh, fangs drenched in blood. I would not step away from this door until I knew it was safe for them.

"Kalen," I called out, hoping my voice would carry on the mist. "I'm here. On the steps of the pub."

He was at the bottom of the steps a heartbeat later, his body heaving, his breaths ragged. Sweat and dirt and blood clung to the skin not covered by black leather armor. His dark hair was pulled back, highlighting the sharp tips of his ears. Shuddering, he dropped his sword onto the sandy ground. Its blade was drenched in blood.

I'd never seen him look more beaten, more tired. Even when he'd been facing the storm in Itchen, there'd been a determined set to his shoulders, a deadly spark in his eye. But now he looked like he'd been wrung out completely. He teetered on his feet, but his eyes never left my face.

My mother gasped and ran back inside.

I stayed frozen where I was, unable to move. "Are you all right?"

"I thought you were dead," he ground out, shuddering. "We went to the castle. The dungeons were empty. There was blood on the floor and fire everywhere. I thought you were dead." His voice cracked on the last word. Something in my heart cracked right along with it.

I made a mistake. I never should have distrusted him, but what was worse, I never should have taken that dagger and shoved it in his heart. If it had been the real Mortal Blade, if he hadn't taken precautions, the man before me now, desperate to ensure my safety, would be dead.

How could he ever forgive me for that?

Tears welling in my eyes, I took one step down. I would finally get to say these words out loud. "Kalen, I'm so sorry. I shouldn't have done it. I wish I could take it back."

I didn't know if he'd understand what I meant, if he'd realize I was talking about that night. But then the exhaustion in his eyes softened into something that curled around me like his mists. And when his lips lifted in the corners, I knew. *I knew.* I didn't deserve his forgiveness, but he would give it to me, anyway.

"Oh, love," he said in his raspy, toe-curling voice.

I launched down the steps, and he opened his arms before I reached him. Our bodies collided, his wall of muscles against my breasts. He pulled me against him with a grunt and lifted me from the ground. I clung on to his neck, my heart pounding, my face buried in his mist-drenched armor.

He was here. And I was here. It seemed to defy the fidelity of this world. Somehow, despite everything, we had both made it back to each other. *Alive.*

I breathed him in. Beneath the mist, he smelled like smoke and blood. He held me strong, but I could hear his rough breathing, could feel the pounding of his heart against me. And when I glanced down, I spotted a scrap of his armor that had been torn off. It looked like something had taken a bite out of him.

I pulled back to see his eyes. "You're hurt."

"I'll heal in no time." He lowered me to the ground, and my boots scuffed the dirt. "There are a lot of pookas out there. They got too close, and we had a big fight on our hands, that's all."

"Us?"

Movement behind Kalen caught my attention, and several forms moved toward us from the mists. I hadn't noticed them before, but they must have been standing there a while. Niamh, Alastair, even Toryn. They all looked weathered and worn, and Toryn's scars had yet to heal. Maybe, like Niamh's, they never would.

"Did you really think we wouldn't come along to rescue you, little dove?" Alastair asked, cracking an easy, familiar grin.

"To be honest, I thought you'd hate me."

"Kal forgave you. That's good enough for me."

I glanced at the others. Toryn nodded. Niamh did, too, and said, "Don't you worry about us, gem thief."

My lips curled. I hadn't realized, until then, just how badly I'd wanted them to forgive me, too. They had every right to hate me. I'd tried to kill their king. Their friend. But they'd gone a step further than that. They'd come all the way here, fighting the monsters in the mists, just to get me away from Oberon's eternal vow.

I turned back to Kalen, fighting the tears in my eyes. He was here. It still didn't feel real.

"And yet it seems we're too late." His sapphire eyes gleamed. "Because you saved yourself."

"I'm still very glad you've come." I smiled, and he smiled right back. My cheeks ached from the unfamiliar expression.

I wanted to leap into his arms again and stay tucked up against his chest for a good, long while, but now that I knew we had an audience, I held back. From behind me, several pairs of footsteps sounded on the hardwood floor. Kalen's eyes flicked up and widened, and then he pulled his sword from the dirt.

My mother stepped up beside me, heaving an axe into the air. "Get away from my daughter."

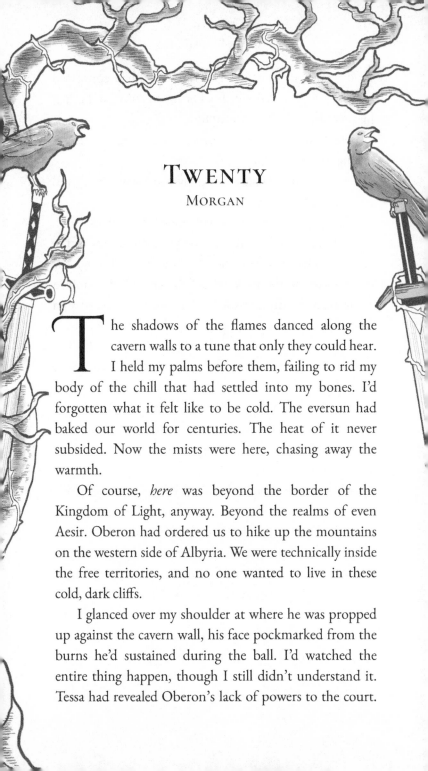

TWENTY

MORGAN

The shadows of the flames danced along the cavern walls to a tune that only they could hear. I held my palms before them, failing to rid my body of the chill that had settled into my bones. I'd forgotten what it felt like to be cold. The eversun had baked our world for centuries. The heat of it never subsided. Now the mists were here, chasing away the warmth.

Of course, *here* was beyond the border of the Kingdom of Light, anyway. Beyond the realms of even Aesir. Oberon had ordered us to hike up the mountains on the western side of Albyria. We were technically inside the free territories, and no one wanted to live in these cold, dark cliffs.

I glanced over my shoulder at where he was propped up against the cavern wall, his face pockmarked from the burns he'd sustained during the ball. I'd watched the entire thing happen, though I still didn't understand it. Tessa had revealed Oberon's lack of powers to the court.

He'd retaliated somehow, but the flames had consumed him as well as everything else. For the first time in his life, his own flames had wounded him.

He'd curled his finger at me, beckoning me closer during the chaos.

"I order you to take me and my wife to our cave," he'd commanded.

The power of our vow had ripped through my soul, and I'd had no other choice. I'd sneaked him out of the Great Hall before anyone noticed. We'd gone through the hidden gate on the back side of the city. He'd stumbled along then, hardly breathing. And then I'd carried him when he could no longer walk. Now here we were.

His wife curled up beside him, her head on his lap. Queen Hannah, our Mortal Queen. She barely spoke these days.

Oberon's eyelids fluttered open, and he caught me staring at him. A shiver of power rippled across his horns. "Morgan, I order you to bring some food to me and my wife."

I let out a long-suffering sigh. I'd grabbed my leather pack on our way out of the city, but it didn't have enough inside for three people. Years ago, I'd decided to get prepared for any eventuality, just in case I ever got free of my vow to him. So, I'd made myself an emergency bag. It held everything I would need for a week spent in the wild. Provisions for my escape from Oberon. Now the king managed to worm his way into that, too.

Oberon had taken everything from me.

I pulled out dried shadowfiend meat I'd wrapped in paper. Every now and then, Oberon had ordered me to hunt in the chasm. I'd saved some of the extra meat over the years, and he'd never noticed. Or, if he had, he'd never said anything about it. I took out three pieces and returned the rest to my pack.

Oberon scowled at me when I handed him the two rations.

"This is not enough food. I need more so I can heal." He glared up at me, blueish-purple bruises around his ember eyes. The air rattled in his lungs as he breathed, and his hand trembled as he lifted the meat to his lips. I'd never seen him this weak before. I was surprised he let me see him like this now, though I was his only option for survival. If it weren't for me, he'd be dead.

That thought did not settle well in my gut. This was the closest Oberon had ever come to dying. The world could be rid of him. *I* could be rid of him. And yet he carried on, because I was forced to cater to his every whim. Eventually, he would heal from this. He was like a festering magical wound. No matter how much ointment or fae healing you poured into it, it persisted.

He was my scar.

He curled his lips at me. "I know what you're thinking."

"That you underestimated Tessa Baran again?"

"Quite the opposite. She failed. Again. I always win when it comes to her." Oberon popped the meat into his mouth, but then coughed, his lungs still full of smoke.

"This doesn't look like a win to me."

I went back to the fire while Oberon fed the other piece of meat to his wife. She whispered a few words to him, but she didn't rouse from her sleep. Her mind and body were failing her now. The years were eating at her, and it wouldn't be long until she slipped away completely. I wondered what he'd do now, with Tessa gone. Would he say goodbye to his queen after all these years? I doubted it. He never gave up.

He was her scar too.

Oberon groaned as he climbed to his feet. I watched him through the flames as he padded over to the cave's entrance and stared out into the mists. A smile tugged at my lips. His worst nightmare had finally come true. King Kalen Denare was inside what was left of his kingdom. And I knew Kalen well, even if he no longer trusted me— I wouldn't trust me, either. He would rip Oberon's head off before he'd ever let him near Tessa again.

"He's going to come for you, you know," I called out to him.

Oberon stiffened, but he kept his back facing me. "Good. I hope he does."

I scoffed. "He will murder the fuck out of you."

"I'll be ready for him."

"I think the smoke has gotten to your head. You're not in fighting shape, to say the least."

He twisted back toward me and smiled. A chill went through me. It was an expression I knew all too well. Already, he was planning something. The gears in his mind moved fast, and he had an idea. Judging by the gleam of his eye, I knew I wouldn't like it.

If only I could reach out to Kalen and warn him. *No.* I wiped away that thought before Oberon could read it on my face. It might give him another idea. If he wanted Kalen to come for him, what better way than to use me to call out to him? Kal wouldn't trust it, of course. He'd expect a trap of some sort. But still, he would come.

Oberon's wife—Queen *Hannah*—moaned and thrashed in her sleep. He was beside her at once, the aches and pains of his many wounds apparently forgotten. I frowned as I watched him. With a soft touch, he brushed her bright blonde hair from her sweat-stained face and whispered sweet words in her ears. This was a side of the king that very few saw. He seemed to think his people would disrespect him if he showed anything other than cruelty and vicious strength. I thought he was wrong about that, but he never listened to me.

"It's all right, my sweet. I'm here."

That was a bit too much, though. I wrinkled my nose.

"I will sort all this out. You'll be fine soon. I will find somewhere for you to go." He lifted his gaze to me. I sucked in a breath. Oberon's eyes sliced through me, his gaze as sharp as the points of his horns, and then he turned back to his catatonic wife. "Just a little bit longer."

I shook my head and stood. The look on his face chilled me. He'd spirited me away to a hidden cave, far from everyone else, and I'd thought he'd only done it because he had nowhere else to go. But now I saw that wasn't it at all. He'd done it to trap me here. For what, I didn't yet know.

While he was distracted by his wife, I grabbed my pack and made for the door, but his voice cut through me before I even got halfway there.

"Stop." The word echoed down the cavernous tunnel. "I command you to stop."

"No." The word ripped from my throat as my boots rooted to the ground, even while my mind screamed against it. Gritting my teeth, I tried to kick out, but my legs wouldn't move. Tears filled my eyes. I tried again and again. Over and over and over, even knowing I was doomed.

I had to try. I would never stop trying.

My entire face burned. The hatred and fear flamed through me like a conflagration. I would get out of here. I would run away from him.

One day, I would be free from his eternal torment.

Oberon stepped up beside me and hissed into my ear. His lavender-scented breath made me gag. "What do you think you're doing, Morgan?"

"Leaving," I moaned. "I got you out of that burning city. You and your wife. And now it's time for me to go."

He chuckled, and it rumbled in his broad chest. "No. You are mine."

Deep, aching tears spilled from my eyes. It had been a long time since he'd made me cry, but *damn him*. He had a desperate look on his face, and he'd do anything to save his wife. If I did not get out of here, I did not know what he would make me do.

Fisting my hands, I tried taking another step. My boot pulled free of the invisible roots, and my breath caught. I took off at a run.

My vision blurred as I raced for the safety of the mists. If I could just put some distance between us, get far enough away that I couldn't hear his commands. He wouldn't be able to control me anymore. He couldn't stop me then.

The moon speared the darkness, so bright and brilliant that it even cut through the dense fog. Just a few more steps. I hated the mists just as much as anyone else, but at least out there I'd be free.

"I command you to stay." Oberon called out after me, almost lazily.

My body shuddered to a stop so violently that I slammed into the rocky ground. Pain lanced through me. I looked back over my shoulder and hissed.

Without another word, Oberon dropped onto the rock where I'd been sitting, just beside the fire. He rummaged through my pack and pulled out the shadow-fiend meat. As he chewed through it, his eyes brightened another shade. The colors deepened. He started to look less like old paint and more like the flames of Albyria.

I sagged against the ground and curled into myself. The cold seeped into my skin once more, even as my life burned down all around me. I would never get away from him.

He would control every moment of my life, even until my last breath.

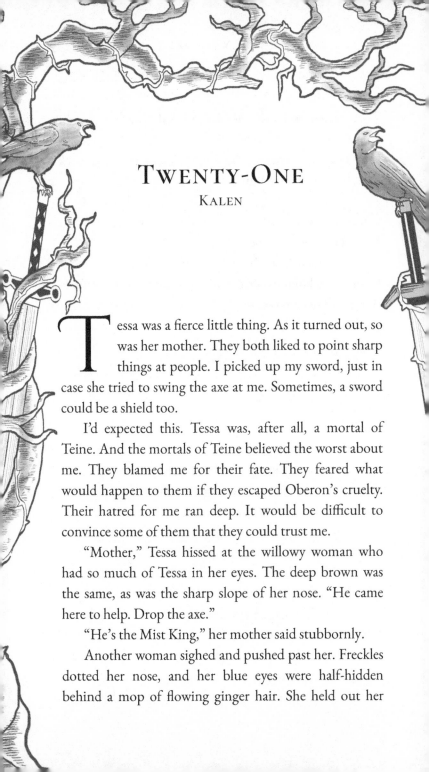

TWENTY-ONE
KALEN

Tessa was a fierce little thing. As it turned out, so was her mother. They both liked to point sharp things at people. I picked up my sword, just in case she tried to swing the axe at me. Sometimes, a sword could be a shield too.

I'd expected this. Tessa was, after all, a mortal of Teine. And the mortals of Teine believed the worst about me. They blamed me for their fate. They feared what would happen to them if they escaped Oberon's cruelty. Their hatred for me ran deep. It would be difficult to convince some of them that they could trust me.

"Mother," Tessa hissed at the willowy woman who had so much of Tessa in her eyes. The deep brown was the same, as was the sharp slope of her nose. "He came here to help. Drop the axe."

"He's the Mist King," her mother said stubbornly.

Another woman sighed and pushed past her. Freckles dotted her nose, and her blue eyes were half-hidden behind a mop of flowing ginger hair. She held out her hand. "I'm Val. Thanks for looking after Tessa while I was stuck in a dungeon."

I smiled and took her hand. "Val. I've heard a lot about you."

"This is insane," Tessa's mother cut in. "Get back here. Get away from him."

"He's not going to hurt any of us." Val eyed me before her gaze drifted to my friends who stood just behind me. "He's come to help."

"He can help us by going back to where he's come from and taking his mists with him. None of us want to be burned or eaten or—"

"Mother, stop," Tessa said gently as she pried her mother's white-knuckled fingers away from the axe handle. She managed to pull the weapon away from her, then handed it to Val. "If he wanted to hurt us, he already would have. He's a good man. I know it's hard for you to trust him after everything we've been told for so long, so just trust *me*. All right?"

Her mother's lips pressed into a thin, white line. She didn't say another word in argument, but I could tell by the flash of hate in her eyes that she wasn't convinced.

Tessa gazed at me. Something in her expression stirred a well of emotions that I rarely allowed to the surface. Unspoken words hung between us in the orange-tinted mists. My thoughts had been consumed by her this past week, as we'd charged toward the Kingdom of Light. I hadn't stopped picturing her face in my mind. Her flushed lips. The curve of her hips. The beauty and strength of her arms.

I'd imagined what this moment might feel like, if I

ever got to gaze upon her again. She looked even better than I remembered. I wouldn't have changed a thing about her then, but I couldn't help but notice a difference in the way she held herself now. Her chin was a little higher, and she stood tall. When I'd met her before, she'd almost seemed bowed over in grief, in uncertainty. Tessa Baran radiated confidence now.

I would kiss her if not for the awkward tension in the air. Several other humans had wandered out of the pub, and some doors on the opposite side of the square had cracked open. Dozens of eyes stared at me in distrust, but only one pair of eyes mattered to me.

Deep brown ones, ringed in burnt orange.

"Kal." Niamh cleared her throat. "We have an audience."

"I can see that."

Tessa took my hand. "There's a lot I want to say to you, but right now, we need to get the mortals out of here. It's not safe for them in Teine anymore. Can you get them to one of the places without mist, like you said before?"

I gazed around at the wide-eyed humans. Many wore old rags. Dirt clung to their hands and bare feet. Some were far too thin, even if Oberon had provided them with everything they needed to survive. But what struck me the most was the haunted look in their eyes. The resignation. They didn't run or scream or try to fight. Instead, they looked as though they were ready to face their deaths.

"They'll never come with me," I said, turning back to her. "They'd rather stay here and die."

Val sauntered up to me with a frown. "Don't be so dramatic. I'll round them up and convince them to follow us across the bridge if you make sure no shadow-fiends attack while I'm doing it."

Out of the corner of my eye, Niamh smiled.

Without waiting for my answer, Val walked across the square to the nearest house. Another mortal, a younger, smaller version of Tessa, darted after her, but her mother continued to stand there on the steps scowling at me as if I'd started the fires myself. After a moment, she sighed and shoved past us to follow Val.

"Looks like that's your answer," Tessa said.

"I know what they all think of me. What makes you believe they'll listen to your friend and leave with the Mist King?"

"Because they won't be leaving with the Mist King. They'll be leaving with Niamh, Toryn, and Alastair."

I arched a brow. "How do you figure that?"

"You and I are going back to Albyria. Did you bring the Mortal Blade?"

"You think Oberon is alive?"

"If he isn't, where's the body? I didn't see one, and I was in the room when the fire started." She stepped close and tipped back her head. "We need to make sure, either way. Because if he's still out there..."

I nodded. "He could still bring back the gods. Can you tell me exactly what happened up there?"

While Val and Nellie gathered the humans in the square, Tessa told the story of how she escaped from a flame-engulfed castle. She'd put Oberon on the spot, revealing the truth about his powers to the courtiers. A smart move. So smart it had actually worked...until Oberon had somehow destroyed the whole damn city with his power.

"The gemstones," I said when she'd finished filling me in. "The barrier worked because he'd poured all his power into the gemstones inside the chasm. And when he pulled his power back out to prove his strength, the barrier failed. There was nothing left to keep the mists out."

"It makes sense," she said. "But he still somehow lost control of it. There was an explosion, and the fires started. He vanished in the smoke."

"He could still be up there, hiding out."

"Look at the castle. It's all on fire, except for the Tower of Crones."

"Where his previous wives are," I murmured, gazing up at the city. Even through the mists, the conflagration was clear. It consumed every inch of the castle, splashing light onto the singular tower that held strong. Only magic could protect a building that way.

"If Oberon is still in that city, he's in the Tower of Crones, Kalen. And he might have his power now, but so do you. Together, we can take him down, once and for all. You use your mists to weaken him, distract him. And then I stab him with the blade."

"It's too dangerous," I said with a shake of my head. This was the second time she'd escaped his grasp. I couldn't risk him getting his hands on her again, especially knowing just how desperate he must be feeling. His entire city was crumbling down around him. His reign had turned to ash. "You should go with the others. They can take the mortals to Endir before traveling on to Sunport, where we can get you all on a ship to the human kingdoms. It will be safe for you there. All of you."

The meaning of my words was not lost on her. "I'm not leaving Aesir. Not until Oberon is dead."

"Tessa..."

"No." She pressed her palms against my blood-drenched chest but did not even react to it. She just took me in, accepting all the violence and darkness that my armor represented. "You told me everything, and I can't walk away from it now. The prophecy. What will become of the world."

"But this is not your burden, love," I said quietly to her, all too aware of the many eyes and ears that surrounded us. "You can leave this place and never again think of fae and blades and cruel kings. Go live your life. Be happy. And it isn't as if we can never speak again. I can still visit you in your dreams."

"It might be my burden more than you could ever imagine," she whispered.

"What do you mean?"

"Kal," Niamh said, striding over to us with her sword propped against her shoulder. "Time to go before more pookas show up."

Behind her, Toryn and Alastair stood with about a hundred humans. They all looked terrified. Val was doing her best to reassure them, but it was clear they were only going along with this out of fear. Not because they wanted to trek across the bridge to Endir.

"Perhaps they'll calm down when I'm no longer here."

She glanced up at the city. "You shouldn't go after Oberon alone."

"He won't be alone," Tessa said. "I'm going with him. With the Mortal Blade."

Niamh arched a brow. "You think I'll just hand the Mortal Blade over to you, of all people?"

"I won't use it against any of you. I know you have no reason to believe me, but I swear it."

"Fantastic." Niamh unhooked a sheathed dagger from her belt and tossed it to Tessa, followed by a small pouch. "Glad we mined some of Oberon's gemstones before he took all his magic out of the ones in the chasm. I think there are eight in there, so use them sparingly. We won't be able to get any more now. So don't stab anyone unless you absolutely have to. That's the real one, by the way. Be careful with it."

"I promise you won't regret this," Tessa said with a smile of surprise. "Thank you for trusting me, Niamh. Even though I don't deserve it."

She gave Tessa slight nod. "I heard what you said to Kal. Your words were laced with truth. It's enough for me."

Folding my arms, I gave Niamh a look. "Tessa is going with you and the others."

Tessa held up the blade and slid the dagger from the sheath. The orange light glinted along the steel. "I'm going with you. It's my decision." She cut her eyes my way. "Are you going to tell me it's not?"

I exhaled, and despite my concern, I could not stop the pride from swelling my chest. She would not be Tessa if she didn't want to risk her life—again—to stop

Oberon. She would never give up. It was stubborn, maybe, but I couldn't help but respect it. Besides, I'd be with her, and I would never let him touch her again.

"I'll agree to it," I finally said. "As long as you swear to listen to me. Don't do anything reckless."

She smiled. "Me? Reckless?"

Niamh just chuckled and wandered back to the human crowd.

"I mean it. We don't know what we'll find up there. Swear that you'll stay beside me and not rush into danger."

She hooked the dagger onto her belt. "I promise. But I won't make a binding vow. Not like before."

"Deal." I held out a hand.

Gazing up into my eyes, she slid her palm into mine. Her fingers squeezed tight, steady and strong. "Deal."

TWENTY-TWO
TESSA

When the others set off for the bridge, Kalen and I held back. We watched them vanish into the dense mist, their forms blurring before us. I whispered goodbye to Val and Nellie, but I avoided my mother. I knew how she'd react if I told her what we planned to do. It was going to take her a long time to accept Kalen's words as truth. Longer than it had taken even me.

"She won't be happy when she realizes you aren't with them," he said as we turned our sights on the burning city up the hill.

"Val and Nellie are with her. She'll listen to them." I checked my dagger at my belt, just to make sure I'd attached it properly, and then nodded. "Let's go."

"Tessa," he said in a deep voice that felt like a fist around my heart. "You don't know how relieved I am to know you're all right."

I glanced up. He smiled and rubbed his thumb against my jaw. Heat filled my neck, and as I leaned into his touch, I wished the world could fall away. We would climb on the wings of dreams and fly far away from here. Away from death and destruction. Away from lies and betrayal. And far, far away from the threat of prophecies and annihilation.

For all my life, I'd expected an average existence. Less than average, really. I would grow up, toil in the fields, keep my head down, and do nothing remarkable at all. The mortals of Teine lived and died just as the bugs in the forest did. No one remembered our names once we were gone. We were nothing. That was how I'd always seen our little slice of the world.

But I'd been wrong. Names *were* remembered. They'd been written in that book.

Mine was one of them.

I still hadn't wrapped my mind around any of it. It seemed impossible that it could mean anything. My father had lost his grip on reality in the last few years of his life. That was the only logical explanation. And yet...I couldn't help but think of Val's words. I was stronger than most mortals. I'd survived several times when I shouldn't have.

And the God of Death had called out to me more than once.

We are so alike, you and me, she'd said.

"Are you all right?" Kalen asked. "If you don't want to do this, we can catch up to the others, and you can go to Endir with them."

I pushed aside my unease. "I'm fine. I want to do this."

Together, we climbed the dirt path up to Albyria.

Smoke filled the air as we drew closer, and the stench of burning flesh clogged my throat. I pressed my hand to my mouth when we reached the open city gates. Kalen's steps slowed to a stop, and he let out an audible gasp at the sight before us. Through the ominous mists, he stood like a beacon in the darkness.

"There is so much death," he said grimly.

We walked through the gates. The fires were easing, just a little, having burned through some of the buildings already. Crooked black beams rained down ash. Soot covered the ground like snow. The streets and castle courtyard were abandoned, other than a scattering of charred bodies. If any light fae had survived, they were either in hiding or they'd fled. Albyria would never again be the same.

Grief weighed heavy on my shoulders as we passed the castle entrance. The stone here had fared better, though the fire still raged inside. All these homes, gone. All that life, gone. I should not feel bad for them, but I did. Many of the fae were cruel and complicit in Oberon's monstrous acts, but if Kalen and the other shadow fae had taught me anything, it was that I couldn't judge all fae by the few who had wronged me.

They were not all Oberon. Some were ordinary people, just like the rest of us. Even if they were not perfect, they were trying. And they had died here this day.

"We're here," Kalen said when we came to a stop outside the curving red door. I'd never been inside the Tower of Crones. I wasn't sure anyone had, other than Oberon. As if to punctuate his ownership of this place, he'd carved his symbol into the wood. The one-eyed dragon, spewing flames from his open jaw.

"He's obsessed with dragons," I said. "He puts that thing everywhere."

"Even on your back." Kalen's voice was as sharp as the blade I carried on my waist.

I had the sudden urge to scratch that spot on my shoulder blade. "I hate that I have to spend the rest of my life marked as his. Even if he dies, I doubt it'll ever go away. It's in my skin. He's branded me forever."

"Not if I have anything to do with it." Kalen tried the door. It creaked and swung wide. Dust motes swirled in the thick air, and a rush of lavender carried with it the sound of crying.

I gave Kalen a sharp glance. "Do you hear that?"

"The Mortal Queens," he said quietly. "The sound is coming from up those stairs."

He indicated toward the spiral stairwell leading from the entranceway to what I assumed was the top of this protected tower. Swallowing, I eased through the doorway and made for the stairs. The sobs grew louder, distinct cries that formed a chorus of pain. These women did not sound like relieved humans whose once-husband had safely joined them in their protected haven.

Kalen reached the stairs just before I did, and he started up first. "Keep an eye on your back. If anyone comes up behind you, whistle."

"I don't know how to whistle," I said as we started the climb.

"Everyone knows how to whistle."

"Blatantly not true, since I don't."

"I'll add that to your training list." He shot a glance over his shoulder. "For now, just say my name if you need to warn me."

"Is that so?" I followed him around the next bend and still the stairs carried on. "Which name? Your Highness? Kalen? Kal? I know better than to call you the...you know."

He chuckled. "Nevermind that anymore. You can call me whatever the fuck you want. I'm just glad you're alive."

I nearly stumbled on the next step as the heat closed in around me. The heat from the flames outside. Definitely from the flames.

"You've changed your tune," I huffed as we neared the top of the stairwell. "I thought you hated that particular name. In fact, you made it pretty clear to me. I remember some shouting and—"

He stopped just ahead of me and then turned. Before I knew what was happening, he had me trapped against the stone wall with his warm breath tickling my neck. He leaned in and whispered into my ear, "I can't hate anything when it's coming from your lips."

My body tensed, anticipation thrumming in my veins. His corded muscles brushed against my breasts, and I nearly shuddered. Mist swirled around us, cool and electric all at once. I wanted to pull him closer and feel his lips on my skin and erase every moment we'd spent apart— erase what I had done to him.

But Oberon could be through that door, now only a few steps away from us.

"Kalen," I whispered, hating that I had to stop...

whatever this was. Maybe it was nothing at all.

He pulled back, his eyes as dark as a moonless night. "I particularly like the sound of that name on your tongue."

I flushed. "Oberon could find us here."

"Good," he said in a growl as his lips skimmed my neck. "I hope he does. And he will see that his claim on you means nothing. You are not his, and you never will be. Fuck his dragon mark."

A thrill went through me. The possessiveness in his words should make me want to run, but it did the opposite. I wanted everything he said. To show Oberon I would never belong to him. To make him understand I would go down in the flames rather than see myself wed to him for eternity. I would have his greatest enemy take me in the stairwell just outside the room where he'd once tried to condemn me for the rest of an immortal life. The Tower of Crones would have been my home if Oberon had gotten his way, after I'd served him in his bed for seventy-five years.

"You are no one's bride," Kalen said fiercely. "Unless you want to be."

Trembling, I tipped back my head, almost daring him to kiss me. His hand skated up the length of my arm before resting against my neck. Fingers spearing my hair, he fisted his hand around the strands and tugged. A flicker of delicious pain jolted through me. I suddenly forgot how to breathe.

"I will never let him touch you again. Do you understand me?"

"It might not be up to you," I whispered back.

"He would have to rip my limbs from my body to stop me from protecting you. And even then, I would find a way." Suddenly, he released his grip on my hair, and then he stepped back. A chasm of cold air yawned between us. "Stay behind me when we walk through that door. Do not run ahead, no matter what you see."

My heart pounded, and I pressed down the front of my gown to steady myself after that...encounter. "What exactly do you think we're going to find in there?"

"I do not know," he said in a grim voice. "Whatever it is, it cannot be good."

I nodded and fell in behind him. My pulse throbbed as Kalen slammed his boot into the door. The sound of splintering wood echoed all around us. The door flew open, and I braced myself for Oberon's destructive power to come racing toward us, but only a handful of sobs answered our arrival.

And then they stopped. The eerie silence rattled my bones.

Kalen went inside. I followed quickly, stepping over a pile of broken wood. A circular room spread out around us, and the chaos of the fire-drenched streets seemed like a distant memory in this cocoon of tranquility. Five beds ran along the nearest wall, all covered in luxurious sheets and plush pillows. A small table sat beside each. Some held books or scrolls. Some were covered in oil lamps and various plants. But two were completely empty.

Movement to the left caught my attention. I turned, half-expecting to find Oberon's gleaming horns aimed toward Kalen. He would curl his fists and throw his fire across the tower. Kalen would have to counter with his mist. Their magic would clash, and another chasm would rip through the world.

But it was only four human women staring back at us. Oberon was nowhere to be seen. Strangely enough, neither was Hannah. I'd assumed she'd been sent here, since I'd seen no sign of her since my return.

I relaxed. "It's the Mortal Queens."

He spoke to me in a low voice. "How much do you know about these Mortal Queens? Do you remember all their names?"

"Of course. The first was a girl named Elise, and then seventy-five years later, we had Layla. Next was Mala and then Hannah, who isn't here. I was to be the...fifth." And yet, there were four humans standing before us. That was one more than there should have been. "Maybe one of them is the maidservant."

I started toward them. As I drew closer, their milky eyes gazed right through me. They all wore matching crimson robes that hung from gaunt forms. Scraggly hair curtained pale faces. Even though they had not aged a day, they looked ancient, their spines curved as if the weight of the entire world rested on their shoulders.

"Hello," I called out. "Are you all right? The castle is on fire. We should get you out of here before the magic protecting the tower fails."

No answer. Each of the crones continued to stare right through me.

"Has Oberon been here?" Kalen tried.

Again, the crones did not speak. They didn't even blink or flinch or make any indication they knew we were standing in front of them.

Frowning, I glanced up at Kalen. "There's something wrong."

"I think we may have just discovered why Oberon swaps out his wives every seventy-five years."

I turned back to the Mortal Queens. Their eyes were so milky that it was impossible to see the browns of the irises any longer. One of them began to hum, a high-pitched tune that sounded like the dying wails of a wounded animal. Shivers stormed across my arms, and I took a step back from pure instinct. My body screamed at me to run, to get as far away from these women as I possibly could.

"Whatever is wrong with them, we can't leave them here. What if the fires break through? I don't think they have the ability to save themselves."

"That might be easier said than done," he said quietly.

Slowly, I approached the Mortal Queens, hands held up before me. I didn't want to startle them, and I wasn't sure how they'd react if I got too close.

"Careful, Tessa," Kalen warned.

The nearest woman stepped toward me. She reached out a hand. Drawing the stale air into my lungs, I took it.

A strange magic surged through me. The intensity of it was like a storm, full of wind and rain and thunderous booms. It knocked me off my feet, my body crumpling like a puppet without strings. Eyes rolling back into my head, I heard, very distantly, the sound of Kalen's roar. And then my mind went blank, and a vision filled my head.

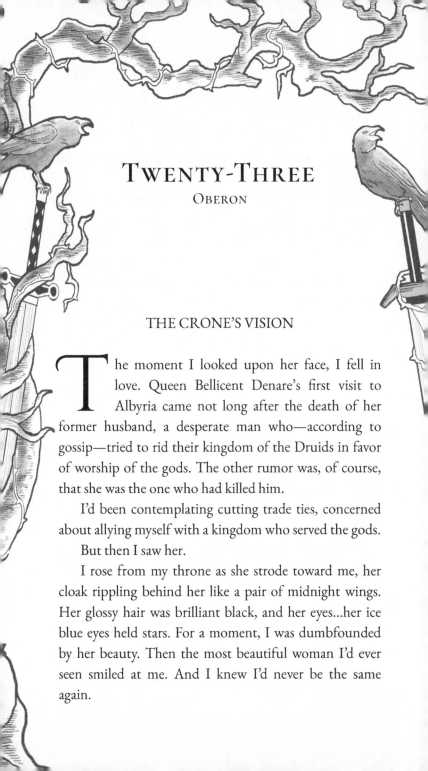

TWENTY-THREE
OBERON

THE CRONE'S VISION

The moment I looked upon her face, I fell in love. Queen Bellicent Denare's first visit to Albyria came not long after the death of her former husband, a desperate man who—according to gossip—tried to rid their kingdom of the Druids in favor of worship of the gods. The other rumor was, of course, that she was the one who had killed him.

I'd been contemplating cutting trade ties, concerned about allying myself with a kingdom who served the gods.

But then I saw her.

I rose from my throne as she strode toward me, her cloak rippling behind her like a pair of midnight wings. Her glossy hair was brilliant black, and her eyes...her ice blue eyes held stars. For a moment, I was dumbfounded by her beauty. Then the most beautiful woman I'd ever seen smiled at me. And I knew I'd never be the same again.

"King Oberon," she said as she came to a stop before me. "I must say, I expected more of a greeting when I arrived in your fair city."

"My apologies, Queen Bellicent." I jogged down the steps of the dais and held out a hand. "Please don't take it as a slight. I—"

"You wanted to make a point. You don't approve of me or the goings on in my kingdom. Trust me, I understand what it looks like. That's why I came to visit you."

She took my hand as if to shake it, but I could not help but lift her delicate fingers to my lips and drop a kiss onto her skin.

Blushing, she cleared her throat and pulled away.

"Again, my apologies." I shook my head at myself. "I don't know what came over me."

"It's all right, King Oberon. I appreciate the warm welcome, even if you didn't greet me at your city gates."

"Just call me Oberon. No need for titles."

She smiled.

I motioned toward the doors leading out of the Great Hall. "Shall we go for a walk? I can show you the city, and you can fill me in on whatever you came here to speak with me about."

Her eyes brightened, although that seemed almost impossible for how bright they already were. "I would like that very much."

Together, we walked along the battlements on top of the wall surrounding my city. I showed her the market full of its bountiful stalls. I pointed out the Temple and the lively inns. And, from a distance, I showed her Teine, where a village full of humans had chosen to build their lives. She told me about her family, her kingdom, her former husband, and his plans to turn to the gods. Gods that she did not worship herself.

And then we moved on to more sensitive topics. We shared our dreams. We shared our loves and what we'd lost over the years. A one-week stay turned into a month. And then another. Six months passed quicker than either of us realized. Long enough for me to memorize every inch of her skin.

But one day, we woke up from our haze of lust and love. Her son had sent a letter.

"I must go. I'm needed back in Dubnos." She climbed out of bed and reached for her robe.

I grabbed her hand and pulled her back to me. "Marry me, Bellicent. I want you to be my wife."

With a sad smile, she palmed my cheek. "My love, I cannot. My kingdom needs me."

"We can join our kingdoms together. Light and Shadow can become one. Together, we could be invincible."

"And who will rule over this joint kingdom?"

"We would rule it together, of course." I searched her eyes. "Or you can rule it all, if that's what you want. I would give it all up for you. That's how much I want you in my life."

"Oberon." She dropped her forehead to mine. Her lavender perfume curled around me, achingly familiar by now. I did not think I could handle never again smelling that scent. *Her* scent. "I will not take your kingdom away from you. And I cannot give you mine. Aesir has been three kingdoms for centuries upon centuries. It should remain that way."

"Then we leave them as they are," I said quickly. "You will rule your kingdom, and I will rule mine, and we can still wed."

She shook her head. "My reign is unstable, and you know it. That's why I came to you in the first place for an alliance. Kalen will make a good king, but he is not ready. If I'm to wed you, it will need to be in the future when I can come live here with you without worry of what might happen."

Bellicent pulled away, grabbed her robe, and padded across the room with the hearth's fire casting an orange glow upon her beauty. Deep down, I'd known her answer. And I understood it was the right thing for her to do. For her kingdom. But selfishly, I would do anything to convince her to stay. Her place was with me. I wanted her by my side for eternity.

She smiled at me while I watched her dress. "I do love you, Oberon."

My heart lifted. "See me again soon. Come back after you take care of your kingdom's business."

"People are already gossiping about my time spent here with you."

"There's a cave," I said. "In the mountains behind Albyria. We can meet there, and no one would have to know. In two months' time?"

Her smile lit up the entire room. "Tell me how to get there."

The two months scraped by. When the day finally arrived, my desperation drove me to leave my guards at the castle so that I could be alone with Bellicent. And when she walked into the cave, glowing like the light of the moon, I told her guards to return to the castle too. I had the power of the sun running through my veins. My protection was all she needed to stay safe.

It was the worst mistake of my life.

We spent a blissful night wrapped in each other's arms. And even though she was used to the cold, I built a fire to keep her warm. We dozed off after hours of passionate bliss.

I fell asleep to her soft snores and awoke to the terror of her screams.

A bandit stood over us, a knife glinting in his hand. He brought it down upon her body, and her blood sprayed in the air. Horror choked me, and for a moment, I could do nothing but stare. My mind did not work. My body could not move. It was as if the world had gone mute, sounds and smells stripped away. All that existed was her blood.

The bandit took one look at me, flicked his eyes at my horns, and then grabbed our packs. He sprinted out of the cave before my mind understood what had happened.

Heart frozen, I stared down at Bellicent's slack form. She stared up at me, her eyes unseeing. I pressed my fingers to her neck, desperate to feel her heartbeat, but I already knew. Blood was everywhere. It coated her skin. My hands were covered in it, and specks clung to my face and eyelids.

Grief consumed me. In a single moment, the world had taken my soul in its brutal fist and crushed me into nothing. The most precious person who'd ever existed was gone. Gone because of me. Because of my selfishness and stupidity.

I'd done this to her. If only I hadn't insisted we meet. If only I hadn't sent away the guards. If only I hadn't frozen when she'd needed me most...

I roared and pounded my fists against the stone ground until my bones cracked and my throat went raw.

I carried her body deep into the caves before returning to the castle, drenched in blood. My guards were the first to see me. They sneaked me inside to a hot bath where I sponged any evidence of her off my skin. Her guards soon came to my quarters and demanded to know where their queen had gone.

I told them she'd headed back to Dubnos without them. The lie came easily, even though the words sounded hollow in my ears. I couldn't tell them the truth. Kalen Denare was fiercely dedicated to his mother. She'd told me this herself. If he knew I was responsible for her death, it could start a war.

So, the guards left, and the flame of my heart sputtered out.

Until I remembered the words of my father, and my father before him. My heritage. My most important responsibility. It had been handed down to me over the years, from king to king, from queen to queen. Keep it safe. Keep it locked up tight. Never let a single soul find out that Albyria was home to the essence—the *dark power*—of half a god.

I found myself standing before the vault hidden deep beneath the halls of my castle. Dust swirled around me, the looming door thrice as tall as me. It had been years since anyone had stepped foot in this place. I'd only come here once when I'd been a boy.

"Never open this vault," my father had told me. "Half of the God of Death's power lives here, trapped inside an onyx gemstone necklace. If she ever escapes, she'll return to her body, and then to this world. She'll bring the other gods back with her. You can never let that happen. Do you understand me, Oberon?"

"Sorry, Father," I whispered now as I turned the handle and tugged open the vault. A deep mist swirled toward me as the wood groaned against my effort. And when the dust settled, a small glittering necklace perched atop a pedestal in the center of the vault.

I walked over to it. Instantly, I felt the intensity of its power thundering toward me.

"Oberon," a woman's voice said. A soft, kind voice that was unlike anything I'd expected. "The ruler of the Kingdom of Light. Why have you come to me?"

"You are the essence of the God of Death," I said around the lump in my throat. "But my father said only half of you is in here, the half that gives life."

"I see. Someone close to you has died. I wondered how long it would take for one of you to come to me."

"So, it's true. You can give life."

"It's all I can give," she said, almost sounding bitter. "That's why they split me in half. That, among other reasons. They believed I might be useful in this form."

I took a step closer to the pedestal. "If someone were to use you, what would happen? Would it release you?"

"Unfortunately not."

"You would stay inside that stone?"

"Unless you destroy this onyx stone, I cannot escape. And yes, I can bring someone to life for you, but there will be...requirements."

Unease thundered through me. "What kind of requirements?"

"First," she said without a moment's pause, "you'll have to take me out of this vault. My magic cannot work inside of it."

I frowned. That was what I'd been afraid of.

"Second, I assume your lost love is a fae?"

I nodded, though I wondered if she could see me or just hear me. That was answered soon enough.

"You only have half of me, and I'm stuck inside of a stone. My power is muted. I cannot do a thing without you willing it. I'm effectively your slave. Do you understand what that means?"

"You won't be able to destroy the world."

"It means there's only so much I can do. I cannot bring your love's body back from the dead. I'll have to transfer her soul into another living body, and it will have to be a mortal one. Now, if I had access to my full power...I could transfer her into the body of another fae, but—"

"Wait," I said, cutting her off. "You can't give life?"

"I can give life. Just not the way you want."

I shook my head. "So, you're saying I'd have to reunite you with the death half of your power. That's the only way to really bring Bellicent back, her body included?"

"How long has she been dead?"

"A few days," I said quietly.

"I'm afraid my power doesn't work like that, even when fully combined. I am the God of Death, not life. I can kill at any time, but I cannot bring a body back unless it has recently died. The only way to save your lover is to transfer her soul into another body."

For a moment, I did nothing but stand there and think. I should have known it wouldn't be as easy as asking this god to return Bellicent to me. No one survived death. Every beautiful thing in the world came to an end. Fae had longer in this world than most, but even we could not avoid the great void forever.

At hearing those words, I should have walked away—should have closed the vault and never again visited this place. It should have been the end of everything.

But a broken heart can lead a desperate man to do terrible things.

"Tell me about the soul transfer," I said to the God of Death.

I could hear the smile in her voice. "You will choose a mortal, and you will carve a mark into her skin to tie her to me."

"Tie her to you?"

"Well, yes. There must be a way to channel my magic through her, or it will never work. Now will you stay quiet and listen to my instructions?"

I pressed my lips together, despite the warning bells clanging in my mind.

"You'll give her a tattoo with my mark, the one-eyed dragon. You'll need to use Comet Dust, which means you'll need to journey to the human kingdoms to find some. They won't much like you taking it, so you'll need to be quiet and careful. Once that's done, you will need to wait for a night when the moon is full in the Kingdom of Shadow's sky. You won't need to leave your borders to check when that is. I can tell you. Then I can do the transfer."

My heart pounded. "And you'll put her soul into another's body. It will really be Bellicent inside?"

"Every glorious aspect of her," the god said. "And with my power channeling through her, she will remain young, never aging, just like you."

My bones shook as I stumbled away from the pedestal to lean against the nearest wall. I couldn't do this, could I? The gods were terrible beings. I'd been warned of them all my life, and I'd been tasked with protecting the world from their return. How could I go against everything I'd always believed?

But how could I not? Bellicent Denare was dead because of me. I'd do anything for her, even risk fucking up the whole world. It wouldn't come to that, though. The solution was simple. I would use the gemstone just this once to bring Bellicent back. And then I would never touch it again. I'd lock it back up in the vault.

Besides, this was only half of the god's power. The other half was stuck in a stone deep beneath the castle in Itchen, and it was fully protected by my soldiers stationed there.

"All right," I said with a nod. "I'll do it."

Bellicent blinked up at me, but the stars had vanished from her eyes. Deep brown eyes looked back at me instead. It was such a human color, but I hadn't grown to hate it just yet. I was too relieved to see her again. Her eyes could have been the color of piss and I would have been happy.

"Oberon?" Bellicent frowned a different pair of lips and gazed around us. "What have you done?"

"I brought you back," I said, my voice rough.

She frowned and clawed at her throat. "This body, this voice. It's wrong. I hate how close the hair is to mine. It feels like me, but it's not. I don't like this. You shouldn't have done it."

It turned out the god had gifted Bellicent with more than just life. She'd given her knowledge, so that she understood at once what I'd done. At first, she was angry with me. The gods are dangerous, she said. I'd cheated death, she argued. She could never again see her son, she cried. She spent a long time alone, stewing in her dark thoughts.

Eventually, she softened against the new reality of her situation. At least she was alive, she finally told me. The years blurred by in happiness, though she rarely spoke unless she had to. The one thing she could never accept was how different her voice sounded in her foreign ears. At first, no one in the castle suspected a thing, but over time, the rumors spread.

And then her mind began to break. Bellicent forgot who she was and even how to speak. Soon, she could not get out of bed without help. Over time, her eyes changed color, from brown to deep purple and now to white.

"It seems the mortal body cannot withstand this kind of magic for long," the god eventually told me. "Even with my power running through her veins, her mind is destroying itself. She will continue to live on like this, but she will become nothing but a vacant shell."

"You have to fix this," I hissed at her. "I took you out of the vault so that you could save her life, so that she could be by my side for centuries. It's only been seventy-five years."

"There is nothing I can do without access to my full power. The mortal body is not strong enough. Now if you would reunite me with my other half, I could put her soul into a fae body. That would withstand the test of time."

The god's essence had done her damndest to tempt me over the years, offering me so much in exchange for her release. She'd sworn to banish the mists beyond our border. To destroy Kalen Denare. She'd even offered to restore the fae women of Albyria with the ability to bear children. And now this.

"Nice try," I said with a bitter laugh. "I will never do it, no matter what you dangle in front of me. You're never getting out of that onyx stone as long as I'm alive."

"Very well," she said with a tsk. "The only other option is to transfer her into another mortal body. And then you'll likely need to continue doing it every seventy-five years or so."

I sagged against the wall. "What becomes of the mortals when we do this to them?"

She laughed. "You should have asked that before the first time you did it. What do you think, Oberon?"

I winced.

"Their little mortal souls die. All so you can save the love of your life. So, what will it be? Say goodbye to Bellicent once and for all? Or shall we do the transfer?"

"Because of the war, there are fewer humans in Aesir now," I said. "Only a hundred or so down in Teine. They'll notice if one goes missing."

"You are the king," she replied. "You can do whatever you want." Then she went quiet for a moment. "Of course, you could promise them something in exchange. Your territory here is so small. Small enough that I could spread my power across it. You could offer them protection from death until they reach old age. In exchange, they give you one of their humans to become your Mortal Queen. Every seventy-five years. You can call it the *Oidhe*."

I closed my eyes. It was wrong. I knew it, and yet I could not bring myself to choose goodbye. The god had trapped me in an impossible situation, and the poison of her power already seeped into my soul. If I'd known seventy-five years ago what would happen, I might have said no.

But now I couldn't. I was a different man.

And so I spoke the words that would condemn me forever. "A mortal's life does not matter compared to hers. I will choose another to die."

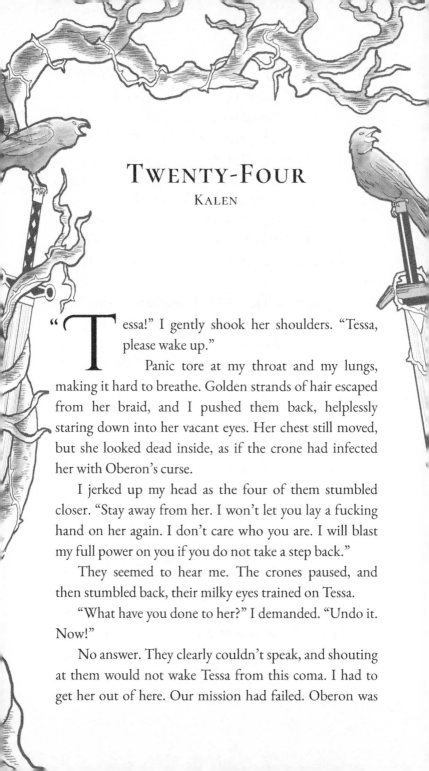

Twenty-Four

Kalen

"Tessa!" I gently shook her shoulders. "Tessa, please wake up."

Panic tore at my throat and my lungs, making it hard to breathe. Golden strands of hair escaped from her braid, and I pushed them back, helplessly staring down into her vacant eyes. Her chest still moved, but she looked dead inside, as if the crone had infected her with Oberon's curse.

I jerked up my head as the four of them stumbled closer. "Stay away from her. I won't let you lay a fucking hand on her again. I don't care who you are. I will blast my full power on you if you do not take a step back."

They seemed to hear me. The crones paused, and then stumbled back, their milky eyes trained on Tessa.

"What have you done to her?" I demanded. "Undo it. Now!"

No answer. They clearly couldn't speak, and shouting at them would not wake Tessa from this coma. I had to get her out of here. Our mission had failed. Oberon was nowhere to be found, and even if he was, I would not fight him with Tessa in this condition. He would see her weakness, and he would try to take her.

I slid my arms beneath her body and lifted her from the floor. Her head rolled against my chest, and her eyes finally slid closed. The beating of my heart was almost painful. I'd fought many enemies through the centuries but none quite like this—helpless women trapped in a burning city by a fae who had used them for his own gain.

"Can you undo what you've done to her?" I asked them.

Four pairs of blank eyes stared back at me. They didn't move. They didn't speak. I shook my head.

"Tessa wanted to get the four of you out of here, but I'm tempted to let you burn for this." I tightened my hold on Tessa's slack body. "But I won't. Only because she wanted to save you. Follow me down these stairs if you want to be free."

Again, no answer. I turned, kicked the door open, and jogged down the spiral stairwell. None of the crones followed. So be it.

When I reached the ground floor, a new dash of fires roared through the streets. Holding my breath, I charged into the smoking ruins of Albyria. A sudden wind caught the flames. They flicked up toward the sky like a serpent's tongue, a bolt of orange through the mists.

I ran through the last remnants of the once-great Kingdom of Light, one of the three remaining strongholds of Aesir. A strange helplessness took seed in my gut as I dodged a building crumbling down. The blackened wood groaned under the weight of its collapse. Yes,

Oberon had been a terrible, cruel king. And yes, many of the light fae had followed his path.

But I'd never intended to bring ruin upon this entire kingdom.

Albyria might rebuild, but it would never be the same. A hollow ache took shape in my chest.

The gods had taken so much from the fae. When the world had forced the gods away, the fae who lived back then must have thought they'd finally won. Things would be better. We would take care of ourselves and each other. Instead, we had continued to destroy one another. Hundreds of years had passed, and nothing had changed.

When I reached the open gates, I slowed. I walked down the hill with Tessa cradled against my chest, alert for any sign of pookas or angry light fae. I carried her across the bridge, and then headed east toward Endir, where the others would be waiting for us.

The burning city on the hill became nothing more than a smudge of orange mist.

We'd left a clutch of horses waiting for us on the other side of the bridge, but they were gone now. The others must have taken them—the humans needed them far more than me. Endir was the closest city to the bridge, but it was still a long way to journey on foot. My arms ached, and my shoulder-blades pinched, but I continued.

I would carry Tessa to the moon and back, if I must.

Halfway to Endir, she squirmed in my arms and cracked open her eyes. She reached up and touched my face. "Is this a dream? Are you really here?"

Relief shook my weary body. "I'm here, love."

She smiled and closed her eyes, sagging against me

once more. With renewed determination, I did not stop to rest until I spotted the familiar shape of Endir's terrain on the horizon. Once the most prosperous city in all of Aesir, Endir had been built into the hills of a lush forest. Curving stone bridges looped between the hills, where the path wound past clusters of slate gray stone houses topped with dark orange roofs. Before my conquest—and the mists—the city had been surrounded by verdant fields full of wildflowers. Now the ground was nothing more than sand.

I found Alastair waiting for me at the towering gated entrance of the city, first built to keep out invading armies. Now it worked to protect the citizens of Endir from the monsters of the mists. A pooka had never succeeded in getting past these walls, and soldiers guarded it day and night.

My old friend relaxed visibly when he spotted me, though his eyes widened in concern when his gaze dropped to Tessa. "What happened?"

"It's an odd story," I told him as I nodded toward the guards who raised the metal gates. After I stepped through and watched the gates close, I felt I could relax for the first time in days. Tessa was alive, even if something strange had happened back in the Tower of Crones. It had weakened her, but it hadn't killed her. Oberon was still out there, but I could deal with him later.

What mattered most was in my arms.

Alastair fell into step beside me as we started up the street toward the castle. "We got most of the humans to Endir, but a few of them ran off screaming when a group of pookas attacked. And three turned out to be allergic to the mists. I'm afraid they didn't make it."

I gave him a sharp glance. "Nellie and Val?"

"Both fine," he said with a nod. "Her mother has been throwing a fit, but she's here too."

"Good. If anything happened to any of them..."

Alastair chuckled. "Trust me, I know. Little dove grows claws when it comes to her family."

I smiled.

"So, what now?" he asked.

"I'll send word to request a ship to meet us in Sunport, and then the humans can sail to the safety of the mortal kingdoms. But it will take weeks for it to get there," I said, glancing down at Tessa. "In the meantime, we'll stay here and regroup. Let everyone rest and learn all is not lost. Maybe we'll even throw a ball, something I doubt any of these humans have ever experienced."

"And Oberon?"

My gaze narrowed. "He's in hiding. I'll send some of our soldiers to seize control of Albyria, and I'll have more patrol Itchen and Vere, as well as the border to the Kingdom of Storms. If Oberon goes anywhere, we'll know about it."

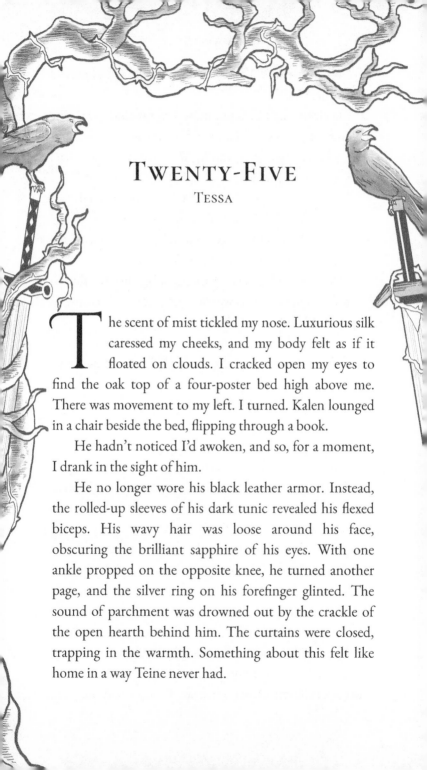

TWENTY-FIVE

TESSA

The scent of mist tickled my nose. Luxurious silk caressed my cheeks, and my body felt as if it floated on clouds. I cracked open my eyes to find the oak top of a four-poster bed high above me. There was movement to my left. I turned. Kalen lounged in a chair beside the bed, flipping through a book.

He hadn't noticed I'd awoken, and so, for a moment, I drank in the sight of him.

He no longer wore his black leather armor. Instead, the rolled-up sleeves of his dark tunic revealed his flexed biceps. His wavy hair was loose around his face, obscuring the brilliant sapphire of his eyes. With one ankle propped on the opposite knee, he turned another page, and the silver ring on his forefinger glinted. The sound of parchment was drowned out by the crackle of the open hearth behind him. The curtains were closed, trapping in the warmth. Something about this felt like home in a way Teine never had.

"Where are we?" I asked him. "Is Nellie all right? And my mother? Val?"

He closed the book and moved to my side. Searching my eyes, he grasped my hand and held it against his thundering heart. "We're in Endir. Your family is here too. They're all safe. But are *you* all right? What happened?"

I smiled. But then I thought back to what I'd seen and heard, and that feeling of home and of safety burned away. "The Mortal Queen who touched me...she gave me a vision of the past. Oberon's past."

"Oh." He visibly relaxed and then brushed his thumb against my cheek. "I was worried she'd done something to hurt you. It made you collapse."

"Kalen," I began, but my throat closed up. How was I going to tell him what I'd witnessed? It would devastate him.

His brow furrowed. "What did you see?"

I slid my hand around his. "It's about your mother. Oberon and your mother."

Kalen tensed, and he started to pull away, but I tightened my hold on him. "You need to hear this. And I want you to stay right here beside me. I want you to look into my eyes and know that I'm with you every step of the way. And if you want me to slow down, I'll slow down. But I won't stop. You need to know the truth about it all."

His jaw tensed.

"I know," I said. "This is hard."

Kalen didn't say another word. He just wrapped his other hand around mine. He listened as I told him the story of Bellicent Denare, the fae queen who'd died and then come back, time and time again, in the bodies of the Mortal Queens. I told him about Oberon's fierce love for her and how it had made him do terrible things.

His eyes were full of anguish when I reached the end of the story. He kept his hold on my hands, clinging with such an intensity that I feared he might break if I let go. It took a long time for him to speak.

"I thought she was dead this entire time," he finally ground out, pain laced through every word. "For some reason, this feels worse. He's kept her hostage—"

"I don't think he's kept her hostage. I think she wants him to do this for her. Maybe she didn't the first time, but what I saw...I don't think she wants it to stop, Kalen."

"But how could she?" Brow furrowed, he shook his head. "She made me vow to fight against the gods, no matter what happened. The mother I knew would never toy with that kind of power, even if it meant saving her own life. It doesn't make any sense."

"I think I might understand why," I said quietly.

"Go on."

"The Oberon I saw in my vision was not the same man he is now. Something changed him. That power, it corrupts. It corrupted my father. It corrupted Oberon. It corrupted your mother too. And I..." I tightened my hold on his hands. "I worry it will get to me eventually, if it hasn't already."

Kalen sat back, frowning. "How? As long as we keep you away from Oberon, you're safe."

"I may have the god's power running through my veins."

I'd wanted to tell him before, but there'd been too much happening. Now did not seem like the best time, either, but I couldn't hold this back from him any longer. If this was true, he deserved to know. It would mean I was dangerous. Maybe he should put me in a dungeon cell, after all.

"What are you talking about? Did you see that in the vision?" he asked.

"I found my father's journal in the pub just before you showed up. Val has it now, I think." I braced myself for my next words. "He'd drawn out a long family tree. *Our* family tree. And it went all the way back to Andromeda and King Ovalis Hinde of the mortal kingdom of Talaven. It said I'm her descendent."

Kalen released my hands and ran his fingers through his wavy hair. "You can't be. The gods wanted to *use* mortals. As food. They wouldn't have…"

"Slept with the livestock?"

"I wouldn't put it that way, but yes. My mother…" A shadow crossed his face. "She didn't come across any of this during her research."

"Did she tell you everything she discovered during her trip to the human kingdoms?"

"Obviously not." He frowned. "But this seems important. If there are descendants of the gods still left in this world, then they're—"

"Dangerous."

"You don't have her power," he countered. "Andromeda is the God of *Death*. She can kill through touch. And trust me, your touch does something to me, Tessa. But it's not death."

I blushed. "Regardless of who and what I am...I am sorry about your mother. I can't even imagine how you must feel. All these years, she's still been here. She's still alive."

His eyes clouded. With a sigh, he stood and moved over to the hearth. His dark silhouette swallowed up his expression. "There might be a fragment of her in there, but it's not her anymore. Not if that power has consumed her to this extent. The mother I knew would never have wanted a mortal to die for her, much less five or six. Whatever is left, it's a twisted version of who she used to be, and Oberon deserves to die for what he's done. He really was playing around with the power of the gods. All this time, I was right." He turned and took a step toward me, power humming from his body. "That mark is still on you."

"I know." I swung my legs over the side of the bed and padded over to him. "The vision didn't tell me everything about the ritual, but I do know I have to be in close proximity to the gemstone in order for it to work. I'm safe, as long as he doesn't find me."

"I'm going to kill him for this."

I couldn't help but smile. "You were already going to kill him."

"Yes, but now I will relish in his death."

A knock sounded on the door. Before Kalen could cross the room, Nellie and Val tumbled inside. They took one look at me and then dashed my way. My mother stepped into the room just behind them, brow pinched. Nellie reached me first and threw her arms around my neck. Val slammed into us a second later. I hugged them just as tightly as they hugged me. They'd made it through the mists. For now, we were safe.

Val finally pulled back, her furrowed gaze scanning my face. "I was worried you weren't going to wake up for days. The way you looked when Kalen carried you inside—"

"Wait." I glanced over at Kalen. "He carried me here?"

"It took him almost two days," Nellie added.

My chest warmed. "Was that not painful?"

"Nothing could be painful enough to stop me from saving you."

Our gazes locked across the room, and fingers of heat crept up my neck. I'd assumed he would never want me the same way he had before I'd...well, *stabbed* him. But the way he looked at me gave me hope. If anything, there was far more in his eyes than there'd been before.

Nellie coughed, and Val shifted awkwardly on her feet. I dragged my gaze from Kalen's and tried to focus on them instead. It was then I noticed their cheeks were free of dirt, their hair was glossy, and they wore fresh linen tunics and trousers, both in gorgeous shades of green. No more crimson, thank the light.

Mother, still in a nightdress, slowly limped over to the bed and clasped my hands when she reached me. Tension tightened the muscles in her face, but the love in her eyes cut through it all. "Oh, Tessa. I was worried I'd lost you again."

I clutched her right back. "I'm not going anywhere. Kalen made certain of that."

Anger flashed in her eyes. She still didn't trust him,

even after he'd carried me back to Endir without stopping to rest. But at least she'd come here. At least she hadn't run, like some of the others. She was alive. We all were. And for the first time in a very long while, we were safe —*fully* safe. I had not felt relief like this in years.

Nellie sat on the bed, brushing her chestnut hair over her shoulders. "Do you feel up to a tour, or would you rather sleep?"

"I feel like I've been asleep for days." I smiled. "What time is it?"

"Late morning. There's still some food set out in the Great Hall for you to break your fast." Kalen opened the wardrobe on the opposite wall to reveal rows of tunics and trousers in varying colors. He then crossed the room to push open a door I hadn't noticed earlier. It led to a second chamber, with a claw-footed tub and a window overlooking the misty landscape.

"You can bathe now or later. I can fetch a maidservant to bring hot water for you."

"You have maidservants here?"

"Dubnos is my home, but I consider Endir my second home. The castle is fully stocked and well staffed. There are many fae, and a few humans, who live in the city. It's protected by a guarded wall, and the pookas do not cross it. You're safe here for as long as you wish to stay."

"And what about—"

"Oberon?" A shadow darkened his expression. "I'll take care of him when we find him. For now, I want you to make yourself at home and try to forget about the darkness of this world for a little while."

That would be easier said than done, but I supposed I

could handle letting go of all my pent-up anger for the time being, especially now that I knew the truth about Oberon's past. Now I felt pity for him more than anything else.

The others left me alone in my bedchamber while I changed into a deep blue tunic and a pair of dark trousers, and then brushed through the tangles in my hair. I'd eat first, see Endir, and then I'd bathe. I was too hungry to wait.

When I was fully dressed, I found everyone except for my mother waiting for me in the corridor outside my room. She'd returned to her own quarters to rest. A lush emerald carpet stretched down the floor, leading to a grand staircase illuminated by a hundred flickering candles, held aloft in chandeliers. The stone walls bore portraits of past queens and kings, but there were also humans scattered amongst them, and fae I did not recognize from my books.

Kalen nodded at one of the human portraits as we passed. "This castle used to belong to a light fae called Lord Cyrus Englewood. He was an avid worshipper of the Druid ways, and he wished for harmony between fae, both common and elite, and humans. So he had his painters do portraits of some of Endir's commoners, and he hung them proudly amongst the portraits of royalty."

"Surprising. There aren't many light fae like him."

"Not anymore."

"What happened to him?" Val asked.

Kalen rubbed a hand along his jaw. "He died when I took this city during the war against Oberon."

Val's eyes widened.

Kalen slowed to a stop at the top of the staircase. The bannisters were polished clean, the silver gleaming beneath the candlelight. "I'll tell you what I told Tessa. I'm not the monster you were warned about, but I'm no savior, either. Many good men and many good fae died as a result of my war with your king. I killed far too many of them myself. Most of this land is left in ruin because of it. But I did not do it out of malicious cruelty. I just wanted to stop Oberon. Take that as you wish."

Val seemed stunned senseless, so it was Nellie who held out her hand. "I've never had an introduction quite like that, but I like the blunt honesty. I'm Tessa's sister, Nellie."

"I know who you are." His eyes softened in a way they rarely did.

"Maybe you aren't a cannibal, but you do know you're still pretty terrifying, right?" Val interjected.

A throaty laugh drifted toward us from the bottom of the stairs. We glanced down to find Alastair, Niamh, and Toryn all looking up at us, clearly eavesdropping on our conversation.

Alastair's gaze caught mine first. As always, he wore black leather armor, and his dark hair was pulled back to show off the rings that dotted both ears. He grinned. "I'm glad to see you're awake, little dove."

"Good to see you didn't get torn apart by pookas," I said, smiling back.

We joined them at the bottom of the stairs, and then they led us toward an open set of looming oak doors. The smell of meat and butter drifted toward us. My stomach growled in eager expectation. I couldn't remember the last time I'd eaten. It must have been days, what with the escape from the castle and our trip through the mists to Endir. I entered a room packed with humans and fae. Sapphire banners hung along the stone walls, embroidered with stars and crescent moons. A silver mask topped with a spiky crown filled the center of each banner. It reminded me of the mask that Kalen had always worn during our first dream meetings, when he hadn't wanted me to know who he was. When he'd just been the captain to me.

"Is that your sigil?" I asked, realizing just how little I knew about the Kingdom of Shadow.

Kalen smiled. "Yes and no. It's the sigil of Endir, to represent those who oppose King Oberon's reign. Some of the residents here are light fae who got stuck on this side of the chasm when Oberon put up the barrier. They've long sought a way into Albyria so they could fight against him."

"Rebels," I said.

"That's right. And I liked the sigil so much, I started using it for my banners."

"So what will happen now? With the light fae? The barrier is gone, the city is destroyed, and Oberon has fled."

"There are many decisions to be made in the coming days. What the light fae rebels do now is one of them."

As I followed Kalen to the head table, past benches packed with humans, I asked him, "Is everyone from Teine staying here, in the castle?"

"I figured this was the best place for them. They were

a little uneasy at first, but they seem to have realized we have no plans to harm them."

In fact, this was the most vigor I'd seen from the residents of Teine in a long time. They were digging into their full plates with gusto, trading laughter and cheerful words. The noise of it all filled the space, making the lofted ceilings and towering walls seem closer than they actually were. It felt snug and safe and so much like home. It was that same feeling I'd had when I'd awoken to find Kalen beside me, reading near the hearth.

I settled into a chair beside Kalen at the head table. Nellie took the seat on my other side while Val perched across from me. Alastair, Toryn, and Niamh joined us, as well as two other fae dressed in all-black fighting leathers. I didn't recognize either of them.

"Ah." Kalen smiled toward them. "Tessa, I want you to meet Fenella and Gaven. Together, with Niamh, Alastair, and Toryn, they make up my Mist Guard. They keep Endir running smoothly when I'm not here."

I held up my hand in a wave. Fenella leaned back in her chair and smirked. Horns that matched the color of Kalen's eyes cut through ash blond hair that fell to her shoulders. A necklace of miniature daggers hung around her neck, glittering like the silver in her eyes.

"Tessa," she said with a narrowed gaze that seemed to pierce right through me. "I heard you stabbed our king."

"You heard right. I stabbed him twice."

Alastair guffawed, and Gaven's lips quirked in amusement, even as he regarded me carefully. He was smaller than the others and less imposing at first glance, but there was a keenness in his attention that made me feel as if he could see my every thought. The silver hair that fell across his dark skin matched the glittering rings that circled each finger. He watched me watching him, and he did not blink a single silver eye.

"Careful where you point your blade next time," he said with a flash of teeth. "Or I might have to rip off the pretty little hand that holds it."

"Gaven," Kalen warned.

"Relax." He turned to Kalen, and as soon as his gaze left my face, the tension throttling my shoulders suddenly vanished. "She has nothing to worry about as long as she doesn't try to kill my king again."

Val caught my gaze and winced. "This is getting awkward. I could use a glass of wine."

"Here." Niamh plucked a bottle from the table and poured amber liquid into Val's glass. "Try that. It's not wine, but it'll take the edge off."

Val lifted the glass to her nose and sniffed. "Smells sweet. What is it?"

"Fion." Niamh grinned. "Technically, it's fae wine, but it's not made from grapes. It tastes like silver and song."

"And it's safe for me to drink?" Val swirled the liquid in her glass.

"One glass will make you very merry. More than that, and you could lose yourself to the magic of it. So stick to just the one."

Val lifted the glass to her lips and took a small sip. After a moment, her eyes widened. "You're right. It does taste like silver and song, though I have no idea how I know what either of those things tastes like."

Niamh turned to me and held up the bottle. "Tessa?"

"None for me, thank you. Maybe another time."

I turned to Kalen, who was deep in conversation with Gaven and Fenella, discussing what he'd seen in Albyria. They were trading ideas on what to do next. Should they send out a hunting party for Oberon? Or should they wait for him to make a move first? Then there were the humans from Teine. How soon should they make for Sunport, where they'd take a ship to the human kingdoms? As Kalen had said, there was much to decide. The future seemed uncertain now.

But I knew one thing above all else. I would not board that ship. Not until all of this was done.

TWENTY-SIX
TESSA

After dining in the Great Hall, I returned to my chambers for a bath. Once clean, I opted for a dress hanging in the wardrobe. It was deep green, darker than the lushest blades of grass and softer than feathers, with long sleeves that hung like bells around my wrists. Golden thread wove along the neckline. Two columns of crescent moons were embroidered down the front of the bodice. I slipped my feet into my leather boots after braiding my wet hair. As I left my room, I ran straight into Fenella.

She lounged against the corridor wall, picking at her fingernails with her dagger. Without shifting her gaze my way, she asked, "Going somewhere?"

"Yes." I folded my arms. "I'm going to take a look around."

"Unaccompanied?"

"I'm not a prisoner, am I?"

She smiled, and only then did she lift her glittering

eyes to my face. "If it were up to me, you would be. But it appears our king has grown soft."

"Kalen and I have both—"

Fenella held up a hand. "Don't. There are few who could stab a fae king and live to tell the tale. Lucky for you, I respect his command, and I will not go against his wishes where you're concerned. But I do not trust you, Tessa Baran, and I will be watching everything you do inside my city."

I swallowed. I'd only been awake for half a day, but I'd already made an enemy. One who was part of Kalen's Mist Guard. One of his closest confidantes. But I could hardly blame her. I wouldn't trust me, either.

"You know what? That's fine. Where is everyone else?"

"My king is having a meeting with the others to discuss what to do about Oberon. Your friends and family have returned to their rooms. I believe they said they wanted to get some rest. The journey here was hard on them."

I nodded. "Why aren't you in the meeting?"

"I opted out. Thought you might try sneaking out of your room to stab someone."

"Lovely. Want to show me where the library is?"

She arched her brow. "Not particularly."

"Well, I'm going to go find it." I started off down the corridor and shot my next words over my shoulder. "You coming?"

Fenella grumbled, but she quickly caught up to me and fell into step by my side. Neither of us spoke as we wound through the maze of passageways, mostly empty except for the occasional maidservant passing by with a pile of fresh linens or a broom in hand. Unlike the morning's meal might have suggested, the castle was calm and quiet. Every now and again, the alluring sound of a harp drifted toward me, or the hush of distant voices. Mostly, though, these halls were as empty as those in Dubnos.

It was an aching reminder of how much this world had lost. The war had taken so many lives, on both sides. Even hundreds of years later, we were paying for it. Hatred and revenge, anger and chaos had wrought devastation. I'd let those emotions live in my heart for far too long, and I'd almost brought that destruction upon everyone I knew and loved. And, if my father was right, they could someday lead me to do far worse things.

After I found myself back outside my bedchamber door, Fenella sighed and motioned me to turn toward the opposite direction. "I can't bear to follow you around in circles for hours. The library is this way."

She led me back down the staircase to the Great Hall, but instead of turning right, we went left. Another set of double doors rose to the lofted ceiling. She took the handles and shoved, revealing a vast room with rows of shelves leading into darkness.

Dust swirled toward us and the familiar scents of parchment and ink almost brought me to tears. I stared ahead, awestruck by the sight, even in the dim lighting. There were so many shelves—so many mountains of books. I could get lost in here for weeks and still not look upon every cover.

Fenella grabbed a lamp from beside the door and dropped a silver gemstone into the center of it. The lamp glowed, spilling brightness into the room. "You look like you've never seen a library before."

"I haven't," I said around a lump in my throat. "But it's more than that. For as long as I can remember, I started every day by reading at least ten pages of a book. Without fail, no matter what was happening. Until that day."

"That day?"

"When everything changed," I said bitterly, "and Oberon chose me to become his next mortal bride."

"Ah, so that's why you wanted to come here." She passed me the lamp and then lit a second one with another gemstone. "You know, I heard you stabbed Oberon too."

"Twice. It didn't work either time."

She surprised me by letting out a laugh. "Just like you did to Kalen. Seems to be a pattern of yours. Let's not make it a third time, though, yeah?"

"I would gladly stab Oberon a third time." There was a viciousness in my tone that almost startled me. My anger was still there, boiling beneath the surface. Despite my every attempt to rein it in, it still bled through whenever I spoke of him, like my veins were full of poison. It felt as if the God of Death was corrupting me the same way she'd twisted the hearts of everyone else. It felt as if my father's journal was right.

"Keep talking that way, and we might just end up being friends after all," Fenella said with a smirk.

Instead of answering, I swept through the library stacks, angling the lantern toward the dusty spines. I found the fiction section and took two books that promised romance and adventure. Fenella seemed distracted by her own handful of books, so I kept searching, hunting the rows for historical tomes.

I moved quietly in the shadows of the stacks. Cobwebs stretched overhead, and the dust tickled my nose, bringing on a sneeze. When I reached the back wall, my eyes landed on the section I was looking for, but there was only one book on the subject. The history of the gods. No wonder Kalen's mother had sailed the seas to find information on what had happened back then if this was all that was available.

Shaking my head, I added the book to the others and backtracked to where Fenella was waiting for me. She swiped a cobweb from her hair. "Damn library never gets cleaned."

"Why not?" I asked. "Kalen said this castle is fully staffed."

"The library is hardly used, and the maidservants have their hands full with everything else. It's not a priority."

I frowned over my shoulder at the darkened stacks. It was beautiful just for being a library, but it could be so much more. With clean shelves and lights spilling through the space, or a hearth blazing in the corner with a cluster of chairs around it...I smiled as the image filled my mind.

"I know what you're thinking," Fenella said, "but there are too few people left in this part of the world for us to devote time and resources to running a library."

"Books are the boards beneath our feet. Without them, we risk wading in mud."

"And I suppose you'll stick around to get the library

up and running yourself?" she asked as she pushed the doors open for us.

I paused, my hand on the door. "I wish. But I don't think that's what fate has in store for me."

"Hmm," was all she said.

Fenella led me back to my chambers and told me that dinner would not be as lively of an affair as the morning's meal, which was just as well with me. Even though I'd recovered from my ordeal at the Tower of Crones, exhaustion had returned, as if my body still bore the weight of that encounter. After leaving her in the corridor, I climbed into bed and cracked open the first book. It did not take long for the words to blur. Sleep soon welcomed me into its embrace.

I awoke with a start. It took me a moment to remember where I was. A bell tolled in the distance, and as the sleep cleared from my eyes, I counted the chimes. It was midnight. I climbed from bed, still wearing the dress from earlier, and moved to the window. The mist was so thick that I could barely see the outline of the waxing moon. Another few days, and it would be full.

Another few days, and I would have been Oberon's newest bride. My soul would have been expelled from my body if I hadn't done something.

Shuddering, I backed away from the window. The truth was, I'd made my move, and I'd gotten out of Albyria, but deep down, I knew it wasn't over yet.

Oberon was still out there. He could be lurking in the mists beyond Endir, watching and waiting for the perfect moment to attack. He would still have supporters. If enough light fae warriors had escaped the city before Kalen's soldiers had shown up, he might have enough of a force to attack this place.

I needed to talk to Kalen. He'd been in that meeting all day, and I wanted to know what they'd decided.

After lacing up my boots, I crossed the room and opened the door. Kalen stood just outside with his fist raised, ready to knock. Still wearing his loose tunic and fitted trousers, he looked nothing like the monstrous king I'd once thought he was. My heart lurched when he smiled.

He dropped his fist to his side. "I wasn't sure if I should knock, but it doesn't look like you're asleep, either."

I glanced down at my dress. "I was until a few minutes ago. I was just about to come find you. How did your meeting go?"

"Can I come in?" he asked in a deep voice that both soothed my nerves and sent my heartbeat racing.

Blushing, I opened the door wider for him to join me inside. He strode into the chambers and glanced around, his eyes lingering on my rumpled sheets for just a moment too long. And then he turned to the cold hearth and knelt, one knee on the floor. He lit the flame and stoked the fire to life. For whatever reason, I couldn't bring myself to speak. I just watched him work, watched the flexing of his forearm muscles and the orange light illuminating the sharp cut of his jaw. I was so consumed by him that I barely noticed I'd begun to drift closer.

He stood and moved to the chair where I'd draped his cloak across the back. With a slight smile, he ran the material through his fingertips. "I'm surprised you still have this. I assumed you'd tossed it into the chasm after you escaped me."

"It kept me warm in the dungeon."

His eyebrows winged upward. "I see."

I took a step toward him. "I'm sorry I took it, but now you can have it back."

"I don't want it, love. It's yours. Keep it with you always."

Chest tight, I just watched him watch me. A lazy smile crept across his face, and he lowered himself into the chair, where he braided his fingers beneath his chin and continued to keep my gaze. I suddenly had no idea what to do with my hands. They felt awkward dangling by my side, but clasping them in front of me felt demure and awkward. Folding them behind my back didn't feel any better. Should I prop my hands on my hips? I landed on just folding my arms, even though I knew it made me look confrontational.

"Relax," Kalen said. "No one is going to harm you here."

"Not everyone is happy with my presence. Fenella followed me around the castle earlier to make sure I didn't stab anyone."

Kalen let out an easy laugh. "Of course she did."

"I don't think she's thrilled that you've forgiven me."

"No, she wouldn't be. She was one of the first light

fae in Endir to offer up support for me and bow before my reign. She has been exceedingly loyal to me ever since."

"She thinks I'm going to stab you again."

He arched a brow. "And are you?"

"Of course not," I said in a soft voice. "You know that, right?"

His gaze scanned my face. "You'd do anything to save the ones you love, and if that meant stabbing me, then I think you would."

I frowned. "You would never harm them. I know that now."

He glanced at the open book on my bed, the book on the gods. I hadn't gotten far into it before I'd fallen asleep, so if any answers were to be found inside, I hadn't seen them yet. All I'd read were a few short paragraphs listing the names of the five: Andromeda, Sirius, Perseus, Callisto, and Orion.

"So, there's the book I was looking for all day," he said quietly. "Did you find what you were searching for?"

Alarm flashed through me. "If you were looking for this book, then you must think my father was right."

"I do wonder," he murmured. "Come here."

I hesitated where I stood, not certain I liked where this was going. "Why? What do you want me to do?"

"I want to look at your hands," he said, as easily as if he were talking about the weather. "They may hold clues about the truth."

Heart pounding, I took slow steps toward him. When I reached him, my boots slid in between his. The difference in our sizes was shockingly apparent. His feet were enormous, dwarfing my own in comparison.

He held out his hand to me, palm up. "Let me see."

I started to reach out to him, but then paused with my fingers hovering above his palm. "The God of Death kills by touch."

"You've already touched me more than once, and I'm still breathing. Let me see your hand."

I dropped my hand into his. The warmth of his skin seeped into me, and a shuddering breath escaped my lungs. He flipped my hand over, bringing my palm up to his eyes. His thumb traced the deep lines in my skin, from the top of my forefinger down to the bottom right where my hand met my wrist.

"Do you see anything?" I whispered to him, wondering at how even the smallest touch could bring such a violent reaction from my heart. It felt as if it might pound its way right out of my chest.

"The rumor was that Andromeda's constellation was etched onto her palms." He sighed and met my gaze. "I'm not sure if this means anything at all, but the lines on your hands are close to that."

I sucked in a breath and snatched my hand to my chest, cradling it there. "So, it's true."

"I did not say that," he countered. "I said those lines are close. I'm sure there are dozens of other palms that look just as similar."

"My father thought it," I said. "There must have been a reason."

"Even if it's true, it's unlikely you would have any of her powers. She was here in this world long ago. Centuries have passed, and generations. The magic would be diluted." He held out his hand toward me once again.

"I can't touch you," I whispered.

"Yes, you can." Kalen gently pulled my hand away from my chest and placed my palm against his face. His gaze stayed firm and steady; his shoulders were relaxed. He had complete faith in me, no matter where I came from, but I did not know if I could have that same faith in myself. "See? I'm still alive."

I let him pull me a little closer, until I stood between his thighs, one hand on his cheek and the other desperate to get tangled in his hair. He wound his arm around my waist and splayed his hand against my lower back. And even though I was standing, our eyes were almost level.

"You don't have to be afraid of touching me, love," he murmured, his chest rumbling against mine.

A desperate need clenched between my thighs as the weight of the past few weeks shattered around me. I'd fought so hard to stay calm and in control, to not give in to my impulses. Not just for my sake, but for the safety of everyone else. I'd bitten my tongue when I'd wanted to fight. I'd followed every order, no matter how much I'd wanted to revolt. I'd stayed my hand when my fingers itched to plunge another dagger into Oberon's heart.

I'd clung to every scrap of control I could muster.

And now I wanted nothing more than to let it all go, to give in and lose myself in the arms of this man. I didn't want to fight anymore. I just wanted him.

Twenty-Seven
Tessa

I leaned into him. The beat of his heart matched the pounding rhythm of mine, and the hands on my back pressed me closer. With a shaky breath, I palmed his chest, feeling the ridges of his muscles through the soft tunic—muscles I'd dreamed of in the dungeon. I'd replayed memories of him, thinking I'd never again touch him like this.

His eyes darkened, and a lazy smile curled his lips.

"Hello, love," he said to me, and just those two words on his lips sent another bolt of fiery need through my core.

"Hello, Kalen."

He practically purred as he slid his hands down my backside, gripped my thighs, and then lifted me from the floor in one fluid motion. The next thing I knew, I was sitting on his lap with my legs around his waist.

"I love the way my name sounds on your tongue." His eyes dipped to my lips, as if he were thinking about more than just his name in my mouth. Truth be told, so was I. "But it's your moans I'm most desperate to hear."

My heart lurched. "Kalen."

"And if you moan *my name*, all the better." Eyes darkening, he reached behind me and lifted my braid over my shoulder and his fingers skimmed its twined strands. I tracked his every move, scarcely daring to breathe. When he reached the end, he curled his hand into a fist and gave the braid a little tug, drawing my lips to his.

Unbidden passion rushed through me as our mouths collided. I released my inhibitions, pressed up against him, and ran my fingers into the lush strands of his dark, wavy hair. He kissed me just as fiercely, his hands gripping my thighs. I wanted more, so much more that I could barely stand the clothing that existed between us.

And then something in his kiss softened. His hand relaxed against my thigh and then traced a line up my side, over my shoulder, until his palm found my jaw. He brushed his thumb against my cheek, and that deep, aching need inside me slickened my thighs.

Suddenly, he stood with my legs still wrapped around his hips. He crossed the room in two strides and lowered me onto the bed with a gentleness that bordered on reverence. The mattress dipped as his broad body hovered over mine, with his forearms braced on either side of my head.

He pulled back, his thumb still pressed against my cheek. "You have consumed me. Everything about you drives me mad, and yet I would not change a thing. I want to give you the greatest pleasure you will ever know, fill you with so much rapture that you forget your own name."

"I don't think I can argue against that," I whispered up to him.

He chuckled. "Well, that's certainly a first."

Gently, he slid the gown's hem up to my waist, and I sat up to help him lift the material over my head. My undergarment barely covered a thing, the cotton slip so thin that my swollen nipples were clearly visible. His eyes darkened as he gazed down at me.

"I want to see all of you," he murmured.

With a boldness I did not know I had, I pulled the undergarment over my head, exposing every inch of my skin.

"Incredible," he whispered as he began to lower himself over me once more.

I pressed my hands to his chest and shook my head. "Your turn."

He smiled. With his eyes locked on my face, he tugged his tunic over his head and tossed it onto the floor. His muscular chest gleamed in the firelight, and the ridges of his abs tensed, leading to a V that begged for my touch. With a flick of his thumb, he unbuttoned his trousers and stepped out of them. When I saw the length of him, I clutched the sheets.

"Like what you see?" he asked with a lazy grin.

Heart fluttering, I nodded. "You could say that."

I started to reach out for him, but he dropped to his knees. "I'm not religious, love, but I am going to worship your body, starting with the altar of your thighs."

I shuddered as he pressed his mouth to my hip. He dropped a soft kiss on the top of my thigh before moving to the other. His lips trailed across my skin, lighting me up with a need I had not known even existed until now. With a gentle touch, he wound his hands around my knees and spread my legs wider. And then his lips moved to my inner thigh. Slowly, he moved closer and closer until...

"Kalen," I gasped just before he reached my core.

He paused and stared up at me from where he knelt between my legs. "Is this too much? We can stop if you don't feel ready for this."

"I'm ready," I said to him, desperately trying to fill my lungs with enough air. "Please. Don't stop now."

With a smile, he dropped another kiss on my inner thigh, and then he shifted to the left, just there and— pure rapture shook my body. His tongue slipped against me, and another shuddering wave of pleasure crashed over me, leaving me gasping for air. I didn't know how I could take much more of this—this *bliss*.

Kalen dragged his tongue across my aching core. My body bucked, my back arching on the bed. His fingers dug into my thighs as he tugged me against his mouth, almost as if he couldn't get enough of the taste of me.

All inhibitions cast aside, I rocked against his mouth, moving in sync with the stroke of his tongue. Stars dotted my vision. Another crash of pleasure thundered through me, driving me so wild that I felt as if I teetered on the brink of a cliff. One small nudge, and I'd fall into the abyss, and I'd never wanted anything more than to plunge into that kind of darkness.

Kalen pulled back, and that heart-shattering crash came to a sudden stop. With a frustrated moan, I tried to tug him toward me with my legs, but he stayed right where he was with a wicked smirk on his lips.

"Not just yet," he murmured as he covered my body with his. A moment later, he slid a finger into my slick core. I shuddered at the new sensation, gasping when he slid a second finger inside. I could feel my wetness coating his fingers, feel his satisfaction when I shuddered beneath his touch.

He lowered his mouth to my breast and sucked my nipple before driving his fingers into the core of me again. A scream of delirious pleasure ripped from my throat, causing his eyes to darken. He thrust his fingers inside me once more, and I moved against him with a feverish abandon. Desperate need clawed through me. That cliff rose up before me once more. I reached for it. I screamed out his name and then—

I shattered like glass.

My nails dug into his back as the world shook around me—or was I the one who was shaking? I couldn't tell anymore. The rumbling consumed me, blinding me, drowning out all but the feel of his hand between my thighs and his mouth on my breast. Violent pulses shook my core. I clung to him so tightly that my fingers scraped into his back.

"I've got you," he murmured, his mouth suddenly at my ear. "I won't let you fall."

The trembling and pulsing began to slow, and my senses came roaring back to life. I opened my eyes—I hadn't realized I'd closed them—to find his face hovering above mine. The deep sapphire of his eyes flared with the heat of a thousand suns, and the entire room was full of mist. Strands of his power caressed my cheek, my stomach, my thighs.

"That was..." I whispered. "More than I thought it would be."

"It certainly was."

"Is it always like that?"

"I don't think so, love."

Something in the tone of his voice made my heart thump. I was not the first woman Kalen had been with, but the look in his eyes suggested this was far different than anything he'd experienced before. But he had not even come yet. I would have to remedy that.

"Your turn," I said with a smile.

He cocked a brow. "Already? I don't want to push you..."

I hooked my leg around his hips and tugged him closer. "I want you inside me, Kalen."

With a wicked glint in his eye, he wrapped his hands around my backside and then—*flip*. My back met the warm air from the hearth, basking me in a heat that matched the fire still burning in my core. Kalen lay beneath me on the bed with my legs spread on either side of his hips. His length stood at attention, ready for whatever I would give him.

"I want to see you take control," he murmured, trailing a finger along my outer thigh.

I read between the lines. Kalen knew my history. Oberon had never touched me like that, but he'd still made a mark on me. He'd threatened me with it more than once, and for a very long time, I was afraid of breaking his rules. The girls of Teine were not allowed to give themselves up to anyone else until after Oberon chose a bride. If they did, the punishment was death.

The last time I'd been alone in a room with Kalen, that past had risen up like a ghastly wraith, haunting me. I'd been hesitant then, because of it. Unsure.

I felt none of that now.

And yet, Kalen wanted to hand me the reins, so that I could stop this at any time.

It only made me want him more.

I lifted my hips and then wound my hand around his cock. He shuddered, hardening even more against my touch. With a trembling heart, I angled myself just right. And then I eased back against him. The tip of him inched inside me. Everything within me tightened, and my walls tensed around him.

"Fucking hell," he growled, gazing up at me with those piercing sapphire eyes.

I shifted further down and took in more of him. A flicker of pain went through me, and I gasped.

Kalen gently caressed my thigh. "Don't rush it. Take your time."

But my need for him was almost overwhelming. I didn't want to take my time. I just wanted to have all of him, filling me until we were as close to each other as we could possibly be. I widened my thighs and lowered myself even more, crying out as his substantial length pushed into me.

I sat there for a moment with my palms flat against

his corded muscles. And then I began to move. A shock-wave of pleasure went through my core, erasing any hint of pain, as I came down on him a second time. He groaned and ran his hands around to my backside, shuddering. Mist stormed around us.

His hips rose up to meet mine as I pushed against him once more, the pace of my movements quickening along with my need. As we rocked together, he pulled my face toward his and brushed a hot kiss across my lips. There was so much more than just lust in his kiss. So much more than what I thought he would be. I kissed back, hungry for him, needy for him. All this time we'd spent apart, I'd wanted nothing but to feel him. To touch him. To taste him. To feel his hardness between my thighs.

"What the fuck are you doing to me, love?" he asked in a gruff voice when we broke apart. Staring into his eyes, I ground my hips against him. His groans fill the room, drowning out the crackle of the fire. The entire world smelled of him. Of mist. Of snow. Of night.

I dropped my head back and moaned.

Because whatever I was doing to him, he was doing the same damn thing to me.

Before I knew it, I was on the edge. I tried to slow my hips, but I couldn't. Just two more thrusts, that was all I wanted. Two more kisses. I didn't want this moment to end. His cock felt so good that I could stay here like this for hours, on every single night of my life. But nothing could stop the pleasure I felt, nothing could put it on hold.

We crashed together, our bodies shuddering in sync. That delicious, all-consuming, universe-ending explosion rocked through me once more. Mist swirled around us like gusts of fog-drenched wind. I held on to him as if I might tumble off the face of the world and into the sky itself, where the pieces of me would scatter across the stars.

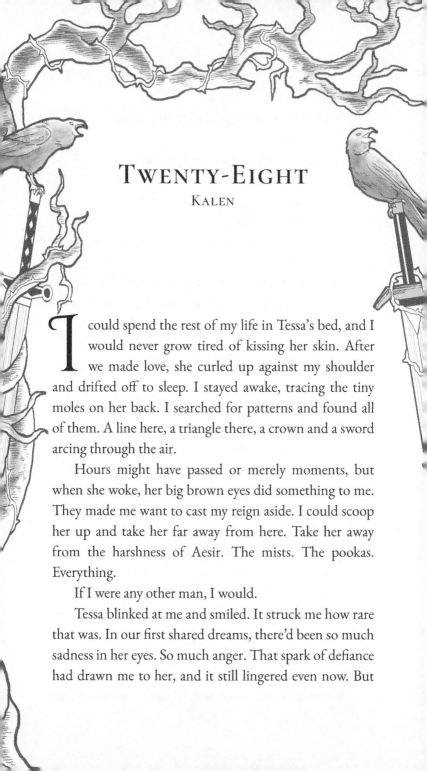

Twenty-Eight
Kalen

I could spend the rest of my life in Tessa's bed, and I would never grow tired of kissing her skin. After we made love, she curled up against my shoulder and drifted off to sleep. I stayed awake, tracing the tiny moles on her back. I searched for patterns and found all of them. A line here, a triangle there, a crown and a sword arcing through the air.

Hours might have passed or merely moments, but when she woke, her big brown eyes did something to me. They made me want to cast my reign aside. I could scoop her up and take her far away from here. Take her away from the harshness of Aesir. The mists. The pookas. Everything.

If I were any other man, I would.

Tessa blinked at me and smiled. It struck me how rare that was. In our first shared dreams, there'd been so much sadness in her eyes. So much anger. That spark of defiance had drawn me to her, and it still lingered even now. But there was more in her expression. And it made me feel smug to know I'd put it there.

"What are you thinking about?" she asked.

I smiled. "You."

Even now, color burst into her cheeks. "Dare I ask what, exactly, is on your mind?"

"All the other things I plan to do with you." I wound my arm around her body and tugged her a little closer, and then I dropped a kiss on her forehead. "Tomorrow, and the next day, and then the day after that."

She arched her brow. "Only three days of things?"

"If I listed all the days, we would be here until the stars consumed this world."

With a sad smile, she looked up at me through her thick lashes. "I worry that will happen sooner than we think."

It was a sobering thought, and as much as I wanted to stay inside this room, locked away from the rest of the world, there was too much to do. There were many lives I must protect, and many decisions I must make, even still. The heaviness of my reign pushed down on me with the weight of an entire city—with the weight of an *entire continent*. But even if I was not king, I would be unable to stand by while so much was still at stake.

"Oberon will be desperate now," I said. "And he has Queen Hannah. No doubt he'll do whatever it takes to transfer her into another body, and I worry that means he'll agree to release his half of the god. He might have no other choice now."

"No other choice but me," she whispered.

I knew she feared what would happen if Oberon got

his hands on her, far more than she had before. Now that we knew the truth about what he did with his Mortal Queens, I could not blame her. It terrified me too. To imagine her soul forced from her own body, only to be replaced by my...

The thought of it brought burning bile to the back of my throat. I did not want to come to terms with the truth —that my mother had chosen eternal life, powered by the God of Death. Yes, it was the side of Andromeda's essence that could give life rather than take it away, but that did not make it any less dangerous. If anything, it was the worst kind of danger. The kind you thought was a gift, only for it to turn around and dig its fangs into your veins, filling you with poison.

"I'm sorry," Tessa said quickly, her eyes scouring my face. "I shouldn't have brought it up."

"You don't need to be sorry for speaking the truth. I need to face this, sooner rather than later, because I must find a way to stop it. I must find a way to stop *her*."

As far as I could see, Oberon had two options. Well, three options, really, but I knew he'd never choose the first. He could let my mother go, let her drift from the realm of the living to wherever the dead souls spent the rest of eternity. It was what should have happened to her all those centuries ago, a fact I had to accept, even if I didn't want to.

"Do you think he's going to come after me?"

"No, he's running scared. I think he's more likely to release the god's power from the gemstone necklace. That way, she'll have the strength to transfer my mother's soul into a permanent fae body."

"But according to the vision I had, he'd still need the other half of the... wait. I didn't release half of the god's essence in Itchen, did I?"

"I don't know." I wrapped my hand around hers. "I didn't think you had. No comet filled the sky. But with everything that has happened recently, I think it's possible."

"Fuck." Tessa tensed, and she started to twist away, but I caught her chin before she could.

"Don't blame yourself. If that part of her escaped, it's only because she tricked you."

"Your vow," she said. "If I released her, you'll be forced to kill me."

"No," I insisted. "Do not go down that path. This does not mean you've brought her back. Someone else would have to destroy Oberon's onyx gemstone. Her other half must escape for her to return to her corporeal form. Only then will the comet fill the sky. That person won't be you, but it could be Oberon."

Or my mother.

It was a truth that had been echoing in my mind ever since Tessa had told me the truth about what had happened all those years ago. My mother had warned me about this very day. She'd tried to prepare me for it, and she wouldn't tell me who I might one day face. For a long time, I thought it was because she didn't know, but now I wasn't so sure.

Had she expected this to happen? Was there more to the prophecy than she'd told me?

Tessa read my face. "You think it could be her. You

think your mother might be the one to release the other half of the god."

"You already know me so well."

For a moment, she didn't speak. But then she said, "I wish I could tell you I don't think it's a possibility, but I won't lie to you. There's a reason she asked you to make that vow."

"Because she knew I would never be able to kill her without it," I finished her thought, even though the words were knives against the ribbons of my soul. Shuddering, I closed my eyes. "And she was right. I don't think I can do this."

She wrapped her arms around my shoulders and pulled me to her chest. With my face nestled between her breasts, I kept my eyes closed and just listened to the thump of her heartbeat against my ear. How had it come to this? I'd fought so hard to protect this world from the return of the gods, convinced I was doing the right thing in my war against Oberon. My hands carried the blood of countless lives. My kingdom, and his, withered beneath a persistent blanket of mist and shadow. I'd destroyed this realm, and for what? It hadn't done any good. Oberon had still gone through with his plan to use the power of the god, and it had taken control of him. Now it seemed he might not even be the enemy I'd sought all these years. That enemy might, instead, be my own mother.

"You can do anything. You're the King of Shadow, the most powerful fae alive. And I will be here to help you."

I lifted my head to gaze up at her. "You should leave these cursed lands. Go to the mortal kingdoms with the others. You don't have to stay and fight a battle that isn't yours."

"It *is* my battle now." That fierce defiance I loved so much rose in her eyes again. "I will not run away from this. And I will not run away from you, from us."

Warmth soothed away the fractured lines around the edges of my heart. She slid her fingers into my hair and tugged me to her breasts again, where I rested my head. We stayed awake for a good long while, but we didn't speak any more about this. We didn't need to. Not now. We just needed to hold each other like two broken rafts tied together, tumbling through a storm-tossed sea. Right now it felt as though we might never find still waters again. But we would find a way to survive this as long as we did not let go.

Together, we would find a way to conquer the storm.

TWENTY-NINE
KALEN

FOUR HUNDRED YEARS AGO

Niamh, the Queen's Shadow, dropped to her knees before me, bowing her head. Her shoulders slumped, and her eyes were streaked red, as if she'd been crying. I sat up straighter on the throne, alarm flashing through me. I'd never seen the stoic warrior display any emotion other than calm determination, steady strength, and fierce competence.

"Do not bow, Niamh. I'm not your king. What's happened? What did you find out?"

Niamh had gone on a mission to bring my mother back to Dubnos after she'd vanished without a trace from Albyria's castle halls. Oberon said she'd left ages ago without her guards. Everyone assumed she'd died somewhere in the wilderness, but I knew that wasn't true. My mother was bold and brave, but she would never travel alone. And we'd been searching for years now. No one—not a single villager or traveler—had seen any sign of her.

Oberon must have taken her captive, or worse. The last time I saw her, she'd told me he'd asked her to marry him, and she'd turned him down. This was his revenge. I grew more convinced of it with every angry beat of my heart.

Niamh lifted her eyes but did not stand. "There are lots of rumors flying around Albyria. I can't make heads or tails of what's true. Some say he was angry about her rejection so he locked her in a dungeon cell. Others say he killed her. Some guards are whispering they saw blood on his tunic, but others insist she left the city and that bandits must have taken her."

A fury I'd never known filled my veins with fire. I rose from my throne—my mother's throne. I'd only taken it in her absence because someone needed to rule. But I was not the king. She was the ruler of this realm. The people loved her. How could they not? She was everything they needed and more. Not me.

"I'm going to Albyria to find out what happened. And if Oberon truly is behind this, it's time for war." I started toward the door.

Niamh jumped up and fell into step beside me. "Kalen—sorry, my prince, I—"

"Just call me Kal."

"All right." She moved in front of me to stop my progress toward the door. "Kal, I don't think that's a good idea. You should stay here and ready yourself, just in case he declares war against the Kingdom of Shadow. Prepare your army. We can send scouts to watch the lands beyond the border." A beat passed. "And we should schedule your coronation."

"You can't mean that."

She winced, her eyes full of sorrow. "This is just as painful for me too."

"I find that hard to believe. She's my mother."

"Fair enough. But it doesn't change the fact I love her too. She was a good queen." She rested her hand on my shoulder. "We have to face the truth now. She is gone, and you must be our king."

I closed my eyes, turmoil cutting through my heart like a scythe. Deep down, I'd known for months she was never coming back. Years, even. And I'd been the one to send her to her death. If I hadn't suggested she visit Oberon, she'd still be here. My knees almost buckled, but I couldn't show weakness in front of the Queen's Shadow. Or anyone, for that matter. Not now. If I were to become king, I had to show enduring strength, even in the worst moment of my life.

"I am going to Albyria," I said firmly. "Quietly, just for a few days. Oberon won't even know I'm there. I want to hear what they're saying with my own ears, and then we will return and begin preparations for the coronation. If necessary."

And then war.

Niamh nodded. "Then I'm coming with you."

It was easier to sneak into Albyria than I'd expected. We approached from the dirt path that led up the hill from Teine, a small human village that had been empty when we'd passed through. The glittering city gates were open, fae and humans walking side by side, chatting amicably as the sun beamed down on us all.

As Niamh and I shuffled in behind them, the armored guards barely gave us a passing glance, though I kept my eyes downcast. Few here would know my face, but they might have heard rumors of my sapphire eyes—a color rarely seen, even in fae. Niamh, who had been here only weeks before, kept her violet hair hidden beneath a dark hood. And soon, we were inside.

I made for the nearest pub first. I'd learned long ago that if you wanted to hear gossip, you went to the drunks. Full tankards led to loose lips, or so my monster of a father used to say. We reached the door of The Red Dragon and pushed inside. Instantly, shadows swallowed up the light from outside, and the pungent scent of ale swirled around us.

Several round tables were scattered throughout the dimly lit room, every single one packed, both with fae and humans. Some were playing cards while others sat sharing stories, their boisterous laughs booming through the small space. I spotted a cloaked human sitting alone near the back and motioned Niamh to follow.

I sat down across from him, wearing false ease to hide the tension pounding in my skull. He was a wiry man with graying hair and a face etched in wrinkles, who at first glance seemed harmless. Just an old man out having a pint. But I did not miss the keen sharpness in his expression or the way he noted Niamh's hood, my eyes, and the dagger I had hidden inside my tunic.

"I know who you are," the man said in a gravelly voice. "And you should not be here."

I dropped my voice to a low whisper. "I'm looking for my mother."

He took a long drink before he answered. "What makes you think you'll find the answer here?"

"This city was the last place she was seen alive."

"I meant in this pub—in that seat right there." His gaze shifted to Niamh. "The Queen's Shadow, a common fae who is far more deadly than many elite fae, as long as you have a bow and arrow. There are songs written about you, you know."

"They're all true," she said with a flash of her teeth.

I leaned across the table. "You look like someone who sees a lot. Hears a lot too, I'm betting. I'm willing to make an exchange. Tell me what you've heard, and I'll make it worth your while."

The man nodded. "I know something. But what if you don't like what I have to say?"

"I'll give you the payment up front."

"I want gemstones. The pale gray ones. I know you have them in your mines."

I glanced at Niamh, and she shrugged. "I've got ten in my pouch."

The man's eyes brightened at that. "Ten communication stones. Up front."

Niamh dug into her armor and extracted a small

leather pouch. Before she handed it over, she gave me a questioning look. "Are you certain?"

"Go on. I want to hear what he has to say."

With a small sigh, she tossed the pouch across the table. It landed beside the man's tankard, the gemstones jingling. Greedily, he grabbed it and peered inside, a slow smile splitting his lined face.

"You know how to use those?" I asked.

"I can manage." He dropped the pouch into his lap and then gave me a wary look. "I don't know what's happened to your mother. No one does. Some stories say she ran off to live with the humans and got killed along the way. Others say Oberon killed her, either by order or by his own hands."

I scowled, dropping two fisted hands on the table with a thump. "That wasn't our deal. I want those gemstones back."

"I said I know something. I never said it was about your mother." He cast a glance around us, and then lowered his voice. "I thought you'd want to hear that King Oberon has been searching for a way to use the power of the gods."

"*What?*" Niamh hissed as she palmed the wooden table and leaned forward. "Where did you hear that?"

I sat back and flared my nostrils to smell any hint of lies in the air. There was none.

Oberon was playing with fire.

A grim realization settled over me as my mother's words echoed in my mind. *Vow to me*, she'd said. She'd looked so worried when she'd told me about the prophecy and the gods. And now here I sat, listening to the last thing I'd expected to hear today. King Oberon was using the power of the gods. My mother was dead.

She must have discovered what he was doing, and he'd killed her for it.

And now I would have to stop him.

I started to ask what else the man knew, but angry voices exploded from a table near the door. The men and fae who had been playing cards were locked in a brutal fight. A knife flashed and then plunged into a fae's neck. His entire body shattered into ash. It rained on the wooden floor like gray confetti.

Niamh gripped my arm. "That's the Mortal Blade."

Shouts erupted as the fae launched themselves on the human who had killed one of their own. The blade leapt from his hand and clattered across the floor, landing only inches from my feet. It was plain and silver, with a cracked gemstone set into the center of it. I snatched it up before anyone else noticed.

"Let me have your cloak," I said to the man.

With a face as pale as bleached sand, he offered up his cloak with no hesitation, his eyes locked on the fight. The fae had stabbed the human to death, and now others had joined in. I swept the material around my shoulders and hid the dagger inside the folds.

"Thanks for the tip." I turned to Niamh. "It's time to gather our army for war."

THIRTY
TESSA

Kalen's heart thumped against my ear, and I sighed into the warmth of his body. He lifted his finger to my cheek and brushed a strand of hair away from my eyes, where it had sprung free from my braid sometime in the night. From the corridor, the sounds of a new day drifted toward us. The murmur of voices. The clattering of carts pushed by maidservants. The steady tap of boots heading toward the staircase that led down to the Great Hall.

"Are you awake?" he asked softly.

"Mmm." I snuggled a little closer, enjoying the warmth of his skin against mine. When my breasts brushed against his chest, my nipples tightened. "I'm awake, but I don't think I'm ready to leave bed just yet. Not as long as you're in it."

A low laugh rumbled in his throat. "You're a little vixen. I'm enjoying seeing this side of you."

At last, I opened my eyes to catch his gaze intent on

my face. "Good. Because I'm feeling extra vixen-y this morning."

With a wicked smile, he pulled me close and ran a hand along my outer thigh. His lips stole across mine, drinking me in. I felt a moan rise up inside me as I hooked my leg around his hip. The hard length of him pressed against my already aching core.

His mouth moved to my neck, kissing me with an urgency that made me gasp for breath. Rocking back, he shifted his cock so that the swollen tip brushed tantalizingly across my sex. My eyes nearly rolled back into my head from the anticipation of it. He brushed against me once more, his tip against my clit.

I shuddered and dug my nails into his back. "I want you inside me."

"Is that so?" he asked before taking my breast in his mouth, his tongue darting across my peaked nipple.

Moaning, I arched against him just as he inched his hips back. I trembled again, delicious, frustrating desire tightening every muscle in my body. His tongue continued to work my nipple while his thumb brushed against the other. I dragged my nails down his back.

He pulled away at the very moment I didn't think I could take any more. A wicked glint lit his hawkish eyes as he swept his gaze across my trembling body. "Is something the matter?"

"You're teasing me," I breathed.

He reached between us and ran his thumb along my thigh before bringing my wetness to his tongue. With his eyes locked on mine, he tasted me. The sapphire suddenly glowed, brighter than the stars. "Don't you worry, love. I am going to bury myself inside you."

A thrill went through me. "Then what are you waiting for?"

After several agonizing moments, his lips finally pressed against mine, rough and hungry. My entire body went weak as his kiss deepened and his tongue explored my mouth. He groaned and dug his hands into my back, pulling me closer to his body. I could feel the planes of his chest shift against me, and the hardness of his cock against my aching core.

I needed him. I wanted him more than I'd ever wanted a man in my life. I didn't know what it was about Kalen Denare, but I felt as if my whole body was drawn to him like the mist was drawn to night.

His mouth moved from my lips to my ear, and he nibbled my lobe with his teeth. Shivers coursed along my skin, and my body trembled. He dipped his head to my neck and dragged his tongue across my skin, my wetness growing with each passing beat.

When he pulled back, his eyes held a heat that made my heart shake dangerously in my chest. Everything inside me felt lit by flames.

And then—at long last—he slid inside me. My walls tightened around him as his length filled every inch of me. He groaned and took my face in his hands, his mouth covering mine in such a rough and hungry way that stars dotted my vision.

"Kalen," I moaned.

He thrust harder and faster, gripping my backside to

keep me in place. As I arched against him, his groans grew louder, and the sound of his pleasure sent thrilling goose-bumps storming across my skin.

"Come with me, love," he growled as he slid his hand up my back and dug his fingers into my hair. "Come with me right now."

My thighs squeezed in response to his command, my whole being yearning to do whatever he said. Pleasure built up inside me, and seconds later, I was shuddering against his chest as wave after wave of delicious release pounded through me, with Kalen groaning out my name.

Shuddering, he held my body close, his mouth pressed against my cheek. Mist unfurled around us, and the light strands of it caressed my cheeks. There was something so intimate about feeling his brutal power like this—in a soft touch rather than a deadly storm.

A knock suddenly sounded on the door, bringing a rush of heat to my cheeks. I had not been quiet. He certainly hadn't been, either. How long had someone been standing out there, waiting for the sounds of our pleasure to subside? If it was Fenella, as I suspected, it might have been all night.

Kalen winked as he climbed from the bed, giving me a full view of his magnificent backside. All corded muscles and rippling strength. As I watched, he tugged on his trousers but didn't bother with his tunic, and then he went to the door.

Fenella stood just outside with her arms folded across her armored chest and an amused smile on her lips. "Are you two done yet?"

"No." Kalen laughed and started to shut the door, but Fenella stuck out her boot to stop it.

"The scouts have returned. I thought you'd want to hear what they've found."

"Ah." The tension in his shoulders suddenly returned. "I'll be there in a few minutes. Just let me get dressed."

After he closed the door, he returned to the bed to trace his finger along the curve of my chin. "I need to go see what they've found. Get bathed and dressed, in trousers instead of a dress. I'll meet you back here in an hour. There's something I want to show you."

After Kalen left, maidservants brought me soothing water and luxurious scented soaps. Unlike in Albyria, the maidservants were called by their names here. They were Alice and Willa, two young humans who had grown up in the castle, sisters with brilliant brown eyes and auburn hair. They handed me a stack of towels and left me to my own devices, thank the light. I'd never enjoyed bathing with an audience back in Albyria.

When the bathwater cooled, I climbed out of the tub and got dressed in a clean pair of dark trousers and a soft green tunic with long sleeves to ward off the cold. Endir had once been part of the Kingdom of Light, before Kalen had attacked these lands and taken them as his— before his mists had consumed the city. Back then, the days had been long and humid and hot, according to the stories. But there was no sun here now to warm our skin, so long sleeves it was.

As promised, Kalen returned about an hour later, his expression darker than it had been before he'd left. The scouts must not have brought good news.

"Where are we going?" I asked as he led me down the stairs, past the entrance to the Great Hall, and toward another long corridor. Humans and fae mingled throughout this space. Some were staring up at a cluster of portraits. Others wandered together, speaking in quiet voices. Most were smiling, even the few residents of Teine we passed.

"I thought you might want to see more of the city." He pressed his hand to the small of my back, and there was something so intimate in the feel of his fingers there. A few fae took notice as we passed, their eyes darting to the point of contact. And I understood the judgment in those gazes for what it meant. It was one thing to have humans in the castle. It was quite another for the king to walk me through a public corridor, making it known I was someone important to him.

I'm someone important to him.

My heart beat a little faster.

Kalen led me outside to a courtyard filled with mist. Vague shapes were unmoving shadows all around us, and the ground was sandy beneath our feet. I tipped back my head to gaze up at the sky, but there was nothing to see. Nothing but fog and mist and darkness. It swallowed up the whole world until there was nothing left in it but us.

"Do you ever get tired of it?" I asked.

As if reading my mind, he said, "I'm so sick of it, I'd be happy if I never saw mist again."

I turned to him, surprised. "But the mist is part of you, isn't it? Part of your power."

"I do not love my power, Tessa. I would be far better off without it. So would the world."

We started off down the path, moving through the vague shapes I could now identify as stone statues. One was in the shape of a tree with drooping branches. Another was a large boulder, a steadying presence amidst the gloom. We passed a few more. Some I still couldn't see well enough to identify. Others made little sense to me.

"What are these?"

"Statues made by the Druids. They crafted these to represent the forces in nature that have lasted for millennia. The things that will rule these lands when we are all gone."

I nodded, falling into step beside him. Instead of heading into the city, he took me down a path that wound around the back of the castle, leading toward the forest. When I realized where we were going, I couldn't help but smile.

"You're taking me to the Ivory Cliff Falls."

"And here I was hoping to surprise you."

"It's still a surprise. I've never seen it before, not even in my dreams. You never showed me this part of the world."

"I thought it better to leave the falls untouched by your mind. It's better to experience some things in person, and this is one of them."

We walked up the hillside, along a dirt path that cut

through tall, weeping grass—browned from lack of sun—that swayed in the breeze. As we climbed, the mists thinned, providing me a hazy view of the moon. A few bright stars poked through the fog, stealing my thoughts away from the walk. After failing to kill Oberon and being locked in that dungeon cell, I'd believed I might never again see the night sky.

"As long as dreams remain, so do the stars," I murmured.

Kalen smiled down at me. "I told you to hold on to that, didn't I? I never would have let him trap you there forever."

I stopped. "What made you forgive me, Kalen?"

His eyes searched mine with that look that always called to me. He brought my hand up to his mouth and brushed his lips against my knuckles. "When I look into your eyes, I see the truth of who you are. I understand why you did what you did, and I cannot hate you for it. We're not that different, you and I. You would rip apart the world to save the ones you love. So would I." He kissed the back of my hand again. "You believed I'd prevented you from saving your family, so you retaliated. It's as simple as that."

"That's hardly simple."

"Oh?" He arched his brow. "Then why did you forgive me for what I did to your father?"

"That's different. Your vow forced you to do it."

"I might have done it regardless, if he'd insisted on following through with his plan," Kalen said. "If the gods return, many of my people will die. I'll do anything to protect them. I went to war with Oberon over it. Look at this city, Tessa. Look at how the mist has ruined everything. I didn't have to do this, but I let my rage consume me to the point where all I cared about was stopping Oberon. And so I took my blade, and I shoved it into the heart of his kingdom."

I pushed up onto my toes and pressed my palm against his cheek. "And that kept this world safe for centuries. You trapped him there, in Albyria. You know what that means, right? He had no way of getting to the other half of the god. The part that is full of death, the part that was trapped in the tunnels beneath Itchen. The part *I* released."

"Stop blaming yourself for something you did accidentally."

"As soon as you stop blaming yourself for something *you* did accidentally. You never meant to drown the world in mist."

A beat passed and then he smiled. "Point taken."

"All we can do is try to make it right," I said. "We will find Oberon, stop him from releasing the other half, and then maybe, just maybe, we can find a way for you to control the mists again. There must be a way."

"How optimistic. Another new side of you." He rubbed his thumb across my cheek. "You contain multitudes, and every new discovery has me utterly destroyed."

"I could say the same about you," I said in a soft voice.

We reached the Ivory Cliff Falls after passing through a gate and then hiking a few hours through hills that grew ever higher and steeper. The swaying grass fell away and bleached rocks rose like the backs of enormous tortoises, flat and smooth on top. The thunderous crash of water drowned out the sounds of our footsteps and the heavy pounding of my heart.

Up here, the mists cleared enough for me to gaze upon the brilliant sight of the cascading waterfalls. The river poured through the mouth of five circular white stones, etched with golden symbols from the ancient world, visible even from this distance. When the water rushed through the holes, the river joined back together, creating a singular sheet of falling water that looked like glass. Down and down and down it went until it crashed into a crystal blue lake that reflected the light of the silver moon above.

The spray drifted toward us on the wind, cooling my warm cheeks. Fireflies darted about as if dancing to the sound of the water. The way the river separated, and then came together, and then fell down to the lake, it almost sounded like...

"It's a song." My eyes widened in awe. "A melody. Each one of those circular rocks is playing a note, and they harmonize."

Kalen smiled. "I thought you'd like it here."

"It's more beautiful than I imagined." I shook my head and then gazed at the empty bank around the lake. "And no one else is here to enjoy it."

He dropped his hand to the hilt of the sword he wore strapped to his waist. "Too dangerous. We're outside the city walls now, and the pookas would not hesitate to attack if they came across someone here."

A chill swept down my spine. "Oh."

"Don't let it worry you." He pulled a second sword from his back and tossed it to me, sheathed. I caught it in both hands and measured the weight of it. This was not the light wood I was so accustomed to.

"Are you handing me an actual sword?"

"You look far too excited about this."

I grinned and pulled the blade from the sheath, practically moaning at the sound of the steel against leather. It whistled, joining with the chorus of the falls. The moon glinted across the blade. With a delighted laugh, I raised the sword and angled the blade at his chest.

"Bad move giving me a sword."

He chuckled and drew his own. The monstrous thing was even bigger than mine. Without even a hint of effort, he tapped my weapon and knocked it out of my hands. It clattered when it hit the stone by my boots.

"Well, that's hardly fair," I told him.

"I want to train you to use a sword. Properly, this time. That means knowing how to handle someone who has a bigger weapon than you."

"You're just overcompensating."

A wicked smile curled his lips. "Now you, of all people, know that is certainly not true."

Heat raced into my cheeks. Did I ever.

"Fine." I collected the sword from the ground and

propped the sharp end against the nearest boulder. "I do want to learn."

"Good. Your first task is carrying that back to the castle."

"Carrying it—wait. Aren't we going to train here?"

"The song of steel could draw pookas, and you aren't ready to fight them yet." With an amused smile, he nodded at where I'd rested the blade against the rock. "Swords are heavy. You need to get used to carrying one before you can even think about wielding one in a battle."

I eyed him warily. "You use straps to carry yours."

"Not at first, I didn't." Kalen took the sheath from where I'd tossed it onto the ground and pressed it into my hand. "Use your strength. You have plenty of it."

Nodding, I strained to shove the blade back into the sheath. The length of it was awkward in my hands, but I managed to get it after a few failed attempts. It was a matter of angling the two components just right. A glimmer of satisfaction glowed within as I held the sword and started off down the path.

Together, we returned to the safety of Endir's streets, where humans and fae could find comfort in the thickness of the walls that kept the shadowfiends—the pookas —from attacking. And a thought struck me as I took one last glance behind us just before we passed through the gates. There was no true barrier here. No protective power to tempt the humans to stay. No magic preventing the fae from leaving. Everyone was free to come and go, but no one left. The people of this place were just as trapped by the mist as I had been—trapped by fear.

I looked up at Kalen with determination in my heart. "We will find a way to fix this."

THIRTY-ONE
MORGAN

Oberon stumbled back and forth at the mouth of the cave, frowning out at the mists as if they held all the answers to his troubles. He'd been at it for hours, and he wore weariness like an anchor around his neck. His body folded in on itself, and his lungs rattled with every step. Burns covered every inch of his skin.

"Just sit down," I said.

"Sitting will not help me work through this maze."

"A maze of your own making," I said with a bitter smile. "Those who play with fire shouldn't be surprised when they get burned."

"Enjoying this, are you?" He folded his arms and narrowed his gaze at me. "You're just as stuck here as I am."

"Yes. Thanks to you, the maze maker."

"What would you have me do?"

"I'm not telling you how to get out of this. Figure it out your fucking self."

His eyes glowed with an orange so bright that it almost hurt to look at him. "Perhaps I should order you to hunt down the Mist King and slit his throat."

I stilled. "Go ahead. He'd murder me before I even raised my blade, and then you'd lose your captive servant."

"It's a shame you have no confidence in your abilities."

"You know as well as I do how powerful he is. Mark my words. If you send me after him, he will kill me, especially after you forced me to trick Tessa into believing he betrayed her."

"If he cares that much for a pitiful human, then he's more twisted than I thought."

"Listen to yourself," I said with a shake of my head. "This power you carry...that's what is twisted. You no longer have a vessel. Just let it go, Oberon. It's over."

As if my words conjured her from sleep, Bellicent stirred. Oberon lumbered over to her side, falling to his knees. He took her hand and clutched it tight, and it was that panic that made me pity him, no matter what he'd done to me. This thing controlled him, just as he controlled me. The difference was, of course, that he did not realize it.

"Bellicent," he said. "Are you all right, my love? Are you here?"

She sighed and blinked open her eyes. The flames of the fire suddenly sputtered out and life filled her cheeks. "For just a few moments. I need to speak with you about my transfer. My mind keeps slipping away from me, and it needs to happen soon."

"I don't have the vessel, and I'm not sure I can get to her. She's...protected."

"The Mist King," she hissed.

I frowned at the ashen remains of our fire. The world thought Oberon had been the one to assign that title to Kalen, as a way to remind his subjects of just how dangerous his power was. Only a few knew the truth. It had been Bellicent, Kalen's mother. She had not dared to speak her son's name, fearing it would bring upon a wave of grief too great for her to bear. It was easier for her to see him as her enemy if she called him something else.

And so The Mist King was born.

"No matter," Bellicent said quickly, before holding up the black gemstone necklace that Oberon and his queens carried with them everywhere. "The other half of the god escaped from her gemstone prison, and she decided to join my half inside this necklace, even though that trapped her again. She'd rather be whole than split in two, even if that means being stuck in here instead. She's much more powerful this way. And she knows how much I'd like to free her."

Startled, I sprang to my feet. "All of her? That's impossible."

The line deepened between Oberon's eyes. He reached out and brushed a finger against the gemstone. With a hiss, he flinched. "When did this happen?"

"It's hard for me to say," Bellicent replied. "I've been in and out of it for so long...perhaps two weeks. Maybe three."

Oberon's hand dropped to his side. He glanced over his shoulder at me. "Did Tessa do this?"

"This is the first I'm hearing it." I frowned. "She and the captain did spend a few days in Itchen. But he would never release the god's power, nor allow Tessa to do it."

Bellicent jingled the necklace. "She only released half the power. Now the God of Death is complete once more. All I have to do is destroy this necklace, and she's finally free. *All* of her."

"That's why the barrier started breaking down," Oberon said, ignoring his wife's suggestion. "With the god whole again, she can work against my power. She can numb my magic, or enhance it. That's why my fire exploded the way it did. She did this." He cut his eyes toward the gemstone. "She was trying to kill me so that the necklace would land in someone else's hands. Someone she could more easily control. Someone who would release all of her."

Someone just like Bellicent.

I gave him a frank look. "You might not want to admit it, but she's found you easy to control for centuries."

"I would never release her, and she knows it." Oberon ripped the necklace from his wife's hands and took a step away from her.

"Enough with all this bickering. You're wasting my time," Bellicent said. "Don't you see what she's done? She has united her two halves. Her power is complete now, and it is far greater like this. It means she can transfer me into an immortal body. A *permanent* immortal body. No more moving me around every seventy-five years."

I stiffened. Bellicent had been desperate for a fae body for as long as I could remember, and it had always been out of reach. With only half of the god's power, she'd been resigned to cycling through mortals every time her mind started to give out. Those poor women were nothing but husks when she got through with them, but Oberon could never bring himself to let them go completely. He got attached to each and every one, squirreling them away in the Tower of Crones, where he visited them regularly.

"That's true." Oberon knelt beside her. "We could transfer you into a fae body now if we had one."

Bellicent smiled and then shifted her gaze to me. Shuddering, I stumbled back. The moment she'd mentioned it, I'd known. Because, of course, it had to be me. We were hidden in the mountains, far away from everyone else. It was either me or Oberon, and the king would never sacrifice himself. That was one step too far, even for him.

Oberon turned toward me, his brow a thick, furrowed line.

"No," I whispered to him, even knowing it was pointless, even hating myself for begging.

But then he turned back to Bellicent and said, "Are you sure this is what you want to do? Morgan has been with us for centuries. She's served me—and you—well. If you do this, it means you'll kill her."

My lips parted in surprise. There was a fondness in his voice I never would have expected to hear from him.

Bellicent laughed, a hollow sound that was far more like the dying bleat of a wounded animal. "I don't care. Her death means nothing to me."

Oberon sat back, a frown etched into his burned face.

"How can you say that? This is Morgan. She's sacrificed so much for you. She's held you as you cried and wiped the tears from your face. Don't you remember?"

"Ages ago," Bellicent said. "I have not cried in at least a hundred years."

The muscles tightened around his eyes. "You are not the Bellicent I once knew. The woman I fell in love with never would have asked me to murder *her*."

I watched their exchange with growing dread. Oberon could see the true depths of his wife's cruelty now, something he'd long insisted wasn't there. No matter how many times I tried to tell him the god's power had corrupted her soul, he wouldn't believe me. He wanted to see her as Bellicent Denare, the queen with stars in her eyes. The woman who wept when she thought she would never see her son again. The one whose remorse was so great for what she'd done that she could barely leave her bed. But that person had died a long time ago.

A monster resided in there now.

Bellicent gave him a flat stare. "Go gaze into the mirror, Oberon. You're not the man I fell in love with, either. Look at all the horror you've wrought."

Oberon sucked in a breath.

She continued, "You've happily sacrificed the lives of innocent mortals to keep me here in this world. You only care now because you think you have a connection to this fae."

Sorrow flashed across his face. He stood. "You're right. We've become the very things we once hated. It has twisted us both."

"Took you long enough to realize," I muttered beneath my breath.

Bellicent glared up at him. "You're the one who started this. It wasn't my choice, and I am who I am because of you. Now are you going to finish this or not? Put me in the last body I'll ever need, and we won't have to do this anymore. No one else will have to die."

I glanced between them, a strange fierce hope gripping my heart. Oberon's constant cruelty had haunted my steps every day for several centuries. He'd forced me into a vow I could not break, and he reminded me of it at every turn. But maybe, just maybe, the fog in his eyes had cleared. Perhaps he would let me go.

Oberon's shoulders slumped. "Very well. I'll make the preparations. Sleep now, my darling love. When you wake, it will be with fresh eyes. The last ones you will ever need."

I crumpled to my knees, and my voice was barely a scratch in my throat. "No."

"Stay where you are," he said, slowly turning from his wife's side. Now that she had burdened me with my fate, her future was decided. Her lungs released their air, and she slumped against the ground, like a ship's sail when the wind goes still. Like this, she looked frail. Her cheeks were sunken, and her eyes were ringed with purple bruises. It was as if the mortal body knew the ancient being living inside her should no longer be there.

It was time for her to pass on.

But she would cling to this life for as long as she could.

Oberon unpacked the special ink—the boiled

remains of a comet—that I'd brought with us. It had always been in my pack for emergencies. Another order from Oberon. My life was full of them. I'd never thought much about this one until now. We had the ink, and we had a knife, and soon, that mark would be etched into my skin.

"Sit still," he ordered. "And do not speak until I am done with this."

I kept my backside rooted to the stone while Oberon took the comet's ink and etched the mark into my upper back. Pain flared, as bright as the comet itself, but I did not cry out. I would not give him the satisfaction of seeing me suffer. The edge of the blade dug into my skin, drawing the lines of the one-eyed dragon. Andromeda's symbol, the one Oberon had co-opted to use himself at the encouragement of Bellicent.

When he was finished, my back felt raw, as if he'd sliced off an entire layer of skin. Soon, the pain would fade, and the wound would heal, but this mark would be on me for the rest of my life. How much time did I have before they made the transfer? Days? Hours? Or even less?

"I am sorry, Morgan. This isn't how I wanted things to end," Oberon whispered as he stepped away from me.

"Don't bother," I said. "You could have released me from my vow decades ago. For the love of light, you could do it now. No one forced you to go through with this but yourself. And don't you dare think that I will not curse your name when you finally take the last thing from me that you can. When I die, I will link your soul to mine and drag you into the underworld with me. You will turn to ash."

Oberon closed his eyes and turned away, striding toward the mouth of the cave. Without another word, he wandered out into the mists. I watched him vanish. Now would be the perfect time to escape, if I could. The transfer could not work if there was too much distance between the gemstone and the vessel. I could run. Get far away from here. Anywhere would do.

Anywhere but here.

But my feet were frozen in place. Oberon had ordered me not to leave.

I looked toward Bellicent's sleeping form. He'd forgotten to order one thing, though.

I held my fingers to my lips and whistled. Moments passed. Soon, they crept into an hour. I whistled, again and again, desperately hoping a nearby bird would hear. I'd given up by the time the flap of wings jolted me from my reverie. Dark feathers rushed toward me. The raven settled onto my shoulder and cawed.

This was not Boudica, but it would do. Most ravens were trained to report to the shadow fae.

I whispered into the bird's ear.

And then my only hope for salvation flew off into the mist on a pair of gleaming black wings.

THIRTY-TWO
TESSA

Nellie followed me into my chambers when I returned to the castle. "We're going to have a celebration tonight!"

I rubbed my shoulder, wincing from the soreness in my muscles. It felt good, satisfying, much like the way I'd felt after a long day scaling the chasm to collect gemstones for the captain, before I'd had any inkling of who he was. And now he had me hauling a sword around for hours. Oddly enough, I had no complaints.

"What are we celebrating?" I asked as I climbed onto my bed and eased into the pillows. After the long hike back to Endir, my body begged for a full night's sleep. Tomorrow, Kalen had said, he'd show me how to swing the sword. I couldn't wait.

"The end of Oberon's reign, of course." Nellie grinned.

I raised my eyebrows and glanced at Val when she walked through the door that still hung open. "Are you partaking in this celebration?"

"Absolutely," Val said, closing the door behind her. "And so are you. Get out of that bed."

Nellie grabbed my hands. "It's an actual ball, Tessa. A *ball*. We've never been to a ball."

My stomach twisted. "*I've* been to many balls. Too many. None of them were enjoyable experiences."

Her face fell. "Oh. Well, surely those don't count. You weren't a real attendee."

No, just a prize on display. A vessel for Oberon's true love.

Val crossed the room and flung open my wardrobe, ignoring my objections. There seemed to be a new collection of gowns inside, four beautiful garments hanging in a neat row. Each was a different shade of blue or silver.

"Consider this a way to banish all those memories of Oberon's balls," Val said. "He can't force you to do anything ever again, and if you hide inside this room all night while everyone else dines and drinks and dances the night away, then that smug bastard has won. The best revenge is enjoying your life now that you're free of him."

"You do have a point," I admitted.

"Of course I do. Now, I'm going to steal one of these for myself. The plain silver one, if that's all right?"

She held up a simple silver dress crafted from silk, and the long bell-shaped sleeves had no embellishments. The brass belt was the only hint of additional color, but when she held it up to her chest, it made her brilliant red hair pop.

"That one is perfect for you," I said before turning to my sister. "Nellie, do you want one as well?"

She trailed over to the gowns. "Which one are you

going to wear?"

They were all beautiful, but one stood out from the rest. It was a sleeveless sapphire gown embroidered with deep gold along the bodice. Its skirt fanned out and was made from pleated paper silk. Golden chains hooked the front of the bodice to the back, to wind over the shoulder, and the front held a rectangular cut trimmed with more golden chains. It was very elaborate and unlike anything I'd ever worn before, but it called to me.

"The sapphire one," I said with a small smile.

Val coughed and then shook her head. "Oh, for the love of light. The one that matches his eyes. You're well and truly gone. Do you know how corny that is?"

"I've spent so much of my life being angry at the world. I don't mind introducing a little corniness to it now."

She laughed. "Well, come on then. Let's get you ready to be your new corny self."

The Great Hall had been transformed. The overhead beams were festooned with sapphire and silver draperies while emblematic shields hung along the walls. Gemstones lit lanterns scattered throughout the room, casting a cozy glow across the party. Along the far corner, a grand table held an assortment of refreshments, from pitchers of ale and fion, to delectable cakes, to buttered rolls and pastries.

Kalen approached me through the crowd, wearing a pair of dark trousers and a silver-and-blue velvet brocade coat, cinched around his waist with a leather belt adorned with silver embellishments. His sword, as always, was strapped to his back, the silver hilt matching the crown atop his head, the one I'd rarely seen him wear. Sometimes, it was easy to think of him as a warrior and nothing more, but he stood with a regality now that only a true king could wield.

With his broad shoulders and piercing sapphire eyes, he commanded attention, and every single person in the room, both fae and human alike, turned.

"This is incredible," I said when he reached me. "When I heard there was a ball, I didn't expect it to be quite so elaborate."

"It's been a while since we had a ball here in Endir, and I thought it was about time." He smiled. "The humans of Teine have been through so much, and so have all those who call this city home. It's time to bring a little light into the darkness of this world. I got the idea when we were up by the falls, and I saw the look on your face. It reminded me that we need more moments like this."

I gazed up at him, so touched by his words that I missed the approach of his Mist Guard. All five of them fanned out behind him, a gathering of some of the most powerful fae in Aesir. Together, they could probably take on a small army themselves. They wore matching outfits: black trousers, black and silver brocade jackets, and embellished leather belts cinched around their waists. All carried swords and had mask-and-crown pins on their jackets that showed allegiance to their king.

"You look incredible, love." Kalen's hawkish eyes dipped to my gown, and a wicked smile curved his lips.

"If it wouldn't be rude to my guests, I'd take you back to my bed right now."

I blushed.

Niamh coughed, but Alastair just laughed. The rest of the Mist Guard merely shook their heads in fond exasperation. At least Fenella was no longer scowling at me.

"Enjoy the party," he said with a nod to me, and then to Val and Nellie. "I'm going to do the rounds, and then I'll find you for a dance."

I started to tell him I had no idea how to dance to any of the songs they might play here—back in Teine, we'd danced, of course, but there were no set moves, no steps to learn and memorize. We just shook our bodies and waved our hands in the air, trying to find whatever pleasure we could in our small lives. But he'd already started across the room with his Mist Guard right on his heels.

"Let's go look at the food," Val said, grabbing my arm and tugging me toward the overflowing table. Laughing, I fell into step beside her and linked arms with Nellie, who had chosen to wear a navy blue sleeveless gown crafted from silk and embroidered with golden birds along the shoulder. With her chestnut hair piled on top of her head, she carried an elegance about her that she'd never had the chance to demonstrate in Teine.

The three of us joined the crowd that surrounded the feast. My stomach growled at the sight of so much luxurious food. I reached for a pastry, but Val smacked my hand.

"Fion first. We need to toast to this night." Her face sobered. "Only a week ago, the three of us were trapped inside Oberon's dungeons. We were facing certain death, in one way or another. It's a wonder we are alive, we are together, and we are safe."

Nellie loosed a ragged breath. "I can toast to that."

"So can I," I said, clutching them both tighter.

With a somber nod, Val found a pitcher of fion and poured each of us an overflowing goblet. I lifted mine from the table and held it aloft. "To surviving."

"To ridding ourselves of King Oberon once and for all," Val said.

"And to finding each other again," Nellie added.

We clinked our goblets, and the dark liquid spilled onto our hands. I took a sip of the fion, and the intoxicating flavors of berries, sugar, and spice coated my tongue. Almost instantly, my head felt lighter, and the music sounded sweeter. Val grinned and did a little dance. I couldn't help but grin back. She was right. We *did* need to celebrate. The odds had been stacked against us from the moment we were born. We'd suffered so much loss, so much heartache. But we were here now, and we had each other.

And that was worth everything.

Nellie beamed. "This is delicious."

"Tastes like honey." I took another sip.

"Honey mixed with...something I can't put my finger on," Val said.

"Magic," a familiar voice murmured into my ear.

My breath caught as I twisted toward Kalen, and a sudden wave of power washed over me. He held out a hand and inclined his head toward an empty space in the middle of the floor where musicians played a sultry tune on their strings, woodwinds, and drums.

"Dance with me," Kalen said as I slipped my fingers into his open palm.

I nodded, something in my chest tightening at the look in his eye. I felt as though he had taken a hammer to my every defensive instinct, to all that hatred and pain that had hardened me against the world—just with this one look. And even though he accepted all that—even though he saw all the worst things about me and understood—the way he looked at me somehow made it all fall away.

There was a lightness in my steps as I followed him to the center of the floor. I could feel every eye in the room on us, but I didn't care. A few whispers drifted toward us, and I caught a handful of fae shooting me scowls—as well as some of the humans from Teine. They didn't understand and didn't have to. All that mattered to me were his sapphire eyes, his strong, rough hands, and the feel of his skin against mine.

When we reached the middle of the empty floor, Kalen wrapped one hand around my waist and tugged me against his chest. I tipped my head back to gaze up at him, placing my palm against his shoulder. With a heated gaze, he started leading me across the floor in a dance.

I tried to move my feet in time with his, but tripped right at the start. One of the nearby fae laughed—a dark-haired man wearing a tailored coat who I'd noticed watching me back at the table. The scowl on his face now made me stumble another step.

Kalen took my chin between his fingers and turned my face back toward him. "Just let go of everything and follow my lead. None of them matter."

We began to dance again, and as our feet flowed from one step to the next, I didn't think about how I might trip, or who in the crowd might be watching us. It didn't matter if they wanted to see me fail or not. With Kalen's hand on my waist and his eyes on mine, I could forget it all.

Our feet moved in sync. Somehow, my body took over and followed his spinning movements across the dance floor. My chest swelled as the music filled my mind and the sweet taste of fion still coated my tongue. Kalen arched his brow when I kept up with a sudden twirl back toward the center of the room.

"You're good at this," he said. "Better than you let on."

I smiled up at him. "I have a good instructor."

A fiery spark lit his eyes. "There are a few other moves I'm dying to show you, though we'll wait until we don't have an audience for that."

My heart pulsed. "No audience? You don't seem like the shy type."

"Oh, I am not shy," he said in a low murmur as he tightened his grip on my waist, "but I can't stand the thought of any other man in this room seeing the beauty of your curves."

"Mmm. So, I shouldn't dance with someone else then?"

"Not unless you want to see me wildly jealous."

"Might be kind of entertaining."

His hand left mine, and he rubbed his thumb against my jaw. "As entertaining as me carrying you back to my bed after this ball, so that I can show you just how many ways I can make you moan?"

"That does sound fairly entertaining," I whispered.

His lips grazed mine. I wound my arms around his neck and kissed him with fion burning through my veins, giving me an extra dose of nerve. Everyone was watching us. They'd likely gossip about this later—the fae king and his mortal lover. But his lips and the heat of the wine banished those thoughts. We kissed there on the dance floor, our arms wrapped around each other, until I could barely breathe.

When we finally broke apart, the music changed. An upbeat tune cut through the strained silence of the Great Hall, and a group of nearby fae sprang into action. Cheeks flaming, I glanced around and spotted my mother with a group of humans, shaking her head with her hand on her chest. It was the first time I'd seen her since her visit to my room. She'd been avoiding me.

"I'm not sure my mother will ever get over watching me kiss the Mist King."

Kalen dropped another kiss on my lips. "She'll have to get used to it."

I smiled as several rowdy fae lurched past us with arms and legs swinging to the beat. Kalen laughed and led me off the floor, back to where Tess and Nellie were feasting on pastries. Little flecks dotted their clothes, and by the widening of their pupils, they were at least another glass of fion into the celebration.

"Toryn is calling me over." He winked as he backed away. "Save another dance for me."

"Only if you swear to do what you mentioned earlier.

After the ball."

A wide grin spread across his face. "With pleasure."

He took several more steps back with his eyes locked on me, almost as if he didn't want to turn away. I'd never seen him so relaxed before, so joyful in the way he moved. Gone was the tension that tightened his shoulders. Gone was the heaviness of his steps. And, as I turned to my sister and my dearest friend, I realized all that was gone from me as well.

"Enjoy your dance?" Val asked, gifting me with a sly smile.

"Don't you start." I held out a hand. "Give me one of those pastries. I'm starving."

But before she could pass me some food, the air behind me shifted.

"Tessa Baran. I've heard a lot about you." The dark-haired fae edged up beside me and leaned against the table with a lazy grin. He was the one who had been watching me dance with Kalen. Like the other fae, he wore fine, tailored attire and had placed a metal pin on his lapel that matched Kalen's mask-crown symbol. It was impossible to tell his age—he could be anywhere from thirty to two hundred. The keen glint in his eyes suggested it was the latter.

"Thank you. I guess."

He narrowed his gaze and stepped closer. That was when I noticed the small dagger hidden just behind his decorative coat. "It wasn't a compliment. The last place our king should be is here, watching over a group of pitiful humans. You're distracting him from what really matters. And that isn't an insect like you."

I blinked and stepped back. A few men from Teine wandered closer, clearly having heard the fae's words.

"There's no need to be rude," Val said with a frown.

He snapped his head her way. "Do not speak unless you're spoken to, *mortal*."

"And here I thought shadow fae were better than light fae," I hissed at him, angling my body between him and Val. "Dismissing humans just because of what they are. That's what Oberon does."

"Well, perhaps Oberon had it right." He grabbed my wrist and gripped it tight. "Because we'd all be better off if you were dead. Did you think we wouldn't hear that you tried to kill our king?"

He whisked out a dagger and pointed the sharp tip at my throat. The edge pierced my skin. Several of the Teine men shouted and started to move toward me, but that only made the fae clutch me tighter.

"Come any closer, any of you, and I will kill her right here in front of everyone," the fae growled.

The music stopped, and an eerie hush fell across the packed ballroom.

Heart pounding, I stared into the depths of the fae's eyes. I should have expected something like this, especially after Fenella's initial reaction to me. She was close to Kalen and followed his lead, despite how she might feel, and she'd still made it known that she did not trust me. Of course others would feel the same, and they might not hold back like she had.

Of course they would want to see me dead.

"You're right," I said, meeting his gaze. "I made a mistake. And I am sorry."

My voice carried through the silent hall.

Fenella charged up to us, fury written in the furrowed lines on her face. I flinched back, worried she'd come to join him, but that only made the fae man grip me tighter.

"Let her go, Asher," Fenella barked.

And then there he was. Mist swirled toward me, caressing my cheek. Power rippled through room, and the scent of snow filled my head until it drowned out everything else. The fae cut his eyes to the side as Kalen strode toward us with his sword unsheathed. His eyes sparked with fury, and a snarl curled his lips.

"Asher. Remove your dagger from her throat." Even though he spoke the words in a quiet voice, they still boomed like a cracked whip snapping through the tense moment. Fenella gritted her teeth and pointed her own dagger at Asher's back.

Asher frowned, and he did not let me go. "You can't allow this, Your Grace. She tried to kill you. This mortal should face a public execution. The world needs to see that *no one* can threaten the life of our king, especially not someone who matters so little. And if you won't do it, *I* will."

Kalen whipped his blade through the air. The sword sliced into Asher's face, from the top of his forehead down to the base of his neck. Blood spurted onto my cheeks and dress as the fae's body tumbled to the ground. The top half of his sliced head fell with a thunk by my feet.

My entire body shook, and I stumbled back into Nellie and Val, who gripped my arms to hold me steady. Gasps peppered the air. Several of the humans screamed and fled from the room, but all I could do was stand there in shock.

Kalen wiped his blade and sheathed it on his back before turning to the crowd. "Tessa is under my protection. Anyone who threatens her life will be viewed as threatening mine, and they will be dealt with accordingly."

Silence hammered the room. Several of the fae bowed their heads, and the rest of the Mist Guard began drifting toward us, each one eyeing the crowd as if they expected a revolt to break out at any moment.

Kalen turned to me and swept his gaze across my neck, where blood dripped from the small wound Asher had inflicted. "Are you all right? Are you hurt?"

"I'm fine," I managed to say. "But Kalen, he—"

"I will not let *anyone* put his blade against your throat." But then his eyes softened, and he brushed away a speck of blood on my cheek with his thumb. "I'm sorry. This is not how I wanted this evening to go."

The fion sat like a heavy stone in my stomach now, and the pastries held no appeal. Neither did the dancing, or the music that had once again begun to play in eerie tones. The entire crowd still watched us, or they stared at the dead fae by my feet. Many of the Teine humans started gathering together and headed toward the open doors. My mother was among them.

The music stopped once more.

Someone in the cluster of fae cleared his throat. A somber cloud hung heavily over them all. Gone was the laughter and the cheer.

The ball was ruined.

Kalen glanced at Fenella's grim face. "Perhaps I was too ambitious to think our two very separate worlds were ready for an event like this."

"I'm sorry, Kal," she said. "I didn't think things would escalate like this."

Niamh, Toryn, Alastair, and Gaven reached us as the rest of the fae started drifting—silently—out of the Great Hall. I started to turn away, certain the Mist Guard would be angry with me for causing yet *another* problem, but Toryn offered me a gentle smile.

"Don't blame yourself," he said. "Asher has been itching for a fight since we arrived."

Alastair gently patted my shoulder. "I hope you're all right."

"I'm fine," I said with a tight smile.

Niamh sighed and knelt beside the dead fae's body. "I can't believe he was bold enough to attack Tessa in front of the entire court."

Gaven frowned. "He's not the only Endirian fae who feels hatred toward the mortals who have taken over their castle, and it seems word has spread about your little... incident with the fake Mortal Blade. I worry others might retaliate."

My hands tightened. "I don't want to cause any issues. Maybe I..." I hated the thought of it, but what else could I do? "Maybe I should leave."

"You will *not* be leaving," Kalen said in a firm voice.

Val came up beside me and took a swig of her drink. "I, for one, think that bastard deserved it. Now, does anyone want to dance?"

THIRTY-THREE
TESSA

SIX MONTHS AGO

Sometimes, I did not know how I could live in Teine for even one more day. My lower back often itched from Oberon's attack, even all these years later. It would throb with pain, and when I touched the raised skin, strange heat would curl into my fingers. It was as if the wounds were alive.

Today was one of those days. And when the scars burned with the heat of the sun, my feet—itching to escape—would carry me to the western edge of the Kingdom of Light, where a wooden wall separated our small piece of the world from the rest. The chasm didn't stretch around this far, but the mists still pushed against Oberon's power-infused barrier. Through a hole in the wall, I watched the haze and wondered at the monsters that lurked in the darkness.

I'd spotted a few hulking forms a few times over the years, but none had ever come close enough for me to get a good view of them. They would be there one moment and gone the next, nothing but a formless blob of silent, gathered shadows, like ancient ghosts sweeping past.

As I leaned against the wall and watched the fog, I wondered what it would be like to live out there, away from the heat of the eversun—away from Oberon and his cruel soldiers.

Was the Mist King truly beyond these borders? Could he be watching me right now? An uneasy rush went through me at the thought.

My father had once left this place to get answers. He must have found something out there, but what? If I followed in his footsteps, would I find them, too? These questions had haunted me for years, but I'd never been brave enough to climb over the wall to find out for myself. Death lurked beyond the borders.

An eerie shriek split the air, breaking me out of my reverie.

With a gasp, I stumbled away from the wall just as the wood shook like a trembling branch in the wind. A yellow eye flashed outside the hole, and a feral howl ripped through my very soul. My mind screamed at me to run, even though the shadowfiend could not get through that wall. It was impossible. Oberon's protective magic kept the monsters from coming over the barrier and into Teine, and yet...

Fear choked me like a beast's talons clutching my throat.

An image flashed in my mind. A small child raced through the mists with a beastly creature bearing down on her. The little girl sobbed. Her face was so, so pale, and her arms flailed in front of her as she reached—desperately—for her father. I shook my head, shoving away the sight. My imagination was getting the better of me again. I was no child, and I was not in the mists.

I'd never been in the mists.

But the image soared back into my mind again, and something about it felt so terrifyingly real.

The shadowfiend's eye vanished from the hole in the wall. The heavy thump of its retreating footsteps soon followed. I exhaled, feeling a little silly for my overreaction.

Shaking my head at myself, I followed the path toward my village, so lost in thought that I failed to notice the fae soldier's approach upon my return. He cut me off just before I reached the front steps of my home, where my sister knelt on the porch washing off the dirt.

The fae man towered over me. They all did. His yellow eyes were as sharp as the tips of his ears, and his snug leather armor highlighted his broad shoulders and impressive chest. But it was his lips I noticed most. They were set into a very thin, very hard line.

"Is there a problem?" I asked, motioning for Nellie to go inside the house. She shot me a fearful glance, but then she scurried in, closing the door quietly behind her.

Good.

"Where were you?"

"Just taking a walk." I folded my arms. "There are no rules against that."

"A walk where?"

"Just...through the village and the woods."

"Turn around," he commanded.

My hands curled into claws. "I have done nothing wrong."

He stepped near, and the heat of his fiery power pulsed against me. Like Oberon, this soldier was an elite fae, and if I did not do what he asked, he could turn his fire on me and burn my body to a crisp. Shaking, I turned and lifted the back of my tunic, knowing what he wanted from me.

He pressed a gloved finger against my throbbing scar, and pain hissed through my back. I dug my teeth into the insides of my cheek.

"Did you go across the bridge?" he asked quietly.

"No," I whispered.

"Over the wall?"

"No, I haven't left. I've *never* left," I choked out as he shoved his finger against my aching wound again.

At long last, his hand fell away. I dropped my tunic, and the material brushed against the raw, pounding scars. Before I could catch my breath, he grabbed my shoulders and forced me to face him. Those flashing eyes cut through me like knives. "I know you think about escape. You all do. But if you go outside the safety of this kingdom, you will die."

He reared back his hand and smacked me in the face. Stars dotted my eyes, the force knocking me sideways. My entire vision went red, rage and helpless terror clashing together inside of me like two cresting waves. The soldier just laughed and wandered off. He'd likely forget about this encounter as soon as he turned the corner, but it imprinted on my mind. I would never forget this day, or any of the others haunted by the fae.

I was done with their viciousness, their disdain toward the mortals of Teine. There had to be something we could do. A way to fight back. A way out.

The rest of the day passed in a blur, and I went through the motions of day-to-day life in Teine. I helped Nellie finish washing the floors and then went into the fields to help my mother carry a bushel of wheat to the gates of the city. After our work was done, Val came over, and we ate a plain meal of grains and root vegetables. It was just like the day before it, and the one before that. Over and over again, nothing ever changed.

I fell asleep with the imprint of the fae's hand on my face. And in my sleep, I called out, even if I did not realize then what I was doing. I screamed for someone to listen to me. For someone to help. For *anyone* to free us from this horrible, twisted place.

And someone answered.

Familiar woods rose up around me in my dream, the sun beaming down from a cloudless sky. Just before me stood a masked fae. He was tall and muscular with dark hair, and he wore some kind of cape around his shoulders over plain clothing.

"Who are you?" I asked, somehow knowing this was real, even if it was a dream.

He cocked his head. "Do you not know?"

"Should I?"

"Interesting." He leaned against the nearest tree and scanned me with piercing eyes. "I'm the captain of some rebel fae living in the mists."

His words startled me. "Rebel fae?"

"Your turn. Who are you?"

I narrowed my gaze. I didn't trust anyone, especially not some strange rebel fae who appeared in my dreams. "I think I'll keep that to myself."

With a chuckle, he folded his arms. "Well, from looking at you, I can tell you're mortal, and your tan tells me you see a lot of sun. You live in Teine. Oberon is your king. And you wish you could escape. Am I close?"

"It's time for you to get out of my head."

"If you live in Teine, you could help the rebels," he countered, pushing away from the tree. "Do something for us, and you and your people will no longer have to live under Oberon's rule."

I stepped back, my heart pounding. "This feels like some kind of trick."

"No trick." He held up his gloved hands. "The rebels have no love for Oberon. You and me, we're on the same side."

This was completely ridiculous. I shouldn't even be entertaining this conversation. But the ghost of the soldier's palm still burned my cheek, reminding me of everything my village had been through in the past ten years—the past *hundred* years and more. We'd been killed. We'd been beaten. We'd had knives in our backs.

Oberon had taken my father from me.

With a shuddering breath, I lifted my chin and said, "I won't promise to do a damn thing for you, but...tell me what you want and I'll think about it."

I could not see his face, but I swore he smiled. "I want you to steal his gemstones from the chasm. And then we'll use that power to free the mortals from him forever."

THIRTY-FOUR
KALEN

It seemed *no one* wanted to dance, and I could not blame them. I'd let my fury get the better of me, and yet I would not take it back. If I hadn't intervened, Asher would have sliced Tessa's throat. Anger still burned in my veins at the thought of it.

Gaven and Alastair stayed behind to clean up the mess while I took the rest of the Mist Guard, including Tessa, into the meeting room to discuss our next steps. Val and Nellie hurried along behind us, and none of us did a damn thing to stop them. I couldn't bear to tell them to go back to their rooms alone after what they'd witnessed this night. I'd brought the mortals here for peace, to provide them with a safe haven from the danger they would have faced back in Teine. But I'd been wrong to assume two very different groups of people could knit together seamlessly.

We pushed inside a room adjacent to the Great Hall. Inside, a fire blazed in the hearth, and several bottles of wine had been set out by the maidservants in anticipation of the night ahead. If the ball had continued the way I'd hoped, my friends and I would have retired to these chambers to continue our celebrations after the party began to die down.

As it was, I didn't have the stomach for any more drink tonight.

Niamh rustled around in a cabinet along the far wall. After she found a bundle of cloths, she crossed the room to Tessa's side. "Here. Let's put this on your wound until it stops bleeding."

"I'm so sorry," Tessa whispered as Niamh wrapped the bandage around her throat.

"Listen here." Niamh clasped her shoulder. "You're one of us now. That means no one can attack you, do you hear me? We take care of our own."

Tessa smiled. She reached up to her shoulder and clutched Niamh's hand. "Thank you."

Warmth flooded me as both Toryn and Fenella moved over to Tessa's side and patted her back. It seemed Fenella had finally given up stalking Tessa's every move, a fact that brought me a measure of relief. I couldn't have them all fighting.

Val and Nellie sank into the armchairs beside the fire while the Mist Guard and I gathered around a smaller version of my war table back in Dubnos. Oberon's glittering crown no longer sat atop Albyria's etched city, but that did not mean this was all over yet.

"Someone please tell me Oberon has been spotted somewhere inside this moon-forsaken kingdom." I turned to Fenella, who merely shrugged.

"I've sent out more scouts. No word. None of the

patrols stationed around the cities saw anything, either. If it didn't sound completely impossible, I'd say he swam across the sea to the human kingdoms."

My frown deepened. "Have you heard from the city guard in Sunport?"

Toryn nodded. "This morning. They said Oberon hasn't shown himself, and no ships have sailed for weeks. So even if he escaped unnoticed, he can't have made it across the seas."

"He has to be somewhere."

Niamh rubbed her scar. "Speaking of ships, I heard some rumblings from the Teine humans during the ball. Several of them don't seem to like the idea of leaving Endir. They feel safe inside these walls, but...then there's another faction. A smaller one."

"Basically, they don't much like you, Kal," Toryn added. "There are whispers they plan to leave on their own. I don't think they trust us to get them safely to Sunport. And tonight's little incident surely didn't help things."

Tessa pushed up from the chair, muscles tightening around her eyes. "They want to leave on their own?"

Sighing, I ran my hand along my jaw. "Don't they realize that if they leave without guards protecting them, they'll die out there?"

Fenella frowned. "Well, they don't seem to care much. To them, you're, well, you know."

"The fucking Mist King," I said through clenched teeth. "We rescued them from Teine and brought them to this city surrounded by impenetrable walls. We've fed them, entertained them. We've done nothing to cause them harm. How can we convince them to trust us?"

"Unfortunately, I don't think there's anything we can do," Niamh said with a sad smile. "They've made up their minds. Sometimes, hatred runs so deep that you can never overcome it, no matter how hard you try to wash it away with kindness."

Tessa shifted on her feet. "Who are they? Maybe I can talk some sense into them."

"Your mother, for one," Toryn told her. "She doesn't trust any of us."

Tessa's face paled.

Her sister jumped to her feet. "Mother? But..."

"You saw how she was when the fae showed up in Teine," Tessa said with quiet resignation. "She threatened Kalen with an axe. I should have known she wouldn't just accept things after that. And she's been avoiding me."

"Well, we need to talk to her. She can't run out into the mists by herself."

Tessa met my gaze, her mouth tight with worry. I hated to see her like this. For a few moments tonight, there'd been so much light in her eyes. So much hope. When I'd seen her gaze at the falls this morning, cheeks flushed, lips parted, I'd known. I'd felt it in my bones. She needed something like this. She needed to see the world for what it could be, for what she'd never had.

I wanted to show her hope.

And all she'd gotten was more of the black sea that dragged her down into the depths of despair.

"How many more are there?" she asked, turning to Toryn. "These humans who want to leave on their own?"

"Ten, maybe, at most."

"All right. I'll go find them and try to talk some sense into them."

Val stood. "I can help."

Niamh moved toward Val's side, and the red-haired mortal cut a nervous glance her way.

"I'll come with you," Niamh said to Val with a smile. "They could be angry and itching for a fight, like Asher was."

Tessa shook her head. "They'll handle it better if it's just us."

The door suddenly flung open. Alastair and Gaven charged into the room, their grim expressions turning my bones to ash.

"Tell me what's happened," I said, crossing the room in two quick strides.

Alastair's lips flattened. "There are screams, coming from outside. I think some of the mortals have tried to flee into the mist."

Tessa gasped.

Tensing, I tossed the words over my shoulder. "Fenella and Niamh, grab your weapons. They may have run into a group of pookas outside the wall."

Toryn shoved away from the table. "I'm coming, too."

The Mist Guard made for the door while I went to Tessa's side. Her cheeks were pale, and as I took her shaking hands in mine, the chill of her fingertips seeped into my skin. "Stay here. I'll do everything in my power to get them back inside the city walls safely."

Her hands tightened around mine. "My mother could be out there."

"I know. I'll look for her first."

I started to pull away, but she held me against her, the fierceness in her expression burning a hole right through me. "I can't stay here being useless, wondering what is happening outside the walls. At least let me come to the gate with you. Let me do something. Please."

Her voice cracked on the last word as her eyes shone with unshed tears. I understood far too well how she felt, how that useless feeling could root itself in your gut like a worm until it carved its way through you, consuming you in slow, agonizing bites.

"Fine." I pulled a dagger from my belt and pressed the hilt into her hands. "Stay behind me. Don't do anything rash—a big ask, I know, but I mean it, Tessa. I cannot save them if I'm distracted by protecting you."

She nodded. "I understand. I'll stay beside you."

I lifted my gaze to Nellie and Val, who huddled by the hearth. The flames splashed orange light onto their faces. "Don't leave this room."

Val swallowed, but it was Nellie—surprisingly—who offered me a lifted chin and flare of nostrils. "I have claws and fangs."

Tessa cast her sister a frantic glance. "Not now, Nellie."

I frowned as we backed toward the door. "What's that all about?"

"I'll explain later," she said before flipping the blade in her hands.

We reached the door and burst out into the corridor.

The others had already made their way down the corridor, and together, we broke out into a run to catch up. As Niamh flung open the front doors, a wailing scream rushed into the castle.

The sound chilled me to my bones. Alastair was right. The pookas were here.

THIRTY-FIVE
TESSA

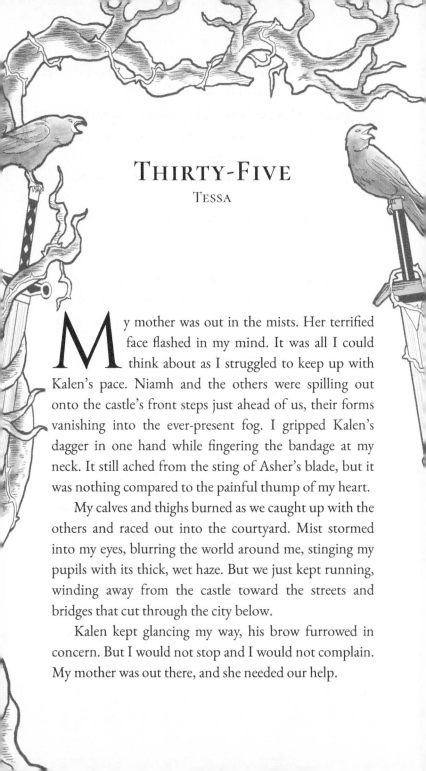

My mother was out in the mists. Her terrified face flashed in my mind. It was all I could think about as I struggled to keep up with Kalen's pace. Niamh and the others were spilling out onto the castle's front steps just ahead of us, their forms vanishing into the ever-present fog. I gripped Kalen's dagger in one hand while fingering the bandage at my neck. It still ached from the sting of Asher's blade, but it was nothing compared to the painful thump of my heart.

My calves and thighs burned as we caught up with the others and raced out into the courtyard. Mist stormed into my eyes, blurring the world around me, stinging my pupils with its thick, wet haze. But we just kept running, winding away from the castle toward the streets and bridges that cut through the city below.

Kalen kept glancing my way, his brow furrowed in concern. But I would not stop and I would not complain. My mother was out there, and she needed our help.

I refused to let myself think the worst, even when another feral shriek rent the murky night.

I'd seen what shadowfiends—pookas—could do. The image of their vicious fangs and claw-like talons was not something I would soon forget.

But I had to hope. I had to believe that it wouldn't be too late.

A main road cut down the side of the hill, right through the heart of the city. We ran past rows of homes built from gray stone, topped with orange roofs. My lungs burned as we continued onward, passing through a small square with a well and merchant stalls that were shut for the night. And still, we kept running, past a pub and an inn and a blacksmith workshop. All dark inside, windows and doors latched tight. A few people looked out their windows as we ran by, no doubt awakened by the screams and the thundering of footsteps.

At long last, we reached the gate. It was a hulking mass of metal. The top of it wasn't even visible from down here. It just vanished into the shadowy mist.

A guard, dressed head to toe in steel armor, rushed toward us, breathless. "A group of humans came through earlier. Eight of them. When the screaming started, I sent two guards out there, but they haven't returned."

"Why did you let them go out there by themselves?" I couldn't help but ask. "They're helpless."

The guard stiffened. "You humans are not prisoners here. If someone wants to leave this city, they can. Unless I've misunderstood our king's commands."

"It's all right, Eitan." Kalen nodded toward the gate. "Open it."

Eitan grunted and stomped away. A moment later, the gate creaked open, and a sudden gust of chilly wind billowed the mist around us. Kalen motioned toward the others.

"Formation," he commanded. "Tessa, stay behind me."

I glanced around as the Mist Guard took up a V-shaped formation with Kalen in the front. Moving just behind him, I gripped my dagger and started walking as the five of them marched out into the darkness. They held their weapons at the ready. Kalen curled his hands out in front of him while Alastair held a sword and Fenella clutched two daggers. In the back row, Toryn carried a spear and Niamh held a bow in one hand and an arrow nocked and ready. Gaven was the only one, other than Kalen, who looked ready to wield magic. With narrowed eyes and open hands, he scanned the mists.

Another scream—this time human—ripped through the night. My feet itched to run as my mind warred against me. I'd made a promise to Kalen not to run ahead, but that vow chafed against my every instinct. We were moving slowly, creeping along in the shadows while my mother was out there somewhere, likely terrified.

Maybe even hurt.

A burning sensation rose up inside me, a desperate need to race forward with no thought to the consequences. The intensity of it choked me like a fist gripping my throat. I struggled to breathe, to think, to keep my footsteps moving forward. And, for a blink of an eye, all I could see was darkness so profound that it felt as if I were no longer even a part of this world.

Kalen stopped short. I crashed into him, and the sudden jolt forced me out of that despairing darkness. The pain and rage flickered away, loosening its hold on me.

I shook my head, wondering what the hell had just happened.

Kalen cast a quick glance over my shoulder. "Everything all right?"

"I'm fine," I said tightly. "Just keep moving. We need to find them."

"Shh." From my right side, Alastair held a finger to his lips as he gazed around us. "One is nearby."

As if to answer his statement, a ball of fangs and fur exploded from the mist. It hurtled toward us with outstretched claws, a wailing shriek ripping from its open mouth. Terror clawed its way up my throat as the Mist Guard shifted toward the beast. Niamh loosed an arrow but missed, the tip punching the sandy ground.

"Alastair, go!" Kalen shouted as the beast landed only a few feet in front of us.

With a roar, the fae swung his sword. His steel sank into the creature's neck and liberated it of its head. A lump clogged my throat as the head tumbled toward us, its vacant yellow eyes staring right through me. It reminded me too much of that day, of that moment I'd thought my sister was dead.

I shook aside those thoughts and turned just as more shadowfiends raced toward us. And then more. My gut twisted as I counted them.

There were at least twenty.

And not a human in sight.

"Mother," I gasped.

"Kal," Niamh shouted out a warning. "There are too many of them!"

"Get back!" he shouted as he braced his feet on the ground. "Take Tessa! NOW!"

Muscular arms wrapped around my waist. Alastair took off at a run, pulling me back, moving faster than I would have expected. Heart pounding, I kept my gaze glued on Kalen as what felt like an entire army of shadow-fiends descended upon him. That horrible helplessness choked me once more. There was nothing I could do. No way that I could help. None of us could.

We were too late.

The beasts drew nearer, so close that I could see the saliva dripping from their bared fangs. Kalen curled his fists. I braced myself, knowing exactly what came next.

He shouted into the wind. His dark power boomed from his body. It felt like a crack in the world opened up, splitting right through my eardrums. I winced at the darkness of it and how strands of pain wrapped around me, tugging me down into the darkness—into death itself.

The ground shook. Sand sprayed against my face, stinging my skin. The power hurtled toward the shadow-fiends and crashed into them with a force that broke every bone in their bodies. They collapsed on the rumbling ground like puppets with cut strings. Then the wave of Kalen's power receded just as quickly as it had washed up against us.

Kalen fell to his knees, body curved, chest heaving.

"Let go of me." I twisted in Alastair's arms.

Alastair released me, and I stumbled forward on trembling legs. Gritting my teeth, I forced my feet to keep moving forward, but it was as if I waded through soup. The remnants of his power still warbled through me.

When I finally made it to his side, I fell to the ground in front of him and searched his tortured gaze. "What's wrong? Are you all right?"

He clasped my hand and shuddered. "I almost lost control that time. I could have ripped open another fucking chasm. It could have…" His voice broke. "I could have killed you."

"But you didn't." I pulled his hand to my chest and rested my forehead against his. "I'm here, safe, because of you. If you hadn't killed all those shadowfiends, I'd be dead."

His sapphire gaze ripped through me. "I shouldn't have brought you out here with me. It's too dangerous."

"It was my decision," I said firmly. "It was a risk I was willing to take. To find my…"

I couldn't say it. Now that I'd seen just how many shadowfiends were out here, I couldn't even mouth the word. *Mother.* Unshed tears burned my eyes, as hot as the flames of Albyria. She and seven other mortals had tried to flee to safety. But there was no such thing as safety out here.

As if reading my mind, Kalen's lips flattened. "Come on. Let's see if we can find them."

He didn't say what we both knew—what *all* of us knew.

I still would not let myself even think it.

We stood and waited for the others to join us. Just as before, they took up their formation and we marched forward, heading further into the darkness beyond the city of Endir. No more shrieks echoed around us. No more terrified screams drifted on the wind. It was silent out here, a heavy sound that weighed on my shoulders like metal chains.

Just ahead of me, Kalen suddenly stiffened. He slowed to a stop and then turned. Tense lines bracketed his mouth, and the sorrowful pinch of his brow caused a whimper to creep up my throat.

"No," I whispered, shaking my head until the world around me was a blur. "No. Please, no."

Toryn let out a strangled noise, and the silence of the others was deafening.

The mist crept along my skin.

"Tell me it's not her," I choked out.

Kalen's cheek tightened. "Toryn and Alastair can take you back to the castle. You don't have to see this."

I started to shake, my teeth knocking together. Words coated my tongue, but I could not find a way to speak them. They just sat there like a lump of bitter sand.

But he knew. He looked into my eyes, and he understood. I could not turn away. I had to face the truth of it all, even if it killed me.

With a heavy sigh, Kalen shifted to the side.

Ten broken bodies littered the ground. Blood was everywhere. A severed arm sat close to my boots, and a pool of blood crept toward me. I swallowed down a lump of nausea, and my eyes blurred. There was so much death. So much fear on the faces looking back at me. Their mouths were still opened wide in silent screams.

Shaking, I stepped over the arm and searched for the

face of the woman who had raised me, who had loved me in spite of everything I'd done to cause her pain. A second ticked by, and then another, and I tried to strangle the hope that threatened to rise up from the dead.

But then...there she was. Her kind eyes stared back at me from beneath a forehead dripping with blood. There was no life inside those eyes. Her body lay still on the sand, and her chest showed no signs of breathing.

Pain shot an arrow through my heart, punching through me so violently that all I could do, for a very long time, was stare.

"Tessa, love," Kalen murmured as he smoothed a stray strand of hair out of my eyes. "Please say something."

I opened my mouth, but nothing came out, not even a whisper. Sorrow rushed over me like a tidal wave, plunging me into the depths of a despair so deep that I thought I might never reach the surface again. My throat burned. My eyes ached. And then something within me *cracked*.

I fell to my knees and sobbed.

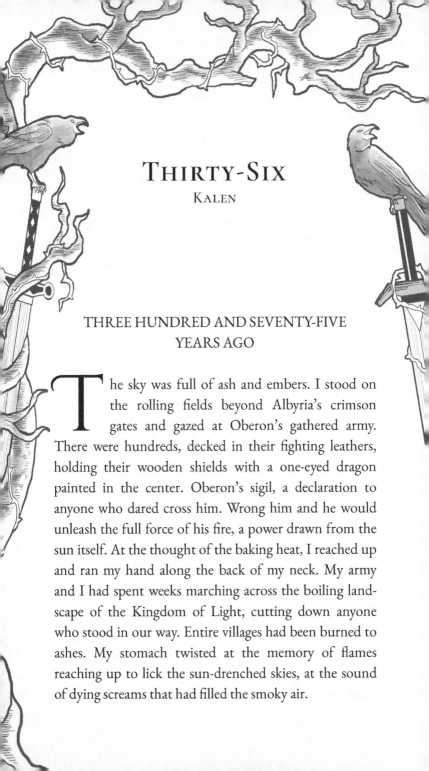

THIRTY-SIX
KALEN

THREE HUNDRED AND SEVENTY-FIVE
YEARS AGO

The sky was full of ash and embers. I stood on the rolling fields beyond Albyria's crimson gates and gazed at Oberon's gathered army. There were hundreds, decked in their fighting leathers, holding their wooden shields with a one-eyed dragon painted in the center. Oberon's sigil, a declaration to anyone who dared cross him. Wrong him and he would unleash the full force of his fire, a power drawn from the sun itself. At the thought of the baking heat, I reached up and ran my hand along the back of my neck. My army and I had spent weeks marching across the boiling landscape of the Kingdom of Light, cutting down anyone who stood in our way. Entire villages had been burned to ashes. My stomach twisted at the memory of flames reaching up to lick the sun-drenched skies, at the sound of dying screams that had filled the smoky air.

I didn't relish in death. Blood and terror and flames—it all added to the nausea that clogged the back of my throat.

But I had no other choice. At least that was what I told myself each time I thought about turning my army around and returning to my homeland, a realm drenched in the cool brush of night. If I did not destroy Oberon, he would find a way to return the gods to Aesir and the human kingdoms beyond the sea. The King of Light threatened the future existence of every single living thing in this world. I would do whatever it took to stop him.

I'd made a vow.

Toryn stepped up beside me and palmed the hilt of the sword strapped to his waist. As the elite fae son of storms, he didn't need a weapon to fight, but he didn't like being unarmed. "What do you think he's going to do?"

"He'll throw the full force of his army against us."

"He should yield," Toryn said, his voice laced with regret. "No more light fae need to die. This war has already taken too many lives."

"Oberon is stubborn and cruel," Niamh said as she joined us, her woolly violet hair twisted into a hundred tiny braids. "But you know that. There's no reasoning with him."

Toryn shook his head. "He is all that, but he's still a king, and he's always acted like one. Regardless of everything he's done, I thought he cared about his people."

"I did too," I said quietly.

Oberon hadn't always been like this. Or, if he had been, he'd hidden it well. He had reigned with a kind smile and generosity, always lending an ear to his people —and assistance where he could. That was the Oberon of a hundred years ago, but something had changed in him these recent years. He'd grown hard and cruel. And he'd taken my mother from me.

Some thought her rejection of his proposal had led him down this path of ruin, but I knew it must have started before that. My father had never liked him. He'd warned us of his treachery. It wasn't until my mother had vanished not long after Oberon's proposal that I'd truly believed this.

Even so, I did not want to destroy the last of the light fae. Yes, some had survived the assaults we'd made against Itchen and Endir, but this realm had suffered so many losses. Most of these fae were just following their king's orders. And there were the humans of Teine not far from the fae city, one of the few mortal villages still left in Aesir. They had nothing to do with any of this. They should not have to pay the price of our war.

I sighed. "Perhaps we could try to draw some of the fae from the front lines for a smaller skirmish. If we win decisively, Oberon might see this battle can only end in the death of his kingdom. He might decide to surrender."

Niamh let out a hollow laugh. "Kal, don't even pretend you believe that. Oberon will never surrender. He won't give up, not even if he has a sword sticking out of his chest."

"The damn gods are more important to him than anything else," Alastair muttered. "Otherwise, he would have given up a long time ago. He's backed into a corner now. He has nowhere to go. And his castle is no fortress."

"We can't discount his power," I said, gazing across the field of his warriors. Oberon still had not shown his face. I'd call him a coward, but I knew there must be a reason. He was planning something, and we had to be prepared. As it stood, Oberon was trapped. Albyria and Teine were backed up against towering mountain peaks along the southern and western edges. Those mountains were not part of the Kingdom of Light. Instead, they were part of the free territory of Albyria—the lands that belonged to no one. The towering, jagged cliffs were deadly, even to elite fae. And the only thing that stood on the other side was the sea. My army waited on the rolling fields that led to the rest of his kingdom, a kingdom that I'd now conquered. Oberon had nowhere to go. And he knew it.

A desperate man was a dangerous man. With nothing to lose, he might be willing to rip his army to shreds.

"Did you find out anything?" I asked Toryn. "About whatever he'd need to do to bring back the gods?"

He shook his head. "I've been combing through the books I brought with us, but a bunch of pages have been torn out. Most likely burned. The fae and humans who drove the gods from this world didn't want us to find a way to bring them back. That information is too danger-ous. So they got rid of it. And whatever your mother found..."

The news settled in my gut like rotten pooka meat. We'd been hoping to find out how Oberon planned to bring back the gods, thinking it would give us a way to stop him. According to Morgan, Oberon knew *something*, but he'd forbidden her to speak of it to anyone, especially me. The only way for me to learn what he knew was to find the answer somewhere else, but all the records had been destroyed. A good thing, in theory. The fae who had burned those pages had hoped to keep the information out of the wrong hands, but they hadn't been thorough enough. Now the wrong hands had it and no one else.

"The only way we're going to stop this is by defeating him," I said. "More slaughter. More blood. More death."

Niamh grabbed my shoulder and squeezed tight. "I'm sorry, Kal. I know you don't want to be the one to order the deaths of all those light fae, but we need you to do it. The world needs you to do it. Because if those light fae live, everyone else dies. It's a few hundred versus thousands."

A few hundred. It was still too many.

Something in the air suddenly shifted, and Niamh's hand tightened on my shoulder. I lifted my gaze to find the army parting to make way for Oberon, who strode through the crowd with his twisted horns and burning ember eyes. They were locked right on my face, and the cruel smile that painted his lips was meant only for me.

I stood my ground, meeting his hard stare with one of my own.

He lifted his hand and curled his fingers. Oberon was calling upon his power.

Dread ripped a hole in my gut. With a grunt of terror, I took off running. "Get everyone behind me!"

"Kal, no!" Toryn cried out, but his voice was as muted as distant thunder. I charged through the army before me, shoving soldiers out of my way. When I reached the front lines, Oberon had widened his arms and tipped back his head. He was going to send his fire across us all.

My mother's words echoed in my ears.

Vow to me, Kalen.

Her glittering eyes flashed in my mind.

You will do whatever it takes to stop them, even if that means killing them. Even if that means using your power against them.

My volatile power burned against my fingertips. I didn't want to use it. I never did. Nothing good came out of my darkness. But if I did not loose this power myself, the vow I'd made with my mother would force me to do it. Oberon threatened every living creature in this world.

Oberon roared. His power ripped from his splayed hands, and a wave of terrifying fire raced across the plains. Gritting my teeth, I opened myself up to the darkness, letting the grim magic build inside me, pressing forward, desperate for release. I imagined the horror the gods would wreak if they returned. I thought of all those inno-cent lives, used and then discarded like a pile of logs burned for heat until they were nothing but ash.

But most of all, I pictured my mother's face, and I let my grief and rage power my magic until all that existed was a pain so great that it shattered my control.

The power slipped from my fingers.

It rushed from my body with a force that knocked me off my feet, hurling me back into my army. I crashed into the front line. Several warriors fell to the ground with me. And then I set my eyes upon the most terrifying, awe-inspiring sight of my life.

Two forces rushed toward each other on the verdant plains. A wave of towering fire, burning every single blade of grass in its path, and a brutal wave of darkness and mist. It rumbled with a power so intense that the ground beneath me shook. I stumbled to my feet and turned toward my silent army.

"Everyone get back!" I shouted. "Run!"

My army descended into chaos. Throwing down their weapons, they turned and raced across the rolling hills, away from Albyria and Oberon's army—away from my horrific power. I followed them, stumbling as the ground jolted beneath my boots, clenching my jaw with the certain knowledge I'd made a very horrible mistake.

Toryn, Alastair, and Niamh were waiting for me off to the side and watching the army struggle against the lurching ground. I ran toward them and grabbed Niamh's arm.

"We have to go," I said. "When those forces hit—"

"It's too late," she whispered, her eyes so wide they rivaled the moon.

I looked over my shoulder. The mist and fire arced toward each other. They were only seconds apart—just long enough for me to wrap my arms around my three closest friends and brace myself.

A tumultuous *boom* ripped through the world.

The ground bucked, and the collision sprayed a rush of mist across us, soaking my face and hair. I glanced down at the earth cracking beneath my boots, grabbed hold of my friends, and started running again. I didn't stop or look back for a very long time.

When I finally slowed and turned to gaze at what I'd done, my heart nearly stopped.

A crack had widened in the ground, so deep it was impossible to see its bottom. My mists swirled against the edge, pushing and shoving against some unseen barrier that separated here from there. I couldn't see any sign of Oberon or his army. And when I looked around us, taking stock of my people, I realized—the mist was everywhere. The sun had vanished from the sky, replaced by the hazy light of the moon spilling through the fog. I tried to push the mist away, but for the first time in my life, it did not respond to me. It continued to swirl around us, transforming the Kingdom of Light into shadowy darkness. In the distance, monstrous beasts began to roar.

I shook my head and stumbled back. "What have I done?"

THIRTY-SEVEN
KALEN

We carried the dead back into the city. The mortals did not deserve to be left out in the mists where any number of creatures might devour them. Their fear of me had driven them into danger, and I would not punish their souls for that. If not for them, then for Tessa.

Nothing could console her. Her grief had hit her so hard that she couldn't even speak. So while the rest of the Mist Guard took care of the bodies, I led her back through the city streets, to the castle, and into my chambers. Someone would need to break the news to her sister, and Val, but I wouldn't leave her alone when she was like this.

She stared through me, unseeing, her teeth chattering. I set her on the bed and moved to the hearth, where I quickly stoked the fire back to life. When I returned to her side, I pressed my palm against her cheek. Her skin was cold and clammy. Lifeless.

"All right, love. I'm here," I murmured as gently as I

could. Kneeling before her, I unlaced her boots and tucked them beneath my bed. I carefully unattached the golden chains that looped over her shoulders and slid the gown from her body. She shook like a leaf.

Her fingers still gripped the hilt of the dagger. Carefully, I unwound each one. I wouldn't force her to let go if she did not want to, but a part of me worried she might snap if someone barged into the room. And someone might. We had eight dead humans and several angry fae from the incident at the ball. Tension crackled through Endir with the threat of further violence.

Tessa released the dagger. I carried it over to my cupboard and then rummaged around for a pair of loose trousers and a warm knit tunic. After I dressed her in those, I pulled some thick socks over her ice-cold feet and then led her to a chair by the hearth.

She stared numbly into the flames.

"I know how you feel," I said. "After my mother vanished, I went in search of her. But deep down, I knew she was gone. For months, I was inconsolable, and I threw myself into preparations for the war. It was the only thing I could do. The only way I could numb the pain."

Tessa blinked.

"I didn't want to talk about it with anyone. So I fought. I killed. I raged across these lands." I let out a heavy sigh, regret thick in my heart. "If you need to rage against something, you can rage against me. I could have better protected your mother. I could have spent more time with the mortals of Teine, showing them I would not harm them."

She turned to me then with glassy eyes. "I don't want to rage against you. I want to rage against *him*."

I nodded. "You and me both, love."

"Then we'll find him, and we'll do it together."

Tears spilled from her eyes, and she turned back to gaze into the flames. I wouldn't push her to speak any more tonight. If there was one thing I knew about grief, it was that it needed time. And so I sat with her in silence, watching the fire dance.

E ventually, Tessa slept. I carried her to the bed and tucked her beneath the heavy quilt, wishing the peaceful expression on her face could carry into her waking moments.

Someone rapped on my door. I crossed the room and opened it to find Toryn with Nellie. Her face was streaked with tears. An even heavier sadness settled in my bones.

"I need to see my sister," she whispered.

I moved aside to show her Tessa's sleeping form. Brushing away her tears, she padded over to the bed and climbed in without another word. When she wrapped her arm around her sister's shoulders, I stepped out into the corridor to give them some privacy.

"What a night," Toryn said grimly.

"Where's Val? Has anyone told her?"

An odd expression crossed Toryn's face. "Niamh is looking after her."

"Niamh?" I arched a brow.

"Apparently."

"And what about the others? Are they done bringing in the bodies?"

Sighing, Toryn ran a hand down his scarred face. "They're inside the guardhouse. What in moon's name are we going to do, Kal?"

"We'll give them a proper funeral." I'd been thinking over this all night. While Tessa mourned her mother the only way she knew how, I had to consider the options for moving forward. I didn't have any choice but to plan. Endir was one of the few cities left in the fae world that had survived the war. So many people depended on the safety of these walls. I couldn't risk that tenuous peace imploding.

"At the waterfalls?" Toryn asked.

"It will demonstrate to the mortals that we have respect for their lives," I said. "We can show them we mean them no harm, that we will protect them if need be."

"You know, after this, none of them will want to leave. A lot of them already don't. This will cement it. The mists are dangerous. Endir is not."

I nodded. "So be it."

"Some of the fae aren't happy with their presence here," Toryn argued. "Too many mouths to feed, I've heard them say. Obviously, I don't agree, but we don't want someone else to follow in Asher's footsteps."

"We'll give them tasks, but we'll let them choose what they'd prefer to do. There are a few empty homes near the rear gates where they can live." I held up my hand when Toryn opened his mouth to argue. "I will not kick them out of this city."

"All right. Giving them tasks might be enough to satisfy everyone." Toryn glanced at the closed door behind me. "How is she?"

"About what you might expect."

"Both parents, gone." A familiar haunted expression crossed his face. "She's strong, though. She'll get through this, especially since she has her sister."

"If Oberon couldn't break her, nothing can."

"Her sister is damn strong too," he said with a fond smile before clearing his throat. "Get some sleep. I'll start preparations for the funeral in the morning."

I gave him my thanks and then cracked open the door of my chambers. Nellie and Tessa were fast asleep on the bed, arms wrapped tight around each other. I went over to the fire, picked up a chair, and then carried it back out into the corridor. Then I settled in and waited for a new day to dawn.

"I want to train."

It was the first thing she said the next morning when she yanked open the door to find me keeping watch in the castle corridor. Her eyes were haunted, but the determined set of her shoulders and the clenching of her hands told a different story. She'd woken from her trance. And knowing Tessa, that meant she needed to fight.

I stood, nodding. "Go to your room and change into some fighting leathers. And then meet me in the courtyard. Bring your sword."

A flicker of relief in her eyes drove aside the grief, if only for a brief moment. "I didn't think you'd agree."

"I've been waiting for you to suggest it. What about your sister?"

Her eyes glazed over once again. "She's still sleeping. I don't want to disturb her."

"That's fine. She can stay there for as long as she needs."

With a grateful nod, she took off down the corridor, still wearing my clothes. I went inside and changed into my own fighting leathers before taking a detour to let Toryn know where Nellie was, so that he could take my place standing watch in the corridor. After leaving his room, I made my way to the castle doors and pushed out into the courtyard.

Tessa was already there, waiting for me. At first, she didn't hear me approach. She stood with the sword raised before her, knees bent, arms trembling from the weight of it. There was ferocity in the tense set of her jaw and the white knuckles of her hands. With a roar, she swung the sword, and the sweet whistle of steel filled the courtyard.

"Not bad," I said, walking toward her. "Good control, but you don't need to use so much force with your arms. More legs, less arms."

She lowered the sword, and the end punched the ground. "It's heavy. I don't know how *not* to use my arms."

"Here." I unsheathed my own sword and held it before me, the dull length resting against both outstretched palms. "Hold it like this and then try to lift it over your head."

Frowning, she did as I asked. And with a deep breath, she managed to raise it into the air.

I arched a brow. "Impressive."

"I'm stronger than I look." She still stood there, chin high, with the sword above her head. Her arms began to tremble.

"You can lower it now."

She exhaled and lowered the sword back to her waist.

"Good. Now bend your knees and use your legs to propel the blade upward." I demonstrated what I meant, and then sheathed my sword, waiting.

Tessa took a deep breath, and I couldn't help but smile at her fierce determination. She had a lot to learn, not just on how to handle a sword, but on how to use it —successfully—in a fight. We had a long way to go before she could be competent, let alone exceptional. But I did not doubt her for one moment. If she wanted to do this, she would.

She bent her knees and then straightened them, pushing the sword over her head. It rose as easily as a leaf in the wind. A gasp of surprise popped from her parted lips, and she was caught so off guard that she dropped the sword at her feet.

Almost smiling, she pointed at the weapon. "That was fucking easy."

I folded my arms, feeling a little smug. "See. Use your legs more. Don't rely on just your arms."

"I understand." She nodded, her smile vanished, and she collected the sword from the ground. "But I don't think lifting a sword like that will help me chop off Oberon's head."

"One step at a time," I told her. "Now do it again."

I spent the rest of the morning taking Tessa through drills. She did everything I asked without complaint, even when it was clear her arms and legs began to ache. Most of the movements were focused on building her strength and showing her how to move in the most efficient way. After we'd been at it for several hours, her legs wobbled when I asked her to run from one end of the courtyard to the next with the sword strapped to her side.

She crashed to the ground on her way back to my side, her chest heaving and palms flat on the sand. "Stupid mortal body."

I knelt beside her. "You pushed hard today, and you've done incredibly well. You need to eat and rest, and then we'll do this again."

She brushed her hair away from her pale, sweat-soaked face and nodded. "Tomorrow?"

I smiled. "I was going to suggest we wait a few days, but yes. If you want to do this again tomorrow, we will."

"Tomorrow," she insisted.

When we went back inside the castle, Tessa went straight for the Great Hall, where she piled her plate with eggs and bacon and bread and dug in without a word. She spent the rest of the afternoon with her sister and Val, wandering through the dusty library, looking for answers I didn't think she would find, especially not in any of the books here. I'd read through the one she'd found on the gods, and there was nothing but basic information between the covers.

The next few days passed, each one the same as the one before. Tessa would knock on my door as soon as she woke, and we would spend hours training. She caught on quickly, growing stronger by the day. But that haunted look did not begin to fade.

The night before the funeral, I sat in my room alone, staring into the flames. Another round of scouts had returned with no word on Oberon's location. It was starting to feel as if he'd escaped Aesir, though how I did not know. He would have needed a ship to survive the stormy seas, and we no longer had any of those here. Not since the war. The only way off this continent was through Sunport or...the Kingdom of Storms.

But someone would have seen him cross the border. I'd had warriors patrolling it for weeks.

A light knock sounded on my door. Frowning, I stood, muscles tensing. I didn't expect anyone tonight. That could only mean one thing: bad news.

"Come in," I said.

The door creaked open, and Tessa stuck her head inside. Instantly, I relaxed.

"I didn't want to bother you, but I can't sleep."

"I'll make good company then. I can't sleep, either." I tried to hide my relief at seeing her here. We'd spent every night alone since the attack. My bed felt cold and far too large, which was utterly ridiculous. I'd slept without company for well over three hundred years. Just one night with Tessa shouldn't have changed everything. And yet...

With a timid nod, she came into the room and closed the door behind her. I tried not to stare, but her thin sleeping garment made that next to impossible. The light, see-through slip cut off at the middle of her thighs, and the little straps on her shoulders exposed the strength of her arms.

She noted the chair beside the hearth and the open book on the table near it. "How long have you been up?"

"I haven't even been to bed yet."

"It's the middle of the night." She started to move toward me, but then stopped, frowning. "Or is it? I find it hard to keep track here."

"It's late. One in the morning. I know it seems like it shouldn't matter, but we try to keep a normal sleep schedule, just like I'm sure you did in Teine." I stuffed my hands into my trouser pockets. "Why are you here, Tessa?"

She sighed. "The funeral is in the morning. I don't want to be alone."

Before I could offer her a seat beside the fire, she toed off her shoes and padded over to my bed. Silently, she slid beneath the covers and curled up on the left-hand side. Something in me softened at that. I pulled off my tunic and climbed in beside her.

Her soft hand slid around my waist. "Could you just hold me?"

I nodded and wrapped my arms around her. She gripped me tighter, burying her face in my chest, a sob choking from her throat. As the fire dimmed and the hours ticked by, I held her until, at long last, she finally found sleep.

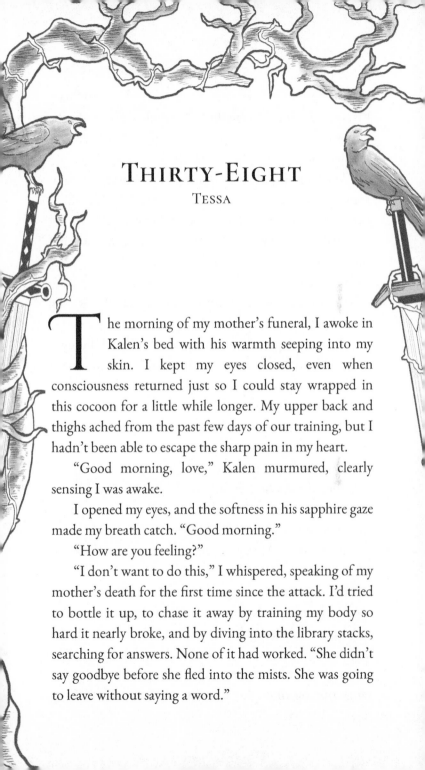

THIRTY-EIGHT
TESSA

The morning of my mother's funeral, I awoke in Kalen's bed with his warmth seeping into my skin. I kept my eyes closed, even when consciousness returned just so I could stay wrapped in this cocoon for a little while longer. My upper back and thighs ached from the past few days of our training, but I hadn't been able to escape the sharp pain in my heart.

"Good morning, love," Kalen murmured, clearly sensing I was awake.

I opened my eyes, and the softness in his sapphire gaze made my breath catch. "Good morning."

"How are you feeling?"

"I don't want to do this," I whispered, speaking of my mother's death for the first time since the attack. I'd tried to bottle it up, to chase it away by training my body so hard it nearly broke, and by diving into the library stacks, searching for answers. None of it had worked. "She didn't say goodbye before she fled into the mists. She was going to leave without saying a word."

And that was the root of it. Deep down, I was more than just grieving. The betrayal stung. I never would have left her like that. If anything, I would have done the opposite. I would have stayed, even if I hated every moment of it.

Tears slipped down my cheeks. "Every time I thought about running away from Teine, I didn't. I couldn't leave her and Nellie and Val. I stayed because of them. I searched the fucking mists, trying to find her when I thought she was lost out there. And then..."

I closed my eyes.

Kalen brushed his thumb across my cheek, clearing away the tears. "I know."

"I stabbed you," I choked out. "When I thought you'd hidden the truth about her captivity from me, I stabbed you."

"I know."

"And she just left me here without saying goodbye. I never would have seen her again!"

The words ripped out of me like trapped steam from a kettle, the boiling emotions desperate for release. I gripped the sheets and shook my head, hating my anger. I didn't want to feel this way. This twisted grief was tearing me apart inside. My heart felt like tattered ribbons, the edges jagged, as if cut by a serrated knife.

Kalen just held me against him. He didn't try to talk me down or wipe away my worst thoughts and fears. He just let me *feel* them. He listened as I talked. And when it was finally time to rise, I did feel a little better. The burning sensation in my heart—that feeling of sharp fangs ripping through me—wasn't gone, but I did feel like I could breathe a little easier, as if I could actually think.

I started to feel a bit more alive.

We held the funeral at the Ivory Cliff Falls, and at least a hundred others—a mixture of fae and mortals—had gathered to bid farewell to the dead. Armed warriors stood along the perimeter, gazes focused out on the mists. Toryn had set out a grand table with ornamental legs, and ten glass jars were lined up in a row down the center of it. Each one held the ashen remains of our loved ones.

A Druid, a man with deep black hair and several rings along his jawline, stepped up to the table, facing the crowd. His long strands blended into his midnight robe, and a swirling tattoo glistened on his hands, etched in a silver ink that matched the color of the moon.

I'd donned a simple black dress, as had Nellie and Val on either side of me. I held on to them both as tightly as I could, but it was Kalen's steady presence just behind me that kept me from breaking down into tears.

"We've come here today to mourn the loss of ten precious souls," Druid Balfor began in a calming voice that sounded like a river running over stones. "Their time has been cut short, but in your grief, you must remember they will never truly perish. On this table, we have their essences, and we will give it back to the waters of this world. They will become one with the earth, and they will forever live on, not just in our hearts, but in the very ground beneath us. Now, repeat after me:

Grant, O Life, the strength to carry on;

And in that strength, give us understanding;

And in understanding, let us know love;

The love of all existences."

"The love of all existences," all the fae repeated. Even Kalen spoke the prayer in his rumbling voice. I whispered the words myself, though I'd never known much about the Druids. In Albyria and Teine, the only deity we worshipped was Oberon himself.

"Now," Druid Balfor said, casting his gaze around us. "We need a loved one for each of these souls."

I stepped forward, along with seven other humans and two fae. One by one, we took a jar and carried it over to the waterfall, scattering the ashes into the lake. When it came my time, my hands shook so hard I worried I might spill the ashes before I even reached the water.

Nellie moved to my side and placed a hand on mine. I met her gaze and nodded, a lump in my throat. Together, we held the jar over the lake. I closed my eyes, picturing my mother's kind smile. I'd always thought of her as so strong, so impossible to ruffle. She took everything the fae threw at us, and it never broke her. And yet, she must have been struggling for so very long. The world became blurry around me, and I shuddered.

"Goodbye, mother," Nellie whispered, her words almost drowned out by the thundering falls.

My tongue felt as if it were made of sand, but I managed to choke out, "Goodbye."

Nellie and I tipped our mother's ashes into the swirling lake, and we watched until every last speck of her was gone.

After I changed out of my funeral attire, I met Kalen in the courtyard for another round of brutal training. I hadn't taken a day off since we'd begun, and my muscles screamed every time I took a step. That wouldn't stop me, though. I wanted to learn to fight. The sooner, the better.

He smiled as I stalked toward him with the tip of my sword dragging a line through the sand. "You're going to blunt the sharpness doing that."

"I thought it might look intimidating."

Kalen chuckled. "It's quite the sight. But you'd be better off taking advantage of people's perceptions of you."

"And that means?" I asked, coming to a stop before him.

"You're mortal. People will underestimate you. I already have numerous times."

I smiled a little at that. With the funeral over, I was feeling much more like myself again. The grief still weighed upon my heart, but it wasn't quite as heavy as it had been. A smile didn't feel as impossible as it had before.

"So you're saying I've surprised you with my abilities. In a good way."

"Now you're just fishing for compliments."

"And I will hook my teeth into you until you give me one."

He arched a brow. "Don't tempt me."

I blushed, feeling a flicker of desire spark inside me once more. Kalen had not pushed for anything from me since the attack. He'd done nothing, not even gaze at me with that fire in his eyes. I'd even slept in his bed last night, and all he'd done was hold me close. He'd asked *nothing* from me, and yet he'd given so much.

Not for the first time, I tried to conjure the words to express just how much his steady, understanding presence had helped me. To thank him for what he'd done. The training, the listening, the lack of pressure and questions and just plain words. But I didn't know how to say all that without breaking down again, and I was done with tears.

So I just let myself smile. "You like to be nibbled. Noted."

"You could do anything to me, and I'd like it, love."

Heat seared me. My sword thumped onto the ground when it slipped from my fingers, and I took two steps toward him just as he strode toward me. My mouth was on his a second later. His tongue slid between my lips, his hands snaking around to my backside. A moan crept from my throat as he lifted me from the ground.

"Ahem." Someone coughed from behind us.

Cheeks flaming, I released my grip on Kalen's shoulders, and he lowered me to the ground. Toryn approached with a raven perched on his shoulder. It was all black with a single white tail feather. Not Boudica then.

"I hate to interrupt," he said, shooting me an apologetic smile, "but a raven arrived with a message. It's for you, I think."

Boudica swirled in from the sky, her all-black wings flexing against the wind. She flew toward us in wide circles before landing softly on Kalen's shoulder. The bird on Toryn's shoulder let out a strange cawing sound, and then Boudica answered, cocking her head.

"What's going on?" I asked.

Kalen's lips flattened. "Some ravens are trained to communicate. This is one of them."

"What she's saying?" Toryn asked.

Kalen turned to Boudica and whispered something to her. A moment later, she nuzzled her head against his cheek. The muscles around his jaw tightened.

"It's Morgan," he said in a low voice. "She's being held captive by Oberon and she needs help."

"Morgan?" I asked, alarmed.

He nodded. "He's hiding out in the mountains behind Albyria. In a cave, apparently. With his Mortal Queen. I didn't know that was an option for him. Those peaks are said to be impassable."

"They are, mostly," I said. "But there's a path on the western side. The mountains aren't as dangerous there."

Toryn frowned. "Or Morgan could be lying at Oberon's request."

"Hmm." Kalen rubbed his jaw. "Perhaps. She also said the full power of the god now resides in that onyx stone necklace. But she could just be saying that to lure us there."

"For what, though?"

Toryn shot me a frank look. "We have something he needs. You're the vessel, remember? I'm surprised it's taken him this long to make a move."

"True, but..." I glanced from Toryn to Kalen. "Even if it's a trap, doesn't that mean he'll still be there, or at least somewhere nearby? You've been looking for him for days, and you have no leads at all. This might be our only chance to track him down."

Kalen folded his arms. "*Our* only chance?"

"Absolutely. I'm going with you."

"Tessa."

"I thought we just established this might be a trap," Toryn said, and then he shook his head. "No, not might. *Most definitely is*. It's absolutely a trap."

"If we're anticipating a trap, it's less of a trap," I argued.

"The word 'trap' is starting to lose all meaning," Kalen muttered.

Toryn and I looked at each other. I pressed my lips together.

And then he whispered, "It's a trap."

I cracked a smile and so did he. Laughter bubbled up inside of me for the first time in days. Toryn tipped back his head, his chuckles blending with mine. Kalen just stared at us with an arched brow, but a moment later, he joined in. Our laughter wound through the courtyard like a song.

The tension in my shoulders released another notch. And when our laughter finally died, there were different tears in my eyes. They washed away another mark of pain.

"All right." Kalen held up his hands. "This is what's

going to happen. I'll look into this, using Boudica to scout ahead. Only a few of us can go. A larger party will be more likely to catch his attention, and I'd rather approach him from behind. If he has soldiers with him, I'll come straight back here so we can gather our own army to send against him."

I opened my mouth to volunteer.

"Tessa," he warned before I could speak.

"No, listen," I insisted. "I've spent my entire life staring up at those mountains. I know which path we should take. You'd be better off with me there. And besides..." I sucked in a sharp breath. "I could take the Mortal Blade with us."

Kalen's gaze pierced through me. "I don't like it. There's no barrier stopping me from reaching him anymore. I could just as easily chop off his head."

"Perhaps." I folded my arms. "But I want another shot at him, same as you."

Over the past weeks, I'd found a way to temper my self-destructive anger, but it still burned bright inside of me. It would never be fully quenched. And so, if I could not be the one to take down Oberon, I at least wanted to be there when the light in his eyes died. Kalen met my stare, unblinking.

"You say you know a path," he began.

Toryn scoffed. "Please don't tell me you're considering this."

"Tessa needs to be there," he said with a knowing glint in his eye. "She's coming with us."

THIRTY-NINE

TESSA

Nellie hovered in my doorway, watching me strap leather armor over my shoulders. She clutched the wood while worry danced in her eyes.

"There's nothing I can say to talk you out of this, is there?" she asked.

"I'm afraid not." I cinched the belt around my waist and slid the Mortal Blade into the sheath. The real one, this time. Kalen and I would journey ahead to the mountains, along with Niamh, Fenella, and Alastair. The others would wait here. Someone needed to keep an eye on things in Endir, since tensions still ran high.

Every member of the Mist Guard had argued against it at first, each one offering to go in our place. The king should stay behind, protected, they argued. Another scout should investigate instead, they suggested. But Kalen and I just looked at each other, and we knew. We had to be the ones to do this.

If Oberon was on that mountain, we needed to find him ourselves.

"You're risking your life for that fool," Nellie said.

Startled, I met her gaze. "Kalen?"

"No, Oberon. You don't have to give him any more of your time. Stay here. Enjoy your life with us. Be free and happy, and never think of him again." Her pleading eyes tugged at my heart, and I wished I could give her what she wanted.

Sighing, I crossed the room and took her hands in mine. "I can't do that, Nellie. Not when I carry his mark on my skin. I *must* face him. One last time. And I will end this for all of us—or Kalen will."

"I just," she whispered, "wish you wouldn't do this to yourself."

"Do what? Fight Oberon?"

She searched my gaze with such intensity, it shot dread through my heart. Her fingers tightened around my hands. "Those mountains. You don't want to go there."

"What are you talking about?"

"You've been there before. I know you don't remember, and for the longest time, I tried to help you see, but now...I think it's just better if you don't. You can move on. Be happy. With Kalen."

I swallowed and pulled my fingers from her grip. "When did I go there?"

"When you were very small. With father."

Something rumbled in my chest, and a strange whimper rose from the back of my throat. Eyes wide, I pressed my hand to my neck and swallowed down the noise. I didn't understand where that had come from. I didn't know why my vision swam and my ears rang with the sound of a thousand bells.

Nellie's shoulders slumped. "I'm sorry. I shouldn't have said anything."

I pressed my hand tighter against my chest and felt the erratic beat of my heart. "Why do I feel this way? What happened out there? Why can't I remember?"

"You pushed it from your mind. I think you did it to protect yourself from the truth. That's why you can't go back there, Tessa. After what's happened with Mother, I think you need some time to heal."

Kalen's muscular form filled the doorframe. "Are you ready to go, Tessa?"

I kept my eyes glued to my sister's face. "Tell me what happened."

"I can't." She shook her head, her voice cracking. "I won't do that to you. You need to remember it yourself, and not right now. Just trust me. Don't go to those mountains."

I looked from Nellie to Kalen and then back to Nellie again. Her words rang with a truth that dug into the depths of my mind—like one of the tools I'd once used on the chasm walls—chipping away at my tenuous grip on reality. For a long time, I'd known there was *something* wrong, like a shadow that shifted in the corner of my vision. But whenever I turned to look, nothing was there. I'd known this, and I'd pretended it didn't exist. Nothing was wrong. Everything was fine.

But looking at Nellie now, I was forced to face the truth.

Those mountains held memories that were so terrible

I'd hidden them deep in my mind. But I could not turn away from this. It was time.

"I'm going with Kalen," I said, stepping away from her. "I'll be back soon. I promise."

Kalen and I met the others at the stables. Alastair, Fenella, and Niamh were armed to the teeth, and their black leather armor turned their forms into shifting shadows that blended with the mists. As I approached them, Alastair shot me an easy grin.

"Glad to see you're with us." He suddenly tossed me an apple. I reacted instantly to catch it. "Some extra food for your pack."

"Thanks. Glad to see you too." I slid the pack around to my front and shoved the apple inside. "How'd you decide which of you would come, anyway?"

Niamh slung an arm around my shoulders and steered me over to the horses that waited beside the stable doors. "Easy. Toryn's still healing. While Gaven is incredibly powerful, he's better at politics than battles. And the people of Endir trust him. He needed to stay."

I had to admit that as much as I wanted Toryn on this journey with us, I was glad he was one of the Mist Guard staying behind. He would keep Val and Nellie safe.

When we reached the horses, there were—thankfully —enough for everyone, and Kalen led one over to me. I started at the sight of his sleek black mane streaked with silver. He looked just like Midnight, but...that was impossible. A chasm opened within my heart as I gazed into the horse's bottomless black eyes. Midnight had been so brave, so selfless. If only I could go back in time and stop him from helping me. He deserved so much better.

"This is Silver," Kalen said, handing me the reins.

I stroked the horse's nose, trying not to show my disappointment. I'd known this could not be Midnight, and yet...for a second, I'd let myself hope. "Hello, Silver."

He nuzzled my hand, and before the tears could fill my eyes, I blinked them away. As the others climbed onto their horses, I leaned in and whispered, "I promise to look after you. And if I run into danger, please don't follow."

"Are you talking to your horse?" Fenella called out as she steered toward me.

"Yes, just sorting some things out."

Alastair's horse trotted up beside us. "You know, most horses don't know how to speak Aesirian."

I glanced up at him. "Is Silver not a joint eater, like the others were?"

"Silver is a just normal horse, I'm afraid," Kalen said with a soft voice, as if he understood the direction of my thoughts. "All of these are."

"Ah." I rubbed Silver's snout again. "Well, he's quite the beauty, whatever he is."

After climbing onto the horse's back, I followed Kalen and the others out the city gates and into the heavy mist. With no more buildings around us, the world was an endless landscape of gray. It was as if nothing else existed but the fog. Out here, everything was gone.

As the horses took off at a gallop, a chill went through me. It had been easy to forget what it was like being out in the nothingness of this place. The city had felt like a different world, one where mist and life existed in tandem. But beyond the safety of the walls, only death remained.

Time passed by in a blur of thundering hooves and foggy haze. When my thighs started screaming, we stopped beside a river to let the horses drink and to give me a brief respite. As I rubbed my legs, I reminded myself that my training needed to be focused on more than just weaponry. I was no more used to spending hours on horseback than I had been the last time. I knew how to ride now, but that didn't mean it was pleasant.

After resting and nibbling on some bread and dried meats, we resumed our charge through the darkness. The hours crawled by, each one slower than the last. At long last, the vague forms of towering mountains rose through the mists, and Kalen slowed his horse to a stop at the front of the group.

I'd never been happier to see those jagged peaks.

I tugged on the reins, bringing my horse to a halt beside his. "I thought I'd be able to see the chasm by now."

"It's just over there." He pointed at the nearby ground as the rest of our party slowed their horses to a stop beside us.

All I saw was endless gray fog. Only a hint of orange pierced the shadows.

"Last time I could see it so clearly," I said. "Even though the darkness is permanent here, the sun from the Kingdom of Light once shone through the mist and showed the path to the bridge. Now, the only thing I can see is..."

The mountain.

Memories suddenly rushed into my mind in fragments. A small girl ran through the mists, screaming. Her long golden hair whipped behind her like frayed ribbons. Her terrified eyes burned holes through my skull. She was so small, so helpless. And then she became me, and I became her. Terror churned within me like a violent storm. In my mind's eye, I fell from the horse and clawed at the ground, but my hands made contact with nothing at all. They plunged through the earth, sucking me inside the dirt until all that existed was a deep black nothingness.

I blinked, and the image whispered away.

Panicked, I looked around. Niamh and Fenella stared back at me, and Alastair gave me a gentle smile. I loosened my tight grip on the reins. I was still here on the horse. Everything was fine.

"Tessa?" Kalen edged his horse closer. "Are you all right?"

I opened my mouth to explain, but I didn't fully understand it myself. Had that little girl been me? And if so, what did it even mean? Nellie said I had experienced something terrible in the mountains, and maybe this was it, but...it still didn't make sense to me. How would I have crossed the bridge that young? Oberon or his guards would have spotted me.

"I just..." I sighed and shook my head. "I don't know. I may have remembered something from my past, but it's not important. Let's keep moving."

He didn't look convinced, but he didn't push, either. I was grateful for that. "Which direction should we go?"

"It's too dark for me to see." I frowned at the looming mountain range. "Remember where we used to meet? We need to go to that hole in the wall."

With a nod, Kalen took the lead again. Our progress was slower now that we'd neared the Kingdom of Light... which I supposed wasn't called that anymore. These lands were Kalen's now. The Kingdom of Shadow had swallowed the light in its mists. Frowning, I gazed up at the distant orange haze. The sun still remained above Alybria, even though the barrier had been destroyed. Why would it be there and not out here? This had once been the Kingdom of Light as well, and the sun had shone brightly in the sky until the day Kalen had lost control of his mist.

I started to ask the Mist Guard what they thought, but Kalen drew his horse up short when Boudica landed on his shoulder, back from scouting ahead.

He turned to us with a frown. "There are light fae warriors just ahead. They've set up a war camp at the base of the mountain, right in our path to Tessa's route through the mountains."

"A war camp?" Fenella asked sharply. "How many are there? Did Boudica spot Oberon with them?"

"A hundred or so, by Boudica's estimation. There's no sign of Oberon, but that doesn't mean he's not in one of the tents."

Niamh rubbed the bottom of her scar, eyes alight. "Could we fight our way through them?"

"It's a war camp, but they're not preparing for battle." Kalen gazed into the darkness, the mists transforming his powerfully built body into a shadowy silhouette. "They must be some of the light fae who survived the fire. They fled here to find safety, not war."

Fenella clucked her tongue. "Are they civilians?"

"They're wearing armor. So I would guess not."

"Then use your power against them." She motioned in the general direction of the camp. "They're our enemies, and they're in our way. Call upon that power of yours and kill them all."

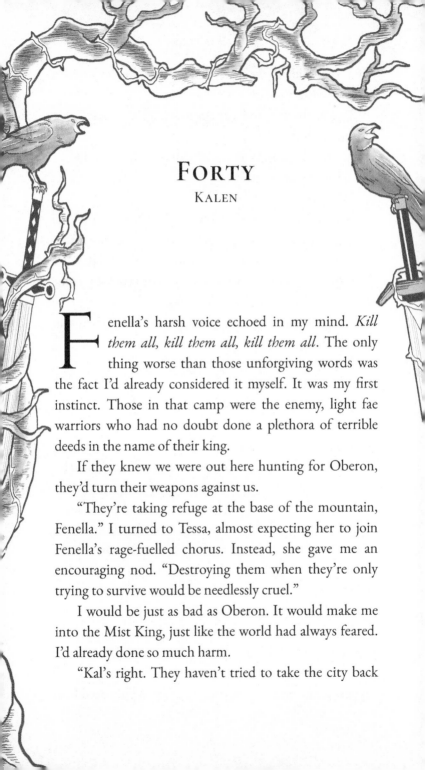

FORTY
KALEN

Fenella's harsh voice echoed in my mind. *Kill them all, kill them all, kill them all.* The only thing worse than those unforgiving words was the fact I'd already considered it myself. It was my first instinct. Those in that camp were the enemy, light fae warriors who had no doubt done a plethora of terrible deeds in the name of their king.

If they knew we were out here hunting for Oberon, they'd turn their weapons against us.

"They're taking refuge at the base of the mountain, Fenella." I turned to Tessa, almost expecting her to join Fenella's rage-fuelled chorus. Instead, she gave me an encouraging nod. "Destroying them when they're only trying to survive would be needlessly cruel."

I would be just as bad as Oberon. It would make me into the Mist King, just like the world had always feared. I'd already done so much harm.

"Kal's right. They haven't tried to take the city back

from the soldiers we sent there. I say we leave them alone," Alastair added.

Fenella huffed and turned away. "Talk some sense into them, Niamh."

"If we don't fight them," Niamh said, "how are we going to get past them?"

We all turned to Tessa.

She shifted uncomfortably on her horse. "I'm the wrong person to ask. I was stuck in Teine my entire life."

"But you know more about those mountains than we do," Alastair said. "That's why you wanted to come along."

"No, I wanted to come along so I can stab Oberon in the fucking heart."

I couldn't help but smile.

"Fair," Alastair chuckled.

"So, you're saying we have no other choice," Fenella said, narrowing her eyes. "Because we either have to go through the army, or we turn back and return to Endir empty-handed. Oberon gets to live and bring back his god."

I closed my eyes. A magic deep inside my bones tugged me toward those mountains while my mother's voice whispered in the back of my mind. I'd made a vow, and now that I knew exactly where Oberon was, I didn't have a choice. I had to go forward, one way or the other. Returning to Endir wasn't an option for me.

It wouldn't be the first time I'd spilled blood—a lot of blood—to influence the future of this world. The ends justified the means. At least, that was what I tried to tell myself when the memories of screams and destroyed flesh haunted my midnight hours. I'd taken so many lives hundreds of years ago, and I'd done it again only a few weeks past. On and on and on it went. When would this end?

Tessa feared she was a descendent of the God of Death, but I was the one whose hands had drained so much life from this world.

"Kal?" Niamh's familiar voice cut through the fog in my mind. The four of them sat on their horses, waiting for an answer, but I didn't have one. As much as I hated death, I could not turn away from this fucking camp.

Tessa speared me with her eyes. She nodded almost imperceptibly, as if she knew—as if she understood the ghosts that haunted my thoughts. "We could approach the mountain from the other side and cross over the western peaks."

"Aren't they impossible to traverse?" Fenella asked.

Tessa smiled thinly. "The southern mountain range is definitely impassable, but this area isn't as bad, according to what I've read about it. We can go around the base of Mount Lumican, which is that big peak over there, and then climb the smaller mountains to reach Oberon's cave. Or where I think it might be."

Alastair nodded. "Sounds good to me."

But Fenella wasn't as easily convinced. "What if you're wrong?"

"Then we'll try something else," Tessa said. "But I think it's worth a shot if it means Kalen doesn't have to kill hundreds of people."

"Kal, it's your call," Niamh said.

The cost of being king. So many envied the power of

absolute authority. But with that power came a responsibility so great that it became stifling at times. Make a mistake—one wrong move—and the aftermath could be cataclysmic, particularly now.

I could sweep through that army within minutes, and we could be on our way up the cliff-side path toward Oberon's hiding place. If the King of Light decided to fight us in the future, he'd have fewer warriors to call to arms. My people would never have to worry about light fae again.

But being here now took me back to that moment when I'd stood in the swaying grass, facing Oberon, and sent my power to collide with his. I'd chosen war over surrender, brutality over mercy. There were so many other choices I could have made instead of charging my army across the Kingdom of Light and destroying everything in our path.

There were so few fae left in Aesir. If I kept killing and killing and killing, what would I even be fighting to protect? A realm of bones and nothing more.

Closing my eyes, I said, "We will go the long way."

Fenella snapped her teeth together, but she didn't argue. I took the lead, with Tessa riding by my side. Niamh and Alastair rounded out the back. We approached the mountain as quietly as we could. As we drew nearer, sounds of life drifted toward us on the wind. We heard the murmur of voices, and the crunch of an axe against wood. Horses whinnied and fire crackled, and just beneath the hum of it all, a fifer played a mournful tune. A familiar song that all fae knew, one that celebrated the souls of the dead.

"You made the right decision," Tessa said, glancing over at me. She held the reins loosely in her hands, and she smiled. "Those light fae don't deserve to die."

"I worried the vow would make me stomp them down anyway. And it still might, if this route is as impossible as Fenella seems to think. But we should remain quiet. If we can hear them, they could hear us."

A hush fell across our party as we neared the base of the mountain where the fae were camping. Through the haze, fires spit sparks into the sky, and the fifer's mournful song of the dead wound through the hills, growing larger and more abundant by the moment. At long last, the distant sight of the camp faded from view as we followed the base of the mountain to the west.

Tessa released a breath when we came upon a sandy shoreline. Water lapped against the horses' hooves, thick with the scents of salt and fish. The wind ruffled the hair around her face, and for a moment, I was captivated by the light that danced across her skin. Here, at the edge of Aesir, the mists were gone, and my body begged to take it in. It was the first time I'd stood in a sun-drenched world, free of mist, in centuries.

And yet, I could not take my eyes off of *her*.

"You're fucking breathtaking, love."

She started, and a brilliant blush filled her cheeks. Such a deep scarlet. The darkness had hidden the true depths of it, and now that I could see it for what it was, I wanted to relish it.

"You're not bad to look at, either."

"Get a room, you two," Alastair said with a laugh as he edged his horse up beside ours and tipped back his head to face the sun. His earrings glinted beneath the light. "For the love of the moon, I forgot what this felt like."

I caught the look of surprise on Tessa's face, so I explained, "The rest of the coastline isn't like this. The mist extends out into the sea for miles, and I haven't sailed anywhere since the war."

"Why would it be any different here?" she asked.

"If I were to guess," Niamh said, nodding at the mountains behind us, "it's the same damn reason the sun persists over Albyria. Oberon's doing something."

"And when we kill him..." Tessa trailed off.

"The Kingdom of Storms will be the only place in Albyria with a sun," I said, the grim certainty settling in my gut like old milk. Aesir would never be the same, even if we won. It was what I had wanted for so long—to see my mists storm across the last shred of Oberon's land.

But now that it had finally happened, the victory tasted bitter.

It didn't matter that fae and humans had once found a way to banish the gods. Those ancient beings still haunted these lands, destroying everything they could, until the only thing left behind was mist, darkness, and death.

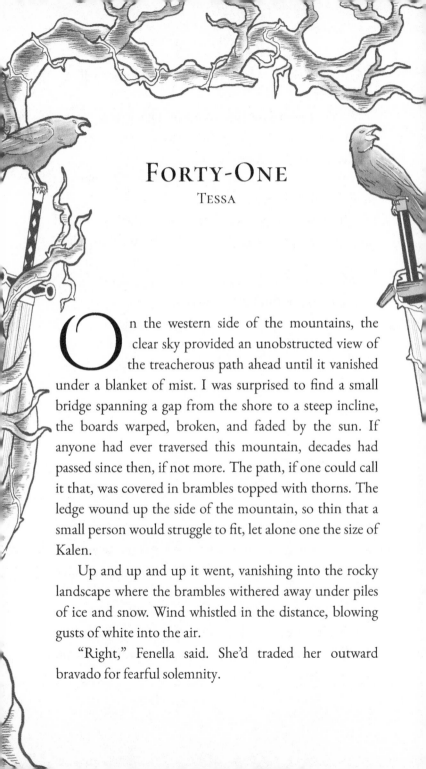

FORTY-ONE

TESSA

On the western side of the mountains, the clear sky provided an unobstructed view of the treacherous path ahead until it vanished under a blanket of mist. I was surprised to find a small bridge spanning a gap from the shore to a steep incline, the boards warped, broken, and faded by the sun. If anyone had ever traversed this mountain, decades had passed since then, if not more. The path, if one could call it that, was covered in brambles topped with thorns. The ledge wound up the side of the mountain, so thin that a small person would struggle to fit, let alone one the size of Kalen.

Up and up and up it went, vanishing into the rocky landscape where the brambles withered away under piles of ice and snow. Wind whistled in the distance, blowing gusts of white into the air.

"Right," Fenella said. She'd traded her outward bravado for fearful solemnity.

Alastair let out a low whistle. "This journey will not be pleasant."

Kalen regarded me for a moment. I knew what he was going to say.

You can turn back now.

"You can turn around," he said quietly. "No one will think you're a coward."

"Just leave it to us. We'll find him." Alastair swung off his horse and gave mine a pat on the rump. "Silver here will get you back to Endir. Just steer clear of that army."

"You'll need to try harder if you want to get rid of me. I need to see this through to the end."

My boots hit the stone. I found the apple in my pack and fed it to Silver, stroking his snout as he made quick work of his snack. He and the other horses could not follow us into the mountains, and we wouldn't leave them stranded alone. It would take us days to reach the other side, and that was even if we managed to do it.

It was time to say goodbye.

Fenella gave me a curious stare when I whispered goodbye and watched Silver charge off into the mist with the other horses. He would return to Endir, where it was safe. My heart heavy, I sat on a boulder and chewed on some dried meat while Kalen and the others sharpened their swords. The song of rock against steel rang in the air, a warning sound that chilled my bones. We'd avoided the light fae army, but we were preparing for battle all the same.

"You know, you talk to that animal like a shadow fae would," Fenella remarked as she settled down beside me. "You sure you don't have fae blood?"

So Kalen hadn't told the others our suspicions about my ancestry. That was just as well. "I'm pretty sure that horse didn't understand a word I said. It just makes me feel better."

"Hmm." She nodded at my back, where we'd strapped my sword. Already the weight felt burdensome. "This journey will be long and arduous, even without carrying a weapon like that on your back. You might want to leave it here. The Mortal Blade is enough to protect you. Plus, you have the four of us."

"I only have a handful of gemstones to power the Mortal Blade, and I don't want to waste them if we get attacked by someone else," I said, gazing up at the towering mountain peaks. "Besides, it's too small. I want something bigger."

She arched her brow and whisked out her double daggers. Both were smaller than the Mortal Blade, but the sharp edges gleamed beneath the eversun's orange light. Without even blinking, Fenella spun the daggers in her hands, and then pressed one blade against my throat while the other hit my back. A glittering smile curled her lips.

"Small is just as deadly. In fact, it can often be deadlier because no one sees us coming. But you should know that better than anyone, shouldn't you?"

I cut my eyes her way. "Wonderful. Thank you. Can you take your dagger off my throat now? You've made your point."

"Fenella," Kalen warned, shoving up to his feet.

"Oh, relax." She rolled her eyes and spun the blades

away. "I'm just trying to show her she doesn't need to haul around a heavy sword."

Frowning, I stood. I glanced at Alastair, who winked. The bastard knew exactly what I was thinking. I took a step back on the rock to position myself just behind Fenella. And then I whipped out my sword and pressed the tip against the back of her neck.

"Looks like you were right. I *can* sneak up on people."

Fenella laughed. "Well played, Tessa. Well played."

I didn't mention that my arms still strained from the weight of the sword and that I fumbled a bit as I tried to shove the blade back into the sheath on my back. Instead, I took a seat beside her and turned to gaze at the glimmering sea. The waters were still, and the sun transformed the crystal blue into a blanket of a thousand stars. I'd only ever seen the sea in my dreams, and it was far more breathtaking in person. If only we could just stay here for a while...

But unless we found Oberon, these seas would turn to blood.

After resting, we crossed the rickety bridge and started up the mountain pass. Alastair went first and hacked at the brambles to create a gap big enough for us to walk through. Still, thorns and twisting branches scraped against our leather armor. Our progress was slow as the rocks crunched beneath our boots.

Despite the eversun beating down on our heads, the air grew colder as we journeyed higher up the mountain. A steady wind pushed from the front, forcing me to bend my body forward, just to give me a brief respite. The hours crawled by. My legs and back ached more and more with every step. With ragged breaths, I sank onto a rock when we finally found a small perch to rest for a few moments.

Kalen sat beside me and handed me some bread. "You're doing well."

Niamh shielded her eyes from the sun and pointed at a distant ridge shrouded in mist. "It looks like there's an outcropping there with some shelter. We could stop and camp there for the night...or day, I suppose. What time is it, anyway?"

"It's evening," I said, without even glancing up at the sky. I could tell from the angle of the light, and I knew the sun's path better than I knew the back of my hand. "A few hours away from what we would consider nighttime. How can you see a ridge, anyway? It's dark up there."

"Fae eyesight." She tapped the side of her face. "We can be there in a few hours."

My entire body groaned at the thought of hiking for even an hour longer. I chewed on the bread, willing my limbs to do what I needed them to do. I did not want to be the one to slow the others down.

So, after a brief rest, we continued onward. The path grew skinny, and the cold stung my cheeks when the mists finally descended. The wind battered my aching body. Shivering, I focused on Kalen, just in front of me. He was all I could see in the sudden darkness. I watched his boots as the rocks crumbled down the cliff-side on our right.

And so I just kept moving, step after laborious step. Exhaustion burned my eyes, and my lungs struggled to pull in enough air. Still, I carried on.

I would not give up. I couldn't.

I took another step, weariness tugging at my eyelids. My boot found nothing but air. I cried out as I stumbled forward, and my foot skidded against the path, lurching me sideways. The ground rose up fast, hurtling toward my face. With a scream, I threw out my hands to brace my fall.

Pain raced through my fingers as they hit the ground. My body tumbled to the side, rolling me off the path— and straight into nothing but cold, thin air.

Rocks blurred by me as I soared off the ledge, my braid whipping around my head. Kalen's roar cut through my heart. Numbing fear flooded my veins. For a moment, the world slowed around me as the reality of my situation sank in.

I'd fallen off the side of the mountain. Soon, I would hit the ground.

Terror knifed my heart. My arms flailed around me as I desperately tried to find something—anything—to grab onto. The raging wind snatched my feet and tossed me sideways. Another scream ripped from my throat, but no sound came out. Fear took my voice and swallowed it whole.

I looked down to meet my fate. And there it was. The face of my death storming up at me from the depths of the shadowy mist.

Two seconds to go.

One.

I sucked in a breath and braced myself.

My shoulder slammed into the ground, and my head snapped to the side, colliding with stone.

The world went dark.

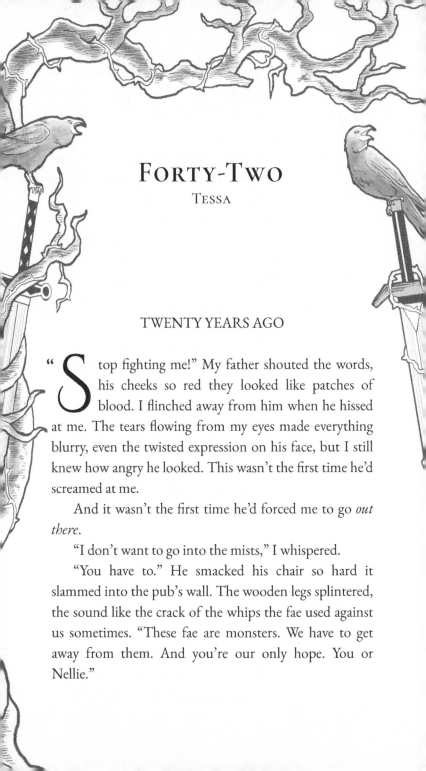

FORTY-TWO
TESSA

TWENTY YEARS AGO

"Stop fighting me!" My father shouted the words, his cheeks so red they looked like patches of blood. I flinched away from him when he hissed at me. The tears flowing from my eyes made everything blurry, even the twisted expression on his face, but I still knew how angry he looked. This wasn't the first time he'd screamed at me.

And it wasn't the first time he'd forced me to go *out there*.

"I don't want to go into the mists," I whispered.

"You have to." He smacked his chair so hard it slammed into the pub's wall. The wooden legs splintered, the sound like the crack of the whips the fae used against us sometimes. "These fae are monsters. We have to get away from them. And you're our only hope. You or Nellie."

"Not Nellie," I said through clenched teeth, my hands shaking so hard that they rattled my skull. "Leave her alone."

"She's stronger than you are," he said with a curled lip before pacing the warped floorboards in front of me. Just like the other times, he'd dragged me here in the middle of the night while my mother and Nellie slept, where no one could hear him shout at me. None of the candles were lit, so creeping shadows filled the entire dusty room.

I closed my eyes. "Please. Leave Nellie out of this."

He wound his hand around my arm and clutched it so tightly that pain cut through my bones. "Then come with me now. If you don't, I'll take her instead."

His words stabbed me in the heart. The last thing I wanted was for him to throw Nellie, only three years old, out into those mists to fend for herself against the monsters. And he knew it.

He'd only done it once, and I'd never let him do it again. She was stronger than me in so many ways, even as little as she was, but the power had warped her in a far different way than it had me. I'd never forget the terror in her eyes when she'd shown me what he'd forced her to do. I wouldn't put her through that again.

Slowly, I opened my eyes and glared up at him—at his stupid, beet-red face. "I'll tell Mother."

"Listen to me." He shoved his finger into my face. "You have the power to save the people of Teine."

"So do you."

He shook his head. "I've been trapped behind Oberon's barrier all my life. It's dulled the magic in my veins, and I'll never get it back. But you and Nellie...

you're young. You need a little push to bring it back to life. Being born behind the barrier has dulled what you can do, but..." His eyes sparked with glee. "It's not too late. We will turn you into a force to be reckoned with."

I did not want to be a force to be reckoned with. All I wanted was to play with the other village children. Splash in the river. Roll in the fields. Race through the woods with the dirt sticking to my bare feet. The fae who lived up the hill were scary, but they mostly left the children alone, especially the girls who would one day be presented in front of Oberon.

I might one day be the king's bride.

But not if he caught me sneaking over the wall. He'd kill me and my father.

"Why can't I just be normal?" I asked.

His anger vanished, replaced by something softer. It was the face he used in front of Mother. He liked to wear a mask so that she'd never suspect what he did out there in the mists. He knelt before me and took my hand in his. My fingers looked so small against his palm. "Because you have a power that can help this village, Tessa. Don't you want to save us?"

I winced and glanced away. "No."

His expression hardened.

"Fine. Just remember you made me do this." Roughly, he hauled me from the chair and tossed me over his shoulder before kicking open the front door.

"Stop!" I screamed, flailing my legs at him. This time, I didn't stay quiet, just like he always asked. I hoped someone heard me this time.

But he just held me tight, carrying me away from the

village. I stared down at the ground beneath his feet with sobs choking my throat. I hated him for this. I hated him so much that I wanted to claw his skin and bite him so hard that he would bleed. Deep down, I knew this wasn't a normal feeling. I had asked the other girls if they ever felt this way. They all looked at me like I was crazy. Even Nellie didn't get this mad, and she'd been through the same thing.

My helpless anger only intensified as we approached the wall behind the village. I braced myself for what I knew would come next. He'd only done this to me a few times before, but already I'd memorized every step of this dance. I opened my mouth to beg him not to do it, but no words came out. He'd made up his mind. It was me or Nellie, and I'd never choose this awful thing for my little sister.

And so I clenched my teeth as tight as I could to brace myself.

"Good luck," he said.

My father threw me over the wall.

For a brief moment in time, my body felt weightless. I soared through the air, from the humid heat and into a wall of cooling mist. My arms splayed out on either side of me. If only I had wings, I could fly away from here.

But instead, I slammed into the dirt. My head hit the ground and darkness filled my mind.

T woke to the sound of inhuman shrieking. Blearily, I cracked open my eyes and peered through the dense fog, but I couldn't see anything. Everything was so dark, and the wet mist clogged my throat as I took in frantic gasps of air.

I pushed up onto my feet and whirled toward the wall. It towered over me. Too tall for me to climb without footholds. And through a small gap in the wood, my father watched.

"A shadowfiend is coming," I pleaded with him. "Father, please. Let me come back in."

With a voice devoid of any emotion, he answered, "You can come back at any time. All you have to do is spread your wings and fly."

But I could not fly. I'd *never* been able to fly any of the times he'd tossed me into the mists. Eventually, he'd grow bored and annoyed with me, and he'd throw me a rope to scrabble up.

"I can't," I whispered as tears spilled down my cheeks.

His eye narrowed in the gap. "The five winged gods could all fly. You have their power in your blood. *Use it.*"

My knees knocked together when another shriek sounded, this time closer. I wound my hands around my back to feel the tiny knobs—scars. A month ago, he'd tried to carve the wings out of me, but that hadn't worked any better than this did. Even if he was right and we were decedents of some long-lost god, I *could not fly*.

Thundering footsteps raced toward me, and yet I still could see nothing but the swirling mists. Clenching my hands into fists, I aimed my attention on my back, straining to shove the wings from my skin. I pushed and pushed and pushed. A little tickle was the only answer. Terror snaking through me, I sobbed.

"I can't do it, Father."

"I won't save you this time," he snarled. "You have to use your power against this creature. It's the only way."

I gasped, whirling back toward him. "No. You can't mean that."

But he was gone. I ran up to the wall and peered through the hole but saw nothing but the distant village bathed in light. Horror thumped through my veins. My father had left me here.

I was all alone.

The creature lurched out of the shadows. I screamed and dropped to the ground, covering my head as it lashed its sharp fangs at my face. A storm of fur and blood-soaked claws hurtled over me. Shaking, I rolled to the side, sand spraying into my eyes.

Sniffing, the beast leaned down and dragged its nose across my cheek, leaving behind a streak of wet saliva. A whimper sounded in the back of my throat as I stared up into the vicious face of the shadowfiend. Even though it was a monster of the mists, I understood it. I recognized the glint in its eyes.

Hunger.

Sobbing, I scrabbled out from under it and took off through the darkness, my feet stumbling upon rock and sand and dirt. The vague shape of the mountain range rose before me like another humongous creature ready to widen its jaws and swallow me whole.

I didn't know where I could go. The mountains were dangerous. Impassable, they said. But the beast was right behind me. I could feel its hot breath on my neck and—

It crashed into me. My legs twisted, and my elbow slammed into the ground. I screamed as I reached overhead. The shadowfiend shoved its paws into my chest. Claws ripped into my skin. Painful venom tore through me. I couldn't even think.

Choking on my sobs, I placed my shaking palms on the beast's sweat-drenched fur and closed my eyes. Its fangs were only inches away from my throat. I had to do something, anything. My powers had never worked before, but if they didn't help me now, I would die.

The shadowfiend would destroy me.

My palms slipped against the beast's fur. I felt nothing—not a hint of magic at all. No rush of power. No spark of electricity on my fingertips. Nothing changed except one important thing.

The shadowfiend's eyes went black. It tensed and then slumped forward, the life draining from its terrifying form. And then it landed heavily right on top of me. The monstrous body pinned me to the sand.

A scent like sweat and must and rotten eggs filled my head. I tried to wriggle out from beneath the creature, but I couldn't move. It was too big and its venom charged through me. Soon, I lost feeling in my legs.

I was trapped there like that for hours.

Days, maybe.

Eventually, my father came for me and dragged me back over the wall.

According to Nellie, I did nothing but read for

months. I didn't cry. I barely ate. I didn't even speak. And then first thing I said to her, after weeks of silence, was, "I can never trust him again. I can't trust anyone."

FORTY-THREE

TESSA

I cracked open my eyes as memories of my childhood tumbled over each other in my mind, flashes of a life I'd blocked out. And now that I remembered— parts of it, at least—the heaviness on my chest made it almost impossible to breathe.

My father had believed Nellie and I were the answer to all the mortals' problems. The barrier had numbed his inherited powers for too long, and he'd never get them back. And so he'd thrown me out into the mists to spark mine to life, over and over, until that one horrible day. I'd killed the beast, but it had also killed me, in a way. It broke me for so many years.

Sudden pain lanced my skull, chasing away the memories. I lifted a shaky hand to my throbbing head, brushing something slick. I hissed through clenched teeth. When I pulled my fingers away, they were stained red.

My right shoulder pounded in time with my head, and when I glanced around, I realized I had no idea where

I was or how far I'd fallen. Heavy mist surrounded me, and I could not see farther than my own hand. Unease slithered down my spine.

I stood on wobbly legs and tipped back my head. I couldn't see anything above me, nor hear anyone shouting my name. Everything was dark and silent and cold, and my head and shoulder hurt so terribly that I struggled to even think, let alone find a way to reach the others.

"Kalen!" I called out, turning in a slow circle.

I was alive, which meant I couldn't have fallen far. I could stand, and I could breathe. That was something, at least. Their hearing was better than mine. So if I just kept shouting, surely they'd be able to locate me.

"Niamh! Alastair! Fenella!" I cupped my hands around my mouth, spinning in place. "Kalen!"

Rocks scattered by my feet, tumbling down from above. A relieved sigh shook my sore body. They'd heard me. It would be all right. I had no idea what we'd do from here, but at least they'd found me.

Heavy feet thumped against the ground to my right, and a strange, uneasy chill swept across the back of my neck, making every hair stand on end. I couldn't see whoever had joined me on this boulder, but still, I knew. This was not Kalen.

My shoulder shot with pain as I slid my sword from the sheath on my back. Tears stung my eyes, less from the fear of whatever lurked inside the thickened mist than from the pain that scraped through every inch of my body. The world blurred before me, and yet I stood my ground.

A feral shriek sounded from my right. I knew that sound. I heard it in my worst nightmares—in my deepest, darkest dreams. Terror gripped my heart as I slowly turned toward the beast that stalked closer. Memories replayed in my mind. A five-year-old girl, screaming as she ran from the monster bearing down on her, its jaws snapping at her back.

My arms trembled as the beast slowly crept into view, the shadows parting around its long, sweat-drenched snout. It sniffed at the air, and its black eyes zeroed in on my head where blood trickled from the fresh wound.

I shuddered. It had smelled my blood, and now it had come to feast on my flesh.

It took another step closer. Claws scraped against stone.

"Stay back," I whispered, angling my sword sideways to protect my chest. "Don't come any closer."

The beast widened its jaws and screamed, its hot breath billowing against my face. I braced myself against the sound and tightened my hold on the sword. My muscles trembled from the weight of it, and my mind begged for me to lower it to the ground, for just a moment of sweet relief.

And that little girl inside my mind cried, pleading with me to turn around and run. She didn't want to face this. She couldn't. Not with her father's angry face flashing in her eyes. Not with his shouts making her cower on her knees. She whispered at him to stop, to just let her be.

The shadowfiend lunged.

With a scream, I held up my sword to protect myself,

but its claws hit my legs and sent me tumbling across the stony ground. My teeth clattered together and sent another wave of blinding pain through my skull. I scrabbled backward, still clinging to my sword as the beast loped toward me.

It would trap me again, just like it had back then. Only this time, I did not know if I could find it within myself to kill it with my hands. I'd spent most of my life in Teine, and like my father, Oberon's protective barrier would have dampened whatever magic I had over the years.

The power wouldn't work.

Steeling myself, I rolled over and jumped to my feet, dodging the beast's lunge. I raised the sword and swung wildly at its head, but it merely whistled through the air, missing by at least a foot.

The beast thundered forward, and I forced myself to focus on everything Kalen had taught me. *Use your legs. Ignore the pain. Focus on your breathing, on the beat of your heart beneath your ribs.* His voice echoed in my mind and soothed away the throttling terror.

Roaring, I swung the sword. At last, it made contact, slicing into the monster's flesh. Blood streamed from the gaping wound as I ripped the blade out of its body.

It screamed, jaws widening and exposing its razor-sharp teeth.

I couldn't let those teeth rip through me. If the venom stormed my veins, it would stun me long enough for the beast to kill me.

I stumbled to the side when it raced for me once more. I barely got out of the way. It whirled on me and sliced its claw at my leg. I danced out of the way just in time. Gritting my teeth, I bent my knees and thrust my sword upward. The beast's paw hit the blade, pushing it down toward my face.

I strained against its weight, desperately trying to fend it off. Sweat pooled on my forehead and dripped down the back of my neck. The pain in my head was so great that I almost passed out.

"*Give up,*" the little girl cried in the back of my mind. "*Run!*"

I wanted so badly to listen to her. I couldn't do this. I wasn't strong enough. I never had been. Tessa Baran was nothing but a rage-filled, colossal failure who ruined everyone's lives. She couldn't protect herself. She should just cower and hide and wait for her death. The world would be better off without her in it.

I ground my teeth together, and then shouted into the mist, "No!"

With a strength I did not know I had, I threw all my force into my legs and arms and *shoved* the shadowfiend across the boulder. I stumbled back as it growled at me, its paw dripping with blood.

Pulling air into my aching lungs, I raised my sword once more, ignoring the pain-drenched protests of my body. And then I swung.

The sword sang, steel through air. It collided with the beast's flesh and sliced deep into its throat. The creature's wail rose up all around me as blood gurgled from its open neck. Its eyes went distant and dark, just as they had back then. With one last gasping breath, the shadowfiend hit the rock and then stilled.

I dropped the sword. It clattered against the rock. And then my knees gave out.

"Tessa, love." Kalen's soft voice wound into my ear, and the scent of snow and mist surrounded me like a gentle cocoon. He pressed his fingers to my neck, and the sigh that scraped from his throat echoed my own relief, even though I could barely open my eyes. Cold seeped into my skin, causing my entire body to tremble.

Someone let out a low whistle.

"Fair play to the mortal," Fenella said. "She cut off the pooka's head."

A warm, rough hand cupped my face. "Tessa, can you hear me?"

I blinked up at his tense face and managed to force the words from my throat. "You found me."

He relaxed visibly, though worry still pinched a line between his eyes. "There's blood on your head and all over your hands."

"Some of that is from the shadowfiend. I got the bastard."

"You really fucking did," he said with a hint of pride in his voice, but then he took notice of my shivers. "Do you think you can sit up?"

"Maybe."

Gently, he helped me ease up from the ground, and then he propped me against a boulder. I caught the others standing just behind him, all staring at me with concern. That probably wasn't a good sign.

He knelt before me and took my hand in his. "I was scared out of my mind."

"I know," I whispered. "Me too. I don't think I should have survived that."

He cast a glance over his shoulder at the dead beast. I hoped they could get rid of it somehow, while I rested. The stench was unpleasant and would only get worse.

"You did more than survive."

I gripped his hand tighter. "I remembered some things. About my past. The journal my father had...he wasn't wrong, Kalen. I am everything he thought I was. I think that's how I survived. The magic isn't strong in me, but it's...it's still there."

I glanced down at where my fingers touched his skin, and I started to pull away. He shook his head, pulling my hand to his chest. "We don't do that, remember? No matter what blood runs through your veins, I do not fear you touching me. We'll find a way through this."

"But how?" I asked, dropping my voice low so the others couldn't hear me. "I'm the descendent of a god, and my fall off that cliff has only slowed you down. You need to find Oberon and stop him, and I don't think I can carry on like this."

"We were going to make camp soon anyway. It's been a long day, and we could all use some sleep," he said. "I'll get a fire started. It'll warm you up, and you can get some rest."

As much as I wanted to argue, I could use a very long sleep. Every inch of my body hurt. Even my bones ached.

The combination of all my training, the ride through the mists, and the fight against the shadowfiend had left me well and truly spent. I could barely keep my eyes open as Kalen started a small fire on the rocks.

My chin dropped to my chest, and the movement jolted me awake. Through my blurry eyes, I watched Kalen kneel beside the fire and cook some meat. Darkness crept into my eyes again. I slumped, head lolling.

Sleep came swiftly.

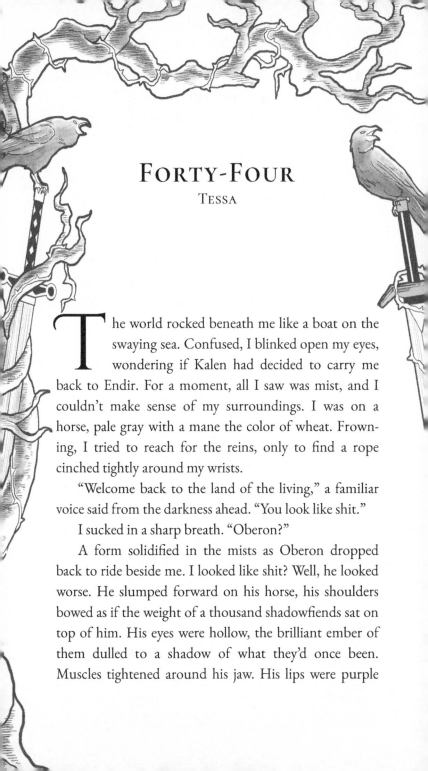

FORTY-FOUR
TESSA

The world rocked beneath me like a boat on the swaying sea. Confused, I blinked open my eyes, wondering if Kalen had decided to carry me back to Endir. For a moment, all I saw was mist, and I couldn't make sense of my surroundings. I was on a horse, pale gray with a mane the color of wheat. Frowning, I tried to reach for the reins, only to find a rope cinched tightly around my wrists.

"Welcome back to the land of the living," a familiar voice said from the darkness ahead. "You look like shit."

I sucked in a sharp breath. "Oberon?"

A form solidified in the mists as Oberon dropped back to ride beside me. I looked like shit? Well, he looked worse. He slumped forward on his horse, his shoulders bowed as if the weight of a thousand shadowfiends sat on top of him. His eyes were hollow, the brilliant ember of them dulled to a shadow of what they'd once been. Muscles tightened around his jaw. His lips were purple and flaked, and the burn scars that covered every inch of his skin looked red and painful and raw.

"I see you still refuse to call me your king," he said roughly.

"Because you are not my king."

"No, I suppose not," he said with a hollow laugh. "Kalen Denare wins once again. He took my kingdom, and now he's taken my last remaining city. I have nothing left."

For once, I was speechless, and it had nothing to do with the orders he'd once given me to keep my lips closed. This was not the brutal monarch who had terrorized me. All that was left was a ghost, and I almost felt pity for him. Still, he had tied me up for a reason.

I pulled at my bonds. "Where are you taking me?"

"Back to my burnt-out husk of a city." He turned his gaze forward, his chest heaving as he clearly struggled to breathe. "There's something I must do."

"Transfer Bellicent's soul into my body." When he cut me a sharp glance, I nodded. "I know all about that."

"I suppose you think I'm a monster for using the god's powers to hold on to the only person who ever made me feel worthy of my title."

I fought the urge to press my fingers to my throbbing temple as we carried on through the mist. "No, I understand it. You loved her. Of course you would do whatever it took to bring her back to you. But you need to stop, Oberon. That necklace doesn't hold half of the god's power anymore. It holds all of it. And if you use it again, with all the power in there...I worry what might happen to this world."

Deep down, I knew there must be a part of Oberon that truly did care. All these years had passed, and he'd never released the god, despite how tempting it must have been. He could have sent humans to destroy the stone in Itchen at any time. He could have smashed open the necklace. The god would have rewarded him for that, and yet, he'd kept her trapped in the gemstone necklace.

Maybe if I could make him see...

"And your very existence doesn't also threaten this world?" he asked in a hiss that prickled the hair on the back of my neck.

I swallowed. "What do you mean?"

Oberon shook his head and let out a hollow laugh. "Don't act coy, Tessa Baran. I watched you fall and fight that creature. You wouldn't have survived if you were just a mortal."

I tried to keep my expression blank, but I could feel his eyes roving across my face. Oberon knew. The question was, for how long?

"I've been training," I said tightly.

His lips curled into a hollow version of his typical smile. "I know what you are and what your father was. Did you truly believe I wouldn't find out why he escaped all those years ago? You and your sister are descendants of Andromeda, the God of Death. Why do you think I chose you to become my bride?"

My body betrayed me. I gasped and turned toward him with parted lips. "Because you wanted to punish me for stealing from you."

He waved his hand dismissively. "I was always going

to choose you. It had been my plan for years. The punishment was merely an excuse."

"And Nellie?" I couldn't help but ask.

"I never would have killed her, knowing what kind of power she might have within her. She was your backup, though not my first choice."

"Why?"

"You know why."

I tensed. "How do you know so much about us?"

He gave me a long-suffering stare. "I am King Oberon, and I've had the power of a god on my side for four hundred years."

My mind churned from the implication of his words. This couldn't possibly be real. I was dreaming—that was the only logical explanation for what I was hearing now. Or I'd gone into some kind of delirium due to the exhaustion, pain, and blood loss. Because if Oberon knew—if he'd chosen me because of my bloodline, then there was only one explanation for his actions based on everything I'd seen in that vision.

"You wanted me to be the final vessel."

It all made sense.

"The half-god said she didn't have the power to transfer Bellicent's soul into a fae body, but she could do it with yours." He spoke his words in a flat voice. "You have mortal blood, and you have *her* blood too. You were the perfect candidate. Mortal enough for her to complete the transfer without access to all her power, but strong enough that your mind would survive longer than the others. The hope was, it would survive forever. I didn't tell Bellicent at first. It was meant to be a surprise when she awoke in her new permanent body. But then you escaped."

And now he was going to take me to Bellicent and finish this once and for all.

I fisted my hands. "What have you done to Kalen?"

"I didn't do anything to him."

"And now I know you're lying." I gripped the rope that twisted around my hands. "He would never let you just take me. He'd *die* trying to stop you. What did you do to him?"

"You know, you are a very tense and angry person."

"Look in the mirror and you'll see why," I snapped.

"Point taken," he said. "But don't worry about your shadow king. He and his Mist Guard have been hit with a dose of valerian fog. They'll be fine when they wake, though they won't be going anywhere for a while. I didn't want to risk them catching up to us."

I scoffed. "*Nothing* will stop him."

"Your faith in him is sweet," he said as his eyes went distant, haunted. "But I have trapped the four of them in iron chains infused with my gemstones. They won't be going anywhere anytime soon."

"Iron chains?" All the blood drained from my face. "But there are shadowfiends out there."

"They have their weapons. They'll be fine."

Eyes narrowing, I jerked my hands apart, and the rope burned my skin. I had to get away from Oberon, not just for me but also for Kalen. I looked down at the ground and made my decision. With a deep breath, I threw my body sideways and launched off the horse. Pain struck me like an anvil when my body hit the ground, my shoulder and head ringing with another wave of torment.

But I didn't let it stop me. Kalen needed my help. I crawled to my knees and then pushed up to my feet.

And then a hand seized me.

Oberon wrenched me around, towering over me with his sharp, curving horns. "Don't make me dose you with more valerian."

I tried to yank my arm out of his grip, but even in his weakened state he was stronger than me. "Let me go!"

"No," he said flatly. "I'm taking you to Albyria and ending this. I'll release the Mist King once it's done."

"You're a monster," I hissed into his face.

Sorrow filled his tired eyes. "I know. Vow to me you'll stop trying to escape, and I'll let you enjoy the rest of this journey awake. Otherwise, I'll have to dose you with the valerian."

"I will never make that vow to you."

"Very well."

Oberon dragged me back over to the horses. The heavy mist stung the wound on my head, but it was nothing compared to the icy terror in my veins. If he dosed me with valerian, I wouldn't be able to fight back. Kalen would remain trapped in those iron shackles, and if a shadowfiend showed up...I didn't want to think what might happen to him. He was so brutally strong and powerful, it seemed impossible that anything could harm him, let alone destroy him completely.

But the iron chains would dampen his magic. He and the others would be powerless against those creatures.

With a growl, I leaned down and clamped my teeth

on Oberon's arm. I bit as hard as I could, giving in to the bloodlust raging through my veins. A momentary victory rushed through me when a shout of pain ripped from his throat. He released me. I stumbled back. And then he slammed his fist into the wound on my head.

The pain took me to my knees. Darkness crept into my vision just as Oberon pressed a cloth against my mouth. I clawed at the ground, desperate to get away. But then the sweet scent of valerian filled my head and took me under.

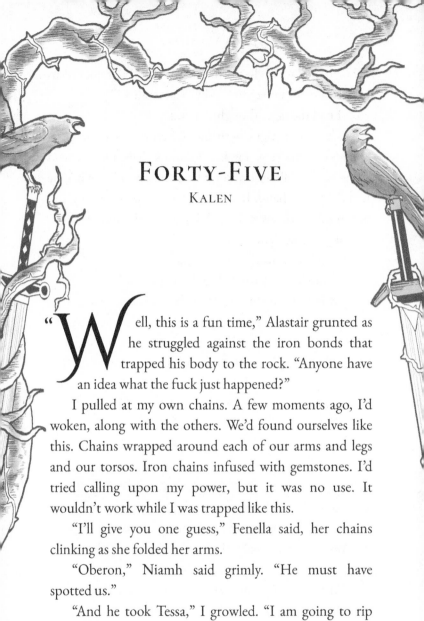

FORTY-FIVE
KALEN

"Well, this is a fun time," Alastair grunted as he struggled against the iron bonds that trapped his body to the rock. "Anyone have an idea what the fuck just happened?"

I pulled at my own chains. A few moments ago, I'd woken, along with the others. We'd found ourselves like this. Chains wrapped around each of our arms and legs and our torsos. Iron chains infused with gemstones. I'd tried calling upon my power, but it was no use. It wouldn't work while I was trapped like this.

"I'll give you one guess," Fenella said, her chains clinking as she folded her arms.

"Oberon," Niamh said grimly. "He must have spotted us."

"And he took Tessa," I growled. "I am going to rip him to shreds for this."

"I'm sure he realizes that," Fenella said. "Hence the chains."

"What I don't understand is why he didn't just kill

us?" Niamh asked, her brow furrowed. "He knocked us out with that valerian fog. Why keep us alive?"

"I had the same thought," I said.

It didn't sit right with me. Oberon and I had been enemies for most of my life. He must have known we'd come here to kill him, and yet he'd chosen mercy when he had the upper hand. It didn't make any sense. And it did not mesh with everything I knew about him. He was brutal and cruel. And he'd—

Realization rushed through me.

A muscle in my jaw ticked. "My mother."

Understanding lifted Alastair's eyebrows. "Ah."

"Even as twisted as this power has made her, she must not want me dead. And Oberon would never go against her wishes, based on what Tessa saw in that vision." My voice rang hollow. It didn't feel right, speaking of her like this. It had been centuries. All this time, I'd thought she was dead.

I wanted to see her alive again, but not like this. There was no happiness when I thought of her now. Just dread. She was just as involved in this as Oberon, even if he'd started it. Would killing the King of Light be enough to fulfill my vow? Or would I be forced to go after her too?

Was my vow really about her, just as I'd begun to suspect?

"Morgan lied. Again. He's going to make the transfer into Tessa's body, isn't he?" Fenella asked.

I ground my teeth. The thought disgusted me.

Niamh shot me a look of pity. "All signs point to yes."

Churning anger boiled within me. I gripped the chains and rattled them as hard as I could, knocking the painful steel against my body. There had to be a way out of this. I couldn't just *sit here*, useless, while Tessa faced her last moments in this world. I couldn't let Oberon take her from me. He'd already taken so fucking much.

The iron bit my skin, even through my armor. I hissed against the pain, but I did not let go. I would not stop trying, not while Oberon had his hands on Tessa.

"Kal," Niamh said gently. "Those chains won't break without a key or a magic-infused axe, no matter what you do. Save your energy."

"I have to get to Tessa."

"You have the ability to get to her any time you want to," Alastair pointed out. "You always have."

"The dreams," I said, understanding at once.

The mists surrounding us were thick, and an orange haze was all I could see of the sun. Even then, I didn't know how to use its path in the sky to tell how much time had passed. It could be an hour or a day. Tessa might not be sleeping right now, but it was worth a try.

I closed my eyes and tilted my head, listening for any sign of her. Black nothingness was my only answer.

"Damn iron chains. Even if she's asleep and calling out for me, I won't be able to hear her. We have to break them."

"That's impossible," Fenella said with a weary sigh. "We don't have a key, and we definitely don't have an axe."

"Lucky for you, *I* have an axe." Toryn strode from the mists with Boudica perched on his shoulder. His lopsided smile and scarred hands were the best things I'd seen in weeks. He held up a small axe with a glittering sapphire gemstone in the center. "Does someone need help from little old Toryn?"

"Thank the fucking moon," I said, hope swelling in my chest. "Get over here and get us out of these things."

"My pleasure, Kal."

He got to work on my bonds first. It took a good five minutes for him to cut through the chains around my ankles, and then he moved on to my hands. When I was finally free, I rubbed my wrists while he slammed the axe against Alastair's shackles. The ring of steel was as loud as thunder.

"How did you get here so fast?" I asked.

He shot me a grim smile. "It's been longer than you think. Boudica saw what happened and came to get me, and I rode flat-out to get here, but that valerian fog really knocked you out."

My heart stopped. "Oberon has Tessa. He wants to transfer my mother's soul into her body." Such a weird fucking thought.

"I know," he said, turning back to Alastair's chains. "Boudica tracked them while I rode here. He's going the long way around—to avoid the army, I think. It looks like he's taking her to Albyria, albeit very slowly. He keeps stopping. I don't think he's well."

I narrowed my gaze. "Then we have a chance of catching up to them. We can stop him from doing this."

And kill him, once and for all.

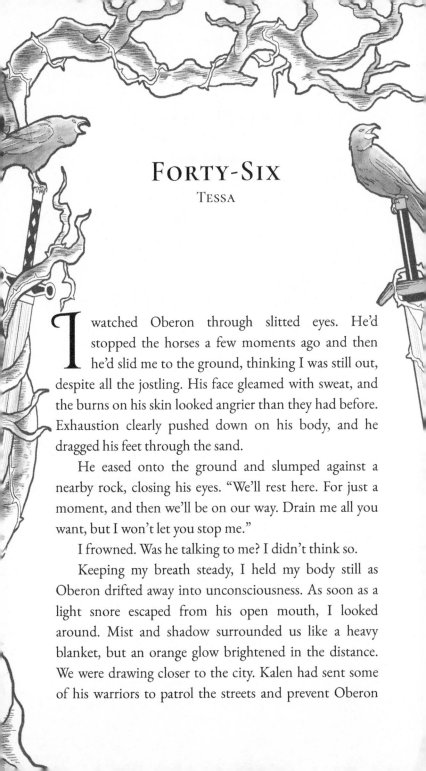

FORTY-SIX
TESSA

I watched Oberon through slitted eyes. He'd stopped the horses a few moments ago and then he'd slid me to the ground, thinking I was still out, despite all the jostling. His face gleamed with sweat, and the burns on his skin looked angrier than they had before. Exhaustion clearly pushed down on his body, and he dragged his feet through the sand.

He eased onto the ground and slumped against a nearby rock, closing his eyes. "We'll rest here. For just a moment, and then we'll be on our way. Drain me all you want, but I won't let you stop me."

I frowned. Was he talking to me? I didn't think so.

Keeping my breath steady, I held my body still as Oberon drifted away into unconsciousness. As soon as a light snore escaped from his open mouth, I looked around. Mist and shadow surrounded us like a heavy blanket, but an orange glow brightened in the distance. We were drawing closer to the city. Kalen had sent some of his warriors to patrol the streets and prevent Oberon from retaking his land. If I shouted loud enough, would they hear me?

I slid my gaze back to Oberon. I couldn't risk waking him, not until I could be sure of my success.

First things first, I needed to get out of these ropes. They cut into my skin every time I moved my hands, and my wrists throbbed as much as my shoulder did. The Mortal Blade wasn't an option. He'd taken it after he'd knocked me out, and it gleamed from the belt around his waist, along with a handful of other small blades. My sword was gone too.

I bit the inside of my cheek. If I could just get my hands on that dagger...

The horse nickered. Oberon's snore cut off.

Stiffening, I closed my eyes and dropped my chin, feigning sleep.

"No," Oberon groaned. "Leave me alone. Let me heal."

I fought the urge to look at him. Who was he talking to now? The horse?

But then silence descended once more, and I risked cracking open one eye. Oberon's head lolled against his chest. His tongue stuck out between his parted lips, and his face shone with sweat. He looked so...small. How had I ever found him terrifying?

Right. I needed to make a move fast, or he'd start leading us toward the city again. And I did not think there'd be another stop along the way—not when we were this close. With one eye on his face, I twisted my hands around in the rope so that I could grip the edges of it with my fingers. Pain shoved through me like the bolt of an arrow, and I took a moment to breathe through my clenched teeth.

My blood painted my hands as I dug my nails into the rope. I pulled at the knots, slowly tugging each strand. Moments ticked by with excruciating torment. Any second now, Oberon would wake, and he'd end my futile escape attempt. I'd barely unraveled one of the knots when my horse stomped his hoof.

I froze, my heart in my chest.

Oberon blinked. I closed my eyes and slumped, but it was too late. He'd already seen me.

"You're awake," he muttered. "More valerian for you."

Well, if we weren't pretending anymore, then I saw no reason to hold back. This was likely my only chance to escape. And I would seize it by the horns.

I opened my eyes and climbed to my feet, standing as he struggled to gain his own footing. His face had turned a sallow gray now, almost like death was eating him from the inside out. Something was preventing him from healing.

I lunged toward him. A startled look crossed his face just before my shoulder hit his. I knocked him sideways, but the pain that shot through me ripped a scream from my throat. The throbbing overtook my mind as he swung a fist at my face. I stumbled out of the way. His fist hurtled through empty air, and he lurched forward, caught off guard.

I hauled up my foot and kicked him in the back. He tumbled to the ground, his cheek smashing against the sand. A dagger flew from his belt and skidded across the ground. I dove toward it without even thinking. It wasn't the Mortal Blade, but it was better than nothing.

My fingers gripped the hilt just as Oberon lumbered back to his feet. He looked at me and laughed.

"You do realize that thing will do nothing against me? Not coming from you anyway. Mortals are too weak to kill fae kings."

"I don't think I'm the weak one here. And as you well know, I'm only *part* mortal."

The muscles tightened around his hollow eyes. "No, you're right. And that's why I have to do this."

He turned his back on me, dragging himself through the sand to his horse. For a moment, I froze with uncertainty. As far as I could tell, I had three options. I could stab him in the back with this pitiful blade. Unfortunately, Oberon was right. It would do very little to harm him.

Alternatively, I could run while he was distracted. I didn't know how far I would get with my pain-wracked body.

The third option was likely my best, but I'd have to move fast if I wanted to avoid another valerian-soaked cloth.

Blowing out a tense breath, I flipped the blade in my hands and sawed at the rope. Oberon took a step closer to his horse. The first strands of the rope broke in two. He took another step and determined tears burned my eyes. More of the rope split apart. I kept sawing and Oberon kept walking, and I ground my teeth so hard that my jaw ached.

Snap. At last, the final remnants of the rope released

me, just as Oberon reached the leather satchel strapped to his horse's back. He reached into a pocket. With a speed I did not know I had, I ran up behind him and put the blade to his neck.

"Don't move," I hissed into his ear.

FORTY-SEVEN
TESSA

T his close, I could see the beads of sweat on the back of Oberon's neck. He swallowed against the blade.

"Take your hand out of the satchel," I commanded.

To my surprise, he actually listened. Carefully, he pulled his fingers out of his bag and dropped them to his side. "You have become quieter than a mortal. You know what that means, don't you?"

"It means nothing. You're just too weak to hear me."

"I wonder, do you have the strength yet to kill me with that thing? I doubt it."

I narrowed my eyes. "Well, then perhaps I should try."

"Listen to yourself. All that rage." He let out a bitter laugh. "You think I'm the dangerous one, and yet you have the blood of a god running through your veins. The God of Death."

I shifted on my feet. "I know what you're trying to do —distract me long enough to think of a way to disarm me. That must mean you're more afraid of me than you care to admit."

I pushed the blade harder against his throat. Blood outlined the edge of the steel. I could stab him now, but this blade wouldn't kill him, and I needed to find out where he'd hidden the necklace. If it fell into the wrong hands, the world would be doomed.

Oberon held up his hands and slowly turned to face me. I ground my teeth, keeping my blade pressed tightly against his skin, but the gleam in his eyes unnerved me.

"Lower the weapon, Tessa Baran," he said calmly, as if we were discussing nothing more than the morning's sun.

"Where's the necklace?"

"What necklace?"

"You know which one. The one that holds the god's power."

He arched his brow. "And if I tell you that, you'll take this blade off my throat?"

I frowned. He'd chosen a pointed question with a yes or no answer. If I lied, he'd know. Damn him.

"Of course you won't," he said. "At least you've learned that lying to me is pointless."

"Where is the necklace?"

"Do you really think, after everything I've done, that I would tell *you*, of all people?"

"Fine. You don't have to tell me where it is as long as you vow to destroy it. You've had four hundred years with your love. Isn't that enough?" I asked. "The necklace isn't as safe as it was before, and I can tell by the look in your eye that you know it. It holds full power now. Life *and* death. And if you aren't careful, she will trick you into releasing her. You *cannot* use it again."

I wasn't entirely sure why I was appealing to him. I should just cut his throat, or at least try to, but...I'd seen him in those visions from the former Mortal Queen. The Oberon of four hundred years ago wanted to protect this world. He *cared*. And even as the power had tried its best to corrupt him—and *oh it had*—he'd still resisted the one temptation that mattered the most.

He never released the god's power, not even to give his love an immortal body. It did not matter how many times the god had asked. Oberon always held tight to his resolve.

Somewhere behind those hollow eyes, the old Oberon was listening to me.

He let out an eerie laugh. "Do you think I'm that stupid? You just want it for yourself. *You'll* release the god."

I shook my head. "Are you out of your mind? That's the last thing I want."

"Your father wanted to release the power." His spittle peppered my face, and he pushed his own neck harder against the edge of the blade. "And so do you. I will never tell you where the necklace is, no matter what weapons you point at me. I am done with this."

Oberon smashed his fist into my gut. Air gusted from my mouth and the force of his blow shoved me away from him. I gripped the dagger and slashed it at his face, but he grabbed my fingers, squeezing so tight that my bones crunched.

Pain flared through my hand, traveling up my arm to

my already wounded shoulder. Hissing between my teeth, I released my grip on the dagger. It fell with a thunk in the sand.

Oberon closed his hand around my throat and lifted me from the ground. As my feet dangled beneath me, I stared into his vicious face.

"There he is," I choked out. "That's the Oberon I know."

Fury rippled across his face. With a grunt, he let me go. My boots hit the ground hard, and my knees buckled beneath me.

"Stop resisting me!" he shouted down at me. "I don't want to hurt you."

I glared up at him. "Actions speak louder than words, Oberon. And you've done nothing but hurt me my entire fucking life."

"That wasn't me. It was the god, warping my mind. She's corrupted me."

"That may explain your actions, but it doesn't excuse them." I spat to clear my mouth and blood painted the sand. Dizziness shook my skull.

"Look at you. Not as strong as you should be yet, eh? Too much time spent behind my barrier." He knelt beside me and shoved a finger into my chest. I tumbled, my backside slamming into the ground. "It's a shame you'll never get to experience the glory of your full power. This will be over soon enough."

I narrowed my eyes. "I thought you didn't want to hurt me."

"And I don't plan to." He wrapped his hand around

the back of my neck and hauled me from the ground again. "Time for more valerian."

"No." I struggled against him, but every inch of my body hurt. It was too much for me to fight—*he* was too much to fight. If I had any enhanced strength or terrifying powers, they'd abandoned me. My body was too weak to conjure anything but pain.

We reached his horse. Once again, he rustled through his leather satchel in search of more valerian-soaked cloths. Any minute now, he would find one, and sleep would claim me once more. I might never wake again. He would take me into his city where his lover waited for him, and then he'd use the power of the god to scrub me from this world. Forever.

I was angry and tired and so very, very sore. It would be easy to just give up, and maybe Oberon was right. Maybe I was too dangerous for this world. I'd seen what the power inside me could do when it was at my fingertips. What if it came back again, only stronger? What if my every touch brought destruction?

What if I became the very thing I feared the most? Someone like Oberon.

"No," I whispered.

Oberon turned toward me. "Don't be so dramatic. This won't hurt a bit."

I yanked my arm out of his grip. "No."

"Don't make me force you," he warned.

I grabbed his arm and used my free hand to yank the Mortal Blade from his belt. The steel slid from the sheath, gleaming even in the murky darkness. Oberon's eyes went wide. He held up his hands and stumbled back.

"This is the real one now," I hissed at him. "And all it will take is one small scrape against your skin."

I lunged with the dagger pointed at his throat. With a shout, he whirled away from me and ran into the mists. I sucked in a breath, taking off after him. Every step shot a new bolt of pain through my body, but I would not fail this time. Just as he'd said, this had to end now.

I raced after him in the darkness. Only the sound of his huffing breaths led the way. Mist stung my eyes and my skin. In the back of my mind, I couldn't help but wonder at what was happening. King Oberon, the powerful fae who had terrorized me for years, was running away from me.

There was a satisfying irony to that.

"No, stop!" he screamed just ahead of me. "Don't make me fall. Please!"

Frowning, I charged forward. I found him only a short way ahead of me. He cowered on his knees, head bent, body trembling with the kind of fear I didn't think someone like him had ever felt. I almost felt sorry for him.

My fingers twitched around the dagger.

He gazed up at me, his graying ember eyes tortured. "Just drop the dagger. I'll do anything you want if you let it go."

"You won't force me to go to Albyria?" I asked, my heart pounding.

"No," he whispered. "You don't have to go."

"And you'll tell me where the necklace is?"

His eyes went wide. "I can't do that. Tessa, please. That's the one thing I can't do."

I closed my eyes, and all the rage I'd felt toward this

fae drifted away like smoke on the wind. For so long, I'd dreamt of this moment. I'd *ached* for it. This was what I thought I wanted—a broken king cowering before me, begging me to spare his life.

But now that this moment was here, it tasted like ash.

As I stared down at his shivering form, I realized I did not want to kill him, but that I would have to do it anyway. He would never let go of his need to save Bellicent's soul from death. Eventually, that necklace would damage him beyond repair, and he'd release the god. Sooner rather than later, judging by the sight of him. He was a broken man.

I knelt before him and took one of his trembling hands in mine. "I'm sorry for what she's done to you."

Relief relaxed the tension on his face. "You understand."

"I do." My fingers tightened around the dagger I held by my side. "You've been fighting her temptation for so long. I understand how hard it's been."

He slumped forward. "Does that mean you'll come with me?"

"To Albyria?"

"I won't force you to go." He lifted his eyes to mine. "But you could come willingly."

I gave him a sad smile. "You just can't let it go, can you?"

"Of course I can't. I started this, and now I have to end it. I'm taking you to Albyria to lock you in the vault, along with the necklace. To keep the world safe, even from Bellicent. I won't let anyone ever use it again. The god's essence has been trying to stop me, dampening my powers and not letting me heal, but—" And then suddenly, he shouted, "No, stop. Just stop!"

He lunged toward me and threw himself against the dagger.

The steel sank into his skin, and blood gushed down his neck. His mouth widened as his hands scrabbled at the blade. And then he met my eyes. The ember glowed bright, like the last gasps of a dying flame.

"No," he choked out, digging a hand into the front of his leather armor. "No, no, no, no, no."

I leapt to my feet and stumbled back, horror snaking through me. The blade's burning magic started at his throat and trailed down the front of him. Flecks of ash drifted off his graying body.

Roaring, he yanked his hand from his armor, and there—the onyx necklace dangled from his fingers. My heart leapt into my throat. Oberon flung the necklace away from him as the ash climbed across his torso. The gemstone landed with a heavy thunk at my feet.

Familiar power thundered across me—heavy, dark, and cold. It scraped against my skin like a hundred tiny knives. Hate seemed to pour off that stone. It wanted to bury itself in my skin.

Suddenly, a gray haze started to creep across the necklace. The onyx gemstone shattered into cinders, and soot-like fingers crept across the chain. Within the blink of an eye, the entire thing was gone.

Dread swept down my spine as I stared at the remnants of the god's prison.

"You have no idea what you've done," Oberon gasped. The ash curled across his face, transforming his fiery features into a colorless gray. Piece by piece, he flecked away, and the light wind scattered his remains across the ground—right beside what was left of the god's necklace.

Stomach turning, I understood at once what had happened. As Oberon had fought to reach Albyria and lock the necklace—and me—inside the vault, the God of Death had numbed his powers and prevented him from healing, just like she'd done to Kalen back in Itchen. And then she'd found a way to throw Oberon against the Mortal Blade. It had destroyed not only the King of Light but also her prison. She was finally free.

A boom shook the ground. I stumbled back from the mound of ash, the only thing left of my greatest enemy, as shadows descended upon me.

I glanced up at the sky. Oberon's sun had vanished, and there were no stars here. Just endless darkness and mist.

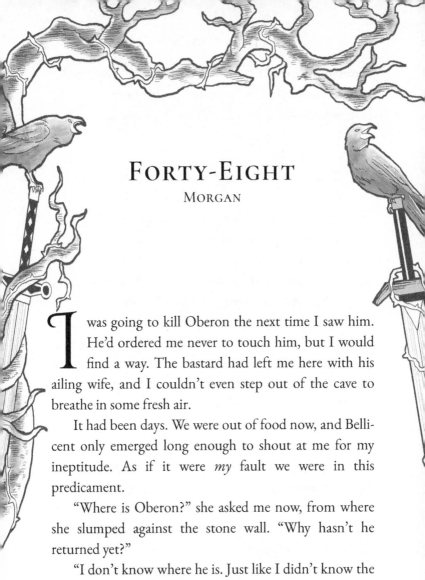

FORTY-EIGHT
MORGAN

I was going to kill Oberon the next time I saw him. He'd ordered me never to touch him, but I would find a way. The bastard had left me here with his ailing wife, and I couldn't even step out of the cave to breathe in some fresh air.

It had been days. We were out of food now, and Bellicent only emerged long enough to shout at me for my ineptitude. As if it were *my* fault we were in this predicament.

"Where is Oberon?" she asked me now, from where she slumped against the stone wall. "Why hasn't he returned yet?"

"I don't know where he is. Just like I didn't know the last time you asked. Or the time before that."

She narrowed her eyes. "I am your queen, and you will show me the proper respect."

"You're going to take over my body," I said bitterly. "I can say whatever I fucking well like."

"Hmm." She shifted against the wall, picking

through the pack Oberon had left behind. "The king has always had a soft spot for you, and it's been one of his biggest weaknesses. It's good that will change now."

"You must be joking."

"I do not joke."

"That much, at least, is true."

"He will be better off without you," she said with a smile that didn't reach her eyes. "And vice versa. You can't tell me you're happy with your current lot."

I stared out into the mists, willing Oberon to return just to put me out of my misery. I'd never enjoyed conversing with Bellicent, least of all now that I knew she'd soon be residing in my body. "No one would be happy with being forced to follow every whim of someone as twisted as Oberon. Free will is an important thing. And I have not had that for a very long time."

"Well, you can have as much free will as you want when you're dead."

I tensed. "If Oberon hadn't ordered me to spare your life, I'd snap your neck. I wish I'd done it when I could have, centuries ago."

A hiss escaped from her lips. "I would have you put to death just for threatening me. Unfortunately for you, your life is already forfeit."

I shoved up from the ground and stormed over to the mouth of the cave. "I've had enough of this. I am going to find a way to leave, even if I have to claw my way out of here with bloody fingernails. There will be a loophole, and I will find it."

A soft breeze rushed into the cave, rustling my hair. And with it came a sense of despair so great I almost sank to my knees and begged for the ground to swallow me whole. I fisted my hands and stared out into the darkness. What was this? Where had it come from? I'd felt nothing quite like it before. It was so...wrong. It tasted of blood and death and hate. Most of all, it was hate.

"Oh!" Delight rippled through Bellicent's voice, a sound that set my frayed nerves on edge. "Well, this is quite unexpected."

I didn't want to give her the satisfaction of turning around, but...

"What is it?" I looked back at her. Unlike me, she smiled. This was the brightest I'd seen her look in weeks. Something in my gut twisted.

"I've just been delivered a *very* important message." Her eyes narrowed on me, and that smile grew wide.

Suddenly, my bones ached to run. I needed to get out of here, now. Oberon hadn't returned, but something else had.

I took a step back, my boots scuffing the stone.

"Andromeda is finally free. *All* of her." Bellicent beamed. "It is time for me to claim your body for my own."

Before I could react, a force slammed into me. Rot and death filled my head until I could see nothing but the deepest shadows in the back of my mind. Trembling, I reached out, desperate to find something—anything— that could anchor me to this world.

Terror gripped my heart. I didn't want to go. It wasn't my time.

All I'd wanted was a year—if that—of freedom. One snippet of an endless life, where I could dance when I wanted to dance, laugh when I wanted to laugh, go where I wanted—even to the land of moon and starlight—and erase the ghosts from my past. All that blood. All that horrible, twisted death.

I had once hoped if I followed Oberon's orders long enough, he would one day let me go. And I could have my year. Just one year. That was all I needed.

But I knew now I would never walk beneath the moon.

The magic stormed through me, consuming my soul and burning away every last scrap of who I was. But then...just before darkness claimed me for the rest of eternity, a blanket of pure, brilliant stars filled my mind. Was this death? Or some kind of afterlife? It didn't matter. Not with a sight like this.

I released my fear, smiled up at the stars, and said hello.

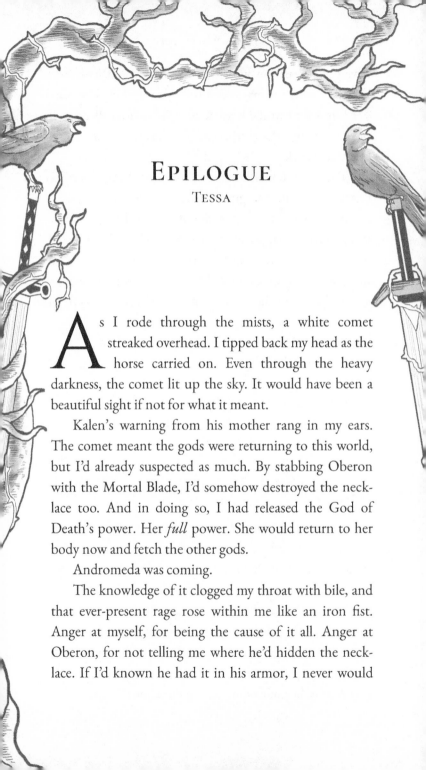

EPILOGUE
TESSA

As I rode through the mists, a white comet streaked overhead. I tipped back my head as the horse carried on. Even through the heavy darkness, the comet lit up the sky. It would have been a beautiful sight if not for what it meant.

Kalen's warning from his mother rang in my ears. The comet meant the gods were returning to this world, but I'd already suspected as much. By stabbing Oberon with the Mortal Blade, I'd somehow destroyed the necklace too. And in doing so, I had released the God of Death's power. Her *full* power. She would return to her body now and fetch the other gods.

Andromeda was coming.

The knowledge of it clogged my throat with bile, and that ever-present rage rose within me like an iron fist. Anger at myself, for being the cause of it all. Anger at Oberon, for not telling me where he'd hidden the necklace. If I'd known he had it in his armor, I never would have gone near him with that blade. I would have held back, knowing the magic of it turned everything into ash.

But what I would have done didn't matter. Because it did not change the truth. The god was free, and I could not take it back.

The next few hours were nothing but a blur of exhaustion, pain, and guilt. I needed to rest, but I had to reach Kalen and the rest of the Mist Guard before something terrible happened to them. And so I hunkered down on the horse and held tight to the reins. Once I made it back to camp, I would rest. Kalen would hold me against his warm chest and tell me everything would be all right.

We would find a way to fight the gods.

The thought of seeing him was the only thing that kept me going.

Hours passed before I finally reached camp. I leapt off the horse and raced to the remnants of the fire, only to find no one there. Broken chains littered the rocks, and ashes were piled on top of the logs. I knelt and pressed my fingers to the charred wood. Completely cold. They'd been gone a while.

Frowning, I glanced around for any sign of them. Had they gone after me and Oberon? It made sense. That would be the first thing Kalen would do once free, but I would have passed him on my way here.

I paced the small camp, wracking my brain. Someone had freed Kalen and the others from their shackles. And then they had...what, exactly? I knew Kalen. He never would have gone anywhere without trying to track me down. Had he gone in the wrong direction?

I sat hard on the rocks. I needed to find him. I had to tell him about the necklace and the comet and...

His words echoed in my mind.

She made me vow to stop it from happening, and to kill anyone who brought them back. I'm to look out for a white comet in the sky.

I sucked in a sharp breath. Kalen had made a vow to kill whoever caused the comet—whoever brought the gods back to this world.

I'd destroyed the necklace. I hadn't meant to, but...I'd held the blade. It was me. I pressed a trembling hand to my chest and tried to catch my anxious breath. Darkness crept into the corners of my vision.

"He's not here," I whispered to no one but myself, "because he's seen the comet, and he somehow knows I destroyed the necklace. He thinks he'll have to kill me."

And he wouldn't be wrong. It had been an accident. A horrible, cruel accident. One crafted by the God of Death herself. Kalen's vow would force him to kill me, and he knew it. And so he'd run the other way, likely with the help of the Mist Guard. He might have needed them to knock him unconscious to stop him from coming after me.

The second he laid eyes on me, he'd be compelled to shove his blade into my heart. There was nothing either of us could do to prevent it.

I slumped against the boulder, my exhaustion so heavy that I could no longer fight it. What was the point of trying? I'd destroyed the necklace and lost the only man I cared for...all in one horrible, brutal day. I had no idea what I would do next. It all seemed achingly impossible to me now. I was wounded and so very, very alone.

And so I gave in to sleep.

Instantly, the blood-soaked, comet-filled world dissolved. That familiar dream forest surrounded me, where chirping birds and whispering crickets sang a song of life. It was an aching reminder of what we would lose if we did not find a way to stop this.

I waited in the tall grass, expecting Kalen to step out of the shadows at any moment. The hours passed and still I waited. My heart ached, but I did not give up, even though I knew deep down that he would not search for me here.

He would stay away. Even if he wanted to come, he wouldn't. It was too big of a risk. He could not kill me in my dreams, but he might be forced to try. The vow could make him interrogate me or press a blade to my neck like before. It could make him terrify me, or even trick me, into telling him where I was.

Kalen would never forgive himself if he did any of that to me. Not now, not after everything that had happened between us.

When I awoke hours later, I did not feel better for the sleep. The mists still hung heavily around me, and I had no one but Oberon's horse to stand by my side. I couldn't return to Endir, not now. Kalen might be there.

Leaving the camp behind, I wandered to the base of the mountain and pushed out onto the sandy beach. Overhead, the comet trailed through the sky, leaving behind a streak of pure, brilliant white. But other than that, the sky was black. The mists had thickened here now, and even the sparkling sea was hidden under a blanket of darkness.

Kalen was gone. I was alone. And I had nowhere in this world to call home.

"As long as dreams remain, so do the stars," I whispered, staring out at the mist-enshrouded sea.

But there were no dreams, and there were no stars. Only night and chaos.

GLOSSARY

Druids - religious fae leaders who worship the sky, the earth, and the seas

Familiar - a bonded animal, usually only shadow fae have this connection

Fion - fae wine that tastes of silver and song

Gemstones - powerful jewels that contain magical properties

Gods - powerful immortal beings who once ruled the world with violence, banished when humans and fae joined together to fight them

Mortal Blade - a blade only a mortal can wield, and whoever is on the receiving end turns to ash

Pookas - the term shadow fae use for the monsters of the mist who feast on human flesh

Shadowfiends - the term light fae and mortals use for the monsters of the mist who feast on human flesh

The Great Rift - the chasm separating the Kingdom of Light from the rest of the world, caused by the clash of powers between King Oberon and the Mist King

The Oidhe - the deal between the mortals of Teine and King Oberon

Valerian - a magic-infused herb that causes dreamless sleep

Acknowledgments

This has been the most challenging book I've ever written, but it has also been the most rewarding. I wanted to do Tessa's journey justice, even though she still has so far to go. This story is just so special to me.

To Josh, first and always, I could not have written this book without your support. You encouraged me and cheered me on and helped me work through plot points. Thank you for reading the book and giving me your feedback and making sure I ate when I worked long into the night.

To my writing buddies, Christine, Anya, Alison, Jen, Marina, and Tammi. Our daily chats keep me sane.

To Sylvia, for the beautiful book cover. It is so perfect for this part of Tessa's story.

To Maggie, for your encouragement and your keen editorial eye. Thank you for making time for me so I could hit my deadline.

And to the readers, most of all. Every message, review, comment on a TikTok or Instagram post, email, share, like, tagged photo, etc. You have no idea how much it means to me. I hope you love this story as much as I've loved writing it for you.

Also by Jenna Wolfhart

The Mist King

Of Mist and Shadow

Of Ash and Embers

Of Night and Chaos

Book Four (Title TBA)

The Fallen Fae

Court of Ruins

Kingdom in Exile

Keeper of Storms

Tower of Thorns

Realm of Ashes

Prince of Shadows (A Novella)

Demons After Dark: Covenant

Devilish Deal

Infernal Games

Wicked Oath

Demons After Dark: Temptation

Sinful Touch

Darkest Fate

Hellish Night

About the Author

Jenna Wolfhart spends her days tucked away in her writing studio in the countryside. When she's not writing, she loves to deadlift, rewatch Game of Thrones, and drink copious amounts of coffee.

Born and raised in America, Jenna now lives in England with her husband and her two dogs, Nero and Vesta.

www.jennawolfhart.com
jenna@jennawolfhart.com
tiktok.com/@jennawolfhart

Made in United States
North Haven, CT
16 July 2024

54832469R00278